DEC

2 ...s *of the Singer Girls*

Secrets

of the

Singer Girls

Kate Thompson

PAN BOOKS

First published 2015 by Pan Books
an imprint of Pan Macmillan
20 New Wharf Road, London N1 9RR
Associated companies throughout the world
www.panmacmillan.com

ISBN 978-1-5098-8187-1

A CIP catalogue record for this book is available from the British Library.

Typeset by Palimpsest Book Production Ltd, Falkirk, Stirlingshire
Printed and bound by CPI Group (UK) Ltd, Croydon, CR0 4YY

Visit www.panmacmillan.com to read more about all our books
and to buy them. You will also find features, author interviews and
news of any author events, and you can sign up for e-newsletters
so that you're always first to hear about our new releases.

*To Ben, for his loyalty and patience,
and to my own Singer Girls, for teaching me
the true value of female friendships.*

One

From the outside it looked like any normal East End factory, but as Poppy Percival allowed her pale blue eyes to travel up the imposing brick exterior to the jumble of soot-stained chimney stacks, she wanted to turn on her well-polished heels and flee. Instead, she stayed rooted to the spot and nervously twisted a lock of her soft brown hair tightly round her fingers. Gracious, it was a sight to turn her pounding heart to stone. The building's brickwork was scorched black from a thousand Blitz incendiary fires, and the high windows of the former workhouse looked as forbidding as the gates of hell.

As twilight bled across the jagged rooftops, a steady rain began to fall. It wasn't crisp spring rain like the type you got in the countryside, Poppy thought uncomfortably. This rain was thick and black, as warm as sour milk, and it coated everything in its path with a dark sheen. The cobbles under Poppy's aching feet were a soupy, sulphurous mess, and the factory shimmered like an oil slick.

Sixteen-year-old Poppy had travelled a long way from the country estate in Norfolk where she had spent the last two years working as a scullery maid. She had left that morning at the crack of dawn, bundled onto a steam train at King's Lynn by her harassed mother, who worked as a lady's maid at the same grand home.

'Don't be shaming me, you hear, my girl,' her mother had muttered as she had swung the heavy train door shut behind Poppy with a resounding thwack. It had slammed so hard it had almost drowned out her words, but not quite . . . 'And remember, no more scandal.' With that her pinched face had disappeared behind a swirl of smoke.

A bit like a dragon who has blown off too much steam, Poppy had thought at the time. She kept that thought to herself, of course. She would sooner carve off her left leg than cheek her mother, especially under the circumstances. The rest of the doors had slammed shut and they had departed, chugging their way through the lush green Norfolk countryside and away from everything Poppy had ever known.

The gentle rhythm of the train had soon lulled Poppy into a deep sleep, but when she had awoken, it had been to sights the like of which she had never before seen. St Pancras Station was charged with energy. Soot-blackened locomotives slid majestically into their platforms, where billowing clouds of silvery-grey smoke swirled above. Every so often the smoke had parted to reveal a tantalizing glimpse of the human lives playing out on the platforms: a sweetheart clinging to a soldier; a mother fussing over a bewildered child.

A tight knot of fear had unfurled in Poppy's heart and she had gripped her canvas bag close to her bosom. Her freshly shone leather shoes, so sparkling she could almost make out the reflection of her freckled nose in them, had seemed rooted to the station concourse.

'Excuse me,' she had said nervously to an elderly-looking porter who was hauling great leather trunks onto barrows. 'Can you tell me the way to get to Bethnal Green, please, sir?'

He had stared at her curiously before a wry grin creased his craggy face. 'Course I can, sweetheart. What's left of it, that is,' he had said with a wink.

Travelling during wartime was an uncertain business, as Poppy had found out. The porter had told her she could take something called the Tube, but the idea of navigating London on an underground train system had seemed too bewildering by half. So bus it was. Except the bus the porter had told her to get had suddenly lurched off the road to avoid a bomb crater and been detoured on a whole new route, past houses that looked to Poppy like grand white wedding cakes and imposing red-brick buildings that soared to the heavens.

Not that Poppy had the faintest idea where she was in any case. She had never been to the city of London before and her heart had thumped in her chest at the overwhelming sights. There was noise, chaos and traffic of all kinds belching out acrid fumes. An eerie greenish fog hung ominously over the city, meaning taxis, trams and utility buses with blacked-out windows loomed out of the smog without warning. The roads were pockmarked with bomb damage, sandbags were bundled up at the end of each street, and every now and then a smart terrace of houses would fall away to nothing but debris.

This was a whole new world to Poppy. The Blitz had been

over for a year now, but the damage was still visible everywhere. As the bus passed a bombsite, a cold, hard fist tightened around Poppy's heart. The uncomfortable thought hit her that every sealed-off site had been someone's private hell. London was awash with brick tombs. In fact, from what she was able to tell, vast swathes of the city had been reduced to rubble. Roped-off roads contained nothing but rain-sodden masonry, the odd twisted skeleton of what might have been a bus embedded within it. Street urchins picked their way through the bombsites, pulling out anything they could salvage to sell. It was a hopeless sight. Nothing like the smart images of London Poppy had seen in magazines. It was all too much and the high emotion of the past few weeks engulfed her.

Tears pricked her eyes and then spilt helplessly down her creamy cheeks as she clutched her bag so tightly her knuckles turned white. Packed in her case, she had only some cotton stays, a vest, two pairs of knickers and three pairs of lisle stockings. Not much to show for sixteen years.

Until recently, she had been safe and cosseted below stairs in a stately home. Back at Framshalton Hall, her days had been filled with hard work. From 6 a.m., when she awoke to black-lead the grate, scrub the passage and light the range fire, her fifteen-hour day had been broken down into a multitude of back-breaking tasks, until she finally finished at 9 p.m. But she had done this with never-ending good cheer. Even marching to the tune of a grumpy cook hadn't dented her ferocious pride in her work. For Poppy's whole sense of worth was rooted in her work ethic. At the age of fourteen, Poppy had left school on a Friday and, as arranged by her mother, started work as a scullery maid on the Monday. From that day forth she had scarcely drawn breath. When she had once made the mistake of sitting down in the servants' hall to rub her feet at the end of service, Cook had swiftly rebuked her. 'If it don't ache, it don't work, madam,' she'd admonished. After that Poppy had never dared to show so much as a flicker of fatigue under her superior's exacting gaze. Fortunately, as the months had rolled out, she had found the harder she worked, the more her confidence in her own ability had grown, until the sight of a sparkling scullery made her heart sing. But life below stairs had also shielded Poppy from the harsh realities of what had been brewing in the dark skies above.

In the sleepy hamlet of Little Framshalton she had barely even been aware there was a war on. Outside events didn't permeate the intense order of a country-house kitchen. She would no more talk to Cook about Hitler than she would dare to sneak onto the family side of the house or take Tommy the frisky hall boy up on his offer to meet behind the woodshed. Of course, she had heard Cook muttering about 'bloody rations', but when it came to world affairs, she was as naive as they came. There was order, security and protection in the hierarchy of the upstairs–downstairs world. The biggest crisis to hit the kitchens of Framshalton Hall was when Lord Framshalton had found a piece of eggshell in his beef consommé.

But then, one evening, everything had changed. Poppy had told no one the truth of what had happened that dark night in the scullery, but the rumour mill had gone into overdrive all the same. Her mother's solution had been to remove Poppy altogether. Far better to pretend it hadn't happened than deal with the ensuing scandal.

'Happen it'll do you good to see another way of life, my

girl,' her mother had muttered, as she had packed her case a few days later with almost indecent speed. 'Besides, now the new National Service Act has come in, you'll have to leave to do essential war work sooner or later. Scrubbing pans won't help to beat the Jerries,' she'd added, conveniently ignoring the fact that her days were spent tending to Her Ladyship's extravagant wardrobe.

And now, after a series of frantic correspondences between Poppy's mother and a second cousin by the name of Archie Gladstone, Poppy had been wrenched, bewildered, from her home to here, this sprawling metropolis. Mr Gladstone was the factory foreman at Trout's garment factory and had agreed, much to her mother's relief, to take Poppy off her hands.

As the bus had lurched its way towards the East End, Poppy had noticed the elegant stuccoed houses and genteel, leafy squares giving way to an altogether different side of London. The housing had grown smaller and more dense and the bombsites more frequent. In fact, as far as Poppy had been able to tell, the whole area was one giant bombsite. The streets were as dark as the skies overhead. In the country, the sky seemed to stretch on forever, and spring had been blossoming when she had left, every field blanketed in bluebells, and wild flowers bursting out in the hedgerows. Here, nothing but the strongest weeds grew, sprouting defiantly through the wreckage of a bomb crater. Finally, the bus had grumbled to a halt.

'Bethnal Green, folks,' the conductor shouted.

Gingerly, Poppy had disembarked. Off the main street, she had just been able to make out rows of identical terraced houses stretching down narrow unlit streets. Poppy's heart had dropped to the soles of her shoes. The smell of sulphur tingled her nostrils as a woman loomed up behind her and, grasping her firmly round the waist, deftly moved her to the side of the pavement as if she were as light as a piece of lace.

'Outta the way, lovey, else you'll get mown down,' the woman had said, grinning broadly to reveal a row of rotten black stumps. Her greasy hair was wrapped round some metal curlers, and she was clutching a string bag in one hand and a cigarette in the other.

'You youngsters,' she cackled. 'You ain't got an ounce of sense in yer whole body.'

'Sorry, ma'am,' Poppy blustered.

''S'right, girlie.' She grinned again.

'Excuse me, ma'am,' Poppy had ventured nervously. 'You couldn't point me in the direction of Trout's factory? All these factories look the same to me.'

'You ain't working with the Singer Girls, are you, love?' the woman had exclaimed, one eyebrow shooting up her wrinkled face. 'Blow me, they'll eat a nice young girl like you alive!' With that, she pointed to a large building at the end of a long road. 'Up towards Commercial Street. Good luck,' she laughed.

Before Poppy had a chance to ask her why she needed the good fortune, the woman was already striding off down the street, shaking her head as her bedroom slippers slapped on the cobbles.

Mother really does want to punish me, Poppy thought sadly, as she made her way in the direction of the factory. The smell of burning filled the narrow cobbled streets, and even though it was early May, a thick smog hung over the factories like a blanket. Everything looked as if it were covered in grime, from the faces of passers-by to the buildings. There was no doubt she was relieved to be away from the eyes of the village gossips, but the dread of being alone in this strange city was causing Poppy's stomach to spasm into a tight knot of fear.

Just then, a wave of noise blasted out from inside Trout's factory to the streets below.

'She's mugging you off,' hollered a shrill voice. 'Lamp her one!'

Gulping, Poppy paused at the factory door. It wasn't covered in the green baize that indicated the upstairs–downstairs divide Poppy was used to. This door was made of heavy-duty wood and was blackened with soot. It also left a nasty splinter in her hand as she finally summoned up the courage to push it open.

'You can do this, Poppy,' she murmured, wincing as she extracted the sharp splinter. But as she hesitatingly made her way up the narrow staircase to the fifth floor of the garment factory, her legs suddenly felt as feeble as a newborn lamb's. As Poppy ascended, the noise she had heard out on the streets intensified, and by the time she reached the top of the stairwell, it had reached a babbling crescendo. The very floor beneath her feet vibrated under the stampede of hobnailed boots. Wild whoops and catcalls whizzed through the air like bullets.

Suddenly, as she digested the astonishing scene, her own problems were forgotten. The room was filled with banks of tables, with rows of sewing machines lined up like soldiers. Under each machine lay bundles of cloth. The high windows afforded little light, and the floor was strewn with cotton and waste material. The small tables were covered in scissors, fabric and thread. Though the room was vast, there was scarcely space to swing a cat. A dank, unwashed smell of bodies hung like a cloud over the room, and through the commotion, Poppy could just make out the distant crackle and hiss of a wireless.

At the centre of the baying crowd, Poppy caught sight of two indomitable women facing off. Both had their hands planted on their considerable hips and were glaring at each other. There must have been thirty other women, of all ages, in the room, but all eyes were on the pair of warring females.

'Who are they?' Poppy whispered to the woman she was standing next to.

'Oh, hello, lovey,' the woman said, grinning. 'You new? Well, you're looking at Pat Doggan – she's the one with the dark hair – and Sal Fowler's the other. You couldn't miss her even in a blackout, could you, not with that red hair. Both fancy themselves as the queen of us Singer Girls.'

'Singer Girls?' asked Poppy. 'That's what the lady outside said. Why do you call yourselves that?'

'You'll see,' she winked. 'Ooh, watch it – we're in for some fun now.'

Poppy gulped. It looked like anything but.

'You leave my Bill outta this,' glowered Pat. 'He's only exempt 'cause of the arthritis in his knees.' Her jowls wobbled indignantly at whatever seemingly outrageous suggestion Sal Fowler had just levelled at her.

Poppy was stunned at the size of Pat. Food may have been rationed, but Pat Doggan was built like a brick outhouse, with huge, hairy arms shaped like legs of mutton. Her dress, which strained to contain her heaving chest, was marked with sweat rings.

Suddenly, a lone voice rang out across the factory floor. 'Didn't seem to be anything wrong with his knees when I saw 'im down on them with Sal at the bombsite out back,' it jeered.

A collective hush fell over the room. The redhead didn't let her gaze leave her enemy's face, but the words obviously hit home, as a malevolent grin slowly curled over her handsome features.

'Ooh-ee,' whistled the woman next to Poppy. 'You watch Sal now. She's got a right temper on 'er. Her and Pat are always at each other's throats. She'll go off like a rocket now, you watch.'

Poppy did, in horrified fascination.

Sal had hair as red as fire and a chip in her front left tooth. Her womanly body had more curves than a rollercoaster, and she was easily the tallest woman in the room. Poppy found herself quite entranced.

'Don't listen to mouth-of-the-south over there,' Sal shot back, quick as a flash. 'I wouldn't touch your Bill if he was the last man on earth, but I wouldn't blame him if he did go looking elsewhere.'

''Ow dare you!' shrieked Pat.

The touchpaper had been lit and it took hold. Pat slammed her fist down into her open palm and in a flash she and Sal Fowler were rolling over the concrete floor, a tangle of limbs, stocking tops and hair.

The spell was broken and suddenly, the crowd rose as one, their voices converging into a shrieking din. 'Fight! Fight! Fight!'

'Should we not try to stop them?' Poppy ventured, but the deafening roars drowned out her words. Poppy had never before seen women behave this way. They'd have been horse-whipped if they carried on like this below stairs. All of a sudden, the crowd parted and a small man frantically fought his way through from the back of the factory floor.

'Watch it!' yelled the woman next to Poppy. 'Mr Patch is coming.'

The man was tiny, barely five foot five inches, and the effort of pushing his way through the scrum of women had turned his face a curious shade of red.

'I don't know why I work here,' he muttered as he passed Poppy. 'It's a bleedin' madhouse.'

'Is that Mr Gladstone?' Poppy asked.

'Yeah, and he's well jibbed,' the woman next to her said, chuckling.

At that moment, a shoe sailed across the factory floor in a perfect arc, striking Archie Gladstone neatly on the side of his balding head. It was the final straw. Rage turned his craggy features purple. Mr Gladstone was small, but he was also nimble and in a flash he had hoisted himself up onto a nearby workbench and was looking out over the sea of women and sewing machines.

'Right, then!' he bellowed. 'Calm down. Is it not enough we're living in a bleedin' war zone without having to work in one?'

Pat opened her mouth to protest.

'Pat, keep your trap shut,' roared Mr Gladstone. 'One more word from either of you and you're out. Get back to your work, everyone. Show's over.' By the time he had finished, the only strand of hair on Archie Gladstone's head, a neatly combed-over sandy lock, had dislodged and was wafting about.

'See why we call him Mr Patch?' nudged the woman next to Poppy.

But the factory foreman's words had the desired effect and slowly the women began to disperse and drift back to their workbenches.

'New girl, follow me,' whistled Mr Gladstone, jumping down and motioning to a small office at the far side of the room.

Perhaps it was the heat, the fug of hormones and angst, but suddenly, Poppy felt overcome with exhaustion. Her introduction to Trout's had been a baptism of fire. With every heavy step she took through the dark factory, she could feel the simmering tension. How on earth would she ever fit in to a place like this? Poppy wasn't sure, but at that moment, she felt dreadfully out of her depth among these feisty women. Her head started to spin as she gazed wide-eyed around the factory floor, and her feet felt too leaden to move.

'Oi, oi!' bellowed Mr Gladstone again, his foghorn voice cutting through her thoughts. 'New girl, don't stand there like a dozy dory.'

As Poppy went to follow, a strange thing happened. The room slid out of focus, turning and shifting like a kaleidoscope.

'I feel a bit . . . a bit queer,' she gasped, reaching out to grab for something to hold on to. But her hands found thin air and the concrete floor rushed up to meet her.

'She's going down – grab her,' echoed a distant voice.

It was too late, though. Poppy fell with a sickening thud.

*

A few minutes later – or was it hours? – muffled voices filtered into Poppy's brain. She blinked as she slowly came to and realized she was laid out on the cold concrete floor on a green stretcher. Humiliation coursed through her. What a fine way to start, Poppy Percival, she scolded herself. Squeezing her eyes shut, Poppy lay motionless, wondering if she could crawl out of the office without the factory foreman noticing. But Mr Gladstone was too busy talking to an older woman sat opposite.

'What on earth am I meant to do with her, Vera?' he sighed. 'I only took her on as a favour to her mother. She's my second cousin. You have to help family out, after all, but she doesn't look like she'll last two minutes.'

'I don't know, Mr Gladstone,' replied the woman. 'Poor little mite, she looked scared out of her wits, and can you blame her? I'll have a word with Sal and Pat. Enough's enough.' The woman's voice took on a brittle edge. 'Those girls need bringing into line. I know Sal's had some hard knocks, but she's pushed it too far this time.'

Poppy groaned at the thought of Sal getting a ticking-off on her account. Hearing her, the woman sprang out of her seat in surprise and crouched down beside her.

'It breathes,' she said, smiling. 'I'm Vera.'

Poppy struggled to sit up.

'It's all right,' soothed Vera. 'Just stop there till you start to feel right again. Got you a nice sweet cup of tea on the way. Nothing tea can't cure, is there?'

Poppy stared up at the older woman and nodded gratefully. 'Thank you,' she whispered. 'You're so kind.'

'You gave us quite a scare. Didn't she, Mr Gladstone?' Vera remarked.

Mr Gladstone rolled his eyes, but managed a weak smile of agreement. 'So, Poppy,' he said, 'this here is my forelady, Vera Shadwell.'

'Please, sir,' she said, 'what's a "forelady"?'

He wiped a hand despairingly over his thin hair. 'This is what happens when you take on a scullery maid. You'd better be as much a hard worker as your mother says you are. Vera is your boss. That's all you need to know. I promised your mother I'd keep you out of trouble and Vera here will do just that for me, won't you?'

Vera narrowed her eyes and regarded Poppy as the girl gingerly got to her feet and sat down on a small wooden chair next to her.

'Indeed I shall, Mr Gladstone. Trouble is something I am fine-tuned to detect. Now, I understand you left your previous position in a hurry.'

Poppy felt herself shifting uncomfortably under the direct line of questioning.

'M–my mother thought it might do me good to get out of the scullery,' she stuttered. 'She, that is to say *I* felt it was high time I did my bit towards the war effort, and the family was talking of tightening their belts, so this was too good an opportunity to pass up.'

'Well, you're certainly right there, Poppy,' Vera said crisply. 'No one young and able should be cleaning family heirlooms when they could be doing essential war work.'

Poppy noted her response seemed to please the forelady and she felt her tension ease.

'I have references too,' she added brightly.

'Well, let me see them, then, child,' Vera demanded

impatiently, holding out her hand as Poppy passed her the sealed brown envelope Cook had given her before she left.

Poppy offered up a silent prayer as Vera scanned the letter: Please don't let her see through the story.

Whatever the forelady had read seemed to satisfy her, though, as she neatly folded the reference and started to give Poppy a rundown of the factory rules.

'I speak my mind, and I run a tight ship here. Mr Gladstone and I hold no truck with slackers. Your hours are eight in the morning until eight in the evening – sharp. Forty-five minutes for dinner and three tea breaks. Six days a week, with your day off on Sunday. Most factories clock off at six. Not us. We're fighting a war, not running a holiday camp. You get one week's holiday a year, unpaid of course. If you're so much as two minutes late to start or back late from your break, that's a morning's pay docked. Your wages are ten shillings a week, and don't be blowing it all on stockings down the market like some of them dolly daydreams out there.'

Poppy shook her head eagerly as her brain attempted to keep up with Vera's rapid-fire speech. 'Oh no, Mrs Shadwell, I shan't,' she promised. 'My mother's packed me plenty of lisle stockings.'

'Very well. I'm not married, by the way, but you can call me "Mrs" as a courtesy. It's come to my attention that behind my back most of the women call me "Kippers and Curtains", which is a harsh assessment of a hard-working woman, but I see no shame in keeping a clean house and a tidy workspace, and I shall insist you do the same. You don't win any popularity contests being a forelady, Poppy. Do I make myself clear?'

Vera folded her hands in her lap and looked at Poppy expectantly. Poppy was saved from answering when the door to Mr Gladstone's office clattered open with a start. A stout charlady wheeled in a tea trolley and, without ceremony, set down three mugs on his desk. Hot tea sloshed over the sides of the mugs as she used her trolley like a battering ram to bash open his office door and march out again.

'Cheers, sweetheart,' Mr Gladstone called after her, using his tie to mop up the spillage. 'I feel just like I'm being served tea at the Ritz.' He was still chuckling as he passed Vera and Poppy tea so strong it looked like it had been laced with creosote.

'Don't look so scared, Poppy.' Mr Gladstone grinned. 'I know we're a bit rough around the edges, but you never know, you may actually end up liking it here.'

Gratefully, she gulped at the steaming-hot tea, all the while thinking that it was a distinctly remote possibility that she would ever grow to like Trout's. She had been here less than an hour and already she had witnessed a savage fight and found herself unconscious on the factory floor. Closing her eyes, she took another long sip from her tea, the thick brown liquid trickling down the back of her throat.

'Listen, love,' Mr Gladstone went on. 'I know what you're probably thinking.'

'You do?' asked Poppy, wide-eyed.

'Yeah – where the hell have I washed up?' He winked. 'But mark my words, Poppy Percival, the women who work here are the backbone of their families and the heartbeat of their communities. They're grafters, each and every one of 'em. They fell out the cradle as machinists. Seventy-hour working weeks we clock up here, week in, week out, even through the Blitz. Not forgetting the girls on the night shift. When this war's over, it's my girls who should be handed the medals.' Pausing to check his words were sinking in, he looked directly into Poppy's eyes.

'I work the girls hard, but I look after 'em too, don't I, Vera?'

'That you do, Mr Gladstone,' Vera agreed. 'Paid us an extra four shillings a week to work through the raids, so he did.'

'What will I be sewing, sir?' Poppy asked.

Mr Gladstone sighed and curled his stubby fingers round his tea mug. 'We used to make the most beautiful girls' dresses.' He tutted. 'Before the war broke out, that is. Nowadays we sew surgical field bandages and uniforms for our boys abroad, both new uniforms and repairs. Some of the uniforms that'll land on your workbench will have bullet holes and damage. It'll be your job to patch 'em up so we can send 'em back to the front. Essential war work it is and we're proud to do it. We clothe our boys in the best uniform known to mankind: that of the serving British soldier. It may not be cut quite as extravagantly as the Americans' uniform, but it damn well serves its purpose.'

Vera nodded stiffly and stared up at the Union Jack poster tacked to the wall behind Mr Gladstone's head. 'And we'll keep doing it until life goes back to normal. Or as normal as can be round these parts.'

'You've got three weeks to learn the ropes or you're out and I'll have to send you back to the sticks, conscription or no conscription. The East End has dozens of clothing factories, so if you don't like it, you can always hotfoot it over to one of them.'

'I'm not afraid of hard work, Mr Gladstone,' Poppy replied, her cheeks flushing pink.

'I dare say.' He smiled, shaking his head. 'There's the door. Shift's nearly over. Tomorrow's a new day.'

Poppy stumbled to the door, rubbing at her head where it had hit the floor, and Vera followed.

'A quick word if I may, Vera,' Mr Gladstone called from behind his desk.

Vera paused at the door.

Mr Gladstone glanced over at Poppy. 'Go on, then, gal. Don't dilly-dally.'

'So sorry. Of course,' blustered Poppy, nearly tripping over herself in her haste to get out of his office. 'I'll wait outside, Mrs Shadwell.'

Outside, she tried her hardest not to look through the crack in the partially open door. But something about the way Mr Gladstone was looking at Vera, the deep tenderness that shone out from his gruff little face, meant she couldn't quite tear her eyes away from the scene. She watched as he rose to his feet and gripped the desk for courage.

'*The Big Blockade* is on at the picture house. It's got that fella in it. You know, what's-his-face, John Mills,' he mumbled. 'I'd be honoured if you'd accompany me.'

Mr Gladstone was hardly a suave star of the silver screen himself, Poppy thought. Squat, balding, with a broken nose that seemed to spread halfway across his pockmarked face like a puddle, he looked more like a bulldog than a film star, but when faced with Vera, his face radiated a gentle warmth.

'Maybe a drink after?' he added.

Vera shook her head. 'I don't think that would be appropriate, Mr Gladstone, do you?'

And with that she turned on her heel and exited his office, leaving a small man to nurse his crushed hopes.

'Women,' Mr Gladstone muttered. 'Next to the wound, what women make best is the bandage.'

From her vantage point on the other side of the door, Poppy heard his words and felt every ounce of his pain as if it were her own. Mr Gladstone may have been a little shopworn, and he was certainly no John Mills, but even Poppy could see he was as decent and honest as the day was long. As for Vera, Poppy had never come across anyone so frank and direct in all her sixteen years. There was something else about her, too, that Poppy couldn't quite put her finger on: an air of sadness that coated her like a fine layer of dust.

Poppy's soul ached for the familiarity of her old life. But then she reminded herself that however intimidating Bethnal Green seemed, it was a hundred miles away from Framshalton Hall, and for that she had to be thankful.

Just then Vera's voice rang out across the factory floor like a siren. 'Poppy,' she hollered, 'don't just stand there gawping. Follow me.'

'Sorry, Mrs Shadwell. Coming,' Poppy said, hurrying after the forelady as she marched off.

Back out on the factory floor, Poppy was stunned to see the women were in full swing again. But this time their battle cries had been replaced with a rousing chorus of 'Bless 'Em All' as *Workers' Playtime* rang out from the wireless. They sang as one, gently pumping the sewing-machine treadles with their feet and nodding their heads in time to the music, never allowing their gazes to slip from their workbenches.

Poppy's eyes could scarcely keep up with the seamless activity. Their fingers were a blur of motion, snipping, sewing, feeding long stretches of material through the sewing machines, as their voices soared and bounced off the high vaulted ceilings. The penny dropped. So that was why they were nicknamed the Singer Girls! Seated behind their Singer sewing machines, sewing and singing in flawless harmony, never had a moniker seemed so apt. It was extraordinary to Poppy. The same cockney voices that had sounded like a gaggle of mating geese just minutes earlier now sounded so gentle, full of warmth and tenderness.

Vera paused at a bank of tables. 'These are some of our long-termers,' she said, with a touch of deference. 'Ivy and Doris. Sixty years' experience at Trout's between them. They can edge-stitch with their eyes shut.'

More names and faces passed in front of Poppy as Vera rattled off further introductions.

Suddenly, the forelady was off again, marching in the other direction. As Poppy followed behind her, she noticed the rain had cleared and the spring evening was giving way to dusk. What little light the tall Victorian warehouse was afforded was already fast fading and soon the area would be plunged into darkness.

A prickle of fear ran up Poppy's spine as she realized she didn't have the faintest clue where her lodgings were or how to get to them. She wasn't scared of the dark. With no street lamps and not even a solitary light from the village twinkling over the fields, Framshalton Hall was always engulfed in a heavy blanket of velvety black by night. But here in London, things were different. Strange men populated this unfamiliar city. She had read about the terrifying

Jack the Ripper, who had once prowled the very streets outside the factory. She didn't fancy walking down those dark, foggy alleys by herself.

As they passed the windows, two women were already standing on high wooden ladders fixing the heavy regulation blackout blinds to the narrow frames. Tears of mirth streamed down their faces, and one screeched with laughter, her body shaking so hard Poppy feared she may topple right off the ladder. It was then she realized that it was Sal Fowler and Pat Doggan. The very same women who had been locked in a vicious fight just an hour earlier. Did that fight mean nothing? What a very strange place this was: full of women who seemed to want to kill each other one moment and hug the next.

As they walked, Vera gave Poppy a rundown of the rules.

'No smoking on the factory floor. You work through air raids, unless I say otherwise. Course, we don't get as many as we used to since the Blitz ended. Fighting, swearing and wearing make-up are expressly forbidden. Keep your head down and your wits about you.'

Poppy nodded furiously. 'Oh, don't worry,' she replied. 'In service, we never wore make-up. Her Ladyship wouldn't allow it.' Poppy hadn't meant anything by that comment other than a desire to assure Vera that she would obey the rules, but at the end of a bank of machines, Vera paused and her green eyes glowed with a fierce intensity.

'You may look down on factory workers,' she replied defensively, 'but it's an honest and decent profession, a damn sight better than charring. I fought to bring in piece-work and an extra four shillings to work through raids so these lot here can earn more money than any other factory girl on Commercial Street. The East End has been built on garment factories for centuries, and you're standing in the best of the lot.'

Poppy couldn't help but notice that the more agitated Vera grew, the more she played with her gold necklace. It was half a heart, and its jagged centre ran straight through the middle. It seemed to Poppy an unusual thing to wear. It was also unfortunate, as it drew her attention to a patchwork of yellowed scars on Vera's chest. Poppy guessed the scars were old. They looked stretched and polished by time, snaking off in all directions over her chest.

'I mean, we ain't the high and mighty lot you're used to working for, but get any fanciful notions out your head, my girl.'

Her voice grew louder as she warmed to her theme. Innocent young Poppy hung on to her every word.

'Our boys abroad are depending on us. We women are enduring the bombs, supplying the troops and keeping the home fires burning, but will they be giving us medals when this thing's over? Will they hell.'

'Oh, give it a break, Vera,' sang a voice from the workbench behind. 'We've had a gutful of your old flannel. Can't you see the poor girl's bored out of her skull?'

Rising from behind her station and extending a slim hand was quite the most beautiful girl Poppy had ever seen. The fingers held in Poppy's hand were long, cool and slender, each nail topped with a slash of crimson varnish. They belonged to a creature so stunning Poppy's mouth fell open.

'I'm Daisy, darling.' The vision smiled, revealing a dazzling bright smile, made all the whiter by a slick of vibrant pillar box-red lipstick.

Poppy's eyes were drawn from her face to the gold necklace sitting round her elegant neck. It was a half-heart pendant . . . the missing half to Vera's.

'I'm Vera's sister,' Daisy purred. How on earth could she be related to Vera? Poppy marvelled secretly. Vera had greying hair and tightly pursed lips. This girl was exquisite and delicate. Only their eyes revealed them to be related: emerald green and crackling with a strange intensity.

'Don't mind her – her bark's worse than her bite,' Daisy went on. 'She got the brains; I got the beauty. I know what you're thinking: how is she related to Vera?'

'Not at all,' lied Poppy, acutely aware of Vera's bristling presence beside her.

'Vera's quite a bit older than me, aincha Vera? Our late mother didn't think she could have any more,' she said, waving her hand dismissively. 'Then along I came. "Miracle baby", they called me, but I assure you I'm real all right,' she beamed, extending a long, slender arm. 'Go on, pinch me.'

Poppy giggled in spite of herself. In all her years she had never seen anyone who oozed such confidence, apart from the odd Hollywood star in Cook's old *Home Companion* magazine.

Daisy's lustrous hair was so black it was almost purple in places, and she had styled it into elegant victory rolls, which framed a face that looked like it had been carved from marble. Her bright green feline eyes sparkled mischievously from over the highest cheekbones Poppy had ever seen. Instinctively, her eyes ran over Daisy's hourglass curves and she gulped. Months of Cook's excellent puddings and pies had left her own small frame comfortably padded, but

Daisy's body went in and out under the cherry-red figure-hugging dress she was wearing. Poppy would need two hot spoons to ease herself into a garment that tight, she thought to herself.

Daisy giggled as she noticed Poppy's gaze travel down to her shapely legs. 'Admiring my nylons, are you?' she winked. She leaned closer to Poppy and whispered in a soft voice, 'Shall I let you in on a secret?'

Poppy nodded wordlessly. She was so enthralled by Daisy she almost felt hypnotized. The clouds of Evening in Paris that were engulfing her only added to the stupefying effect.

'They're not real. I paint my legs in gravy browning and get Sal to draw the seams in with an eyebrow pencil. They look like the real thing, though, don't they, Poppy?' she smiled, arching one leg and stretching it out brazenly in front of her.

Poppy swallowed hard and looked away. There was more flesh on show than she had ever been exposed to in her whole life.

'Oh, put it away, Daisy, for goodness' sake,' snapped Vera. 'Can't you see you're embarrassing the poor girl? You're behaving like a cheap trollop, and take that muck off your face while you're at it. How many times have I told you about wearing make-up at work?'

Despite the dressing-down from her sister, Daisy didn't look the slightest bit uncomfortable. In fact, she completely ignored Vera as she smoothed down her dress and turned her attentions back to Poppy. She spoke with just a touch of laughter in her voice.

'You stick with me, and don't listen to my sister. We'll have much more fun, won't we, Poppy?'

'Will we?' Poppy replied.

'Oh yes,' she oozed. 'I know all the best dances. You know,' she smiled, as she looked Poppy up and down, 'you're awful pretty. If you'd let me do you up a bit, shorten that skirt, touch of rouge . . . you'd scrub up a treat. Just you leave it to me. Not that I'm going to be here for long, mind you. I'm going to marry an officer and move to corned-beef city.'

'There's a city named after corned beef?' Poppy asked, astonished.

Daisy threw her head back and laughed throatily. It was a wonderful laugh, rich and contagious. Soon Poppy was helpless with giggles.

'No, sweetheart. Dagenham, I mean,' replied Daisy. 'I'm going to get married and move into one of those lovely semis in the suburbs. I'm going to have beautiful children and be the perfect wife.'

Her confidence was unshakeable.

'Soon as the war's over, I'm leaving. I don't want to grow old in Bethnal Green,' she said, laughing again and tossing a casual glance at her older sister. But this time, the laughter was mocking. 'Anything to get away from this dump,' she added.

Vera looked as if she were about to implode with rage.

The slow, wretched wail was haunting, rising up from the very bowels of the factory, its droning sound deafening everything like a scream. For a second Poppy was confused. Was it Vera? But no, she was rooted to the spot, still staring at her younger sister, her face a ghostly white. No sound came from her thin lips.

Mr Gladstone burst out of his office. 'All right, ladies!' he shouted. 'Evacuate.'

The penny dropped. 'An air-raid siren?' gasped Poppy.

'You come with me, sweetheart,' Daisy said. 'Something tells me you won't last two minutes out there without me.'

'I-I've never heard one before. They don't go off where I come from,' Poppy stuttered.

'Thought not,' grinned Daisy. 'Looks like the war's finally found you, Poppy. What did you say your surname was?'

'P-Percival,' Poppy stammered over the siren.

'Well, Poppy Percival, Sal's got a mate with a pub – we can shelter in the cellar. Everyone else usually goes down the church crypts or Bethnal Green Tube.' She sniffed in disdain. 'All crammed in like sardines, they are, thousands of them. No, darling, you stick with us.'

Poppy knew better than to argue with this assertive young lady and stuck close behind her as, together, they joined the tidal wave of workers clattering down the stairwell and out into the unknown.

Two

Outside on the streets, the air hummed with nervous tension as people scurried to the nearest shelter, clutching bundles of bedding and sleepy children to their chests. Bodies jostled and bumped in the sticky evening air, and all the while the dreaded siren sounded. Its sickening drone ran through Poppy's brain on a loop, disorientating her.

Poppy had never known an evening like it. If there was even a single shaft of moonlight, it would have helped, but the sky was thick with clouds and brick dust; she could taste it in her mouth.

'Where's Mrs Shadwell?' Poppy asked suddenly.

'Oh, don't worry about Vera,' drifted back the voice of Daisy. 'What you need to know about my sister is, she's a bit peculiar. She never comes down to the shelters. She was the same all through the Blitz. Reckons she suffers from claustrophobia. More like she can't bear to leave her good room. We got precious little space in our house as it is and she treats our front parlour like a shrine.'

'What do you mean?' asked Poppy.

'Well, we're only allowed in there on Christmas or birthdays, but she scrubs it most days. It's only got an old chaise longue, which she covers with a dust sheet, and a poxy aspidistra, yet the way she carries on, you'd think it was Buckingham Palace. What a joke.' Poppy heard a tinge of bitterness creep into Daisy's voice.

Poppy heard Sal call back to them, 'To give her credit, though, Dais, she does have the cleanest nets on the street.'

'What good is having pearly-white nets when you've got half the German Army trying to kill you?' Daisy snorted.

Poppy could just make out Sal's muffled laughter from somewhere up ahead.

In the dark, Poppy could feel Daisy's shoulders stiffen and faintly heard an angry sigh. Poppy didn't know yet what history lay between the warring sisters, what had happened in their past to shape them into the two very different women they were today, but she felt sure that Vera's scarred chest held the answer. For now, though, she let the matter lie, and followed in her new friend's footsteps as she led her to shelter.

Two minutes later, they arrived at the Dog and Duck. The East End was filled with pubs. Poppy must have seen the shadow of one on every street corner, at least, but Sal assured her this one was special.

'I know the landlord, Alfie Bow,' she winked, rapping on the door.

The door opened and Poppy found herself descending a narrow staircase.

'Make yourselves at home,' a gruff voice called out after them.

Inside the cellar, it was cold and dank, and the stench of beer was suffocating. Even the heavy odour of Daisy's Evening in Paris perfume did little to disguise the smell. Poppy had never set foot in a pub in her life, but she kept that to herself.

Shivering, she sat down on a small wooden stool. Daisy pulled a stack of warm blankets from behind a barrel and gently placed one over Poppy's knees.

'You must think me a sorry creature,' Poppy said between chattering teeth.

'Don't worry, darlin'.' Daisy smiled. 'It's the shock of hearing the siren.'

Sal lit some candles and soon the gloomy basement was filled with a soft, comforting glow.

'What's your poison?' asked Sal, as she rummaged around inside a wooden crate for some glasses. 'Good old Alfie always leaves us out a little tipple, doesn't he, Dais?'

'Golly, I should say,' she smiled, kicking her long legs out in front of her.

'Oh, I don't drink,' muttered Poppy. 'My mother doesn't approve.'

'Your mother isn't here now, is she?' insisted Sal, placing a small glass of honey-coloured liquid in Poppy's hands. 'Come on, girl – wet your whistle. It'll do you good.'

'May as well enjoy it,' agreed Daisy. 'Goodness knows how long we'll be down here for.'

Poppy took a sip and a second later, her cheeks were flushed with heat. 'Cor, blast me,' she spluttered, clutching her chest and coughing. 'What is this?'

'It's whisky,' laughed Sal, tossing her tumbler back in a mouthful and reaching for the bottle to refill their glasses. 'Warms the cockles like nothing else I know.'

Overcome with tiredness, Poppy leaned back against the dank brick cellar wall and took another, bigger sip. The red-hot liquid slowly trickled down the back of her throat, warming her, numbing her emotions.

Cast in the flickering candlelight, Poppy got the chance to observe Sal Fowler close up for the first time. She was not as pretty as porcelain doll-like Daisy, but she was handsome all right. A cloud of fiery red hair was pulled back from her face with a jade-green headscarf, and every feature seemed exaggerated, from her strong jawline to her full, sensuous ruby-red lips. As she talked, Poppy was transfixed by the chip in her front left tooth.

'Admiring my war wounds, are you, Poppy?' Sal smiled, pouring more whisky into Poppy's glass.

'I really shouldn't,' Poppy murmured.

Sal blithely ignored her protestations and carried on chatting as she poured. 'Got hit by a bit of flying debris during the bombings. We were running to a shelter when it just nicked my mouth.'

'Were the Germans really dropping bombs here?' Poppy gulped, wide-eyed, noticing a strange glowing feeling starting in her stomach.

Daisy and Sal stared at her with undisguised shock.

'Well, they weren't dropping pineapples,' snorted Sal. 'Blimey, you're green, aincha? My home was flattened to the ground during the Blitz. It was a tenement flat in the old Peabody building. Took a direct hit from the Luftwaffe when I was at work – thank God for that at least. Good riddance, mind you – it was a dump. One way to deal with the lice, I suppose. In fact, half of Bethnal Green's gone. Best thing Hitler ever did was to bomb the slums. He did us a favour. Now I've got myself a brand-new Nissen hut, and best of all, my good-for-nothing husband has no idea where it is. He's fighting abroad, and long may that continue.'

Daisy bumped her glass against Sal's. 'Hear, hear,' she murmured.

'How long has your husband been away?' asked Poppy.

'Let's not ruin the night by talking about Reggie,' Sal replied. Her mouth tightened, and as she lit a cigarette, Poppy got the distinct impression that subject was firmly off limits.

Sal blew out a long stream of blue smoke, then suddenly smiled and flicked an impish look at Daisy. 'Are you thinking what I'm thinking, Dais?' she asked.

'I should say,' Daisy replied, with a wink. 'Now, then, sweet Poppy,' she gushed, as she fished around inside her bag. 'While we're all stuck down here, why don't we do you up a little? Just a touch of rouge.'

Before she knew it, Daisy and Sal were unscrewing pots of rouge and powder. Poppy had protested. She really had. Along with drinking alcohol, wearing make-up had been banned for servants at Framshalton Hall.

'Oh no, I couldn't,' she said vigorously. 'I'm not allowed. Make-up is forbidden below stairs.'

Daisy and Sal exchanged a wicked laugh.

'Nah, you put it on your face, Poppy,' Sal quipped. 'Besides, got to stay lovely. There's a war on, after all.'

'Absolutely,' agreed Daisy enthusiastically. 'We're gonna make you look so pretty, Poppy Percival, your own mother wouldn't recognize you.'

Poppy smiled sadly. 'Maybe that wouldn't be so bad.' The words were out of her mouth before she had a chance to stop herself.

Daisy cocked her head. 'Now why ever would you say such a thing, Poppy?'

'She's ashamed of me,' replied Poppy miserably. 'She couldn't wait to get rid of me.'

'Whatever did you do?' gasped Sal and Daisy as one.

Poppy clammed up. 'Oh, nothing of any consequence,' she lied. 'You know what mothers are like – nothing's ever good enough. Now then, I thought you were going to make me look like a film star.'

In no time at all Sal and Daisy were dolling her up like a shop mannequin, Daisy's radiant smile dispelling Poppy's fears. Somehow she had found herself unable to say no to Sal and Daisy, and maybe, she reflected, allowing a little guilty thought to slip unbidden into her mind, she hadn't wanted to. Saying no wasn't something she was terribly good at, after all. Soon the dark cellar was filled with giggles. By the time the all-clear sounded, she no longer resembled the girl who had nervously ventured up the factory stairs. Her soft brown curls were now styled into elegant finger rolls. Her flawless creamy skin had been accentuated with rouge, and a liberal coating of panstick completely disguised her dusting of freckles. Only Poppy's wide blue eyes remained the same. A little glazed from the alcohol that was coursing through her veins, but otherwise bright and beautiful.

The girls led Poppy back up the cellar stairs and she emerged blinking into the brightly lit saloon bar of the Dog and Duck, which Poppy was surprised to see was already fast filling up. A glass of port and lemon was pressed into her hand as the girls chatted and waved cheerily to people on other tables. They seemed to know most of the drinkers in the pub and bantered back and forth good-naturedly with the landlord.

They had been there no time at all before Poppy spotted a familiar face weaving her way through the tables towards them.

'There you are, Poppy,' sighed Vera, visibly relieved. 'I came as fast as I could. I promised Mr Gladstone I'd keep my eye on you.' She paused as she took in Poppy's new appearance. 'Are you all right, my dear?' she asked, her eyes narrowing.

'Hello, Mrs Shadwell,' mumbled Poppy. 'Sal and Daisy have been looking after me. We've been having a gay old time.'

With that, she hiccupped and leaned back against the bar. Frantically, she fought to stay upright, but with a couple of glasses of whisky inside her, it was like trying to balance on two pins. Instead, she slithered slowly down to the floor.

'Oh, for goodness' sake, Daisy and Sal,' snapped Vera, grabbing Poppy before she crumpled into a heap at her feet. She wrenched the glass of port from Poppy's hand and whistled to the landlord. 'Bitter lemon over here when you're ready.' Then she whirled on Daisy. 'She's nothing but an innocent up from the countryside. How could you corrupt her like this?'

'Sssnot an innocent,' protested Poppy, though no one was listening.

Vera was glaring with ill-disguised disgust at her younger sister, but Daisy met her gaze with a challenging look, her proud chin thrust defiantly in the air.

'Mr Gladstone entrusted me to look after her, and what do you two do?' Vera said angrily.

'Oh, do calm down, won't you, Vera,' sighed Daisy. 'It's just a bit of make-up. You wanna try it yourself.'

'But look at her, for pity's sake,' said Vera, ignoring Daisy's cruel jibe about her looks. 'She looks like she should be working the docks.'

'Steady on,' said Sal.

'Don't waste your breath, Sal,' tutted Daisy. 'I reckon our young friend here would sooner be bombed out than look like my old sister.'

'That's enough of your sauce, my girl,' Vera snapped.

Mercifully the conversation was brought to an abrupt halt when in the corner of the smoky room, someone struck up a song on the piano. In no time at all half the pub was swaying and singing along to the lively tune, the voices drowning out the bickering sisters.

'Oh good, I love a sing-song,' enthused Sal, relieved at the interruption. 'Come on. Let's grab a table before it gets too rammed. I reckon young Poppy here could do with a sit-down.' She winked at Poppy and gently guided her to the nearest table.

As Poppy sat and sipped her bitter lemon, attempting to gather her wits, she took in the pub's customers. Men and women of all ages, relieved to have escaped unharmed from their shelters, were pouring into the warmth and safety of the Dog and Duck, ordering drinks, laughing and telling jokes. The tiny room was packed, the blacked-out windows steamed up, and the air was alive with the babble of cockney voices competing for airspace.

Poppy soon lost count of how many people she was introduced to.

'Gracious,' she smiled, 'you girls are popular.'

'You better believe it,' grinned Sal, waving at Pat, Ivy and Doris from Trout's as they walked in.

'Budge up, Poppy, there's a good gal,' cackled Ivy, when she reached their table.

'Yeah, that's the way, sweetheart,' piped up Pat, easing her gigantic bosom round the pub table until she was rammed in on the other side. Hapless Poppy found herself wedged in between the layers of a human sandwich.

'Don't look so worried, Poppy,' whispered Sal from across the table. 'Everyone likes you, I can tell. All you need to know about the East End is if people like you, you're all right, but if you cross 'em . . .' she paused to exhale her cigarette in perfect smoke rings, 'forget about it – your life will be a misery.'

'But how will I know?'

'Trust me,' winked Sal, 'you'll know. You'll be sent to Coventry.'

'But I've only just got to London,' Poppy pleaded, but Sal was no longer listening.

Sitting back in her chair, Sal sighed contentedly. 'Can't beat this,' she said. 'It'd be perfect right now if only my boys were here. I don't know why you want to leave, Daisy. I'm going to end my days here.'

'Couldn't agree more,' piped up Vera. 'Everything we need is right here.'

Daisy laughed with scorn in her voice. 'No imagination – that's your problem,' she said, shrugging her delicate shoulders. As she spoke, Poppy noticed how, nearby, a table of men were gazing rapt at Daisy, hanging on her every word. Her beauty had that effect on people. The tumbling raven curls, sensuous, inviting mouth and glittering emerald eyes gave her an almost cartoonish beauty, which seemed exaggerated next to the stout, matronly figures of Pat, Doris and Ivy.

What must it be like to be the most beautiful woman in any room you walk into? Poppy wondered.

'I may be an East End girl, but I got big aspirations, see,' Daisy went on in her wonderful breathy voice. As she spoke, she absent-mindedly played with the hem of her red dress, her fingers seductively toying with the silky folds of the gown. The men on the neighbouring table looked like they were about to expire.

'I want an inside toilet, a proper garden, hot running water. My old mate Sandra's family upped sticks to Jaywick Sands. Expect she's living the life of Riley. Eighteen thousand people have left Bethnal Green in the last ten years alone, they reckon. I just wish I was one of 'em.'

'Yeah,' interrupted Vera. 'And you know how many have come back?' Without waiting for anyone to answer, she went on, her scarred chest heaving with indignation. 'A third, that's how many. And I'll tell you for why – there's no community. An inside toilet can't compensate for not being with your own.'

'That's right,' agreed Ivy, while Sal nodded.

'Where's the markets, the pubs and the music halls in the suburbs?' Vera said. 'Who'd look after your kids if you were ill, or run stuff down the pawnbroker's? You pay a high price for indoor plumbing.'

'But that's the point,' protested Daisy. 'I want to look out at green fields, not pawnbrokers. As soon as this war's over, I'm making a better life for myself. I want to raise my nippers out in the fresh air, do a proper job of it.'

Vera stared hard at a puddle of beer that was creeping

towards the side of the table, dangerously close to spilling over the edge.

Poppy watched the older woman's face flicker with emotion. Vera fished out a hanky and furiously wiped at the mess on the table.

'You don't know you're born, young lady,' she spat. 'You're too young to really remember the days before this war changed our neighbourhood.'

Daisy tutted and rolled her eyes.

Sensing that the sisters were about to engage in round two, Poppy focused her gaze on Sal.

'You mentioned your boys, Sal,' she ventured sweetly. 'I'd love to hear about them.'

Sal's expression changed in a heartbeat. Her mouth stretched into a dazzling smile. Even her halo of copper hair seemed to shine more brightly at the mention of her sons.

'Well, there's Billy – he's seven – and Joey, who's five. Lil' bleeders they are,' she said.

'Don't listen to her,' chuckled Daisy. 'She loves the bones of them. Don't you, Sal?'

'That I do,' she grinned. 'I might be biased, but they are gorgeous. You want to see?'

'Oh yes.'

Placing her glass down, Sal pulled a crumpled black-and-white photo from inside her blouse and proudly thrust it at Poppy. Staring back at her were two adorable little boys. They had quite the grubbiest faces she had ever seen – street urchins, Cook would have called them – but beneath the dyed-in grime shone a sweetness and intelligence. At least they have a mother who would quite obviously fight like a lioness if anyone so much as harmed a hair on their heads, thought Poppy. More than could be said for her own mother, who had spent every day of Poppy's childhood scrubbing her with carbolic soap and washing the fun clean out of her life. And when danger had come knocking, how had her mother helped her?

'They're beautiful, Sal,' said Poppy, as she carefully handed her back the photo.

Sal took her picture and traced her finger down it with a touching fervour, as if she was stroking her sons' warm cheeks and not just a faded black-and-white image of them. Her mothering instincts were beyond reproach and Poppy felt humbled by such a strong love, displayed so honestly.

'You must be very proud of them – angels with dirty faces,' she blurted, so moved she couldn't stop herself speaking her mind.

'Angels with dirty faces? I like that, Poppy.'

'So where are they now?'

'I had them evacuated a year before the Blitz began, as soon as the first wave of evacuations started,' Sal replied. 'It made sense. And I'm glad of it too. They're safe now, staying with a postmistress down in Devon.'

'You must miss them very much,' said Poppy.

'You have no idea. But I know it's the right thing for them. And I know I'll see them again.' Her voice cracked and Sal allowed Daisy to fold her into a hug.

Poppy watched the touching scene in awe. Gently, Daisy rocked her like a mother might a sick child.

'It's all right,' Daisy soothed. 'Better out than in, I always say.'

And there they remained, wrapped in a cuddle, bound

by deep ties of care and loyalty that Poppy could never even begin to fathom. Their friendship left her breathless with admiration and envy. East End women clearly made friends for life. What real friends did she have back in Norfolk? None that she knew of. And her mother? At least Sal had sent her boys away to keep them safe; her mum had got shot of her the first chance she had simply to save face.

'I'm sorry,' Sal sniffed, composing herself. 'It's like a part of myself has gone. And every single day I wonder what it is they're doing, what I'm missing. Joey lost his first tooth the other day and it wasn't me pretending to be the tooth fairy. But I don't regret it,' she blazed. 'Oh no. Three days after the Blitz began, a junior school over in Canning Town, near the docks, copped it. Hundreds of poor souls buried alive. The East End was ringed with fire that night, wasn't it, girls? We saw the flames billowing up into the night sky from the top of Trout's.'

Daisy nodded sadly. 'They were piling the dead up in the street. Those poor little kiddies.'

The table fell silent. Even Vera's usually brisk expression seemed haunted by the memory.

'That day changed the East End forever,' murmured Pat.

'So you see why I sent them away, Poppy?' said Sal.

'I do,' Poppy replied softly. 'Sounds like you've done the right thing. At least you evacuated your kids out of London. My mum evacuated me *into* London.'

Sal screamed with laughter and slung her arm around Poppy. 'I like you, Poppy Percival. I reckon you and me are going to be all right. What do you reckon, girls?'

She turned to the rest of the Singer Girls, who Poppy realized were all staring at her curiously. She found she was holding her breath as she waited for their response. She yearned for the approval of her new workmates. Suddenly, it seemed to matter very much what they thought of her.

'I think she's the prettiest, sweetest little thing I ever saw, Sal.' Daisy grinned and a deep ripple of warmth spread through Poppy's stomach, this time not caused by whisky. Even Vera was smiling warmly at her from across the pub table.

By the time the last-orders bell sounded, Poppy was happy but plainly exhausted.

'You look dead on your feet, Poppy,' remarked Vera. 'Tonight you will stay with me. It's too late to find your new lodgings now.'

'I don't wish to be a burden, Mrs Shadwell.'

'Nonsense. I promised Mr Gladstone I would look out for you and that's precisely what I intend to do,' she said, and then as an afterthought she added, 'I just hope he's out tonight on a night shift.'

Poppy was about to enquire who *he* was when she noticed the smile had frozen on Vera's face and she was staring hard at something.

'Talk of the devil and you summon him up,' she muttered, hurriedly draining her drink. 'Come on, Poppy, let's go.'

Poppy turned and found herself staring up at the face of a strange man.

'Well, this is a cosy scene, ain't it.' He grinned, revealing a set of cracked yellow teeth. It wasn't a warm smile, more of a sneer, and judging by the way he was swaying, he was full of drink. Instinctively Poppy drew her arms around herself.

'Evening, ladies,' he said, nodding to the rest of the Singer Girls. 'How's my favourite girl?' he said to Daisy, completely ignoring Vera.

'Dad!' Daisy gushed.

Poppy was flabbergasted. This drunk man was Vera and Daisy's father?

'Sit down, Dad,' Daisy smiled. 'Make room, everyone.'

Everyone begrudgingly shifted up. The atmosphere had changed from one of easy warmth to a strained silence.

'Don't worry,' snapped Vera, reverting back to the prickly woman Poppy first met in the factory earlier that evening. 'We're just leaving, aren't we, Poppy? Have my seat, Frank.'

How odd, thought Poppy, that she referred to her father by his name, unlike Daisy. There was clearly no love lost between her and Frank.

'Don't go on my account, Vera,' he said icily. 'Who's your new friend? Ain't you going to introduce me?'

'This is Poppy Percival and she just started work at the factory,' Vera said tersely. 'Now come on, Poppy – we really ought to be getting you home.'

But Frank wasn't letting them go that easily.

'Delighted to make your acquaintance, Poppy,' he said slowly, letting his eyes roam unashamedly over her body. Taking Poppy's hand in his, he gripped it so firmly she felt her hand begin to tremble.

'You're a pretty young thing, aincha,' he leered, leaning in so close Poppy could smell stale tobacco and sweat. 'And look at this lovely fresh skin,' he went on, clearly revelling in her discomfort. 'Straight up from the countryside I dare say, by the looks of you. Don't you be letting these girls corrupt you. You need *anything*, you just come to your uncle Frank.'

'Behave, Dad,' laughed Daisy, seemingly oblivious to Poppy's unease.

'You've had your fun, Frank. Come on, Poppy, let's go,' said Vera, rising sharply to her feet.

Gratefully Poppy stood, her head spinning from the smoke-filled air and Frank's close attention.

'I'm just going to nip to the toilet before we go, Mrs Shadwell, if I may.'

'Of course, Poppy,' she replied. 'They're out back in the yard. Don't be long. It really is getting late now.'

Poppy went as fast as her feet would take her through the bar and out into the pitch black of the yard, gasping as the fresh night air hit her lungs. Frantically she groped her way through the darkness until she found the outhouse door. Experience taught her not to hang about too long in outdoor toilets. If the icy cold of the outhouse brick toilet wasn't bad enough, rats scuttled about yards like this. Trembling, she made her way back towards the warmth of the pub and gasped as she bumped straight into a solid force.

'Going somewhere in a hurry?' rang out a gravelly voice. The tip of a cigarette glowed before her and suddenly Frank's face was illuminated in front of hers. Had he followed her outside?

'F-Frank,' Poppy stammered eventually. 'Would you let me pass, please?'

'Course I will, sweetheart,' he said, an unnerving softness creeping into his voice. 'I just wanted to let you know that I meant what I said back then.'

Poppy's skin crawled as he took a gnarled, tobacco-stained finger and traced it slowly down her cheek. She stood rooted to the spot, her heart thundering in her chest. Her fear seemed to arouse Frank further, as his breathing grew shallow.

'You're a good girl. I like that,' he rasped, edging closer forward.

In horror, Poppy realized he was about to kiss her; his dry lips were hovering just inches from hers. Frank made a strange guttural sound in his throat as he wiped his mouth with the back of his hand.

'I'll look after you, Poppy,' he croaked, reaching out in the darkness for her body.

Fear exploded in Poppy's chest, yet she remained motionless. Why could she not run?

'That is enough.' A sharp voice rang out through the darkness and Frank sprang back. 'For goodness' sake, Frank, Poppy is young enough to be your granddaughter.'

'Oh, piss off, Vera,' groaned Frank, staggering backwards.

In a flash, Vera was by Poppy's side. She took her arm and guided her back across the yard. Poppy could feel Vera's hand shaking on her arm as they walked and suddenly she realized: Vera was as scared of her father as she was.

'Where are you going in such a hurry?' Daisy exclaimed, as they reached the pub table and Vera quickly gathered their bags and coats.

'Ask him,' Vera spat, gesturing to the back door of the pub, where Frank had entered. 'I just caught him trying it on with Poppy,' she blazed. 'He's so full of drink a barrage balloon couldn't even hold him up.'

'Shut your mouth, my girl, unless you want to feel the

cut of my hand across your backside,' Frank muttered as he reached the table.

Poppy felt herself drowning in despair. Oh, please, Lord, not again. Why did trouble follow her wherever she went?

'You wouldn't dare, not in public,' Vera snapped back, hastily fastening the buttons on her coat, her fingers shaking.

The pub fell silent and Poppy wished the ground would open up and swallow her.

'I don't want to cause any trouble,' she said quietly.

'You're not,' said Daisy firmly, glaring at Vera. 'This is between Vera and our dad. For some reason, she has a real bee in her bonnet when it comes to him.'

'That's right, love,' said Frank, coming up behind Daisy and placing a hand on her shoulder. 'I was just being friendly to young Poppy here and Vera goes and accuses me of all sorts of tripe. Ain't that right, Poppy?'

His dark eyes were full of menace as they bored into hers.

'I-I, er, yes,' she stammered, hardly able to meet Vera's gaze.

'It's all right, Poppy,' snapped Vera. 'You're not the first young woman he's tried to corrupt, and I dare say you shan't be the last. The problem is, Daisy can't see him for what he really is. Rotten to the core.'

In a flash Daisy was on her feet. 'Oh, for pity's sake, Vera, not this again,' she yelled. 'He's our old man. He's the only parent I've got and I'm sick of you slagging him off.'

Along with the rest of the pub Poppy held her breath waiting for Vera's reaction. Frank sat back down and crossed his arms, a malevolent smile curling over his cruel face. He's enjoying this, thought Poppy in dismay.

'Parent?' Vera spluttered, her fear giving way to outrage. 'Don't make me laugh. I've seen rats with more nurturing instincts. Don't you remember?' she shouted. 'He knew I was terrified of mice so he'd sit outside our bedroom at night scratching at the bare boards. He was the real vermin. Or the time you were crying so he took you down Wheeler Street Arch and threatened to leave you there for the ghost of Jack the Ripper. Or all the times he gave me a hiding for leaving a plate out or for not having his dinner ready on time.'

'You're making this up, you sad old spinster,' Daisy scoffed.

'So help me, God, I'm not.' Vera trembled. 'You were just too young to remember. You were a nipper; I was sixteen, don't forget. Ask Dor, or Ivy, or anyone round here for that matter – they'll tell you. They all know he's a bad apple. But worse than the beatings were his mind games. They made my life a misery, and Mum's too. She worked twelve-hour shifts to put food on our table 'cause he was too drunk most of the time to get work. She felt the wrath of his temper every bit as much as me. You think he loves you, but trust me, he doesn't. That man doesn't know what real love is.'

'It's not true,' Daisy wept, hot tears spilling down her face. 'I was his miracle baby girl – he told me that constantly.'

'The only miracle is how he's scraped through life at all. He wasn't even around when you were growing up,' Vera insisted. 'He was only interested in finding a stray bit of skirt or gambling. Any money he ever did earn he chucked down his neck.'

'Maybe because he knew you'd bend his ear whenever

he stepped foot across the doorstep,' blazed Daisy. 'No one ever felt comfortable in our house. You saw to that all right. We breathed and you bleached the air. If my childhood were a smell, you know what it'd be, Vera? Carbolic soap and disinfectant! Where was the love? The cuddles? I didn't care that we had the cleanest doorstep on the street. Dad's been the only person to show me any love, so don't you dare make up such poisonous lies about him.'

'You tell her,' piped up Frank, who had been watching in satisfied silence up until now. He was clearly enjoying the sour twist in the evening, that he had brought about. He turned to Vera with a gloating grin. 'You heard your sister, it's only me who showed her any affection growing up. You never had any cuddles for her.'

'Be that as it may, it was me who raised you, Daisy,' Vera countered.

'Suffocated me more like,' Daisy snapped back. 'Oh, you were always there all right, Vera, watching over me. Afraid I might make the wrong choice in life, pick the wrong friends, afraid to let me have the smallest measure of freedom.' Her words were falling over themselves. 'You tried to be mother to me until I could bear it no longer. Don't you get it? I'm eighteen now. I'm going to go my own way in life.'

Vera's face was wrung with despair, haunted by her sister's cruel outburst. 'I was only trying to raise you the way I know Mother would have wanted,' she whispered.

'Yeah? Well, I wish it was you and not our mother who burned that night in the fire,' Daisy spat. 'Then me and Dad would be happy.'

Quick as a flash, Vera struck Daisy full force with a stinging slap round her cheek. A crimson flush immediately coloured the place where Vera's palm had made its impact. Poppy winced, and Sal shook her head sadly.

Deathly white, Vera stepped backwards as if it were her who had been struck. Try as she might, Poppy couldn't reconcile this defeated wretch of a woman with the strong lady she had met in the factory earlier that day.

Frank's eyes darted from his older child to his younger, wicked amusement flickering over his face.

'Now, now, Vera. Play nicely with your sister,' he taunted.

'That's enough,' she whispered. 'It's late and we've all got work tomorrow. Come on, Daisy, we're going home.'

But Daisy shook her head and stepped back. 'Forget it. I'm not coming home with you. You can't tell me what to do anymore.'

With that, she turned and, in a flash of crimson, strode out of the pub. Sal grabbed her bag and, with a last despairing look at the group, ran after her friend.

'I'm off, then,' muttered Frank, glaring at Vera. 'Don't wait up. I've picked up a night shift. We'll talk about your little display later.'

Poppy stared at the wreckage of the night, from the defeated figure of Vera gazing heartbroken after her sister to the stunned faces of the Singer Girls. Cold fingers gripped Poppy's heart as she surveyed the scene. She realized that her new friend Daisy, though beautiful, was capable of cruelty, and her elder sister, Vera, was frailer than her tough outer shell indicated. She may have been the boss of the Singer Girls, but in matters of the heart, her younger sister held all the cards.

By the time they made it back to the Shadwells' terrace in nearby Tavern Street, Poppy and Vera were spent. Poppy sat in silence and watched as Vera bustled around the tiny kitchen and prepared tea on the old range, heaping tea leaves into a vast brown pot. Despite its humble appearance, the kitchen was spotlessly clean and the range freshly black-leaded. Vera's nickname suddenly made sense to Poppy. It was no leafy country estate, but to Vera her home was her castle.

'Toilet's in the outhouse out back, and there's some torn-up newspaper hanging on a nail,' said Vera, motioning to the scullery wall as she brought a steaming pot of tea to the table. 'I'd offer you something to eat, but we don't have much in. I can give you a biscuit, though.'

She reached up to the shelf and pulled down a King George V Silver Jubilee commemorative tin.

Poppy hesitated. 'No, thank you, Mrs Shadwell. I'm not hungry. I'm . . . I'm just so dreadfully sorry,' she blurted. 'I should have defended you earlier, but I simply didn't know what to say when he was staring at me like that, and now I've caused you and your sister to fall out.' Exhausted tears streamed down her face as she cradled her teacup in both hands for comfort. 'I wanted to say what really happened, Mrs Shadwell, but I just couldn't seem to find the words. Your father, he's . . . Well, he's—'

'An animal is what he is, Poppy,' Vera said firmly, cutting her off. 'None of this is your fault, child. That man causes trouble wherever he goes.'

For all the fear and angst of the evening, another more terrifying thought flashed through Poppy's mind.

'You're not going to send me home, are you?' she pleaded. 'My mother will go spare. I can't go home – I would never survive the scandal.'

Vera looked at her, baffled. 'Why on earth would I do

that, Poppy?' she asked, perplexed. 'I told you, none of this is your fault, my dear. This is Frank's style. He likes to cause misery at every turn. Trust me.'

Poppy slumped back in her chair, relaxing just a little.

'Thank you, Mrs Shadwell. I . . . I don't mean to sound nosy . . . but did he, well, did he really do all those things you said?'

Vera's green eyes glowed in the firelight. 'Yes, and more, Poppy,' she said quietly. 'He's a bad man. Not that Daisy seems to see, or maybe she chooses not to remember. He can do no wrong in her eyes.'

'She'll see his true colours at some point,' Poppy said softly, reaching her hand across the kitchen table instinctively and gently closing her palm over Vera's fist. Vera's hand shot away as if she had been electrocuted.

'I'm sorry,' she snapped, folding her arms across her chest defensively. 'It's complicated, that's all.'

'Life often is,' agreed Poppy, thinking of her old home, which in such a short space of time already seemed so far away. 'Daisy will come to her senses. She doesn't strike me as a daft girl.'

'Maybe not, but she is a handful,' admitted Vera. 'I do love her, dearly, though, and that's why I won't leave this house. Daisy may not realize it yet, but she needs my protection.'

Poppy was taken aback at the tone of her voice. It was loaded with a fierce passion. As she had said the words, Vera's hand had leaped to her necklace. The chain was as much an emotional crutch as a piece of jewellery, Poppy thought.

'That's beautiful, Mrs Shadwell,' she said, nodding to her necklace.

'Thank you,' Vera replied. 'It's my pride and joy. Shortly

after Mum had Daisy, she bought one for us both. Us girls were her life. "You're the two halves of my heart," she told me when she gave it to me. It was the last thing she ever gave us. I owe it to Mum to stay put here and deal with this.'

Sighing, Vera collected their teacups and rose to take them to the small sink.

'Frank definitely won't return tonight, will he?' Poppy's voice shook.

Vera's expression soured again. 'I shouldn't think so for a moment. My father's a creature of the night, you might say. He's rarely ever home before dawn. Says he's out working the docks, but I suspect he's out thieving.'

Poppy breathed a sigh of relief and allowed her head to rest on the paper tablecloth. Her tiredness was suddenly overwhelming and no matter how hard she battled, her eyelids were as heavy as sheets of metal. Her first day in Bethnal Green had been a baptism of fire. And now suddenly weariness engulfed her.

*

Vera guided her young houseguest through to the front parlour. Laying her down on the chaise longue, she took out a candlewick bedspread and carefully placed it over Poppy and tucked it in around her. As she slept and dreamed, Poppy's freckled nose twitched. Vera gazed down at her and shook her head.

How different this innocent little creature was from her own wayward sister. There were no sharp edges to her; even her voice was as soft and warm as porridge.

A steady rage built inside her as she cast her mind back

over the dreadful events of the night. How dare her father try to corrupt this vulnerable young girl in her care? When she had found Poppy trapped with him in the backyard of the pub, the poor mite had been rigid with terror. With a jolt she realized Poppy was only a year older than she had been when she lost her mother. How different things could have been had she had a maternal hand to guide her along life's bewildering path.

As she turned to tiptoe out of the room, her reflection in the mirror over the fireplace caught her attention. Vera was not a vain woman and scarcely gave her reflection the time of day, but now she forced herself to really look at her face, to try and see how Daisy saw her, how others at Trout's viewed her.

Her fingers trailed down her chest, tracing the contours of her scars, her sister's words echoing through her mind. *Sad old spinster.* And the most heart-wrenching of all, which had been like a sledgehammer to her solar plexus, *I wish it was you and not our mother who burned that night in the fire.*

There and then a desire for revenge settled over Vera's heart. A tight ball of hatred formed in her chest and burned like fire. Despite everything that her father had done to her, she would stay put. She would not allow him to harm one hair on her little sister's head, or on Poppy's for that matter. No. Vera's place was under her father's roof, until he got what was coming to him, however hard that might be to suffer. She would endure it all, for Daisy's sake.

Three

The next day on the factory floor of Trout's, all was quiet but for the humming of thirty sewing machines. The mood was decidedly subdued. Poppy wasn't sure what time Daisy had returned the night before, but conversation over the breakfast table that morning had been stilted.

Poppy still couldn't shake the memory of Vera's revelations about her father's detestable behaviour, and thankfully, Frank hadn't made an appearance at Tavern Street. Poppy felt so desperately for Vera. How unimaginably awful to have a man so cruel for a father, and worse still to have a sister who either didn't see it or refused to acknowledge his actions. No wonder poor Vera had a brittle outer shell, being forced to live in such a hard environment.

Daisy, meanwhile, seemed utterly unfazed by the turmoil of the previous evening, and as soon as mid-morning tea break was announced, she shot out of her seat.

'Girls!' she whistled excitedly from the window. 'Come and have a butcher's at this.'

'Ooh, what is it, Dais?' piped up a young girl by the name of Betty from her seat next to Poppy.

'GIs at one o'clock,' announced Daisy.

Soon the room was filled with the sound of chairs being

scraped back eagerly as the younger members of Trout's flocked to the windowsill to take in the spectacle of the American soldiers walking on the streets outside.

'Come on, Poppy,' Betty giggled, her quick eyes shining with glee. 'You don't want to miss this.'

'I ought not to,' she replied timidly. 'Mrs Shadwell might see.'

After the kindness Vera had shown her last night, Poppy didn't want to do anything to make her regret her hospitality, but Betty wouldn't take no for an answer and soon she found herself being dragged over to join the sea of clamouring women by the window ledge.

From the tips of their highly polished leather boots to their dazzling toothpaste-bright smiles, the soldiers were handsome, suave and oozed testosterone from every pore. The four GIs sauntered down the road like Hollywood film stars, oblivious to the hungry eyes drinking in the sight of them.

'Goodness.' Poppy got her first glimpse of the American soldiers she had heard were flooding British shores. 'They're ever so smart, aren't they? Look at their uniforms.'

'It's not the uniforms I'm looking at,' Daisy quipped. Frantically wiping the condensation from the glass, she let out a low whistle under her breath. 'Having all these Yanks about is better than Christmas. Over a million of them are going to be arriving, I heard on the wireless the other day. They're billeted all over, from stately homes to tents in parks. Food might be rationed, but at least men aren't anymore.'

'That's for sure,' Betty added, nudging Poppy to one side so she could get a better view. 'It's just nice to see some young fellas about the place at last. My mum says the whole of East Hanglia is filled with 'em.'

'You mean East Anglia, you nit,' interjected Sal, with an amused smile.

'That's what I said.'

'And what fellas indeed,' Daisy went on, scarcely able to tear her gaze from the window. 'Look at that blond one. He's got muscles on his muscles.'

'Too right,' Betty bantered back. 'You could bounce a penny off that bum.'

A chorus of laughter erupted, causing a flush of colour to rise up Poppy's chest. She wasn't accustomed to such frank talk, and though part of her admired the women for their boldness, she would never dare to speak with such a brazen tongue.

'Come on, girls,' chided Sal. 'Watch the language in front of Poppy. We don't want to scare the poor girl back to Norfolk.' Sal winked at Poppy to show her support.

Daisy seemed not to have heard this, as a second later, she flung open the window, plunged her fingers between her lips and wolf-whistled so loudly Poppy jumped two inches off the floor.

'Cooee, up here!' Daisy hollered.

'Daisy, don't,' Poppy blurted, wide-eyed. 'He might hear you.'

Too late. The object of Daisy's affections whirled round and stared up at the open window of Trout's. A wide smile creased his cheeks as he took in his attentive audience.

Poppy had to stop herself from ducking down under the ledge. 'Now you've done it,' she hissed fearfully.

'Well, hello there, miss,' called up the GI, exuding charm

and confidence. 'Why don't you all come on down here and say hello in person?' A cigarette dangled languidly from the corner of his mouth.

Poppy stared in disbelief as Daisy smoothed down her shiny black tresses.

'You're on,' Daisy said, grinning and banging shut the window. 'Come on, girls. What we waiting for?'

'I better not,' Poppy replied, her voice quavering. 'What if Vera sees us? She'll dock our pay if we're late back from break.'

Daisy rounded on her. 'So what if she does see us?' she blazed. 'It's our break – we can do what we like. Besides, we've heaps of time.'

'All the same,' said Poppy earnestly, eyeing her workbench, 'I best not. It is my first proper day here after all and I want to make a good impression.'

'Suit yerself,' shrugged Daisy. Striding over to her workbench, she reached into her bag, pulled out a bottle of Evening in Paris and dabbed some along her collarbone. 'Now I'm dressed,' she said with a wink. 'Come along, Sal – I'm not going down there without you.'

'You are barmy, Daisy Shadwell,' replied Sal, shaking her head and laughing. Poppy was surprised to see Sal follow after Daisy, nervously smoothing down her red hair.

By the time the two friends had clattered down five flights of stairs in a whirl of giggly excitement, the four soldiers were leaning up against the side of a green truck filled with yet more GIs, hanging over the edge.

Poppy watched and listened intently from the window ledge. She knew she should return to her workbench as she had said she would, but curiosity was rooting her to the spot.

*

Five floors down on the cobbled street, Daisy grabbed her opportunity with both hands.

'Well, hello, beautiful,' the GI grinned as he allowed his grey eyes to roam appreciatively over Daisy's shapely body. 'You smell like the jasmine flowers on my porch back home,' he smiled silkily.

Sal was laughing at the pair's brazen performance when suddenly she too found herself broadsided by a cocky Yank.

'And what about you, miss?' drawled a GI as he leaped athletically from the jeep and planted himself in front of Sal, hands on hips. 'You're staying awful quiet. Cat got your tongue, as you Brits say?'

Sal knew it was a line: she wasn't as naive as some of the young girls these soldiers had no doubt been practising their lines on. She was a married woman, for goodness' sake, and old enough to know better, and yet, when faced with the GI's dazzling charisma, a little piece of her reacted to his attentions. It had been a long while since a young man had spoken to her with such charm.

'I speak when there's something worth responding to,' she replied with a shrug.

His eyebrow shot up and he started to laugh, revealing the widest white smile Sal had ever seen.

'I like you, Red. You're a real firecracker,' he laughed. 'Should have known with hair like that. And there was me thinking you were all shy English roses. Anyway, how's about you both meet us at Dirty Dick's later? It's opposite Liverpool Street Station.'

'Do you mind?' said Daisy in mock horror. 'We're not those kind of girls.'

'All right, then,' he said, changing tack. 'There's a big dance on tonight in Leicester Square. Meet us there instead?'

'Maybe,' grinned Daisy, as if butter wouldn't melt. 'Come on, Sal – we best get back upstairs.'

'See you later, then, doll,' winked the first GI.

Daisy didn't need to look back to know the soldiers were watching as she sashayed over the cobbles.

As they ran giggling up the stairs, Sal's laughter disguised her deepest fears. She could talk the talk all right, but finding the strength to step out from her husband's shadow? That was another thing entirely.

*

From her vantage point five floors up, Vera watched the whole performance and shook her head. She didn't mean to be an old-fashioned fuddy-duddy, but it wasn't right, not in her eyes. Their mother had been so ladylike, despite the poverty in which she had raised them, and she always knew the right way to behave. Dignity, respect, hard work and cleanliness were the bywords that had governed Anne Shadwell's life, and she had passed those virtues down to her elder daughter.

A horrible sense of foreboding swept over Vera. With every silly row, she felt her little sister pull ever further away from her, and yet she felt powerless to do anything to prevent it. Daisy seemed to be growing more reckless and restless with each passing day.

What was it she had said last night? *You can't tell me what to do anymore.* Maybe not, but Vera would never stop trying to protect her, if only from herself. She had a feeling these Yanks were going to be trouble.

The factory door burst open and Daisy and Sal fell through it, flushed with giggles and euphoria. As they drew level with Vera, they saw her thin lips were pursed in a rigid line.

'Mother would be turning in her grave,' she hissed as Daisy sauntered past her to her workbench.

Daisy flicked her hair nonchalantly as she sat down. 'Don't be bitter, Vera,' she snapped. 'It'll show on your face.'

'I mean it, Daisy. She would never have conducted herself like that,' Vera went on, determined that her words would hit some small fragment of Daisy's conscience.

Daisy merely shrugged and fished her compact mirror from her pocket. Pinching her cheeks and fluffing her hair, she smiled sweetly. 'Life's for the living, and trust me, I intend to live it.'

Before Vera had a chance to respond, a chorus of whistles flooded the factory floor as Sal sat down behind her machine.

'Been out soldiering again, girls, have we?' piped up Pat, her face wreathed in a wicked smile. 'Any more of that and you'll end up with a reputation as a soldier's groundsheet. Just watch your step, girls.'

Mr Gladstone strode onto the factory floor and silenced Pat with a glare.

'All right, ladies. Tea break's over,' he boomed. 'Back to work. And how about a bit of "Take Me Back to Dear Old

Blighty" while you're at it? I haven't heard that in a while. And make it nice and loud so everyone can hear. Come on, let's show 'em what we're made of.'

'Right you are, Mr Gladstone,' chirruped Daisy, who never needed an excuse to show off her beautiful singing voice.

Vera nodded, satisfied at the sight of the women resuming work, and was just about to return to her duties when Mr Gladstone pulled her back gently.

'I heard about your row with Daisy last night,' he said.

Her face clouded. 'Nothing I can't handle, Mr Gladstone,' she snapped defensively.

'I know. But she's only young still. She didn't mean it. She loves the bones of you. Everyone does.' His gruff voice softened. 'You're not the only one with a nickname,' he smiled. 'I know they all call me Mr Patch.' He grinned and tapped his bald patch. 'On the subject of which, I do wish you'd call me Archie and not Mr Gladstone. Makes me feel even more ancient than I am. I'm only forty-five, you know.'

Vera's proud face stiffened. 'I don't wish to suspend formalities, thank you.' She bristled. 'We may be fighting a war, but that's no reason not to uphold standards.' Vera straightened herself up. 'Now, if you don't mind, we've at least a dozen bundles waiting to be signed off.'

'Of course,' Mr Gladstone mumbled, flushing red. 'But I'm still here if you need me. To talk . . .' His voice trailed off as he nervously smoothed down his hair. 'So, how many bundles did we get through this morning?' he said briskly.

Much to Vera's relief, they got back to the business of the day.

*

Back at her workbench, Poppy's slight fingers trembled as she tried and failed to thread a needle. Factory life went on around her as usual, but inside, her mind was in ceaseless turmoil. She had watched in wonder Daisy and Sal's confidence around the American soldiers. They handled themselves with such aplomb and poise, as if all the world were their stage. If it had been her, she would have been a gibbering wreck.

Every situation Poppy found herself in seemed to scare her senseless. What hope had she of meeting a man when she could barely string a sentence together without stuttering or flushing? Would she ever meet a man who didn't frighten her, or for that matter find the confidence to deal with men like Frank? Why did she not possess even one ounce of Daisy's beauty or assurance? Perhaps her mother was right: maybe she really didn't know how to do anything but skivvy.

At the thought of her mother, Poppy's heart broke all over again. In the short time she had been here, she had already realized her cool behaviour towards her only daughter hadn't been right. She had cast her out into this strange new world with not so much as a by-your-leave. Vera had shown more maternal instinct towards her in the past twenty-four hours than her own mother had in sixteen years, and now what? How on earth was she to cope living alone in complicated, bomb-shattered London? Life below stairs in a scullery hadn't prepared her for this. The thought of a future alone here in the East End scared her rigid.

Suddenly, the thread in her hand snapped as she tugged it too hard.

'Oh, dash it all,' she mumbled, tears filling her eyes. 'I'm such a silly goat. I can't do anything right.'

So absorbed in her own turmoil was she, she barely noticed Vera looming over her.

'I said, are you all right, Poppy?' she repeated.

'What?' She jumped, startled. 'Oh, sorry. I was away with the fairies.'

'You were very quiet over breakfast this morning.' Vera's direct manner took Poppy by surprise.

'Oh, gracious, no, Vera, I mean Mrs Shadwell. No, I was just a little tired. I hope I didn't come across as ungrateful, because I owe you so much for all the kindness you've shown me, really I do,' she stammered. 'I'm just feeling a little out of my depth.'

Vera's face softened. 'I promised I would look after you, Poppy, and that's exactly what I intend to do, so chin up, please.' Without waiting for Poppy to reply, she went on, 'I'll help you move in after work tonight, and I'll also make sure Mr Gladstone gives you an advance on your wages, just enough to buy a bit of food. I understand your mother's paid your first month's rent upfront?'

Poppy nodded and bit her lip hard to stop the grateful tears that were fast filling her eyes again.

'Are you sure you're all right, Poppy?' asked Vera again. 'Is there something else you'd like to tell me?'

'No, I'm fine, really I am,' she reassured her. 'You've been so kind to me, all of you, and I really am so grateful.'

When Vera moved on, Poppy lost herself in the strange comfort of repetitive work: sewing, folding and stacking, over and over. Poppy had been nervous at the prospect of her new duties, but she was rather pleased to find she had taken to sewing like a duck to water. The whirring of the machine and the women's song wrapped her in a comforting rhythm.

The rest of the day passed mercifully without incident, and by the time the skies darkened to dusk, Poppy's soul was calm again.

At precisely eight that night, the shrill bell that signalled the end of the shift rang and Daisy jumped from her seat like a scalded cat.

'Gracious, Daisy,' Poppy chuckled. 'You'll do yourself an injury moving that fast.'

Daisy smiled and grabbed her purse before whistling over to Sal. 'Sorry, Poppy. I didn't mean to startle you. Are you joining me and Sal tonight? I'm sure they'll have a friend for you. We've just got time to stick a bit of warpaint on, and if we hurry, we can get the number 22 to Leicester Square.'

'Leicester Square? Oh no, I really can't,' Poppy replied, growing flustered. 'Besides,' she blushed, silently cursing the ease with which she turned red, 'I've got to move into my new lodgings.'

Sal, however, needed no encouragement and was already pulling on her coat. Poppy would never dare admit out loud that next to them she felt like a frumpy little country mouse. Drinks in an East End pub were one thing, but big showy nights out in the centre of London were quite another.

Besides which, Daisy was radiant; her beauty was so luminous that Poppy would pale into invisibility next to her.

Poppy spotted Vera approaching out of the corner of her eye and swiftly went back to her sewing.

'You out again, Daisy?' Vera asked. 'I thought after last night you might stop in. There are chores to be done, and once we'd done the washing, I thought I'd treat us. I've saved up my coupons and was going to pick us up some pie and mash. There's *Dancing Club* on the wireless too. You used to love that, remember?'

Poppy listened sadly as Vera's peace offering was shot down. She knew enough of Vera's home life already to realize that she quite clearly didn't want to be left on her own with Frank.

'No offence, Vera,' Daisy replied airily, 'but why would I stop in with you and a stale pie when I could be out meeting the man of my dreams? I'll do my chores tomorrow night, I promise. The washing can wait. This could be my shot at true love.' With one final look in her compact mirror, she snapped it shut and picked up her handbag. 'Don't wait up.' The remark was tossed in her sister's direction as the door slammed shut behind her.

An awkward silence hung between Vera and Poppy, who grappled to say something that would ease Vera's torment. She was about to tell her to ignore her younger sister's exasperating behaviour when the forelady suddenly dashed to the window. Poppy realized that in Daisy's haste to escape, she had forgotten her coat.

'Your coat!' shouted Vera, flinging open the window. 'You'll catch your death of cold.'

But Poppy could see that Daisy was already too far out

of earshot, tripping down the road, her arm linked through Sal's, their faces lit up with mischief.

'When will she learn, Poppy?' Vera sighed. 'She's always leaving it behind, the little madam. I spent weeks sewing that coat. It's not fashionable, I'll grant you, but I used up fourteen clothing coupons buying the softest wool from Brick Lane.'

Sniffing, Vera tugged on her scratchy old coat and muttered half to herself, 'It's practical and serves its purpose – what more do you need?' A little like Vera herself, Poppy thought.

'Don't worry, Mrs Shadwell,' she smiled, patting her on the arm reassuringly. 'She'll come home when she gets cold enough.'

The older woman smiled back at her and shook her head as if she were seeing her for the first time. 'Such a level head for one so young.' And with that, she slipped her arm through Poppy's. 'Come on, then. Let's find your new lodgings.'

Grateful for the help, Poppy took her arm and together she and Vera picked their way down the darkened stairwell.

As they walked, Poppy sensed Vera had a question on the tip of her tongue.

'You said you couldn't go to the dance earlier. Why?' The directness of the question took Poppy by surprise.

'Not can't. I meant won't,' she replied, flustered. 'I'm far too tired.'

Poppy knew the stairwell was too dark for Vera to be able to read her expression, but her cheeks coloured immediately.

When they reached the factory doors, Vera turned to her. 'Not all secrets are best kept to yourself, Poppy,' she said softly, and then, with a catch in her voice, 'Take it from one who knows.' In the gloom Poppy felt Vera's hand reach out and squeeze hers. 'Would you like to talk about it?'

Poppy went to reply but faltered at the last moment, pressing her lips together. 'Come on.' She shivered. 'It's getting dark. I don't really want to be out again like last night.'

As they turned into the street, the wind became fierce, and rain started to pour relentlessly from a blackening sky.

'Out there in this weather and no warm coat,' muttered Vera to herself. 'Daft little article.'

Number 42 Burnham Street was a fine, strong house that had remained unscathed from the Nazi onslaught. In fact, it looked like it might just remain standing forever. The same couldn't be said for its landlady, a woman with finger-nails as black as her teeth and a full head of greasy grey hair. Poppy smiled at her nervously.

'My name's Mrs Brown,' the landlady rasped. 'I was expecting yer last night. Follow me.'

Poppy shot a nervous look at Vera before stepping inside the house. Mrs Brown staggered slightly as she walked down a long, dark hallway, then stopped in front of a door. Poppy sniffed and immediately wished she had a handkerchief. The hall smelt of cabbages and mothballs.

'This is yer room. Yer board's five shillings a week, and make sure yer keep the place nice and tidy. And no male visitors. I got a reputation to keep and standards to uphold.' With that she absent-mindedly scratched her left armpit.

'Anyways,' she grinned, turning the key in the lock,

'toilet's out back in the yard, but I think yer'll find it's got all yer need, lovey.'

The door swung open to reveal the most miserable fleapit Poppy had ever seen. A damp brown stain of water was creeping down the peeling walls, and a deep stench of decay emanated from the rotting floorboards. Tatty, torn grey net curtains hung forlornly from the window, and a small gas stove sat in the corner.

'Make yerself at home,' gestured Mrs Brown, handing her the key.

'It's lovely,' smiled Poppy weakly.

'It's a disgrace,' snapped Vera from behind. 'Fetch me a pan of boiling water and a scrubbing brush immediately.'

Mrs Brown was clearly affronted. ''Ow dare you,' she shrieked, raising a hand to her stained housecoat. Despite her dressing-down, she sloped off along the hallway to fetch some water.

'I'm sure she's very nice really,' remarked Poppy generously, once her new landlady was out of earshot.

'She's the most slovenly woman I've ever come across. An affront to decent East End women,' snapped Vera. And then, more brightly, 'But don't worry, love. We'll get this place spick and span in no time.'

After the hot water had been delivered, Poppy and Vera set to work. They cleared what furniture the room contained to one side and set about sweeping the place clean before scrubbing it with steaming-hot water. Before long their faces were coloured with heat and grime. They worked with quiet determination, feeding off one another's energy.

'By, scrubbing like this makes me feel like I'm a scullery

maid again,' chuckled Poppy, sitting back on her haunches and wiping a tendril from her pretty face. 'I'm sopping.'

'Me and all,' laughed Vera. 'But there's no work quite like hard work, is there? Nourishes the soul, I say.'

Poppy didn't know about that, but the effort of all the physical work felt good, and for an hour at least, her troubles ceased to haunt her. They dissolved and melted to nothing in the soapy suds.

When at last the floor was swabbed, Vera popped down to the corner shop and came back brandishing a mop, a brown paper bag of borax soap flakes, some dusters and a tub of Mansion Polish.

'We'll have this place looking like home soon,' she smiled, setting down her purchases on the bed.

'Oh, Mrs Shadwell, you shouldn't have. I thought you were saving your coupons for a special tea?'

'Don't worry, love,' she soothed. 'It's nice to help someone who I know appreciates my efforts.'

'And I do.' The gesture put fire in Poppy's belly and she set about the place with fresh determination. As she polished the glass with newspaper and vinegar, Vera ripped the old nets from the window and scrubbed down the walls.

After three hours of polishing, scrubbing and mopping, Poppy was exhausted, but she had to admit their hard work had made a difference. The old place gleamed like a new penny. Poppy noticed Vera had even managed to polish away the grime on the old iron bedstead to reveal pretty ceramic knobs atop each post.

'See, there's always something good to be found in the grimmest of places,' Poppy said thoughtfully, gazing at her new friend.

When they were finally finished, Vera swept out the hearth and lit a small fire, and the two women sat down to rest in front of it with a steaming mug of Bournvita each.

'A job well done,' Vera grinned, bumping her mug against Poppy's.

'Thank you, for everything you've done for me,' Poppy said in a soft voice. 'I'm so lucky to have found you, and the other girls too, of course.' She watched as a weary but satisfied smile chased over Vera's face as she stared into the crackling flames.

'I don't know about that, Poppy,' she said. 'But us girls have got to stick together.'

The warmth of the fire seeped deep into Poppy's bones and for the first time since her arrival she felt a glimmer of hope for her future. What serendipity to have found Sal, Daisy and especially Vera. Vera, for whom life was so full of troubles, but who still found the time to help her and show concern. Taking a sip of her milky drink, Poppy closed her eyes and sighed contentedly. Perhaps, just perhaps she had made a friend for life, someone with whom she could share her dark past. Not tonight, but maybe in the foreseeable future. Over the soap flakes and elbow grease, Poppy knew she had made a friendship to treasure.

Opening her eyes, she glanced down at her watch. 'Good grief, look at the time,' she said with a start. 'Here's me yattering away. I'm keeping you from a warm bed.'

Vera yawned and slowly got to her feet. 'You're a terror, Poppy Percival,' she teased. 'Keeping me up talking half the night – I don't know.' Smiling, she stifled another yawn. 'It's nice to have some company, though. I'm glad of it. Just don't be shocked if I'm not so familiar with you on the factory floor. Don't want the other girls accusing me of playing favourites.'

Poppy smiled to hide her sadness. Was Vera lonely? Goodness only knows she'd felt enough of that herself after spending hour after wretched hour alone in a scullery.

'I quite understand,' she reassured her. 'You're a professional with a reputation to uphold.'

Vera nodded approvingly. 'Very good.' As she spoke, she touched her heart pendant necklace and pensively rubbed it between her thumb and forefinger. 'I wonder if Daisy's back yet.'

Wearily, Poppy rose and took their teacups to the tiny sink.

'Don't worry – I'm sure they'll be fine,' she said as she softly set down the cups in an enamel bowl. 'And thanks. Thanks for everything you've done for me tonight. I know Mother would be worried sick if she knew I was living in a place like this,' Poppy said, frowning. Actually, deep down she wondered whether her mother cared where she was at all.

'Course she would, Poppy – you're right,' smiled Vera reassuringly as she shrugged on her coat. 'All any mother wants is for her daughter to be safe. That's all our mother worried about when she was alive. Sleep tight. Don't let the bedbugs bite.' Vera paused and her smile grew wistful. 'Or as mine and Daisy's mother – God rest her soul – used to say, "Up the wooden hill to Bedfordshire and I'll come up and tuck you in."'

Poppy smiled. 'That's sweet. She must have loved you very much.'

'That she did,' Vera replied sadly.

Poppy saw her to the door and instinctively the two women moved towards each other, arms outstretched. When they had finished hugging, Vera hurried out into the night.

'Night-night. Sweet dreams.' Poppy's soft voice sang out into the darkness, and yawning, she padded back to her room.

Once she heard the front door bang shut, she hastily double-locked her bedroom door, then ran to the fireside. Taking the small wooden chair beside it, she wedged it firmly up and under the doorknob. Poppy frowned and tested the doorknob, rattling it hard to make certain she was safely barricaded in. She knew it was daft, dangerous even, to lock herself away like this. What if an air-raid siren went off in the night and she had to escape in a rush? But even the very real threat of bombing attacks paled into comparison with the terrible haunting fear she felt in her heart.

Climbing into bed, she quickly pulled the covers over her head and snuggled down under her eiderdown, hoping and praying that tonight would bring respite from the nightmares.

Four

Earlier that night, four miles across town, Daisy stepped off the bus at Charing Cross Road and looked into the gloom of Leicester Square eagerly. Sal hesitated behind her, her bum firmly placed on the bus's slatted wooden seat.

'Oh, do come on, slowpoke,' Daisy urged impatiently. 'At this rate it'll be time to turn round.'

'Coming,' Sal sighed, gingerly feeling her way through the darkness and onto the pavement.

'Where's your arm, Dais?' she called out. 'I don't want to break my neck on a crater.'

Daisy reached out to her friend, and arm in arm they teetered their way through the darkness towards the dance hall. Daisy moved at such a pace her heels clacked over the pavement in a blur.

'Steady on, girl,' laughed Sal. 'Lover boy can wait. I want to get there in one piece.'

The rain came down from the sky in great sheets, cascading from the gutters, leaving the pavements slick, grey and deadly in the blackout. The West End, usually ablaze with neon light, lay under a heavy blanket of darkness.

Daisy paused in front of a shadowy doorway in which a

small group of young servicemen and civilian women were huddled.

'This it?' Sal sniffed impatiently. 'Don't look like much to me.'

A single column of pale light spilt out from the club's entrance like a beacon in the steamy darkness. It may have been wet, but that was doing little to dull Daisy's ardour. If anything, the smell of damp hair and bodies bumping in the blackness was heightening her senses. Madness and magic were palpable in the air, and Daisy could feel it coursing through her veins like electricity and setting her heart alight. After twelve hours in a stuffy factory under the watchful eye of her sister, the rain felt fresh and invigorating on her skin. It felt good to be young. It felt good to be alive. Anything was possible on a night such as this. Could tonight be the night she would find true love, the type of love that would help her escape the East End? Maybe not, but the excitement of the unknown felt like tiny bubbles popping inside her tummy. If nothing else, the war had shown them that no one's fate was certain. In some ways, that unpredictability made the war almost exciting. Not that Daisy would admit as much to Vera. She couldn't hope to understand. In Daisy's eyes, her big sister was ancient, her life's path already mapped out. But not Daisy! She was just eighteen and on the cusp of great change, ready to take a leap into the tantalizing unknown.

Just then a gleaming black chauffeur-driven Jaguar purred to a halt outside and two immaculately dressed RAF officers got out.

Daisy dug Sal in the ribs with her elbow. 'Out of my league, do you reckon?' she giggled.

'You're punching above your weight again, Dais. They're more your type,' Sal grinned, gesturing to two servicemen footslogging it up the road.

'Ambition – that's what you lack, Mrs Fowler,' teased Daisy.

'I'm just here to support you, remember?' Sal gestured to her wedding ring. 'I'll leave the romance to you, thank you very much.'

At that moment a ripple of excitement ran through the queue. A jeep packed full of demob-happy GIs was racing up the road, all muscles and wolf whistles. They flashed past in a blur of green.

'Things are looking up.' Daisy grinned.

For the benefit of the crowd, the soldiers turned and drove back down the road. As the jeep drew level with the girls, Daisy gazed coyly out from under her long, dark lashes, her green eyes sparkling invitingly. A chorus of wolf whistles and catcalls sang through the air. Suddenly, she was seized by a mad urge.

'Evening, chaps,' she called, her figure perfectly outlined in the light spilling from the doorway.

'Holy moly,' mouthed the driver of the jeep, his eyes on stalks. The screeching of his brakes wailed through the air as he narrowly avoided collision with a huddle of dustbins. Collapsing into shrieks of laughter, Sal linked arms with Daisy and made her way inside.

'Whatever was you thinking, Daisy?' laughed Sal, inside the foyer, as they tossed thruppence into a saucer by the cloakroom and handed the assistant their bags. Daisy turned the question over in her mind.

'I honestly don't know, Sal,' she gasped, her cheeks dewy

with excitement. 'I just feel like I've got the devil in me. Tonight's the night I'm going to find the One.'

As she spoke, Daisy caught sight of her reflection in a small mirror behind the coat check. She knew she was pretty as a picture. She didn't consider it vain to admit that; in her mind, denying it was like saying the world was square. But even she had to admit that tonight she was giving off a certain radiance.

'Tonight I feel like I might just find my way out of the East End.'

With that, she turned on her heel and swept towards the main dance hall, leaving Sal speechless in her wake.

Inside the dimly lit, oak-panelled room, the club oozed sophistication. A soft light glowed from the red lampshades dotted around the small tables, and the glint of metal buttons flashed from the soldiers' uniforms. Handsome, smiling couples glided past Sal and Daisy as they waltzed their way round the highly polished parquet dance floor.

Daisy sighed happily. Nothing bad could reach her here; not even her big sister's oppressive presence could touch her. The very thought of Vera's face popping up uninvited in her brain made her wince. She felt a momentary pang of guilt at her outburst in the pub last night. Then she remembered Vera's stinging retaliation and a steady rage built inside her. How dare she? Striking her like that and spouting all those wicked lies about their father. No, Vera was nothing but a bitter old shrew. Daisy shivered slightly.

'You cold?' asked Sal, wrenching her back to reality. 'You left your coat at work, you dozy mare. Why ever don't you wear it?'

'What, and ruin my silhouette in that lumpy old thing?'

she replied scornfully. 'Come on,' she urged. 'Let's not talk about the East End. Isn't this place wonderful, Sal? I just love it. All the men so dashing in their uniforms.'

Sal smiled but said nothing, and together, they surveyed the scene. Groups of uniformed men and women huddled together on the darkened edges of the dance floor, plucking up the courage to ask each other to dance. The working-class factory girls, like her and Sal, clustered in groups. Better dressed and flash, they cut a dash in bright red and green figure-hugging dresses. The Wrens were a different kettle of fish. Upper middle class and quietly sophisticated, with a love of beige and navy blue, they were cut from a very different cloth.

'Look at them,' sighed Daisy enviously. 'Ain't they classy? I wish I could talk like them. Maybe when I've moved to Dagenham, I'll have elocution lessons.'

'Why?' blazed Sal. 'Be proud of your roots. Just because we don't talk with plums in our mouths doesn't mean we haven't got something worthwhile to say.'

'I know that, Sal,' Daisy blustered. 'It's just that . . . Oh, I don't know. They're a class act, that's all. I bet they don't have to use an outdoor lav.'

'No, you're right – they probably have a butler in white gloves to do it for them,' laughed Sal.

'Be serious,' Daisy giggled, taking a playful swipe at her friend.

'I am being serious,' Sal protested. 'You look at them and see gilt edging. I see plain and over-privileged. Social class!' She almost spat the word 'class' onto the parquet flooring. 'It's only perception. This whole war's based around class if you ask me.' Sal sniffed in disgust. 'That's the one good thing to come from having all these Americans about the place, I suppose – it's breaking down the divide between the classes. These GIs wouldn't know a tart from a title.'

'Boy, are you two ever a sight for sore eyes.' A smooth male voice cut across the music.

Daisy whirled round and found herself staring into a pair of inviting grey eyes. It was the GI they'd met outside Trout's earlier that day.

'Glad you could make it,' he grinned.

For a second Daisy was struck dumb. Inside the club, he looked even more handsome than on the streets of the East End. Compared to the tongue-tied English soldiers in their ill-fitting, scratchy uniforms, this one was from a different planet. All loose-limbed and smelling of soap and lemons, even his uniform looked more expensive. He was the picture of glamour.

'That was some performance earlier.' He winked at Daisy, but she was scarcely listening. Her gaze was fixed six inches behind him, at his friend and comrade. Following her gaze, the GI's face lit up with an understanding smile.

'This is my buddy Robert. Robert, meet Daisy and Sal. We met them in the East End earlier. And I'm Sam.'

Sam extended his hand, but Daisy ignored it. She was rendered speechless at the sight of Robert. Robert was black, his skin the colour of gleaming mahogany. He was quite delicious, and for the first time ever she found herself lost for words.

'Say something, then,' hissed Sal.

'W-where's your other pal?' Daisy stuttered self-consciously.

'Chuck, you mean?' replied Sam. 'Oh, he got waylaid by

a couple of, er, ladies of the night, shall we say? They shone their flashlights at their ankles and that was the last we saw of him. Think he planned on taking them to the Windmill dance club in Soho. What is it you Brits say – never knowingly clothed in the Blitz?'

Daisy smiled awkwardly – she hadn't really understood half of what just came out of Sam's mouth – but Sal threw her head back and roared with laughter. Daisy searched for something half decent to say, gave up and instead smiled spellbound at Robert.

'Care to dance, Red?' Sam smiled.

'I don't think so,' Sal replied. Harmless chat was one thing, but dancing was another.

'Come on,' he urged. 'I'm a terrific dancer.'

'And so modest too,' Sal grinned, shaking her head. 'Very well, but it's a dance only – no funny business.'

'Like I'd dare with you, Red,' he grinned back, leading her to the dance floor.

Alone at last, Daisy continued to gaze longingly at Robert. His powerful face looked like it had been chiselled from stone and she couldn't wrench her eyes away from staring at every glorious inch of it. A part of her hoped he wouldn't speak in case the words were somehow disappointing. He leaned casually against a darkened alcove, yet his shoulders were so wide they seemed to fill the room.

'Do you mind being seen with a black man, miss?' He grinned curiously.

Daisy shook her head slowly, her eyes fixed on his.

'Are you walking out with anyone?' he asked politely.

Daisy shook her head again.

'Boy, I sure can't get a word in edgeways with you,' he joked, with a wide grin.

This time it was Daisy's turn to laugh.

'Sorry.' She smiled, feeling shy for the first time in her life. 'It's just that, well, I haven't seen a black soldier before. There aren't too many where I come from.'

Robert smiled back and nodded. 'I understand. I get that reaction a lot.'

'Don't you mind?' asked Daisy.

'It's fine. Most British people, with the exception of a few, are awful polite. Where are my manners?' he said, suddenly standing upright. 'Can I get you a drink?'

As he stood to attention, Daisy noticed his uniform tighten round his strong chest and felt her throat constrict again.

'A lemonade would be lovely,' she gulped, dry-mouthed.

By the time he returned with her drink and carefully handed it to her, Daisy had recovered herself.

'So, you one of these gangster types from Chicago?'

Robert laughed and shook his head.

'All right, then, you're a gun-toting Texan?'

'Actually, I'm neither,' he replied. 'I'm from Missouri. Me and my daddy, we work together on an apple orchard. Picking the fruit, then moving bushels of apples onto pickup trucks. You like apples, miss?'

Something about Robert's deep voice was having a stupefying effect on her, so she just nodded.

'It's a simple life,' he went on, 'but I miss it so much, truth be told. We only just arrived here and I'm a little lonely. The people are nice and all, but it rains a lot and your beer's warm.' He grinned, holding up his glass.

Daisy smiled and cocked her head to one side. 'So why did you join the army, Robert?'

'I don't know really. I guess, and this may sound a little strange to you, I wanted to get out and see the world. See what life there is beyond Missouri. Back in America, you know, black and white don't mix much. It's just the way it is. Same here, for that matter – black and white troops are segregated.'

'But you're here with a white fella?' Daisy said, puzzled.

'Sam's different.' He shrugged. 'We know each other from back home, and he's my buddy, but he's taking a risk being seen out with me. As are you, miss.'

'I don't care,' said Daisy defiantly. 'We're all fighting the same war, aren't we?'

Robert looked surprised. 'You're more enlightened than the folks back home. You Brits are an awful lot more tolerant. You don't even have a colour bar in place. Here, I can go where I like, even get on the same bus as whites.'

He looked at her and took a tentative sip of his beer. 'Well, I just wanted to broaden my horizons and here I am. The Depression hit us hard. Back home, we cook over a wood stove, the only running water comes from a well, and when the tornadoes come, you better hunker down in the cellar. It's a good life and all, but I want a better one for myself. Talking to you, such a beautiful, clever woman, well, that's just swell.'

Daisy glowed. 'I know just what you mean. I've spent the last year hiding in shelters. Not from tornadoes, mind you, but bombs. If ever there was a girl who wanted to broaden her horizons, it's me. I want a better life too. I hear America's magical.'

Robert returned her smile and just like that she was overcome with an emotion so powerful she couldn't put a name to it. Escapism, freedom, kinship? Daisy didn't know, but she knew this: she had come searching for her destiny, and tonight, in this small, dark alcove in a West End night-club, she had found it. The world was suddenly bigger than Bethnal Green, Dagenham even. Perhaps her future lay across the ocean with this dashing soldier?

They talked and talked. The hours slipped by like minutes. Huddled together, the outside world melted away. She didn't hear the music whipping the dance floor into an energetic jitterbug, or Sal and Sam calling them to join in. Likewise, the disapproving stares of strangers went completely unobserved. After a while, Daisy didn't even register Robert's army uniform, and for a brief time she was no longer living in a war zone. She was simply Daisy, and he was Robert. An East End girl and a Midwest boy. The soldier with the melting brown eyes and voice as rich as treacle who wore his heart on his sleeve. His stories of hunger, hardship and happiness wove such a familiar tapestry Daisy half wondered if he wasn't recounting her own childhood. But above all, she was won over by his strength. To her, Robert was a man of the soil, rugged and proud, yet humble enough to admit to his fears and loneliness. She was intoxicated by the whole package and her heart was aflutter.

'I'd love to kiss you, Daisy.' His strong voice pulled her from her reverie and she gazed at him in awe. He wanted to kiss her. Right here in public?

She knew she should retort with something witty and she frantically searched her mind to think what Sal might say, but no words came. Instead, she allowed her heart to guide her.

Closing her eyes, she tilted up her neat chin and held her breath. Suddenly, she felt herself being pulled into his powerful arms. His body was a force of nature and she felt as if she had been sucked into a cyclone, but his kiss, when it came, was as gentle as the rustling of autumn leaves.

Robert's embrace was so warm, his lips as soft as velvet, and yet his muscular body had total control over hers.

A vision of Vera's face flashed through her mind. *Mother would be turning in her grave.* Daisy knew that the sight of her kissing a black man in public would be enough to give her big sister a coronary on the spot. Somehow that just made it all the more attractive. Besides, she reasoned, war justified spontaneity in a world where tomorrow was never certain.

Squeezing her eyes shut, she tuned out Vera. Two years of rationing, queuing, slaving and sheltering had taken their toll. She needed so desperately to live.

'Time to go,' screeched a voice.

'Sal,' groaned Daisy, letting her forehead rest against Robert's chest.

'I hate to break up the party, but we gotta go, otherwise we'll miss the last bus home.'

'Do we have to?' Daisy protested.

'Yes, unless you want to walk all the way home. Besides, Vera will string you up if you're late.' She took Daisy by the arm. 'Now come on – give lover boy a last kiss goodbye and look lively.'

'Will I see you again?' Daisy murmured to Robert.

'I sure hope so,' he grinned. 'We're to be stationed in

London for a little longer, while we complete our training here. I'll look you up. Trout's is near Bethnal Green, isn't it?'

'Yes, and make sure you do,' whispered Daisy, before reaching up on her tiptoes to whisper in his ear, 'And thank you for the most wonderful evening.'

'It's me who should be thanking you,' he said. 'I never met anyone like you before.'

'I'm not like most girls,' she smiled breathlessly.

'Let's go, Cinderella,' snapped Sal.

Laughing, Daisy ran to the exit. Pausing at the door, she managed a last backwards glance. Robert's eyes were still fixed on hers through the crowded dance hall, full of hunger. She stopped in her tracks, her heart pounding fiercely. No. No. No. Her fairy-tale night wasn't ending like this. On impulse, she unclipped her heart necklace and, turning back, weaved her way frantically through the crowd.

'Dais, what you doing?' Sal called after her.

Robert's eyes widened in surprise when she reached his side. Taking his hand in hers, she pressed the necklace into his palm and closed his fingers over it.

'Now you have my heart – don't be careless with it,' she urged. And with that, she took her leave.

Five

Two days, thirteen hours, thirty-seven minutes and fifteen seconds. That was how long it had been since Daisy had kissed Robert. Not that she was counting, but his silence was causing her agony. She hadn't even touched the Spam sandwich laid out on a plate in front of her in the factory canteen.

'Why hasn't he visited?' she sighed to Sal during their dinner break. 'I gave him my heart, for pity's sake.' Forlorn, her fingers traced the spot on her neck where her necklace used to lie. 'I told Vera I took it off to clean it and then forgot to put it back on, but there's only so long I can keep fobbing her off,' she said, her voice breaking a little. 'She's getting suspicious already.'

Sal faltered. Daisy knew she was trying to find the words to let her down gently.

'Who knows, Dais?' she said at last, stirring her tea and staring thoughtfully at the swirling brown liquid. 'Maybe he's forgotten where you work.'

Daisy felt herself growing impatient. 'Don't give me that flannel,' she snapped, instantly regretting her outburst. 'Oh, I'm sorry, Sal,' she cried, exasperated. 'I shouldn't take it out on you. It's just that he said he'd get in touch and now . . .

nothing. I should have heeded Pat's warnings, but I've never met anyone like him in all my life.'

'Phooey,' scoffed Sal. 'Don't listen to anything Pat's got to say about men. What does she know? Empty vessels make the most noise.'

And then, closing her hand over Daisy's, she lowered her voice to a whisper. 'I understand why he's turned your head, but maybe it's better we stick to our own kind, Dais. Those soldiers never know where they'll be from one day to the next. Besides, they ain't going to want to settle down here when the war's over, are they? There's nothing left but rubble. They'll return to their world and leave us to ours.'

'I suppose,' sniffed Daisy. 'It's just that . . . Oh, I don't know.' She shook her head in frustration and her sleek dark hair shimmered as her eyes drifted to the window. 'I really thought he was my ticket out of here. And that kiss. It was something else.'

Sal's eyes lit up with mischief, and a second later, she had whipped the piece of Spam out of Daisy's uneaten sandwich and clamped it between her lips so that it flopped out like a tongue.

'Give us a kiss, Daisy,' she said in a gruff voice.

Daisy's laughter nearly took the roof off Trout's.

'Oh, stop it, Sal,' she roared. 'You really are the giddy limit sometimes.'

'Cheered you up, though, didn't it,' Sal grinned, flinging the pink luncheon meat back on the plate with a slap.

*

The parcel landed with such a thud on the table in front of Poppy that she jumped.

'Cor, blast me,' she cried, clutching her chest. 'You gave me a fright.'

'Nervy little thing, aren't you? You've been jumping around all morning like you've got a touch of the St Vitus's dance,' chirped a young machinist by the name of Kathy. 'We're used to loud bangs round here.'

Vera silenced Kathy with a glare and placed a gentle hand on Poppy's shoulder.

'Sorry, Poppy. It's just the post. I didn't mean to alarm you.'

'The post?' murmured Poppy in a trance.

'Yes, post, letters,' laughed Kathy. 'You know, a paper affair usually with a stamp on the front.'

'All right, Kathy,' snapped Vera. 'See those boxes of bandages over there? Take them down to the loading bay to be collected, would you? The delivery boy's off sick.'

'But it'll take me forever,' Kathy protested.

'Not if you put your back and your heart into it,' Vera replied swiftly. 'Chop-chop.'

Kathy moved off begrudgingly and Vera crouched down beside Poppy.

'Are you sure you're all right, my dear?' she asked in a low voice.

'I'm fine, Vera . . . Mrs Shadwell,' she blustered. 'I just feel a bit on edge, that's all. I'm not sleeping so well. The noise of the artillery guns in the park is fearful.'

'But your lodgings, they're suitable now, aren't they?' Vera persisted. 'That slattern of a landlady's not giving you any grief, is she?'

'No, no. She's perfectly nice,' Poppy reassured her, omitting to tell Vera that the loathsome Mrs Brown had taken one look at the new, improved room and promptly put up the rent.

'Well, if you're sure,' Vera replied.

Poppy knew that her new friend was only displaying concern, but at times she had the strangest sensation that Vera was trying to open up her thoughts and fish out her secrets.

'Quite sure,' she said. 'Can I be of any assistance?' She motioned to the pile of mail.

'Well, yes, actually. A lot of the workers have their mail directed here. During the Blitz, a number of the women and their families were bombed out and were forced to move to temporary accommodation, so many have their correspondence sent here. Would you be so kind as to hand the letters round, Poppy?'

Poppy smiled and sprang to her feet. 'I'd be happy to.' Judging by the eager looks on the faces of the Singer Girls, she would have a warmer greeting than Santa Claus himself. Another heartening thought struck her: perhaps her mother would have written to her. She was longing to hear news from home and half felt like flicking through there and then, but she resisted. It would be so selfish to put her own needs before those of these women.

Poppy spent a very happy half-hour handing round the post. She knew from the daily chat that nearly every woman in the place had a husband, sweetheart, brother or son away fighting and news of their well-being was eagerly received. Soon the floor was filled with relieved exclamations of joy and tears of happiness as letters from all corners of the globe were swapped or quietly read in a corner.

Happiness swelled in Poppy's chest, and with a jolt, she realized how much she was starting to like working in this community of lively women. Their spirit was something to behold. To see the women's pride in their menfolk was humbling too, though Poppy was also in awe of how they fought the war on the home front. It rather put her own problems into perspective, she thought sadly.

As she approached Sal's bench, she piped up, 'Anything for me from my boys?'

Poppy quickly riffled through the envelopes and produced one with a Devon postmark on it.

'"Sal Fowler" and in brackets "Mum". This must be yours,' she chuckled.

Frantically Sal ripped it open and a photo fell out. Sal gazed at it, then her legs abruptly gave way beneath her, and she sank heavily into her chair.

'Oh look, Poppy,' she breathed. 'It's a picture.'

Poppy looked at the photo Sal had just handed her with a trembling hand. Two little boys stared back at her from outside a well-kept cottage. The elder boy grinned self-consciously, showing off a big, gappy grin. The younger boy raised a chubby little hand to wave at the camera.

'Is this Joey and Billy?' Poppy gasped, for she barely recognized Sal's sons from the previous photo she had shown her in the pub. Gone was the dyed-in grime. These little lambs were squeaky clean and as hale and hearty as they come.

'My, haven't they changed?' she said.

Sal's face crumpled as she read aloud from the letter.

'Oh, my days,' she wept. 'Joey's lost two more teeth, and Billy's learned to swim. Whatever next? Says the lady they're billeted with even lets Billy help out in the village post office counting the day's takings.' Her face fell. 'He couldn't count when he lived with me,' she said sadly. 'So that's something, isn't it?' Her voice trailed off to a barely perceptible whisper. 'Maybe he's better off without me, or maybe when this war's over, he won't want to come home.'

'What rot, Sal,' interrupted Vera, as she bustled past on her way to Mr Gladstone's office. 'You're his mother. There's no replacement on earth for your own flesh and blood.'

Her eyes narrowed as she glanced over at a subdued Daisy. 'Talking of which, Daisy, for the umpteenth time, just where is Mother's necklace?'

Daisy's stricken face glanced up, then she fled from the floor in tears.

'What did I say?' asked Vera in dismay.

'I'll go,' sighed Sal, leaping up and running after her.

'Oh look,' said Poppy brightly, trying to avoid another confrontation. 'One left and it's for you, Betty.'

Hurt stabbed at Poppy's heart as she walked over to her workbench to deliver the letter. Nothing at all from her own mother. Oh well, she was obviously too busy tending to Her Ladyship, or maybe she had been caught up with her WVS work since she left, Poppy thought charitably, but in her heart she knew this wasn't true. For all her mother's aloofness, Poppy still missed her desperately, just as much as she missed the endless skies of Norfolk. She thought with a pang of her half-day off, and how she would pull her rattly old bike out from the stable block and tear down the country lanes, her hair flowing behind her in the breeze, the tang of sea salt from the wash tingling her nostrils. The wild strawberries would be ripening in the meadows and the fens groaning with wild flowers. But those innocent, carefree days were over now.

A sudden feeling of homesickness mingled with the harsher taste of abandonment washed over Poppy. There was no escaping the truth. Her own mother had banished her from the village in which she was born and failed to stand by her in her greatest hour of need. What, Poppy wondered, with an aching sadness, did that say about her? Surely if even her own mother didn't want her anywhere near, then she must be very hard to love?

Shaking herself a little, she painted a brave smile on her face and handed Betty her letter. The young girl greedily tore open the envelope.

'You didn't?' gasped Kathy. 'Have you taken leave of your senses?'

'I only did,' Betty replied.

'You little bleeder,' giggled Kathy, full of admiration.

'Did what?' asked Poppy.

'Well, why should Daisy get to have all the fun?' Betty shrugged. Checking to see Vera was out of earshot, she leaned forward conspiratorially. 'I wrote to a serviceman,' she giggled. 'Nicked his name and address off my big sister. He thinks I'm a twenty-one-year-old seamstress who can do the jitterbug. I even squirted the letter with some of my sister's perfume.'

'Betty,' admonished Poppy, 'whatever will he say when he finds out his pen-pal sweetheart is a fourteen-year-old apprentice?'

'He won't find out,' she shot back. 'There ain't a snowball's chance in hell of me actually meeting him. Besides, what hope have I got of getting a sweetheart? I'm plain as a pikestaff – I don't have Daisy's good looks or Sal's banter, so I've got to use what I can. That's the beauty of letters, Poppy,' she said. 'You can be whoever you want to be.'

Poppy said nothing, but the young girl's words had filtered into her brain. She had to admit that to a girl as shy as her, a letter had an almost irresistible allure.

'All right, girls,' said Mr Gladstone as he bowled in from his office, 'gather round.'

His gruff voice wrenched Poppy reluctantly from her train of thought.

'I need some volunteers to go up to the children's hospital this Sunday. Let's have a show of hands, then.'

'To do what, Mr Gladstone?' asked Betty.

'To perform an enema, what do you think?' He laughed, shaking his head. 'To sing, of course. Your reputation as Bethnal Green's most talented singers precedes you. I'm forever telling people about your voices.'

'Saying what?' heckled Pat. 'That we ought to use 'em less?'

Laughter rang out across the floor. Poppy giggled along too as Mr Gladstone's head slumped into his hands in a gesture of mock despair. But when he lifted his head, their boss had fire in his eyes.

'Seriously, girls, you have to know that I'm proud of you. You have some decent lungs on yer, and what better way to use them than to cheer up some sick kiddies? Let's show them Jerries we'll never be silenced.'

A loud cheer erupted from the women. Even Daisy had re-emerged and, after fixing her face, was chatting excitedly at the prospect. The only person not joining in the revelry was Vera.

'I thought that hospital had been evacuated out of London,' she said cautiously.

'Parts of it were,' replied Mr Gladstone, 'but there are some kiddies too sick to move.'

'I'm not sure it's a suitable place for our girls to visit,' Vera warned. 'They'll be some sad sights.'

'Vera,' chided Mr Gladstone gently, 'I thought you'd be the first to want to do your bit to help.'

'I can't . . . I'm too busy on Sunday – I'm helping out at the Red Cross jumble sale at the Methodist Mission,' she blustered.

'Starching her curtains, most probably,' muttered Betty under her breath to Poppy.

'Sorry to hear that, Vera,' Mr Gladstone replied. 'You'll be missed.'

'Yeah. Only by him,' whispered Betty. 'Mr Patch has it bad for old Kippers and Curtains.'

Poppy nudged her hard in the ribs. 'Ssh,' she scolded.

'Who else would like to go?' asked Mr Gladstone.

A sea of hands shot up.

'I'll organize it,' offered Sal, over the clamour of voices. 'Be a real treat to cheer the little mites up.'

'That's the ticket, Sal,' grinned Mr Gladstone. 'I'll go and ring Matron now and tell her I've got some of my best girls lined up.'

News of the hospital visit caused a real stir, and Poppy watched as Sal rallied the troops.

'Now, I reckon we start with "Run, Rabbit, Run" and

then how about "Climb, Climb Up Sunshine Mountain"? My boys loved that one.'

'Ooh yes. How about "Lay a Little Egg for Me"?' ventured Daisy, all memory of her earlier outburst seemingly forgotten.

'I could knit them some little teddies,' offered Doris.

'And I'll help you,' added Ivy.

'That's the spirit, Dor,' said Sal, clapping her hands. 'We'll put a smile on those children's faces and give them a show to remember.'

'Poppy, you'll join in, won't you?' asked Daisy.

'Course I will,' she murmured. But Poppy wasn't really giving them her full attention. She was too busy staring at Vera, who in the commotion had been quite forgotten by the other ladies. She had her back to the floor and was busy counting bundles, but as Poppy looked closer at her friend's face, she could have sworn that her eyes were misted over.

Six

The day dawned bright and gin clear. A perfect, sunny spring morning full of promise. The cherry trees were bursting into life, and Poppy noted with a smile that even the buddleia bushes sprouting through the wreckage of the bombsites were in full flower, their vivid purple blossom poking a defiant tongue at Hitler's best efforts.

Gradually, and thanks to the warmth and camaraderie of the Singer Girls, Poppy was starting to feel more at home in the East End. Being away from Framshalton Hall and a life consigned to the isolation of the scullery was actually doing her good. That awful night had taken her apart piece by piece, but slowly her fragile self-esteem was being restored. The memories of what happened, and the scandal that followed, were starting to fade.

She had taken extra care with her appearance as she dressed that morning, pinning a lovely sparkly brooch to her coat and even washing with her bar of rose-scented soap, which Cook had given her as a leaving present. Soap had just been rationed to three ounces per month and that scented bar was like gold dust. But Poppy figured if the children enduring so much in the hospital wards could manage without, then the least she could do was make an extra effort for them.

Waiting for her outside Bethnal Green Tube Station were Daisy, Sal, Doris, Ivy, Betty and Kathy. The group was chatting excitedly in a rabble of noise.

When Poppy spotted them, she painted a bright smile on her face and quickened her pace.

'Hello, girls.' She smiled shyly. 'Sorry I'm late.'

Within seconds she found herself wrapped in a tangle of kisses and hugs.

'Hello, dearie,' grinned Ivy. 'Ooh, you're a tonic on the eyes.'

'You look pretty as a picture today,' agreed Daisy, standing at arm's length to appraise her. 'What have you done different to yourself?'

'Oh, nothing really,' Poppy replied, blushing furiously and secretly thinking that she could never match up to Daisy, who today looked ravishing, with her hair in victory rolls and wearing an emerald dress that clung to her shape. She was the spit of Vivien Leigh.

'That dress matches your eyes perfectly, Daisy,' Poppy breathed.

'What, this old thing?' Daisy exclaimed, twirling round. 'Made it out of some old curtain material.'

'Well, it will certainly cheer up all the children,' Poppy ventured.

'That's the spirit,' grinned Sal. 'Now, let's go entertain the troops, as they say.'

'Have you always sung?' Poppy asked as they walked. 'You have the most terrific voices.'

'Oh, we've always loved a good sing-song,' Sal replied.

'When war broke out, we just sang louder. It's like whistling in the dark – keeps a good face on things. We're not professional.'

'Yet,' added Daisy brightly. 'But who knows what tomorrow might bring?'

'That's right,' cackled Doris. 'If *Workers' Playtime* ever visit Trout's, they'll be signing us all up to tour with 'em.'

'Here, isn't that your old man over there?' Kathy asked, nudging Daisy.

The group stopped and suddenly Poppy recognized the figure of Daisy and Vera's father weaving his way up the road towards them.

'Hello, girls,' grinned Frank, when he reached them. 'You look proper lovely all dolled up. Where you off to?'

The group's excited chatter tailed off as he barred their way, and Poppy stared uncomfortably at the ground. Her heart started to thud as she smelt his familiar waft of stale sweat wash over her. Daisy leaned forward to give her father a kiss on the cheek.

'We're off up the hospital to do a sing-song for the kiddies,' she said brightly.

'That's my girl,' he grinned. 'Regular little ray of sunshine, she is.'

As he spoke, his eyes fixed on Poppy, before flickering up and down her body. 'The sight of this angel would be enough to raise any man from his sickbed, so it would,' he leered.

Poppy gripped Sal's arm tighter in fear.

'Sorry to be rude, Mr Shadwell, but I better get these

girls off or else we'll be late,' interrupted Sal. Poppy noticed her usually chipper voice was cold and guarded.

'See you later, Dad,' called Daisy.

'So long, darlin',' Frank replied, still staring at Poppy. 'Don't be late – got us a nice bit of liver for our tea.'

As Frank drew level with Poppy, he winked.

'No guessing where he got that liver from,' Ivy spat as soon as he was out of earshot. 'Still hanging out with villains, is he, and dabbling in the black market? Men like that give decent East End fellas a bad name.' Her voice dripped with pure vitriol.

'Oh, leave it out, Ivy,' sighed Daisy. 'Why is everyone always slagging off my old man? I get enough of that from Vera. He has a dicky heart.'

'All right, girls,' said Sal. 'Let's not forget why we're out on this beautiful spring morning. To bring some joy to some little 'uns. So turn that frown upside down.'

'Sorry, Sal,' mumbled Daisy, contrite.

'Yeah, me and all,' said Ivy.

How does that vile man cause upset wherever he goes? Poppy thought, but wisely held her tongue.

Not two minutes later, they stopped abruptly in front of an imposing Georgian building. The hospital had taken a few hits and looked as if it was in need of some tender loving care itself, never mind the patients.

Sal climbed the steps to the door, then paused, raising one foot up to rest on a sandbag.

'Now, girls,' she announced, looking for all the world like a general going into battle, 'there might be some sad sights in here, but it's important we only bring smiles into this building. So if you can't put a merry face on it, now's the time to sling yer hook.'

Poppy realized Sal was staring straight at her.

'Understood.' She gulped. 'I won't let you down, Sal.'

Sal touched Poppy softly on the cheek. 'That's my girl.'

Inside, Poppy and the group struggled to keep pace with a nurse as she led them down a series of long tiled corridors, until finally they reached an office.

'Matron's office,' the nurse announced.

The matron, a white-haired lady with kind but tired eyes, greeted them warmly.

'Oh, but I can't tell you how excited the children are to have some visitors,' she smiled.

'Many of them have terribly sad stories and have lost whole families in the Blitz. They are here until they are recovered enough or until new homes can be found for them. We do what we can, but . . .' Her voice trailed off. 'It's not easy. On the bright side, it's jam sandwiches for tea today, and they have some other visitors who may cheer them up too. Now, come – please do follow me.'

Poppy was about to ask who the other visitors were, but there was no time, as soon they were being led down another maze of corridors. At a set of double swing doors, Matron halted.

'The children are ready for you.' She smiled at the group. 'You'll be amazed at how wonderfully they cope with their predicaments, so it's important you don't pity them.'

'But how about you, Matron?' asked Sal quizzically. 'How do you cope? It can't be easy looking after patients in a war zone.'

Poppy watched as her kindly face clouded.

'Simple, really. The needs of our patients must call forth all our love and devotion. You are merely a pair of hands for service, to minister to the suffering and make them as comfortable as you can in their hour of need. One's own comfort and well-being simply must not come into it.' She sighed and her face fell into a spider web of fine lines. 'After all, most women's lives are one of self-sacrifice, and never has that been more true than today.'

Poppy absorbed her words but found no solace in them. 'But the future looks so grim – we aren't safe anywhere,' she blurted. The girls stared at her in surprise. 'I'm sorry,' she said. 'I don't mean to sound morose.'

Poppy could have kicked herself. How could she have been so reckless to have shown her true colours?

'Please do not trouble yourself, young lady.' Matron smiled kindly. 'It's true. These days of war are anxious for everyone. Fear and uncertainty are at every turn, and the future seems to hold so little to cling to.'

She paused and gazed deeply into Poppy's blue eyes. 'But we must never surrender to our fears, or abandon hope. We are British, after all. Now, shall we meet the children?'

The double doors swung open and Poppy gasped. Her heart melted at the pitiful sight. Row after row of little children confined to iron beds. Some looked so listless they could scarcely walk. Others were still recovering from bomb blasts and wore heavy slings and bandages that concealed their wounds and burns.

'Oh, my,' Poppy murmured. Some of the poor little scraps had every limb encased in plaster casts but still wore sunny smiles that broke her heart.

Sal stepped forward. 'Hello, children,' she grinned. 'My two boys have been evacuated, so what am I going to do with all these?' She sighed with mock despair. From behind her back, she produced a basket of second-hand toys and knitted teddies.

An excited cheer rang round the ward.

'That's what I like to hear.' Sal laughed over the noise.

'Now, my friend Poppy here is going to hand these round while we sing you a few little songs.'

Poppy paused at the bed of a girl with her leg in plaster and handed her a small knitted bear.

'Poor little mite lost her mum in a bomb blast, and her dad's missing,' whispered the nurse.

'Missing?' asked Poppy, puzzled.

'Missing in action,' explained the nurse. 'She's just here until we can find space in a children's home. I dare say that's the first gift she's had for a long time.'

Poppy shook her head in sorrow. At least she had a mother, even if she didn't seem to want her near. There and then Poppy made a decision. No more feeling sorry for herself. Plastering a bright smile on her face, she sat down on the little girl's bed.

'You have the prettiest hair,' she beamed.

'That's what the other lady who visits from Trout's says,' the girl replied.

'What lady?' Poppy asked curiously.

'Vera, I think her name is,' she replied. 'She visits every Sunday morning. Very friendly with Matron too. I'm surprised she's not here today.'

'So am I,' murmured Poppy. How strange that Vera had not mentioned she visited so regularly. Poppy couldn't understand the secrecy, but resolved to ask her in a quiet moment.

A happier morning Poppy had not known. Two hours slipped by like two minutes. She had to hand it to the girls, they proved themselves natural performers as they sang a medley of songs, danced and sprinkled a little magic and cheer over the ward.

'I hate to break up the party, but the next lot of visitors has arrived,' said Matron. Her announcement was met with a chorus of groans and boos. 'All right,' she chuckled, holding up her hands in defeat. 'One more song, but these young men have been waiting ten minutes already.'

'Any requests?' asked Sal.

'"We'll Meet Again"?' piped up the orphan girl Poppy had befriended. Her little voice echoed down the ward and its resonance touched Poppy's heart. 'Can the pretty one who looks like Vivien Leigh sing it?' she smiled shyly.

Without a trace of bashfulness Daisy stepped forward.

'I'd be honoured, sweetheart,' she smiled, striding into the middle of the ward like it was the stage at the Albert Hall.

Poppy giggled to herself. Gracious but her friend was full of herself.

Her laughter dissolved as Daisy's clear voice began to float through the ward. She really could sing. Poppy had heard her sing before, of course, but never on her own. Her voice was so exquisitely beautiful and her diction so perfect that if Poppy closed her eyes, it was almost as if she were in the room with Vera Lynn herself.

Daisy was just reaching the crescendo of the song when

the doors burst open and a hulking great figure of a man stumbled in with his cap in hand. Behind him stood the mischievous faces of his comrades, who had just shoved him in as a prank.

Poppy did a double take. She had never seen a black man in uniform before. In fact, she had never seen a black man full stop, much less one as handsome as this fella. She waited for the fallout. Daisy would be furious at this chap for interrupting her grand finale. But it wasn't anger flitting across Daisy's flawless face; it was total shock.

'Robert?' Daisy breathed. Then her radiant face lit up.

The GI tipped his head in deference.

'Miss, I'm so sorry for this rude interruption.'

'Oh, I don't give a fig about that,' she gasped. And to the absolute amazement of Poppy and everyone else in the room, she flew across the ward and into his outstretched arms. The force of her hug nearly knocked the six-foot soldier off his feet and dislodged the packet of sweets he had been holding out in his hands.

'Whoa there,' he chuckled, as a shower of gobstoppers bounced onto the floor. It was all too much. The kids on the ward went wild, hollering and clapping as nurses scurried about collecting the runaway sweets.

Poppy was struck dumb at Daisy's display, but there was no denying that the exuberance in the air was infectious. She was still grinning madly when she felt a little hand tug at her sleeve and found herself looking down into the orphan's inquisitive eyes.

'Excuse me, miss,' the child babbled excitedly, 'but is this part of the show?'

'No,' muttered the despairing voice of Ivy from behind Poppy's back. 'But after that little performance, you can bet it'll be curtains for Daisy when Vera finds out.'

Seven

Daisy left the hospital in such a giddy whirl she felt as though her feet had barely touched the ground.

'Can you believe it, girls?' she gabbled to Sal and Poppy as they clattered down the tiled corridors. 'What are the chances of bumping into Robert like that? I knew he and his comrades had to visit hospitals in the East End to boost morale, but I never imagined for a minute it would be that one.'

Her hand flew to her heart. 'Fate has a role in this,' she gushed breathlessly. 'I just know it. Meeting Robert has to be my destiny, and better yet, he's invited me for tea later.'

Sal smiled at her friend's happiness, but her voice was guarded. 'I'm pleased for you, Daisy, but what about Vera? She won't like this one little bit.'

Daisy tutted. 'Oh, don't take the shine off this for me, Sal. I'll tell her I'm going out with you.'

Sal frowned. 'I'm not comfortable lying to Vera.'

Daisy looked like she might burst into tears. 'Oh, Sal, I beg of you. This could be my one chance at true love. You surely wouldn't deny me that, would you?' Her green eyes misted over. 'I'll simply die of heartbreak if I don't get to see Robert later.'

Sal's shoulders sank. 'All right, then, but promise me you won't stay out late.'

'Oh, Sal, I promise,' Daisy cried, flinging her arms around her. 'You're the best friend a girl could ever have.'

'Yes, I am,' she sighed ruefully, untangling herself from Daisy's embrace and turning to Poppy. 'What do you think, Poppy? Should Daisy sneak off to meet this GI chap later?'

'Don't ask me,' she replied with a tremor in her voice. 'I should never have the nerve.'

'Well, you two might be too scared to follow your heart, but I'm not,' asserted Daisy.

As they went to part ways, Sal gripped Daisy's arm. 'Please don't make me regret this.'

Sal's words were long forgotten, as two hours later, Daisy found herself facing Robert across a starched white table-cloth, nervously holding his hand. The image of her slender white fingers laced through his strong black ones painted a sharp contrast. She knew they stuck out like a sore thumb and the thought made her giggle nervously.

'Hark at me, sitting in a Lyons Corner House with you,' she babbled. 'Talk about posh. They've even got carpet on the walls in the lav. I'm all in a lather. You sure you can afford this?'

Daisy realized she was starting to sound like an over-excited schoolgirl and her voice trailed off. But Robert didn't mock her. Instead, he gently returned her smile.

'I'm not exactly used to this level of refinement either, Daisy, and yes, don't worry – this is my treat.'

She watched his brown eyes scan the room and take in

the glittering chandeliers and the men in tuxedos serenading them from the orchestra.

'Back home, I wouldn't even be *allowed* to sit in a fine place like this, much less with a girl like you.'

At that moment, a waitress in a white apron and white-peaked cap delivered the most mouth-watering afternoon tea Daisy had ever seen. Dainty scones and silver dishes oozing with strawberry jam. If Robert hadn't been there, Daisy would have torn into it, but she was so nervous she was sure she could scarcely eat a thing.

The waitress paused as she gently placed the silver tray on the table and looked pointedly from Daisy to Robert.

'That'll be all, thank you,' said Daisy in the haughtiest voice she could effect. 'Daft little bint,' she muttered under her breath when the waitress left. 'Hasn't she ever seen a black man and a white woman eating sandwiches together before?'

'Is that what you call these?' Robert smiled quizzically as he held up a tiny cucumber sandwich. Daisy giggled helplessly. It looked like a postage stamp in his hands.

'If you're well-to-do, you eat them with the crusts cut off in this country,' she grinned, suddenly feeling more at ease. 'And that little madam of a waitress is called a "nippy", and when you drink your tea, you cock your finger just so.' Picking up her china cup, she raised her little finger like she had seen Vera do at the Jubilee street party.

Robert laughed so loudly the ladies taking tea nearby interrupted their restrained chatter to look their way and raise their eyebrows.

'Guess I have a lot to learn about your British customs,' he smiled, lowering his voice. 'Though I think I'm going to struggle to get my finger through the hole in this cup,' he added, cradling the delicate cup of tea in both his hands instead. 'Back home, it's coffee us Yanks drink, not tea.'

Daisy gazed at Robert's face through the fragrant steam. He was so handsome in his uniform he looked like a Hollywood actor of the silver screen.

'Why did you not get in touch?' she blurted suddenly. 'I waited for you.'

His face fell. 'Believe me, Daisy, I wanted to,' he said in his soft drawl. 'You're just about the prettiest girl I ever saw.' Slowly Robert raised his eyes to meet hers and Daisy felt her heart melt like warm butter. 'You're so brave. I never met anyone like you. Moreover, and I know this is going to sound crazy, Daisy, but darn it all, what have I got to lose now? I felt that first night we met as if you and I are cut from the same cloth. I know we come from very different places, but we want the same things out of life. We're not content to just play the cards that fate has dealt us, do what's expected of us—'

'I get that,' interrupted Daisy breathlessly, her face lighting up like a string of fairy lights. 'Truly I do. Most men I know in Bethnal Green just want to tie me to the kitchen sink and expect me to pop out a brood of babies, but I want more out of life. So, so much more. I want to work, to travel, to explore life beyond the East End and have amazing adventures.'

'Me too, Daisy,' replied Robert. His voice was soft and tender, turning her insides to caramel. 'If you were my wife, I should never want to confine you to the kitchen. Hell, I'd want to show you off in every city on earth. I guess what I'm saying is, I don't want to die in the place I was born, and I certainly don't want to pick apples for the rest of my life like my poor daddy. I want to leave my mark on the world, and I sense that need in you too. This war is going to change the future for the likes of me and you, Daisy, I just know it. We can rise above our station in life, aspire beyond the ordinary. Anything is possible.'

And just like that a golden thread wound its way round Daisy's heart, connecting her to Robert. A deep current of understanding flowed between the soldier and the seamstress, and Daisy knew she had met a man with whom she could happily end her days.

But then Robert hesitated and Daisy watched his giant shoulders sink two inches.

'But I'm so sorry, Daisy. For all that I really do feel about you, when it comes to you and me, I'm afraid it just can't be.' With that he dug around in the pocket of his smart green uniform, pulled out Daisy's necklace and slid it back across the tablecloth towards her. Daisy's heart started to thump painfully, and her eyes filled with tears.

'But why?' she replied tremulously, frustrated and offended in the same moment. 'Unless, of course, you already have a sweetheart back home?'

'Oh no,' he said, shaking his head vigorously. 'I swear I haven't.'

'Then why in heavens not?' she blurted.

'Because, Daisy,' he sighed, 'men like *me* can't go out with women like *you*. After we left the dance, my buddy Sam pointed out the trouble I'd get us both in. White women ain't supposed to fraternize with Negro Americans. He said it could lead to ill feeling. And he's right. I don't want to make trouble for anyone while I'm in someone else's country.

The British folks have been awful kind to me, but I'm not sure that hospitality would stretch to me walking out with one of their women. Besides which, our posting in London is coming to an end soon. We'll be getting moved someplace else to continue our training.'

Daisy felt her body stiffen in frustration.

'Who is anyone to say whom we should and shouldn't see?' she blazed. 'If this war has taught me anything, it's not to give a fig for what I ought to do. I've spent the last year of my life terrified out of my wits, always wondering if today's the day I'll cop it. Well, excuse me if I want to grab my chance at happiness. I don't care if you're black, white or purple quite honestly, Robert. I love the colour of your skin. Everything in London's grey, from the buildings to people's faces. Even the bleedin' bread's grey. What's more, I'm sick to the back teeth of people telling me what to do. I can't even have a bath in more than five inches of water, and I can't remember the last time I saw a banana. Well, I'm tired of going without. I won't go without love!'

By now the tears were streaming down her face, but she couldn't hold back.

'My life was dull and boring, and you brought me hope,' she wept. 'I actually thought I had finally met someone I liked and who liked me back. Anything is possible, you just said. So why not us?'

After her little outburst, Daisy trembled. She had not opened her heart like that to anyone before, but by golly, she had meant every word. She picked up her cup, but her hands were shaking so much tea sloshed over the sides and into the saucer.

Robert gently took the cup from her and set it down on

the saucer. Then he leaned over the table, took her face in his hands and kissed her. Right there in the middle of a Lyons Corner House, over the scones and the dainty sandwiches, with the orchestra and the nippies looking on, this handsome, strong man actually kissed *her*, and Daisy knew she had lost her heart for good.

By the time his lips left hers, Daisy was so breathless she could scarcely speak.

'All right, then, Daisy,' he said softly. 'What else can I say to that but maybe we *should* grab our chance at happiness? I'm only stationed here for a brief time, but I want to see you again when I next get a pass out.' His face clouded. 'Beyond that, I can't make any more promises. Once we leave, I don't know when – or if – we will return to London.'

Daisy refused to be brought down. That kiss had sent her soaring to the heavens and she wasn't ready to face reality just yet.

'We can write, can't we? And you're bound to get leave at some point surely. Besides which, let's not worry about the future. Let's live for the moment.'

Her green eyes shone with possibilities. 'There's plenty of sweethearts coping with separation the world over, and trust me, I'm tough enough to cope with it.'

Robert shook his head in amazement. 'You're an incredible girl, Daisy Shadwell. I never met a girl with such fire.'

All too soon tea was over and Daisy glanced at the clock on the wall. 'Crumbs, I ought to be getting home. My sister, Vera, will be getting herself in a right tizzy if I'm late.'

'Tizzy?' Robert smiled, baffled, as he walked round to Daisy's side and pulled out her chair.

'British saying,' she laughed, while marvelling at what lovely manners Robert had.

When they stepped outside onto the busy London street, Daisy's heart sank. 'How much longer are you in London for?' she asked.

'Ten days. After that, who knows . . . ? I couldn't say even if I did, I'm afraid. Loose lips . . .'

'Sink ships,' finished Daisy, with a smile. 'I know.' She took a sharp intake of breath. 'Well, in that case, I see I'm going to have to make the most of you while I've got you.' She smiled brightly, shivering slightly as the early evening sun started to dip behind a tall building.

Robert gently turned up the collar of her jacket to keep her warm.

'Yes, you will,' he murmured. 'While we're here training, we're also under orders to visit hospitals, rest stations and Red Cross centres in the East End to boost morale. 'Say,' he added with a grin, 'why don't you try and time it so your singing coincides with our visits?'

'What a wonderful idea.' Daisy beamed back. If he could boost her spirits this much in two hours, think what he could do for the sick and injured.

'Now, if you please –' Robert held out his arm with a flourish '– I'd be honoured to escort you home safely.'

'Don't be daft,' she chided. 'It's a long walk from here to Bethnal Green.'

As deliriously happy as Daisy was, she wasn't sure if she was quite ready to face Vera's wrath if her sister spotted her in the neighbourhood with Robert.

'Well, no girl of mine is going to go out walking after

dark on her own,' he retorted, carefully placing his coat around her shoulders.

No gesture had ever left Daisy feeling more loved or safe, and as they stepped out in the direction of the East End, she felt as if she were walking on little clouds.

Robert made sure to walk on the side of the traffic, and on his arm she felt like royalty. When they reached the Thames, they paused to take in the view and his jaw dropped. Tower Bridge and the Tower of London loomed larger than life through the hazy spring evening. Dusk was creeping through the sky, drenching the river in a soft orange glow.

'Oh my,' he marvelled, his eyes widening at the historical landmarks he had only seen on picture postcards.

'And there's St Paul's Cathedral the other way,' Daisy said proudly. 'Managed to survive more or less unscathed throughout the Blitz, thanks to the fire-watchers up on the roof.'

'Whoever should want to bomb something so magnificent?' Robert said in dismay. He swept his arm along the length of the Thames and fell silent. Seeing it through his eyes, Daisy also felt a little heady.

'The sights of London are nearly as beautiful as you,' he said, impulsively bending down to kiss her.

Daisy felt as if she were floating on air as they continued the walk back to Bethnal Green and she chattered brightly all the way, pointing out the churches and buildings that had survived the raids.

'You folks sure did cop it,' he said as they passed yet another sealed-off street, peppered with roofless houses and rubble. 'However did you manage to survive this, Daisy?'

'Camaraderie,' she answered, without hesitation. 'Singing

in the shelters and at work gave us a common purpose – you know, like we were all in it together. It still does.'

Robert nodded his head thoughtfully. 'I'll remember that when we get posted abroad.'

But all too soon the walk was over and they arrived back at Bethnal Green.

'You can leave me here,' Daisy said reluctantly, when they reached the Tube station. 'I don't live far from here, and I'm not sure you're ready to face my sister or the neighbours just yet.'

'I understand,' Robert replied.

Thank goodness the blackout was useful for one thing, thought Daisy as Robert planted a lingering kiss on her lips in the shadows of the doorway.

'Until we meet again, Daisy,' Robert breathed, reaching round and clipping her heart pendant round her neck before planting a last kiss as soft and sweet as marshmallow on her lips. 'May God go with you.'

No matter that the odds were well and truly stacked against them – it truly had been the most magical night of Daisy's life, and Robert had already left an indelible mark on her heart.

The next morning, Daisy could scarcely wipe the silly grin off her face as she sat at the table and played with her bowl of porridge laced with Bemax.

'Eat up,' urged Vera from across the table. 'Rationing's kicking in something awful now. Do you know how long I had to queue at the butcher's for, after work on Saturday? I had hoped to get us some pork chops for our tea, but after queuing for nearly an hour, all I came away with was a tin of corned beef.'

Her big sister's talk of tinned meat floated clean over Daisy's head, and in a trance she took a mouthful of porridge. Even the Bemax food supplement she loathed so much didn't seem to leave such a nasty taste in her mouth this morning. All she could taste were Robert's kisses, and all she could feel was his hand still warm in hers.

'Glad to see you've got Mum's necklace back on,' Vera remarked. 'Where did you find it?'

'Do you know,' Daisy replied with an enigmatic smile on her face, 'it turned up in the last place you'd expect. Talking of which, the kids loved our sing-song at the hospital yesterday.'

'Did they?' Vera replied guardedly.

'Oh, absolutely.' Daisy nodded enthusiastically. 'Matron said we were welcome back anytime. As a matter of fact, Vera,' she said, rising to her feet and taking her bowl out to the scullery so her sister couldn't see her face, 'I offered to nip back quickly on my dinner break today to say hello to the kiddies.'

She had tried to keep her voice light, but she still felt her sister bristle behind her.

Vera frowned. 'Well, you don't need my permission, but you had better make sure you're back before your forty-five minutes is up. If you're even one minute late, I shall be docking your pay. Rules are rules. The fact that you're family means, if anything, I shall have to impose them more firmly. Besides,' she added suspiciously, 'you've never showed much interest in this sort of thing before.'

'I know, but I like to do my bit, Vera,' Daisy said, turning to face her with a bright smile on her face. It was only half a lie, she reasoned. She *had* actually loved their trip to sing to the children in hospital. She had already resolved to corner Ivy, Doris, Betty and Kathy at work that morning and apologize for her sudden display of affection for the visiting soldier. She would blame it on the emotion of the visit and say it was to put a smile on the children's faces. A sudden thought flashed alarmingly through her mind.

'You're not planning on joining us, are you?'

Vera's body stiffened. 'I don't think so. Mr Gladstone's asked me to do some overtime.'

At that moment, a bleary-eyed Frank walked into the kitchen.

'Morning, Dad. What plans have you for the day?' Daisy asked.

'They're hiring down the docks,' he replied, greedily wolfing back his porridge.

Vera went to speak but clearly thought better of it. Turning away from their father, she gathered her coat from where it was neatly folded over the back of her chair and quickly pinned on her hat.

'Fetch us a couple of brown ales on your way back from work tonight, will you, sweetheart? Your sister's working late. Reckon she's set her cap on that old windbag Mr Gladstone.'

'He's more of a man than you'll ever be,' Vera said defiantly.

'Come on, Vera, or else we'll be late,' Daisy said, taking her sister's arm and deftly guiding her from the house.

She loved their father, but Daisy did wish he wouldn't rile Vera so. Never mind the battlefields abroad, sometimes she felt like she was living on the front line at number 24 Tavern Street. Daisy had often found herself wondering why it was that Vera loathed their father. He wasn't perfect, but what man was? Daisy suspected that Vera's bitterness at having to take over the running of the house after their mother's death was the real reason behind her dislike of their father. She could not blame her for that, she supposed. Having to be a mother, sister and housekeeper rolled into one at such a tender age was enough to make any woman weep, but that was hardly their father's fault, was it? Just as much as it wasn't that he suffered a heart condition that made work difficult.

A sudden sadness crept into Daisy's heart as she and Vera strode in the direction of Trout's. How different life would be today if her mother were still alive and hadn't perished in that awful fire. She knew from the framed picture in the good room that she was pretty, all right, and Vera never tired of saying what a hard worker she had been. But with a sudden jolt of anguish, Daisy realized that was all she knew. Had she liked sugar in her tea? Did she prefer her toast with the crusts on or off? What was her favourite scent? And it wasn't just the silly little details she was missing. Had she loved their father with the intensity she knew she already felt in her heart for Robert? She longed to ask her big sister, but she knew she would get short shrift like she always did when she tried to talk to her about anything emotional. Thanks to Vera, her past was a sealed envelope, and its memories were shut within.

But none of that mattered any longer. A sweet rush of delirium flooded through Daisy's veins as she relived her evening with the handsome GI all over again. She couldn't wait to tell Sal and Poppy, but she had an agonizing three-hour wait until their eleven-o'clock tea break. No sooner were they seated at the canteen table than she was away, rattling off the details.

'Robert bought me scones with real jam. Did I tell you he works in an orchard back in America, picking apples? Perhaps I could help him during harvesting. Imagine that. And his kiss . . . Oh my.' She touched her cherry-red lips and smiled dreamily.

'Slow down, Dais,' said Sal. 'I hate to bring you down to earth, but surely he's being posted out to fight soon?'

Daisy's face hardened. 'Oh, where's your sense of romance?' she replied peevishly.

'Well, I think it's all terribly romantic,' smiled Poppy shyly. 'He's ever so handsome.'

'Oh, he is, isn't he?' gushed Daisy. 'I know it's all happening so fast and we've only met twice, but honestly, girls, I think I love him.'

'I dare say you think you do,' sighed Sal with a heavy heart. 'But there's no future in it. All men are pretty much the same in the end. Limbs, loins and a roving eye, and that's if you're lucky. Besides, I thought you were marrying an officer, not an apple-picker?'

'Oh, I'm not talking to you,' Daisy snapped back. 'You're obviously in a lousy mood.' She turned back to Poppy. 'Only the other day I was reading a report in the *News of the World* about all these women engaged to GIs. War brides, they call 'em. They'll be setting off across the Atlantic soon as this wretched war's over, and do you know what?' Her green eyes flashed with determination. 'I'm going to be setting sail with them.' With that she flounced from the canteen with the sound of wedding bells in her head and the whiff of sea salt in her nose.

Sal turned to Poppy with a weary look in her eye. 'Never mind apples. That's a forbidden fruit that's going to taste sour when she takes a bite. You mark my words.'

Eight

Over the course of the following week, Daisy managed to meet Robert for a few snatched moments, stealing a clandestine kiss under the secluded arches by the train station, but she had to wait until Sunday for their first proper date, when Robert had a pass to leave his base.

When the morning dawned, she rose early to complete her chores so she could escape the house in time to meet him.

Vera looked as if she might faint on the spot when she came down into the backyard to find Daisy running sopping-wet clothes through the mangle.

'Good heavens,' she exclaimed. 'It usually takes wild horses to drag you from your bed at this hour on a Sunday. Whatever has come over you?'

Daisy looked up, flushed from her efforts. 'I just thought I'd seize the day, Vera,' she puffed. 'You're always asking me to help out more, so I've done all my chores. When I've finished this, do you mind if I nip to the hospital? I said I'd put in a few hours up at the Red Cross aid centre after, so I might be late back. Is that all right?'

'I don't see why not,' replied Vera, flabbergasted at the

sea change in her sister. 'As long as you've completed all your jobs.'

'Guide's honour,' Daisy replied brightly. 'I've done the washing, scrubbed down the scullery and black-leaded the stove. Now, am I free to go?'

'Very well, then,' sighed Vera, picking up the mangled clothes to peg out on the line. She watched in total astonishment as her little sister breezed out of the house. 'Well, I'll be,' she murmured.

Free at last, Daisy hopped on a bus in the direction of the West End. She felt a momentary pang of guilt for lying to her sister, but she squashed it down just as quickly. Robert didn't have long left of his time in London and she was determined to enjoy every single precious second.

Daisy's heart skipped a beat when she saw her handsome soldier leaning against the wall outside Piccadilly Tube Station. Everything about him gleamed, from the shine on his boots to the sparkle on his silver buttons.

'Daisy, you look beautiful.' He took her hand in his to kiss. 'Shall we get out of here?'

'Yes, let's.' She smiled back, marvelling at the effect this dashing man had on her. Even her hand was tingling from where he had kissed it.

Despite the early hour, the place was teeming with soldiers of every creed and colour, all intent on finding fun, and Daisy noted with a wry grin that there were no end of Piccadilly commandos, as the prostitutes of this area were called, happy to aid them in that search.

No one else was staking a claim on her man, though, and she gripped Robert's hand tightly.

'Where we going, then?' she grinned, fizzing with excitement.

'It's a surprise,' he winked.

By the time they drew level with the Ritz, Daisy must have seen at least fifteen different uniforms, from Poles and Swedes through to Australians and Canadians. They hadn't called it the 'friendly invasion' for nothing. The city was swarming with foreign soldiers all babbling away in a hundred different tongues.

'Oh my,' she breathed, as they slowed down to look at the grand hotel at number 150 Piccadilly. With its liveried doormen and marble foyer, this was definitely up Daisy's street. 'Are we taking tea in the Palm Court?' she asked excitedly.

'Sorry, but we're not going to the Ritz,' Robert replied. 'Boy, but you sure can beat your gums, Miss Shadwell. All will be revealed soon,' he teased. 'Besides, this area of London is swarming with GIs – they're calling Mayfair "Little America" now – so I'd actually like to get out of here.'

They walked and walked, taking in Berkeley Square, where Daisy couldn't help but sing a few bars of 'A Nightingale Sang in Berkeley Square', which Robert likened to having honey poured in his ears.

Finally, he stopped in front of the beautiful stretch of water that ran through Hyde Park.

'Why are we at the Serpentine?' Daisy puzzled.

'We're having a picnic on the other side,' Robert beamed. 'Your cruise ship awaits, madam.' He pointed to a small wooden rowing boat.

'I'm not getting in that.' Daisy screeched with laughter. 'I'll rip my nylons.'

Suddenly, she found herself being swung high up into the air as Robert swept her off her feet. 'Come on,' he laughed. 'Where's your sense of adventure?'

Giggling helplessly, she let Robert lower her into the boat and watched admiringly as he used his strong arms to row them along the glittering waters. Robert had thought of everything and when they alighted on the other side, he produced a picnic blanket and a mouth-watering spread of food.

'I was the first at the American post exchange this morning to get this. Gotta spoil my girl,' he said excitedly, laying out things Daisy had never seen before. There was macaroni salad, potato salad, pickles and even a big box of chocolates, and Daisy feasted.

'After years of corned beef and cabbage, this is like the food of the gods,' she said appreciatively between mouthfuls. 'Who needs the Ritz with this?'

'I'm glad you're happy, Daisy,' Robert smiled. 'You sure do deserve it.'

Afterwards, they lay on their backs holding hands, full and content, watching the barrage balloons hovering over the park. Despite the spectre of Robert's departure hanging over them, Daisy realized there was nowhere else on earth she would rather be and she may as well enjoy the moment. She longed to kiss Robert, but decided that might be a stretch too far for the Air Raid Precaution wardens patrolling the park. Robert smiled lazily as he traced their initials into a dry patch of dirt on the ground with his finger. An R and a D, and a heart with an arrow through it.

'I know you love the pictures, Daisy,' he said, propping himself up on one elbow, 'so I got us tickets to see *Reap the Wild Wind*. John Wayne's in it. We better . . . What is it? Oh yeah . . . "shake a leg" if we're to make the performance.'

By the time they walked arm in arm down the sweeping staircase at the Troxy on Commercial Road, the desire to kiss Robert was gripping her like a fever.

Daisy caught a flash of their reflections in the floor-to-ceiling mirrors and marvelled at how glamorous they looked together. In fact, after the day she had just had, she felt like she was living in a Hollywood film, not about to watch one.

When the lights dimmed, Robert rustled around in his pocket and produced a Hershey's chocolate bar.

'You'll make me fat,' she scolded.

'You'd still be beautiful,' he whispered.

As they settled back to watch the film, Daisy could scarcely concentrate. Was it the heady escapism of sitting next to a man who sounded like a film star or the sweet chocolate melting on her tongue? She didn't know, but when the final credits rolled, she was certain of one thing: Robert had absolutely bewitched her. Even the sight of John Wayne on the big screen hadn't been enough to stop her sneaking sly sideways glances at her dashing sweetheart. To Daisy, it was as if the cinema had just burst into life.

'I suppose I'd better get back home now,' she sighed reluctantly. 'I don't want to be—'

Suddenly, Robert pulled her into his strong arms and silenced her with a deep, lingering kiss. By the time his lips left hers, Daisy's head was spinning.

'. . . late.'

'No,' he grinned ruefully. 'As much as I never want to let you go, I had better get you home.'

They had just exited the picture house when Daisy spotted a troop of white GIs sitting on a bench further up the road. They seemed in high spirits and were laughing and arm-wrestling one another.

'Looks like someone's lost a bout with British beer,' she remarked to Robert. He didn't reply, but she felt his body tense beside her. As they drew level with the group, one of the GIs stepped in front of them, blocking their path.

'Hey, beautiful, lemme buy you a drink,' he leered.

'If it's all the same to you, no, thanks,' she replied, neatly stepping round him.

But the GI was persistent, jogging after her.

'Aah, c'mon, sugar, don't be like that.'

Daisy had dealt with worse sorts than him.

'Maybe that big old head of yours is so heavy you can't turn it round, but if you look to my left, you'll see I've already got a date. Now hop it.'

His beady eyes narrowed as he glared at Robert.

'Lady, you have got to be kidding me,' he snapped. 'You're dating this uppity Negro? Why in the hell would you walk out with him?'

Daisy felt her patience wearing thin. 'Look here, you little twerp. Last I heard, his blood was the same colour as ours,' she snapped. 'And I happen to like gentlemen who know how to treat a lady. Now, if you will please excuse us, we have places to go.'

Robert stepped in front of Daisy. 'You heard the lady,' he said quietly.

'Shut up.' The GI scowled. 'Either get back in the gutter where you belong or me and my buddies will put you there.'

By the way he was grinding his teeth Daisy could tell he was spoiling for a fight. Oh, why was this happening now to ruin their magical day?

Robert was so strong he could have halved an apple with his bare hands, but he simply shrugged. 'I don't fight in front of ladies.'

The GI took a step closer to Robert and pushed him hard. Robert didn't flinch. Just then a patrolling military policeman, ever on the alert for trouble, slowed his jeep to a halt by the kerb.

'Everything all right, fellas?' he asked.

'Yes, sir,' the GI barked back. 'No problem here.'

'Good,' he snapped. 'Keep it that way.'

But as he drove away, the GI spat on the pavement in front of them. 'Stay out of my way, darkie,' he warned, before disappearing up the street with his pals.

'I'm so sorry you had to see that,' Robert said quietly.

'Does that happen a lot?' she gasped.

'Most days.' He shrugged. 'You British folks are awful good; it's my own countrymen who give me the most trouble. Back home, we're not allowed in the same stores, but here in London, it's different and I can go where I like. Them white fellas can't get used to it, I suppose.'

'But that's awful!' she replied, disturbed at the humiliating treatment meted out to Robert because of his skin colour. 'You're over here fighting the same war, aren't you?'

Robert shrugged. 'Who knows? I just hope things will be different after the war.'

The incident was never mentioned again, but it cemented

what Daisy already knew in her head and her heart. Not only was Robert fighting a war on all fronts, he was also as decent, strong and honourable a man as she was likely to find anywhere.

'Thank you,' she smiled when they reached Bethnal Green Tube. 'I had a really terrific day.'

'Me too, Daisy.'

'Even after what happened earlier?' she asked worriedly.

'Nothing could take the shine off being with you,' he grinned back. Then the smile left his handsome face. 'I suppose next Saturday night will be our last proper date before I leave.'

'Please don't,' she replied. 'I can't bear to think about it.'

'What would you like to do?' he asked. 'I got a twelve-hour furlough before we're moved on.'

'Well, I don't think my nerves are up to another wobbly rowing boat,' she admitted, 'but I'd love to go dancing.'

'Your wish is my command.' He took her in his arms and waltzed her up and down the pavement right outside the Tube.

'Not now, you daft beggar,' she shrieked. As he whirled her round, Daisy pushed all thought of the horrible encounter from her mind and lost herself in the romance of the moment, relishing the feel of his strong arms wrapped tightly round her waist.

*

Poppy watched them dancing right there in the street and felt a pang of jealousy. She had taken herself out for a little walk and had spotted Daisy and Robert outside the Tube and instinctively hidden behind a bus shelter.

Sundays were the day she dreaded above all. For the rest of the week Trout's provided the perfect distraction, but left alone all Sunday in that poky room by herself she found the loneliness crippling. The fresh air would do her good, she had thought, as she had walked up in the direction of the Tube.

She watched spellbound from the shelter as Robert pulled Daisy into his arms. They looked so glamorous together, he in his dashing uniform and her in her beautiful dress, those shapely nylon-clad legs brushing up against his gaberdine trousers. They gazed deep into one another's eyes as if they had a secret that they alone knew. Daisy's gleaming hair was flecked with grass at the back, and they were giggling like a couple of kids.

Suddenly, a red bus flashed past, obscuring her vision, and when it passed, they were kissing. Poppy's heart lurched.

'They're in love,' she whispered out loud. Myriad emotions flashed through her mind. She thought the world of Daisy and was so happy to see such joy etched on her friend's face, but the kiss just compounded her own aching loneliness. Would she ever know a love like that, wrapped up in such a grand passion that a man felt compelled to waltz her down the pavement and kiss her in broad daylight?

Crossing the road, Poppy went on her way, eyes cast down to the pavement. If she hadn't been feeling furtive before, she certainly was now. She couldn't turn back, though. She had been planning it all week after all. It had been easy enough to get the keys to the factory. She had told Vera she wanted to go in on her only day off as she sorely needed to practise her sewing. Impressed with her dedication, Vera had willingly handed her the keys. Poppy felt guilty deceiving the woman who had shown her nothing but kindness, but she simply couldn't think of any other way to carry out her plan.

The factory floor was deserted and as Poppy settled herself behind her workbench, the silence was deafening. Being here all on her own was a little unsettling and she shivered as the sounds of the night descended. The forlorn drip, drip of a leaky tap in the kitchen. The rattle and groan of the ancient Victorian pipework, like a wheezy old man sinking into a chair. Up above, a rat scuttled noisily over the slate roof tiles.

Poppy carefully took the note out of her bag and read over her own immaculate handwriting.

My name is Poppy and I'm a sixteen-year-old machinist looking for a friend to write to. I work at Trout's garment factory in Bethnal Green. I used to be a scullery maid in Norfolk before the war, so I'll understand if I'm not the glamorous sort you want to get involved with, but I would so dearly love a friend to write to. I don't have many friends here, you see. I suppose on account of the fact that I'm not very confident. Gracious, I'm not selling myself terribly well, am I?

Anyway, I don't suppose you shall write back, but I think you boys are awfully brave. Three cheers to the red, white and blue.

Poppy

PS If you did write, I would write back.

Poppy frowned. It wasn't the stuff of high romance like the flowery prose she used to read in Cook's sentimental novels, but it would have to do.

Carefully, she tucked the note between the snowy folds of cotton and started to stitch it up. As her foot gently pressed down on the treadle, a whisper of a smile played over her pretty features.

It was Betty who had first given her the idea, when she had written to a soldier passing herself off as a twenty-one-year-old. Poppy replayed her words over in her mind. *That's the beauty of letters . . . You can be whoever you want to be.*

The seed of an idea Betty had inadvertently planted had taken hold and grown. Feeling more reckless than she ever had in her life, Poppy finished stitching in the note and then examined her handiwork. Perfect. There was no way Vera could guess at what the bandage contained.

Pretty soon it would be winging its way to an unknown soldier on the battlefield. And then what? Who knew? She didn't dare to presume she might find the grand kind of love consuming Daisy and Robert, but a soldier to write to, well, it was a start.

Hiding the letter had given her an addictive frisson of excitement, but also filled her with inestimable sadness. Why could she not summon the nerve to go to a dance and meet a man like any normal girl? In her heart she knew why. Because the memory that haunted her like no other had stolen away her right to a normal, happy courtship. Sighing heavily, little Poppy flicked off the factory lights and scurried out under cover of darkness as fast as her legs would take her.

Nine

One week on from Daisy's whirlwind date and Vera was still reeling from her sister's apparent change in attitude. Gone was the churlish, petulant and self-centred young girl and in her place was a thoughtful, hard-working lady. Vera was particularly impressed with her volunteering efforts at the children's hospital. It seemed to agree with Daisy too, as she always returned brimming over with smiles.

She shared her news with Mr Gladstone on a Saturday-morning tea break.

'I've got to admit,' she confided in the privacy of the foreman's office, 'our Daisy's a changed woman. She talks to me with a civil tongue in her head, and do you know? Last Sunday, I found her running sheets through the mangle without my even asking.' Vera broke off and shook her head in amazement at the memory. 'Volunteering at the hospital's doing her the world of good.'

Mr Gladstone's round little face was filled with joy. 'What did I tell you, Vera?' he beamed, rising from behind his desk and joining her at the glass door. 'I dare say she's finally growing up. This war's ageing us all and no mistake. I mean, look at me.'

Vera turned to look and saw his crinkly blue eyes sparkle with mischief.

'I had hair when this war started.'

A rare smile washed over her face.

'Get away with you,' she chuckled.

'Seriously, though, she's a proper songbird, your Daisy,' Mr Gladstone went on. 'Voice of an angel. I reckon singing up the hospital has been the making of her. Perhaps she's found her vocation in performing.'

Vera frowned. 'Oh, I'm not sure I'd want her on stage, Mr Gladstone.'

'Well, maybe she could join the ENSA lot. She's certainly good enough,' he reasoned. 'They're doing some sterling work entertaining the troops.'

'We'll see,' said Vera, her usual look of stern foreboding returning.

'Well, think about it, Vera,' he urged. 'I bumped into Matron the other day and she thanked me most heartily for the first-rate efforts of the Singer Girls, in particular Daisy. Told me she was a hit with everyone on the ward. Your sister has a talent. Doesn't she have a duty to share it?'

'Right now her duties lie here, making sure we have sufficient surgical bandages and uniforms for our troops,' she replied firmly. She paused and in a warier tone added, 'Did Matron say anything else?'

'Nothing really,' he said. 'Just that they look forward to her visits enormously.'

'That's as may be,' Vera retorted, 'but I like her where I can keep an eye on her.' As much as Vera wished to believe her sister's apparent turn of mood could be attributed to a growing maturity, the cynical side of her simply refused to believe it.

Mr Gladstone went to reply but clearly thought better of it and the two fell into a comfortable silence as together they stared out over the sea of workers.

Vera felt a sense of protectiveness stir in her heart. The women were listening to *Music While You Work* on the Home Service and the crackly old wireless was playing 'We'll Meet Again'.

'So much solace and companionship in music, ain't there,' mused Mr Gladstone. 'It stops me from getting lonely, that's for sure. I miss their singing when I'm home on my own. Don't tell them that, though.'

Vera chuckled, then on impulse, she turned to face him. 'Why don't you come to ours for your tea tonight?' she said. 'It's a Saturday night after all. Daisy's invited Sal and Poppy round to eat after they've done their stint at the hospital and before they go off to a dance. It's only corned beef hash, but I'm sure I can eke out another plateful for you.'

Mr Gladstone's face lit up as if he had been invited to take tea with the King himself.

'Corned beef hash, you say?' he grinned, rubbing his rotund belly. 'Why, it's my very favourite – a rare treat. I'd be delighted. And there was me thinking it was just a plate of bread and dripping to keep me company tonight. What time shall I present myself?'

Vera was taken aback at his reaction and instantly found herself regretting her uncharacteristic act of spontaneity. She liked to keep her private and work lives separate, and now she worried this would send out the wrong message, but she couldn't very well withdraw the invite.

'Eight thirty prompt, Mr Gladstone.'

He grinned and his top lip twitched mischievously. 'Does this mean you'll call me Archie now?' he twinkled.

'Don't push your luck, Mr Gladstone,' she retorted, and, with that, took her leave of his office.

At a quarter past eight that evening, Vera spooned loose tea into her giant brown pot, poured in boiling water, then popped a tea cosy on top before standing back to admire her handiwork. The tiny kitchen was as clean as a new pin and filled with the delicious smell of a mutton stew bubbling away on the stove. In another act of spontaneity, her second of the day, she had popped to the butcher's at dinnertime and blown half a week's rations on some mutton. She had even managed to get her hands on a loaf of bread, not fresh admittedly, but Vera had a nifty trick of dabbing it with a bit of water and putting it in the range to warm through, making it taste just baked. Never let it be said she had fallen foul of the squanderbug!

Vera took the lid off the stew and pondered her impulsive behaviour as she stirred a wooden spoon through the rich, meaty juices. Why was she making such an effort? Was it because Daisy seemed to be trying so hard to turn over a new leaf that she felt compelled to try herself? Another alarming thought popped into her head. Or was it to impress Mr Gladstone?

Don't be so daft, Vera, she chided herself. You haven't needed a man so far, so why ever would you start behaving like a simpering girl now?

No, it was all for the benefit of her little sister. With a resounding clatter she replaced the lid on the pot.

When she heard the front door open, Vera instinctively froze. Her father always returned at the same time. His routine rarely changed. He spent his days pawning whatever he could lay his hands on, gambling and dabbling in the black market to provide himself with enough money to spend the afternoon with his cronies down the pub.

At around eight in the evening, he returned like a bad omen to take his paper to the toilet in the yard, gobble down some tea and then go out again, to where exactly Vera shuddered to think. Usually he came up with some cock-and-bull story about working a night shift, but after years of living with Frank, Vera was wise to his ways.

From local gossip and experience she knew that the only place Frank headed was to a local drinking den or boxing club. At times he seemed to have plenty of money, showering Daisy with gifts of perfume and magazines; other times he was penniless and it was left to Vera to make up the shortfall in the housekeeping. She could usually tell immediately by his voice whether his horse had come in or his scheme had paid off.

'Hello, Vera,' he slurred behind her in a voice thick with drink and danger. Without turning round, she could already picture the look of malice lurking in her father's eyes. Tonight he was vexed, and instinctively, Vera felt her body stiffen.

'Something smells delicious,' he said slowly, walking up behind her and standing so close she felt the hairs on the back of her neck rise, one by one. The rancid odour of ale and Woodbines swept over her, intensifying the chilling feeling of foreboding. 'Enough of that for your old man?'

he asked. Without waiting for an answer, he took the lid off Vera's pot of stew.

She whirled round. 'Don't do that,' she snapped, regretting the words even before they were out of her mouth.

Retribution was fast and furious. In a flash Frank had his hands round her neck and she was pinned up against the kitchen wall. Even when he was drunk, her father seemed to have unnerving accuracy and his rough fingers had her gripped tightly round the jugular.

'Or what?' he seethed, pressing his face so close to hers she could see every broken and bloodshot vein in his eyes. 'What you going to do, you stupid little busybody?' he growled. 'Show me up like you did at the pub? Yeah, don't think I've forgotten about that. I ought to have given you a bloody good hiding for shaming me like that. You're nothing, my girl. You hear me? A silly, worthless cow, just like your stupid mother.'

In horror Vera realized her father was shaking with an uncontrollable rage, his fingers tightening round her neck, tiny flecks of spittle showering her face.

'Frank,' she spluttered, 'I can't breathe. Let me go.'

'Let you go?' he mimicked. 'I should have drowned you at birth, you useless witch. Don't you ever talk back to me in public again. You should take a leaf out of your sister's book.'

His mouth twisted spitefully; then he smiled as he gouged his thumb into the side of her neck so hard she felt the vein underneath pulsing.

'It's about time you showed your old man some respect. I'm the guv'nor, the man of the house! Do I make myself clear?' he roared.

Vera's head was starting to tingle. Her field of vision was obscured as her father's fingers gripped her windpipe like a vice. Hot shards of pain sliced down her throat; she realized she could black out at any moment.

'I said, do I make myself clear?' he bellowed.

'Yes,' she rasped, attempting to nod her head.

'Good,' he snapped, releasing his grip. Vera slumped to the floor, gasping for breath and clawing at her blouse. The fear was all-consuming. She wanted to crawl away, but staring at her father's heavy hobnailed boots, Vera knew exactly what he would do if she tried to escape.

Suddenly, he knelt down and his face loomed into view. 'Look at you,' he sneered, roughly pulling her blouse down to reveal the scars that covered her chest.

'Frank, please don't,' she whimpered, mortified.

'It's no bloody wonder you ain't got a fella,' he taunted, flicking her chest. 'Look atcha. You're deformed. What man would want to wake up next to a woman like you? You're probably barren and all after everything that's happened.' Frank Shadwell looked down at his elder daughter with a look of utter contempt.

'Right. I'm off out, but I'm warning you, Vera, you breathe a word of this to our Daisy and I might pay a little visit to your new friend Poppy.'

Vera sat bolt upright in alarm. 'What she's got to do with this?'

A hideous smile creased Frank's face. 'Lovely little thing,' he grunted. 'She and I got unfinished business. You turn Daisy against me and I might just see my way to finishing it. Know what I mean?'

Frank's threat was veiled, but with a sinking despair Vera knew exactly what he meant. She nodded wordlessly.

'Good,' he snapped. 'I'm off to work. See you in the morning.'

A minute later, the door slammed shut and Vera hauled herself to her feet and sank trembling into a chair. She felt a solitary tear course down her cheek. Angrily, she brushed it away. No, she could not start crying now, for if she did, Vera knew she would never stop.

Instead, she rose to her feet and carefully replaced the lid on the pot of stew. Next she walked to the mirror over the mantel and, with a shaking hand, did up the buttons on her blouse and smoothed down her hair. She took a moment to regard her appearance. Mr Gladstone and the girls would be here shortly and she could not for a moment let her feelings betray her. But there was no disguising the ancient pain in her eyes, as another piece of her heart hardened to stone. Against all odds she must protect her younger sister from that monster, and if that meant keeping his violence and dark side a secret, then so be it. That was the heavy burden she must now carry. For all their safety depended on it, including, Vera realized with a wrench, sweet Poppy's.

Ten minutes later, the girls burst through the door in a giggly whirlwind, their apple cheeks glowing fresh from the spring evening air.

'Cooee,' grinned Sal. 'We in time for tea?'

Vera took a deep breath and painted a bright smile on her face. 'Get in, get in, and shut that door else you'll let out all the hot air,' she fussed, collecting their coats and neatly storing them away in the good room.

Sal paused and sniffed the air. 'Vera,' she breathed, 'that isn't what I think, is it? Oh, it is! You're a ruddy marvel.' With that, she grabbed Vera about the waist and playfully danced her round the tiny kitchen.

'Get away with you, you scoundrel, Sal Fowler.' Vera smiled awkwardly. 'Now, go and wash your hands in the scullery, girls. We're just waiting on one more; then I can dish up.'

'Who's that?' asked Daisy, crinkling her elegant nose as she touched up her lipstick in a compact.

'Is it Frank?' Poppy asked fearfully.

Vera felt her tears bubbling just below the surface, and using every ounce of self-control, she blinked them back. 'No, love, he's at work,' she reassured Poppy.

'Oh, that's good news,' gushed Daisy. 'He must have picked up a night shift down the docks. See, Vera, I told you he's trying hard.'

Vera was saved from answering by two swift raps at the door.

'I'll go,' sang Daisy, leaping from her seat.

Seconds later, a sheepish Mr Gladstone stood at the door clutching a withered bunch of violets in one hand and a bottle of port in the other. His shoes had been buffed to a high shine and were gleaming almost as much as his blue eyes.

'I've been looking for an excuse to crack this open,' he smiled, passing the bottle to Vera. 'Sorry about the flowers, though,' he said, gazing at the limp bunch apologetically. 'There wasn't much choice at the market.'

'That's ever so kind of you, Mr Gladstone,' Vera smiled back, taking the flowers quickly with a trembling hand.

Mr Gladstone hesitated. 'Are you quite well, Vera? You look a little pale,' he said, concerned.

'Why ever wouldn't I be?' she replied, turning quickly. 'I'll just go and put them in water.'

With that, she bustled to the yard to fetch water from the outside tap, relieved to be out from under Mr Gladstone's scrutiny. She knew the foreman was sweet on her, and that little episode showed her why she must keep him at arm's length. How could she afford to let anyone get too close, least of all someone as kind and perceptive as he? Archie wasn't daft, and if she let him into her heart, he would surely dig out her secrets. That was unimaginable.

When Vera returned, she noticed with gratitude that Archie was seated at the wooden kitchen table deep in conversation with Poppy.

'Did the gentry *really* have the butler ring a gong to summon them up to dinner, Poppy?' he asked.

'Oh yes,' she said, shifting a little awkwardly, clearly uncomfortable at being the centre of attention.

'How wonderful,' breathed Daisy. 'Every single night?'

'Oh yes.' She nodded. 'He even had a menu in a silver frame on the table with all the courses written on it.'

'What, every day?' squawked Sal in disbelief.

'Yes,' replied Poppy. 'Even if His Lordship was up in London and Her Ladyship was dining alone. They upheld their traditions rather rigidly.'

'Well, they won't be holding on to them for much longer,' muttered Sal darkly. 'The war will see to that. Though I doubt *His Lordship*'s much affected by rationing and bombs. Bloody toffs.'

'Watch your language,' Vera warned.

'Sorry, Vera,' Sal replied quickly.

'That's all right,' said Vera, patting her softly on the shoulder as she went to dish up.

'So that's upstairs,' smiled Daisy. 'But what was life like below stairs, Poppy?'

'Nothing much to say really, Daisy,' Poppy blustered.

'Well, I tell you summat for nothing. I reckons as 'ow it'll be His Lordship envying us tonight,' beamed Mr Gladstone as Vera spooned a piping-hot ladleful of stew into his bowl. 'This is an absolute feast, Vera. You've done us proud. My tummy's grumbling like a tank.'

'Oh yes,' gushed Poppy. 'Cook's stews never looked as good as this.'

Vera waved a dismissive hand. 'Well, I dare say I don't match up to a butler in white gloves, but it'll have to suffice.'

'Shall I do the honours, Vera?' asked Mr Gladstone.

'If you would be so kind.'

Gently lowering her eyes to the table, she mouthed the Lord's Prayer alongside the factory foreman. Being immersed in the silence of prayer, Vera finally felt a peace wash over her.

'Amen,' she whispered reverently when Mr Gladstone had finished.

Seconds later, the room was filled with sounds that brought joy to Vera's heart: the eager scraping of cutlery on bowls and appreciative murmurings.

'This is ever so good, Vera,' said Daisy brightly, as she used a hunk of bread to mop up her left-over gravy. 'Thanks.'

Vera felt so taken aback at her younger sister's gratitude she looked up in surprise. Had she heard the girl right? Happen this war had one blessed side effect. Her self-centred little sister was finally growing up. She caught Mr Gladstone wink at her from across the table and felt a wave of happiness wash over her.

After tea, Mr Gladstone filled up five glasses with port as the girls stretched themselves out on the hearthrug in front of the fire.

'Vera, that tasted beyond heavenly,' Poppy said, smiling sweetly.

Maybe it was the crackling flames and the warmth of the port snaking through her veins but Vera felt herself relax. At least this proved her father couldn't ruin everything.

'Come on, girls,' said Daisy impatiently, draining her drink. 'If we get a wriggle on, we can get to the dance before the queues build up. You coming, Poppy?'

Poppy smiled and shook her head, as did Vera. They never tired of trying to get the poor girl out with them. When would they see she wasn't like them? Poppy didn't like the high life. She preferred the simple pleasures, like Vera did.

'No, thanks, girls.' Poppy yawned sleepily. 'If it's all the same with you, I'll stop here with Vera and finish off the rug I've been weaving. It's coming on a treat, isn't it, Vera?'

Vera smiled tenderly at the girl. 'That it is, Poppy. You've got a natural talent in those hands. I've not seen many handle a dolly peg like you can.'

Suddenly, the door to the kitchen opened, letting in a blast of cold air.

'Someone forget to invite me to the party?' grinned Frank, his dark outline blocking the light from the fire.

Vera felt her bubble of happiness burst. 'I thought you

were doing nightwatching at the docks?' she blustered, sitting up stiffly in her chair.

'They laid me off,' he snapped. 'Not enough work.' His gruff voice was grating in the gloom.

'Oh, rough luck, Dad.' Daisy smiled up at her father.

'But I thought you said work was plentiful at the moment,' Vera replied, her voice guarded.

'What did I say about showing respect, Vera?' he warned in a low voice, helping himself to a generous glass of Mr Gladstone's port. 'And what's he doing here? Trying to get his feet under the table?' Frank gestured rudely to the foreman.

'I think it was time I was off, Vera,' Mr Gladstone said warily, rising to his feet. 'The food and company have been delicious. I really can't thank you enough.'

Vera felt like crying as she showed him to the door.

'You're welcome,' she replied.

On the doorstep, he hesitated, before picking up Vera's hand and planting a small kiss on it. 'I hope we can do it again sometime,' he said quietly, then quickly strode off.

Vera watched until the darkness of the blackout consumed him before returning to the smoky kitchen. She had not been gone two minutes, but in her absence, Poppy had got her coat and her hat on and Daisy and Sal were ushering her out.

'But I thought you were stopping in with me, love?' she spluttered, unable to contain the panic in her voice.

'I really am awfully sorry,' Poppy said apologetically, shooting a nervous glance back at the kitchen, 'but I've changed my mind and I will go to the dance after all. Besides, perhaps it's better I leave –' she lowered her voice to a whisper '– under the circumstances.'

Vera gulped and feverishly began to wring the hem of her apron between her fingers. 'Of course, Poppy. I understand, and you're right – perhaps it's for the best.'

Poppy hesitated and swallowed hard. 'Unless of course you prefer me to stay, that is, and keep you company, Mrs Shadwell.'

Vera smiled sadly. Dear, sweet Poppy, putting aside her own fear to think of Vera and her well-being. She glanced over at her father and remembered his veiled threats of earlier.

'I'll be absolutely fine,' she said, a touch too brightly. 'Now off you go.' She shooed them all out onto the doorstep.

'Daisy and Sal, look after Poppy, won't you?' she ordered.

'We will, Vera, don't worry,' promised Sal, linking her arm through Poppy's.

Poppy shot Vera one last concerned look before she was led off down the cobbled street.

Vera stood on the doorstep and watched them go, the giant barrage balloons floating over their heads casting them in an ominous shadow. She closed her eyes and felt a strong wave of nostalgia wash over her. A plump, rosy-cheeked baby swaddled in a coach pram, old ladies shelling peas in their pinafore laps and sipping stout. The next-door neighbour whitening her step while shrieking children chanted as they turned a giant skipping rope over the cobbles. She could picture the East End she loved so clearly in her mind's eye.

Except, years on, it had all changed. The children had gone, as had half the houses, what doorsteps were left were covered with sandbags, and the chalky outline of hopscotch games on the cobbles were now blackened from the Blitz fires. So many houses had been reduced to rubble that the street looked like a smile with missing teeth. The close-knit community was now battling for survival, yet for Vera, conflict raged outside *and* inside her home. Sighing heavily, she gripped the door frame for support and forced herself back across the threshold.

Back in the kitchen, her father had discarded his hobnailed boots, leaving a fresh trail of mud over her kitchen floor, and was sitting in her easy chair with the bottle of port resting on his tummy while he gobbled back the last of the stew. She watched him shove the food in his mouth, barely chewing before he swallowed.

The beautiful violets Mr Gladstone had thoughtfully brought had been upended when Frank had tossed his coat over them, and the water from the vase dripped into a pool on the floor. Even the room smelt sour. At that moment, Vera loathed him. He was as ugly as war itself. How could this animal be her father? Frank tainted everything he touched. That evening, she had searched for stardust and he had reduced it all to nothing but smouldering ashes. Like he always did.

Grunting and shifting in the chair, Frank looked up at her and, with a mawkish grin, raised his glass in a mock toast.

'Lovely stew, Vera,' he grinned. 'Hope you don't mind me interrupting your cosy night, but I thought it best I come home and make sure you haven't been filling Daisy's head with rubbish.' He paused and the smile stretched further.

'Blimey, but that Poppy's a treasure. Almost worth coming home for, to catch sight of her pretty young face. How's your neck, by the way?'

Vera's hand leaped to her throat, where already she could feel a tender bruise spreading down her neck. Without saying a word, she fled up the stairs, bolting the bedroom door behind her.

Ten

The dance was in full swing by the time the girls got there, and Poppy's eyes went out on stalks when she saw the dance floor heaving with Americans all doing the jitterbug.

'What do you think, Poppy?' Daisy grinned excitedly, tapping her feet as she scanned the floor for Robert. She had never checked her bag and coat so quickly, and as for that meal . . . She had thought it would never end. It had been a blessed relief when Frank walked in, as at least it had given her an excuse to get away. She didn't mean to come across as ungrateful – Vera had gone to a lot of effort to cook a delicious meal – but this was Robert's last night, after all. She had a lifetime of nights with Vera stretching ahead of her, but her time with Robert was uncertain at best. Her heart thumped painfully at the very thought of him leaving, but she forced her attention back to Poppy.

'It's awfully busy.' Poppy gulped, sitting down quickly at a table. 'In the country, we just did the waltz, and you were lucky to get a cup of tea.' She looked about her nervously. 'The cook used to chaperone us to the village hall and have a whist drive with her friends while they waited. I think I'm a little out of my depth here.'

'You haven't a thing to worry about, Poppy,' Sal said,

raising her voice to be heard over the music. ''Cause we're your chaperones now, and this one will be a whole lot more fun than a dusty old village hall.'

With that, she lit a cigarette and clamped it between her teeth as she rummaged around in her bag for her purse. 'Gin and tonic, is it, Daisy?' she asked.

'Ooh, I should say, but hold the gin for Poppy, Sal,' she replied. 'Remember, she's only sixteen.'

'Crikey, yes,' she said. 'Vera would have my guts if we got her drunk again.'

Daisy stared curiously at Poppy as Sal went off to fetch their drinks. Little by little she felt the mysterious newcomer from the country was starting to trust her, but still there was something about Poppy she could not fathom. An aching sadness hidden under the surface. Daisy had the queerest feeling that ever since Vera's fuss in the pub that night, Poppy was scared of her father. Not that there was any need – Frank came across as a bit gruff, but Daisy knew there was a heart of gold deep down. She wanted to explain all this to Poppy, but she was such a timid little thing, and when it came to men, she seemed simply thunderstruck.

'Look here, you do trust me, don't you, Poppy?' Daisy said softly.

Poppy gazed back up at her with those huge, vulnerable blue eyes and blinked.

'It's just that I can't help but notice that you seem a little nervous, particularly around men,' Daisy said, pressing her. 'You know, my father really meant you no harm at the pub that night. He was just being friendly. Not all men have their brains below their belts.'

Daisy had been joking, but she was taken aback by Poppy's reaction.

'Don't they?' she whispered, turning her head away quickly.

'No, Poppy,' Daisy replied, surprised. 'Why ever would you say such a thing?'

'Never mind,' Poppy said hastily. 'Now, I wonder where Sal is with our drinks.'

Suddenly, the tall figure of a man loomed over the table and Poppy jumped.

'Here's my little songbird. I thought you'd gone AWOL on me,' said a deep voice.

'Robert!' screamed Daisy, leaping to her feet. 'Oh, darling, I'm so sorry I'm late.' She flung herself into his arms and the couple embraced for a long time before Daisy turned back round.

'Doesn't he look handsome tonight, Poppy? . . . Poppy?'

Poppy was busy gathering her bag and making to leave.

'Oh, please don't go, Poppy,' Daisy urged. 'You've only just got here.'

'Sorry, Daisy. I . . . I suddenly don't feel very well. It's best I take myself home.'

'But you can't go on your own, Poppy,' Robert piped up, concerned. 'Please, let me escort you home safely. I insist.'

'Thank you, sir, that's kind of you, but no,' Poppy replied, looking flustered. 'Please, I really don't wish to be any trouble.'

'It's no trouble at all, Poppy,' Daisy urged.

'Honestly,' said Poppy with a brave smile. 'I'm getting used to London now, and I feel quite confident getting the bus home by myself. Besides, it's your last night together and you don't want to waste half of it getting me back to Bethnal Green. I promise you I shall be perfectly fine. You just enjoy yourselves.'

'Very well.' Daisy smiled back. 'We shall in that case.' She reached down and wrapped Poppy in a hug. 'Farewell and take care, sweetheart,' she whispered.

When Poppy had left, a frown creased Daisy's pretty face.

'What's wrong, Daisy?' asked Robert.

'Oh, I don't know, nothing really,' she replied. 'I was just thinking I'll make a bit more of an effort with Poppy at work. I think she's missing home.'

'Poor thing,' nodded Robert. 'She seems a swell girl, but a little on the shy side.'

'Talking of missing . . .' sighed Daisy, wrapping her arms around her sweetheart's broad shoulders. 'Is it really your last night? Please tell me it was all just a dreadful dream and you can stay in London forever.'

Robert grinned ruefully and shook his head. 'Afraid not, Daisy. Uncle Sam has plans for us.'

'Oh, please let's not talk about the war, Robert,' Daisy urged, pressing her finger lightly over his lips. 'I simply can't bear to think about it. This is your last night in London and nothing is more important than that.'

The past two weeks had been the most magical she had ever known. They had managed to see each other as often as time and circumstances had permitted, thanks to the morale-boosting trips to the hospital. Not to mention that wonderful date in Hyde Park. Even Robert's brutal treatment at the hands of his fellow countrymen outside the pictures hadn't dented what had been the best days of her life. In fact, it had merely solidified what she already felt towards the dashing soldier, for she adored Robert with all her heart. He had utterly bewitched her. And best of all, he seemed just as spellbound by her.

Initially, Daisy had to admit her head had been turned by Robert's striking good looks, but now that attraction had mellowed to something that she instinctively knew could last a lifetime. All his life Robert had fought prejudice over the colour of his skin. Even now, while fighting for his country, he faced a barrage of hatred and abuse. And yet Robert remained as dignified and fearless as any man she had ever met. He certainly treated her with more gentle-manly reverence than she was used to.

A strong sense of protectiveness stirred inside her heart, and if she was honest, something about his predicament resonated deep within her. All her life Daisy had felt like an outcast in Bethnal Green. She longed for so much more than the four walls of the factory and her stifling terrace that at times she swore she could almost hear the frustration drumming in every cell in her body.

Perhaps this urge to escape came from growing up without a mother to anchor her. Her big sister could never hope to understand . . . but Robert did. He hadn't laughed at her dreams; he had encouraged them. Before, she had only dared to imagine a life in the growing suburbs of Essex, but now, thanks to Robert, the whole world had suddenly opened up to her, and oh, how she longed for a future with him in it.

Something else about her family had always puzzled Daisy too: her sister's ferocious protectiveness towards her and disgust towards their father . . . It didn't make much sense. But now, none of that mattered anymore. Her feelings for

Robert were honest and pure. They at least made perfect sense. He may have arrived in a jeep, not astride a white horse, but in Daisy's heart, Robert was the man to whisk her away from the East End.

'I'll give you a penny for them.' He smiled down at her.

'For what?' she frowned, shaking herself out of her reverie.

'Your thoughts.' He grinned.

'Oh, sorry, Robert,' she replied. 'I'm all yours.'

'Good,' he said, taking her hand and leading her to the dance floor. 'In that case, let's dance.'

When the music slowed to a waltz, she nestled her head on his strong chest. He smelt delicious, of fresh-baked biscuits and cut grass.

'I can't stand to think of you going away, putting yourself in danger,' she sighed. 'Everything will feel so flat. Even Vera seems to have herself a new fella now.'

'Don't begrudge her some happiness,' Robert replied. 'After all, it will be nice for her to have someone after we marry.'

Daisy stared up at Robert and her hand flew to her mouth in surprise. 'Oh, Robert,' she gushed. 'Do you really mean that? Will we truly have a future together? You must have read my mind!'

'I sure hope so. I won't lie. Like I've said all along, it will be hard, but I'll move heaven and earth to make it happen.' He smiled down gently. 'I don't know when or how, but once this war is over, I intend to make you my wife, Daisy Shadwell . . . if you'll have me, that is?'

'Have you?' she breathed. 'Nothing would make me happier than to start a new life with you.'

They sealed the proposal, for Daisy was sure that was what it was, with a lingering kiss.

*

Sal arrived back from the bar clutching their drinks to find Poppy missing and Daisy on the dance floor with Robert.

'Daisy!' she called out to her. 'Where on earth is Poppy?'

'She wasn't feeling well,' Daisy called over her shoulder. 'She's left.'

'But she can't simply just go on her own!' Sal protested. 'We promised Vera we'd chaperone her.'

'We did try our hardest to stop her,' Daisy replied, shrugging, 'but she seemed in a dreadful hurry.'

'I'm going to follow her, Daisy,' Sal muttered, trying to hide her irritation. 'Enjoy your last night with Robert.'

'I will,' Daisy sang back, oblivious, and the love-struck pair melted into the sea of young people crowding the dance floor.

Sal put the drinks down on the table and sighed heavily. She loved Daisy with all her heart, but she could be a little self-centred at times. Fancy letting Poppy hotfoot it out of there like that, all alone. There was no way on earth she would have allowed Poppy to travel back to the East End on her own. Perhaps it was the strong maternal urge in her, but at times she felt Poppy wasn't much more mature than her own boys. She was certainly less streetwise than them. The thought of her out there on her own made Sal shudder.

Sal said a hasty goodbye to Daisy and Robert before reaching for her bag and scurrying from the club, her heels clicking down the parquet stairs. She burst out of the door and onto the pavement, just in time to see Poppy board a bus bound for the East End. Running as fast as her legs could carry her, she chased after the bus.

'Poppy!' she yelled, but the bus rumbled on ahead until it was swallowed up by the darkened street. 'Curses,' she mumbled.

Vera wouldn't like it one little bit, but then neither did she. Poppy was far too young to be travelling alone at night and Sal knew she had let her young friend down. She glanced back at the dance hall. Cigarette smoke and raucous laughter spilled out as servicemen stood huddled by the entrance. Sal suddenly felt a deep and aching tiredness. She had no desire to return and fend off the attentions of amorous GIs. No, she would get the bus back to the East End, check Poppy had got home safely, then retire to the warmth of her bed. She had a half-written letter to her boys she was dying to finish.

Alighting the bus back in the East End, Sal's route to Poppy's lodgings took her past Trout's. Blearily, she glanced up at the darkened facade of the factory and saw something that made her stop in her tracks. A chink of light spilt out from behind the badly drawn blackout curtain.

Must be Mr Gladstone working late, she mused. But it was not like him to be so sloppy with the blackouts. He was usually meticulous with these things.

Trout's worked a night shift throughout the week, but not usually on a Saturday or Sunday, so Sal simply couldn't imagine why her boss would be there at this time of night.

Shocked to find the factory door unlocked, she silently picked her way up the darkened stairs, moving softly so as not to disturb whoever was there. Scarcely breathing for fear of disturbing an intruder, she pushed open the door to the fifth floor and gasped.

'Poppy . . .' she breathed, astonished. 'Whatever are you doing here?'

Poppy looked like a rabbit caught in the full glare of headlights. 'Sal!' Panic flitted over her pretty face. 'Oh, Sal . . . I . . . I . . .' but Poppy couldn't finish her sentence. Fat tears ran from her blue eyes as she gazed, stricken, at Sal. 'I've done something so dreadful. Promise me you won't tell Vera I was here so late at night?'

Sal could see she was consumed with terror. Her heart filled with compassion for the young girl and she moved quickly to her side.

'Dear, sweet Poppy.' She smiled tenderly, pulling a hanky from her handbag and gently dabbing away Poppy's tears. 'Are you going to tell me why you're here? You gave me an awful fright, you know. Whatever it is, it really can't be that bad, surely?'

Poppy's eyes widened. 'Oh, but it is, Sal, and Vera will give me my marching orders on the spot when she finds out,' she whispered. 'I've . . . I've . . . Well, I've been coming in here after hours, you see. Sewing little notes into bandages.'

'Sewing notes into bandages?' repeated Sal.

'Well, not just bandages, sometimes into the hems of army jackets and trousers, but mainly the field bandages. This is only my second time, but oh . . . you must think me so foolish.'

Sal felt her mouth twitch, but she couldn't contain herself and soon her shoulders were shaking with laughter.

'Oh, Poppy, you daft cow,' she chuckled. 'If I had

tuppence for every note or love letter sewn into the lining of a jacket or a bandage, I'd be a rich woman by now.'

'You mean—'

'Yes,' she replied. 'I reckon half the young women in this place have done it at one time or another, and in broad daylight on a shift too. Young Betty and Kathy do it all the time. Vera suspects, but she's never caught anyone red-handed. I even found some saucy piece slipping a note that said, "If you're in the mood, come to me and I'll be in the nude", with her address on the back. She's got more front than Blackpool that one!'

Poppy blanched a shade whiter. 'Oh my! I can assure you my note wasn't smutty, Sal. You have to believe me,' she begged.

'It's all right,' Sal said soothingly. 'I do. To be honest, most of the women just do it for a laugh, you know, to boost morale or find a sweetheart. There's quite a shortage of young British men on the streets at the moment, in case you hadn't noticed.' Sal broke off and stared curiously at Poppy. 'But that doesn't strike me as your style, Poppy,' she said quizzically.

'No,' replied Poppy, with a drop in her voice. 'I don't really do it for fun.'

'Then just why are you doing it?' asked Sal directly. 'It makes no sense to run from a dance hall packed full of eligible young men to come here and write to anonymous soldiers. I don't get it, Poppy, really I don't. You're such a pretty young thing – you could be courting any number of men by now.'

'Because I'm scared,' Poppy replied, in a voice so quiet Sal could scarcely hear it.

Instinct told Sal not to reply. If there was a silence, Poppy would eventually fill it. As she waited with bated breath, you could have heard a pin drop.

Poppy cast her eyes to the floor and took a shaky breath. 'I'm scared, Sal,' she repeated. Her words were almost lost in the cavernous factory.

Sal gently took Poppy's face in her hands and tilted it up until their eyes met. The look of hopelessness and fear lurking there nearly took her breath away.

'What are you running from, Poppy?' she urged quietly, holding her gaze. 'You can tell me anything.'

'But that's just it, Sal. I can't tell you.' Poppy started to cry, shaking her head in bitter frustration.

Sal could feel Poppy's whole body quivering and sensed she could push no further. Whatever it was that scared her would reveal itself in time. Secrets could not be forced out against their will.

Instead, she summoned up all her courage and did something she knew would shock the young girl to her very core.

'You're not the only one with secrets, Poppy,' Sal admitted.

With trembling hands she slowly pulled up the hem of her skirt to reveal the tops of her thighs. Poppy gasped and a startled squawk escaped her lips.

The skin at the top and inside of Sal's thighs had bubbled clean off. What was left was raw and exposed, the scars snaking up inside her pants and nearly down to her knees. The flesh that remained was stained from brown to purple like a tidemark, the skin so thin and stretched you could almost make out the tendons and bones beneath. It was barbaric and unspeakably sad.

Sal stared down at her deformed legs, her face etched with an ancient pain. The terrible silence in the room turned Poppy's heart over as her mind grappled to make sense of what she was looking at.

'Who did this to you, Sal?' she asked tremulously.

Sal looked up at Poppy, her expression changing from shame to blazing fury in the blink of an eye.

'The man who pledged to love, honour and protect me,' she flashed back. 'Reggie, my *beloved* husband.' She spat the words out as if she had a fish bone stuck in her throat.

'But . . . but why?' Poppy stuttered, confused.

'Why do you think?' Sal shrugged. 'Most men in Bethnal Green like to beat ten bells out of each other in the ring down York Hall boxing club, but my Reggie didn't need a punchbag, not when he had me. It was almost like a second job to him. When he weren't working the docks, he was busy knocking the stuffing out of me. Started seven years ago, when I was pregnant with our Billy. He reckoned I gave the baby more attention than him. What kind of man's jealous of his own child?' She shook her head so fiercely at the memory that her red curls tumbled about her pale face.

'Oh, Sal,' cried Poppy. 'Why didn't you tell the police?'

'The police,' she snorted. 'Don't make me laugh. I did to begin with, but I couldn't call them every time it happened, could I? They used to call Saturday night – when Reggie got back from the pub – "flying plate" night, but they stopped coming out. Besides, if I did tell anyone, my Reggie would give me a right good hiding, so I quickly learned to keep my mouth shut. It was the only way to survive, see. And you want to hear the funniest thing?'

Poppy stared back at her, struck dumb with horror.

'I don't think he even really thought he was doing anything wrong,' she went on. 'One night, we were walking down the street and he dropped his bag of chips. He was that jibbed he turned round and, without saying a word, belted me across the face. Talk about a wallop! It was so hard it knocked me clean off my feet. When a passer-by helped me up and gave Reggie a piece of his mind, he turned to the fella, completely baffled, and said, "But she's my wife," as if that somehow excused it.'

She let rip with a hollow laugh and fished a cigarette out of her bag, lighting it with a shaky hand. Drawing heavily on her cigarette, her eyes narrowed to slits. The crackling of the cigarette caused the tip to burn more brightly, illuminating her scars even more vividly.

'But your legs . . .' murmured Poppy, gesturing to her thighs. 'That's more than a slap and a kick.'

'Another hardship of the war,' Sal replied in a voice as dead as dry leaves. 'It happened on his last night at home before he was sent off for army training, a few days after Chamberlain's announcement. He was drunk, of course. Reckoned he was due some how's-your-father, his conjugal rights, seeing as he was going away and didn't know when he'd next be getting it. I denied him. I knew it was my unsafe time. Last thing I wanted was another mouth to feed in the middle of a war. He won't wear a sheath, of course. Mind you, show me an East End man that will.'

The effort of recounting the story was almost too much and Sal took a deep, shaky breath before continuing.

'He went mental. Told me I was silly whore. I turned my back on him and next thing I know –' her voice cracked a little '– he did this. Poured boiling water from the kettle straight over my thighs. Told me if he couldn't go there, he didn't want anyone else going there either. His way of marking out his property, I suppose. He marched off to war the very next day. It's taken two years to heal. I've had infection after infection, and the doctors don't reckon it will ever look any better than this. Vera and Daisy came to my rescue while I was in hospital, looked after my boys until they were evacuated. I owe them both a great debt.' With that, she angrily tugged down the hem of her skirt.

'So there you have it,' she spat, so fiercely the breath whistled through the chip in her left tooth. 'All I can hope is that he never comes back and my boys can return to a home free from violence. Reggie's been serving abroad since the war broke out, and I haven't written to him once. He has no idea our flat took a direct hit during the Blitz, or that I evacuated the boys the first chance I got, and I have no intention of telling him, not that *he*'s written once to see how they are.'

Rising sharply from her seat, Sal ground out her cigarette and started to pace the factory floor, her body as tense as a coiled spring. Poppy remained rooted to her seat, listening in horrified silence.

'The night the flat was bombed, I didn't dare show it, of course, but inside I was jubilant,' Sal went on. 'It wasn't a home, you see, Poppy – just a place crawling with bad memories. I couldn't wait to see the back of it. Most of the neighbours returned after the all-clear sounded, to salvage whatever they could. Me, I just walked right away with only the clothes on my back. My boys were safe in the country by then, so nothing else mattered. I spent a week sleeping on the floor of the Salvation Army rest centre before the council rehoused me into my new place. They asked if I'd like my husband to be notified, but I told them that I would write instead. Only my friends and my boys know my new address and that's the way it's staying.'

Sal paused and drummed her finger on the workbench as if to underline her point. Suddenly, it struck Poppy that her friend was in hiding, living with the terrible spectre of Reggie's return.

'But that's awful, Sal. What if he comes back?' Poppy asked fearfully.

Sal shook her head despairingly. 'If he survives the war, he'll return to the East End at some point, but by then, Poppy, I hope I'll be strong enough to fight back or else will have upped sticks and left. It's not much of a plan, I'll grant you, but what else can I do?

'Maybe I'm being naive, but a part of me hopes he will just vanish and the boys will forget they even had a father. How much they took in I couldn't tell you. I tried my hardest to protect them from the worst of it. I even learned how to take a beating without screaming so they wouldn't hear.

'I love my sons with all my heart, you see, and I would do anything, *anything* to keep them safe and happy. Being their mother is the only thing that has made my life worth living. Every spare penny I earn from this place I've put aside in a biscuit tin under the bed, so that maybe one day, when we're all reunited, we can escape the East End and I can give them a better life. I've managed to save enough for three train tickets to the West Country and three months' lodgings for us all, which should tide us over until I've found work. Soon as the war's over, we're leaving. My escape fund, I call it. Makes me feel stronger just knowing it's there. Daft, ain't it?'

Sal's speech seemed to have sapped all her strength and she sank down heavily into the chair next to Poppy.

'I don't think it's daft at all, Sal,' Poppy whispered, in a voice full of awe. 'Your boys are lucky to have a mother like you.'

'That's sweet of you to say.' Sal smiled back. 'But don't you think me weak for putting up with Reggie?'

'On the contrary,' she replied, taking Sal's hands in hers. 'I think you are the strongest, bravest woman I know. If anyone can find a way to a new life, it's you.'

'Bless you,' Sal murmured, comforted by the warmth of Poppy's tiny fingers wrapped around hers. 'Now that you know *everything* about me, is there anything you'd like to tell me about your past? A problem shared is a problem halved. I should know,' she added with a wry smile.

'I know that too, Sal,' Poppy replied quietly. 'And I appreciate your concern, really I do, but my worries are nothing next to what you've been through. I'm just being silly.'

Sal shook her head slowly. 'You're a long way from silly, Poppy Percival. There's an old saying, you know: in a storm, you should open your front and back doors. Don't let your troubles find a home. Do you understand what I'm saying?'

Poppy stared back at her for what felt like an age before answering. 'I understand, and I'm grateful for your wisdom . . . but I really am dead on my feet. Shall we both go home? It's been ever such a long day, and that landlady'll give me what for if I'm late back.'

'If that's what you want.' Sal smiled back sadly. 'If Vera

gets wind that old Mrs Brown's been boxing your chops, she'll have her guts for garters.'

Together the two women rose wearily to their feet, but when they reached the doorway, Poppy paused and Sal spotted the fear she had seen earlier flash over Poppy's face.

'Promise me you won't tell Vera about my secret letters?' she implored. 'She might send me home to Framshalton Hall, and I can't go back there, Sal. Not ever.'

'No one's sending you back there,' Sal reassured her. 'Your secret's safe with me. You have my word.'

Poppy's shoulders sank in relief and together the two friends left the factory and walked out into the dead of night. Sal had laid herself bare to Poppy. She just hoped that in time the young girl would trust her enough to do the same.

Eleven

In a strange way, Sal found that she was relieved to have unburdened herself. Aside from Vera and Daisy, no one else knew the full extent of her husband's abuse or of the scars she hid so well. She hoped one day she could repay the favour to Poppy. They were as different as chalk and cheese all right, she thought with a smile. Sal was a smart-mouthed East End factory girl, while Poppy was as timid as a country mouse, and yet somehow, Sal realized, their friendship worked. She felt nothing but genuine affection towards the young girl and prayed she would spill her secrets. Time will out, she thought sagely, as she turned the corner of her street and saw the outline of her temporary housing loom into view.

It was a welcome sight. After the drama of the night and seeing Poppy safely home, she was shattered, and the balls of her feet were throbbing. The thought of a hot, sweet cup of tea and a warm bed had never felt so promising.

'That's strange,' she muttered to herself as she walked up to the door. 'I could have sworn I didn't draw the curtains before I went out.'

Curtains were just one of the things Sal was so pleased to own. Her prefab home was nothing but a glorified single-storey hut made from reconstituted bits of damaged aircraft. But glory of glories, it did at least have a tiny bathroom, so no more stumbling about in the dark groping for the communal lavatory door. She was proud as punch of her little home and prayed each night that it heralded a new beginning.

Sal pushed her door open with a yawn. She hadn't bothered to lock it. No one in the East End ever did. She stepped into the prefab and lit the tiny oil lamp that barely threw out enough light by which to make tea.

Suddenly, through the soft orange glow, she made out the figure of a man sitting in the dark at the far end of the room.

She froze. The kettle slipped from her fingers and landed with a clatter on the floor.

'Hello, sweetheart. Why don't you come over here, then, and give your old man a welcome-home kiss?'

Reggie stepped out of the shadows and walked towards her, placing both hands on her shoulders. A scream caught in her throat as her husband's fingers tightened round her neck. A crawling feeling of despair prickled the length of her spine.

'It's been two and a half long years and you ain't written me,' he hissed. 'Not once.' The smile on his face was at odds with the menace in his voice as he trailed his fingers up and down her cheek.

Sal froze, barely able to utter a word. How could it be? Reggie was standing right here in her new home, a monster in her midst again.

Why had she been so stupid to imagine he would never

get leave or come home? And how on earth had he found her?

'All my comrades lived for their letters from back home,' Reggie went on. 'Made the hell we were enduring so much easier to bear, so they said. But then, I wouldn't know.' His smile froze and a vein twitched on the side of his head. 'Because my darling wife didn't write so much as one word to me.'

Sal gulped and tried her hardest to stay calm, but inside she was preparing for the very worst. How could this be happening? War had done her husband no favours and looking into his brittle features, she realized if he wasn't unstable enough before he left, his mind was certainly completely warped now.

'So I gets to thinking . . .' he said softly, picking up a lock of her red hair and twirling it tightly between his fingers, 'perhaps my darling wife don't love me no more. Perhaps she's even met someone else while I'm out there risking my life.'

His calloused fingers carried on winding her lock of hair, tighter and tighter, drawing her face closer to his.

'Don't, Reggie,' she whimpered.

Finally, his fingers were blood red from twisting her hair painfully round them and her face was inches from his. She was so close now she could smell the beer on his breath. She felt trapped and utterly helpless.

'All my army mates will have come home to a hero's welcome, I dare say. I come home to find my home bombed to smithereens and my wife and kids missing. So I goes up the council offices this morning and they tell me you've been rehoused here and the boys have been evacuated.

Apparently, you informed them that you would notify me of the new address, but that's funny, I says to myself, 'cause I didn't get no letter.'

He wrenched Sal's head back so hard her neck strained at the jugular.

'Not a single, solitary bloody letter,' he seethed, poison dripping from his every word. 'You ran like a dirty little deserter the first chance you got. You can't just walk out on our marriage and not pay the price. Do you take me for a fool?'

'Please, Reggie,' she croaked, her head spinning as she wondered what lie she could tell him. 'Let me go and I'll explain.'

'Shut up and don't speak until I say you can,' he roared, his dark eyes flashing. 'I ain't done with you yet. Whatever was you thinking? That you were free? Got shot of the boys so you could gallivant off with a fancy man? Got yourself set up in a nice new gaff – everything's coming up roses for Sal while her old man's away fighting, ain't it? Having yourself a lovely old war, aincha?'

'No, Reggie,' she quivered. 'It's not like that. You don't know what it was like here. No one's been safe. I had the boys evacuated out for their own safety. I've got myself a job as a machinist too, at Trout's factory.'

His eyes snapped open in surprise. 'A *job*?' he thundered, as if he couldn't quite believe his ears. 'My wife has a job?'

She nodded, mute with fear.

'So that's where you got all this money from?' He motioned to the bed and Sal's heart plunged when she saw her biscuit tin sitting with the lid off, completely empty. In that moment, her fragile dreams of a new life crumbled to dust. Her precious escape fund, the money she had so diligently saved these past two years, to plan a new life, all gone, probably sitting in Reggie's back pocket.

A painful smile twisted over his face as he took in Sal's reaction. 'What's the matter, girl? Think I wouldn't find it under the bed?' he goaded. 'Not a very original hiding place, is it? But then, you always was a bit stupid.'

The new strength that she had talked of not half an hour ago in the factory with Poppy had all but deserted her. Her secret stash of money had imbued her with a false sense of security, and just like that, she knew . . . it was over. Trembling, the tears filled her eyes. Deep, desolate tears, as a tight ball of pain unfurled inside her. A road of misery stretched ahead, with no end in sight. She had stupidly thought the war had freed her. How foolish was she?

The fear of what Reggie would do next was utterly paralysing.

'Good at keeping secrets, aincha? Well, I'll tell you this, my girl. If I found out you've so much as looked at another fella, the Blitz will have nothing on me. You hear me? I will kill you with my bare hands.'

His eyes bulged in rage and Sal realized he was now capable of anything. War had turned him from a cruel monster into a full-blown killer.

Drawing back his fist, he brought it crashing down against her cheek. Her head snapped sideways and her lip burst open like a ripe watermelon.

'That's for running away,' he growled, 'and for not writing.'

Sal staggered back, clutching her lip, but in a flash, Reggie dragged her back to him, swinging her round by her hair.

'I am going to teach you a lesson you'll never forget. I own you, see – you, Joey and Billy, you all belong to me.'

Ripping off his thick army belt, he tightened it between his hands and got ready to unleash two years of pent-up violence.

At the mention of her boys' names, something deep inside Sal snapped. The emotion thundering inside her now was almost primal in its intensity.

No matter how many times he beat her, or how hard, he would not break her spirit. Let him do his worst. She could take it. She had survived Hitler's bombs, so help her God she would survive this and she would escape him again. As she watched his deranged face, bathed in the flickering gaslight, she knew with a certainty he would try to kill her. If not now, then later. She would never really be free of him.

Sal lost track of time as he unleashed his fury. Ignoring the hot shards of pain slicing through her and the roaring in her head, she used every fibre of her being to stay conscious.

I will survive this, she told herself over and over, like a mantra.

Eventually, Reggie exhausted himself and sank back onto the bed, tossing his blood-spattered army belt behind him.

'Now say it,' he ordered. 'I own you.'

Sal groaned and hauled herself unsteadily to her feet, her limbs pulsing with pain. 'You own me,' she whispered, staring at the floor.

'Louder,' he demanded.

Drawing strength from every corner of her being, she

gritted her teeth and acquiesced to his demand. 'You own me.'

He smiled. 'That's better.'

Reggie glanced at his watch and yawned. 'Oh, past midnight. Sunday now, day of rest. I'm getting my head down for some kip, and when I wake up, you and me gonna get reacquainted. Understand?'

Reggie issued Sal with a lecherous smile before turning his back on her and stretching out on the bed, grunting as he kicked off his boots. Sal knew exactly what Reggie meant and what would happen if she was foolish enough to say no. The fear of what lay ahead turned her stomach. Helplessness and despair blazed through her, but then she spotted it, flung casually on the bed within inches of her fingertips. Reggie's thick army belt. The deep welts on her back testified as to its handiness as a weapon.

This could be her only chance of escape. It was now or never. What had gone before was bad enough, but what lay ahead was simply unimaginable.

A vision of her boys' faces floated into her brain and a voice screamed in her head, *Do it!* But her body was as rigid as stone. Try as she might, she could not move a muscle.

Run. Run. Run, urged the voice. Sal started to whimper as the scrambled pathways of her brain struggled to think. If she left it any longer, she risked him locking the door, or worse . . .

Then, just like that, his nicotine-stained fingers crept along the bed sheet and began to paw at the mottled flesh on her thigh. 'Actually,' he grunted, in a voice thick with lust, 'why wait?'

The time for indecision was over. Quick as a flash, she reached out and, using all her strength, brought the belt down hard on his back. The belt buckle landed with a crack on his spine.

'You bitch,' he howled in rage, curling into a ball of pain.

Sal was up and out of the bed in seconds, adrenaline pumping in her chest as she tore across the room.

Her hands were trembling so much she could scarcely turn the door handle, and she was certain that any second a heavy hand would wrench her back.

'Come on!' she screamed hysterically, rattling at the handle. Suddenly, it sprang open and Sal threw herself through it like her limbs were on fire.

It wasn't until she was running down the cobbled street, her breath ragged in her chest, that she realized she wasn't even wearing shoes. Instinct told her to run to the only woman she could really trust.

*

Across town at the dance hall, Daisy and Robert returned to their table and the GI gallantly pulled out a chair for Daisy to sit on.

'Thank you,' she murmured, nibbling her bottom lip nervously.

'What's wrong, Daisy?' Robert asked.

'I just feel a bit bad letting Poppy and Sal go all alone like that,' she replied.

'Don't you worry about Sal,' he soothed. 'From what I've seen, Sal's a ballsy broad. Something tells me she can look after herself. Besides, she left straight after Poppy – she will have caught up with her for sure and they're probably both tucked up in bed by now.'

'Sal's not as strong as she'd have you believe,' Daisy said, shaking her head.

'I bet she's just fine,' insisted Robert. 'But if you like, we can go and check to be on the safe side?'

Daisy shook her head. 'You're probably right. Besides, the selfish side of me just wants you all to myself this evening. I don't even know where the time is going. It will be over before we know it.' Heartbroken tears filled her green eyes. 'Who's going to take me on picnics and dance with me in the street now?' She giggled through her tears.

Robert smiled tenderly. 'When you are in my arms, Daisy, all is right with the world. I've been waiting my whole life to meet a woman like you, a woman not afraid to want more. Doesn't hurt that you are so beautiful either,' he whispered, pulling out a hanky and passing it to her. 'Even when you're crying. Come on, let's get out of here. I want to walk the streets of London with my favourite girl.'

Sniffing, Daisy dabbed at her eyes with the hanky and smiled up at her soldier sweetheart.

'Remember what you told me, on our first date at the teahouse? That anything is possible. I truly believe that, Robert, now more than ever. For the first time since this war began I actually feel hope for the future.'

And then, with a cheeky wink, 'It doesn't hurt that you're so handsome either.'

Outside, the streets were bathed in soft silver moonlight and Robert draped his coat around her shoulders. They walked in silence, their footsteps echoing off the pavement, until they found a leafy square flanked by smart white hotels and guesthouses.

Finding a quiet bench, they sat down. Robert drew Daisy to his broad chest and kissed her softly on the lips. A nightingale sang down from the branches of a tree above them, and at that moment, Daisy felt as if they were the only two people in the city.

'I wish we could stay like this forever,' he smiled down at her, tracing his finger gently over her top lip. 'Just you and me in this deserted square.'

Daisy's heart splintered into thousands of tiny pieces.

Robert understood her and loved her in a way she had never experienced before, and soon he would be gone and there would be nothing left to fill the aching void. Even the long hours behind a sewing machine hadn't felt quite so monotonous these past two weeks, because she had felt truly alive for the first time in her life, his kisses playing over and over in her mind until she had felt delightfully delirious.

There were no words left, and as Robert stood up and held out his hand, Daisy took it and rose too. Utterly spellbound, they walked in silence to the nearest hotel and smiled at each other nervously as Robert held the door open for her.

Daisy felt her heart pounding in her chest as she anxiously looked about the quiet reception, with its gleaming brass bell on the polished mahogany countertop. Everything about the place looked discreet and expensive. She had never been in a hotel before, and had only dreamed of being in one as smart as this.

'A double room, please, sir,' Robert said respectfully to the gentleman behind the desk.

'Of course, sir,' he replied, discreetly averting his gaze from Daisy's to lift a set of keys from a large wooden board behind the counter. 'And under what name shall I book the room?' His tone of voice suggested that Daisy and Robert weren't the only English girl and GI soldier to step through these doors.

'Mr and Mrs Taylor,' Robert replied swiftly.

Daisy felt herself stifle a nervous giggle as they followed the bellboy up the plush carpeted stairs.

'Do you have any luggage you need assistance with tonight, sir?' asked the boy when they reached the room.

'No, that will be all, thank you,' Robert replied, handing him a generous tip. Only once the door clicked softly shut behind them and Daisy took in the large double bed did she let her nerves swamp her.

'This is frightfully grand, *Mr Taylor*,' she giggled, sinking onto the edge of the bed. 'You could fit our whole house in this room.'

Robert sat down next to her and the air crackled with nervous tension.

'Daisy,' he said softly, 'we don't have to do this. I don't wish to take advantage of you. I love you so much I don't want to do anything to hurt you. I'll be gone by first light tomorrow, and I daren't risk being even a minute late returning to base.'

'All the more reason to make the most of our time together,' she whispered nervously.

Robert sighed and rested his chin on her head; then he closed his eyes and drew her body to his.

'Daisy Shadwell,' he murmured, breathing into her hair as his fingers trailed down her spine. 'I want to remember this moment, whatever the future holds. I want to wake up next to you every morning for the rest of my days, only not in some strange hotel room.'

'Then promise me you'll come back for me, Robert,' she said fiercely.

'I'd be a fraud, Daisy, if I said those words to you,' he replied sadly. 'But on my honour, *if* I can find a way back to you, I will.'

'No more words,' she whispered.

Tenderly he bent down and brushed his lips against hers, and no more words were said.

Afterwards, they lay naked in each other's arms, their limbs entwined, but Daisy didn't dare to drift off. She wanted to savour every second of this bittersweet time, but as the clock ticked ominously on the wall and the first fingers of dawn crept in through the bottom of the blackout blind, her heart shattered like glass. Daisy knew with absolute certainty she was now more helplessly in love with her dashing American soldier than ever. She had given him something so precious to remember her by and she prayed that this was just the beginning, not the end.

Twelve

It was gone midnight when Vera opened the door. In a candlewick dressing gown and with her hair clad in metal rollers, she blinked groggily out into the darkened street. When she spotted the pitiful sight in front of her, her eyes widened in horror.

'Whatever's happened, Sal?' She clutched her dressing gown tightly around her.

Nearly mute with exhaustion, Sal clung to the door frame. 'It's Reggie,' she whimpered. 'He's back.'

Vera's face paled and she ushered Sal in. She shot a look up and down the street. Thank goodness it was pitch black and not a soul was about. Last thing either of them needed was one of the neighbours spotting Sal and word getting back to Reggie.

Once inside the kitchen, Vera bustled to the stove and lit the flame under the kettle, blinking back the tears that were welling up as she did so.

When she turned round, Sal was sat in a chair by the coal fire, rocking back and forth and hugging her body tight. Her face and chest were a patchwork of bloody bruises.

Vera never stopped marvelling at the wickedness of some men. She knew better than most the fear and shock that would be consuming Sal right now. Frank, in all his cruelty, was no match for Reggie, but she still felt every ounce of Sal's pain.

Rushing upstairs to her bedroom, Vera fetched Sal a warm blanket and draped it round her shoulders before pouring her a tumbler of Frank's whisky.

She pressed it into her shaking hands. 'Drink this, love,' she urged. 'You're in shock.'

When she had finished it, Vera carefully drew Sal into her arms and allowed her shattered body to relax. She could feel Sal's whole being shivering and her teeth chattering as the full trauma of her night washed over her.

'It's all right, love,' she soothed over and over. 'You're safe now.'

It was a whole hour before Sal stopped violently shaking, which gave Vera time to work out a plan.

'I can't stay here, Vera,' Sal whispered. 'He'll find me. Please help me.'

'You have to go to the police, Sal,' Vera urged. 'It's the only way. He could have killed you.'

'No, Vera, and I forbid you from doing it either,' she said sharply. 'If I do that, they may charge him, then bail him, and then what do you think's going to happen? He will kill me on the spot. He's a serving soldier. You know as well as I do, Vera, the police just regard it as a personal matter to be settled behind closed doors. They'd probably even blame me for not informing him I'd moved when he was serving abroad, reckon I goaded him into it.' Her words spat out the wisdom of someone with bitter experience.

Vera shook her head sadly. Deep down, she knew Sal was right.

'In that case, we have to get you out of London,' she said, thinking fast. 'I'll come with you to the station at first light and we're going to get you on a train down to stay with your boys in the countryside. Reggie doesn't know where they're billeted, does he?'

Sal shook her head scornfully. 'He never even thought to ask. He doesn't care about them. He could find me there too, I suppose, but I have nowhere else to go. Besides, I shudder to think of him anywhere near the boys without me being there.'

'That's settled, then,' she replied.

Another alarming thought occurred to Sal. 'But what about the state of me?' she cried, pointing to the purple bruises that were slowly spreading over her body like a storm cloud. 'I can't let the boys see me like this – they'll be terrified.'

'You tell them you've been bombed out and you have no place else to go. You're their mother; they'll be thrilled just to have you with them.'

Sal turned the information over in her mind, until another thought came to her. 'But work: Mr Gladstone will never let me have time off, and I've no money.'

Vera held up her hand. 'You leave Mr Gladstone to me. I'll square it with him. We'll cover your workload for you.'

Then she rose to her feet and reached over to her biscuit tin. Fishing about, she pulled a ten-bob note from the bottom. She pressed it into Sal's trembling hand. 'This should get you down there and see you right. Just until the coast is clear and Reggie's leave is up. Write me in a week or two and hopefully it will be safe for you to return.'

'I can't take this, Vera,' said Sal tearfully. 'This is all the money you have in the world. You and Daisy will need it.'

'Nonsense,' she replied flatly. 'You can and you will. Your need is greater than ours.'

At this show of kindness, Sal started to weep again. 'I don't know how I can ever thank you, Vera,' she cried.

'You don't need to, Sal,' Vera replied. 'We're friends, aren't we? And friends stick together. Besides,' she added, 'I know a little of what you're feeling.'

'What do you mean?' asked Sal, groaning softly as she shifted her aching body to face Vera.

'Oh, nothing. Forget I said anything,' she blustered, absent-mindedly playing with the gold necklace that fell over her scars.

'Come on, Vera, I know you better than that,' replied Sal. 'What did you mean?'

Vera sighed heavily, her weary face framed by the flickering light. She stared down at her hands: rough, calloused and parchment-dry from a lifetime spent scrubbing, sweeping and polishing, not to mention the heavy toil that came from factory work. These were the hands of a working-class woman. They looked ancient, as if they belonged to a sixty-year-old, not a thirty-four-year-old woman, but then, inside she felt ancient.

'You're not the only one who suffers at the hands of a cruel man,' Vera stated, in a voice devoid of emotion.

'Frank?' Sal shot back.

Vera nodded.

Suddenly, another thought occurred to Sal and her eyes widened in alarm. 'Where is he?' she gasped.

'Out,' said Vera flatly. 'Don't worry – he never usually returns before morning.'

Sal relaxed a little. 'I knew all was not well, ever since

that night at the pub when you accused him of trying it on with Poppy. Has he raised his hand to you, Vera?'

Vera nodded. 'Yes,' she whispered. 'Nothing on the scale of your Reggie, mind you, but I've been on the receiving end of his fists. But it's his mind I fear more than anything; he's twisted in the head, Sal.'

Vera omitted to tell Sal of Frank's threats to visit Poppy if she revealed his cruelty to Daisy, and nothing of the dark pain of her adolescence. She said just enough so Sal would know she wasn't alone.

'But why didn't you say anything?' gasped Sal.

'Same reason as you, more likely as not,' she whispered. 'He's a terrible man, and I don't think I really know half of what he's capable of. And then there's Daisy. She worships her father and I have to protect her. For all her bravado, she's young still. She could never handle knowing the truth about her father.'

Sal nodded thoughtfully. 'I understand, Vera.'

A current of love flowed between the two women, the sad, shared understanding of what it felt like to be terrorized by a cruel man.

'Now then, love,' said Vera, shivering despite the warmth of the fire, 'let's get you patched up.'

With that, she hurried to the kitchen and filled a bowl with steaming-hot water from the kettle. Once she had bathed Sal's cuts and bruises and applied a hot poultice to the worst of her wounds, she fixed her more hot, sweet tea using the last of her sugar rations. After Sal had drunk her tea, Vera insisted she lie down.

'Just rest for an hour or so, love,' she insisted. 'You need to gather some strength for the journey. I'll wake you in an hour. Then we must wake up Daisy and be on our way before Frank returns home.'

Sal fell into a shattered sleep, as Vera hurried to her room and packed her a small case of clothes. No matter that they would be a little on the tight side. Vera's figure went straight up and down like a piece of paper, whereas Sal was blessed with womanly curves, but there was no time to worry about that, or purchase her some that would fit. Sooner or later Reggie was sure to come here looking for her. There was not a moment to lose.

Hurriedly, Vera changed out of her nightgown and tore out her curlers, before tying a headscarf round her head. On impulse, she took another scarf from her chest of drawers for Sal to wear. Her flaming-red curls would stand out like a beacon and it was imperative she get out of Bethnal Green without being recognized.

Next, she tiptoed back down the stairs to the kitchen. Working quickly, she filled a flask with Bovril, prepared some sandwiches with what little potted meat she had and tucked some more money carefully into Sal's case. Hopefully it would tide her over until she reached the safety of the countryside.

She walked into the front parlour and drew aside her blackout blinds. With a jolt Vera spotted the first blush of dawn bleeding over the chimney pots of Tavern Street. Sunrise was creeping over the East End. Loose skeins of smoke drifted over from the nearby factories, and shortly the night-shift workers would blearily be clocking off, Vera realized in alarm. That meant if her father had been telling the truth about picking up a night shift, he would be on his way home soon. Frank knew Reggie well from the boxing clubs and drinking dens of Bethnal Green, and would surely delight at informing him of Sal's whereabouts.

'Sal,' she urged, gently shaking her from sleep, 'it's getting on. We must wake Daisy and be on our way.'

Vera hurried up the stairs, but a minute later returned, ashen-faced.

'She's not there,' she gasped to Sal. 'Her bed's not been slept in.'

'She was with Robert when I left her at the dance . . .' Sal blurted, trailing off as she realized what she had inadvertently revealed.

'And who the devil might Robert be?' Vera demanded to know.

Sal closed her eyes. 'I'm sorry, Vera . . . I . . .' She faltered, racked with guilt for hiding Daisy's secret, especially after all the kindness Vera had just shown.

At that moment, the front door clicked and they heard soft, furtive footsteps tiptoeing down the passage, the aged wooden boards gently creaking underfoot.

'Stop right there, madam,' Vera called out from the parlour. 'Don't worry, Sal,' she muttered. 'Now it's up to Daisy to explain exactly where she's been instead of using you to cover her tracks.'

A second later, the door swung open and Daisy stood pale-faced and stunned to find an audience in the parlour.

'Well, look what the cat dragged in,' Vera tutted.

Daisy went to protest, but Vera silenced her with a single icy glare. 'I knew you were up to something all along. Don't tell me where you've been, because quite frankly I don't want to know right now.'

No sooner had Vera dealt with one problem than another

was following hot on its heels. 'Men,' she muttered despairingly as she marched through the kitchen to get Sal's case and her coat. 'I wouldn't give you tuppence for the lot of them.'

By the time she had gathered their things and returned to the parlour, Sal was telling Daisy all about her night.

'Reggie's back, Dais,' she said in a shaky voice. Sal pulled down her blouse and Daisy paled even further when she spotted the bruises that had already deepened to the colour of coal. Her face crumpled in anguish at the sight of her friend's injuries.

One look at Daisy's tear-stained cheeks and Vera felt her anger at her little sister's behaviour melt away.

'This is all my fault, Sal,' Daisy sobbed inconsolably. 'I should never have let you leave the dance hall on your own.'

'Don't be so daft,' soothed Sal. 'You weren't to know he was coming home on leave; none of us could have known. He decided to keep it secret and surprise me in the only way he knows how.'

Sal got up to hug Daisy, wincing as she did so. 'Ooh, that sod's got a mean right hook on him,' she laughed sourly. 'His time in the army's obviously taught him some new skills.'

Vera wasn't fooled by her gallows humour. She could read Sal like a map and she could see the fear lurking behind her smile.

'But couldn't you just stay here with us? We'll keep you safe,' pleaded Daisy. 'We'll go to the army police, get him reported.'

Vera shot Sal a warning look, a look that implored her not to reveal that she would be no safer under their roof with Frank than she would be back with Reggie. Fortunately, Sal did not betray her confidence.

'I've been through all this with Vera already, Dais,' she said wearily. 'I just don't trust the police to protect me. Besides, you didn't hear him. He was bad before, but now he's unhinged. I've seen boys go to war and come back as men. Tonight, I saw a man go to war and come back a monster.'

Vera stepped to the window and nervously shot a glance up the slowly lightening street. Already she could hear the distant clanking of glass bottles as the milkman trundled up the cobbled street in his horse and cart.

'Come on,' she urged. 'We can discuss all this once we're safely on our way. There is no time to waste. Sal, put this headscarf on and be quick about it. We must get you on a train out of London.'

It took them three buses to get to Paddington Station and for the first time ever Vera thanked the chaos that war had thrown up. None of the buses was running to its usual route. Many of the streets were nothing but rubble and roped-off bombsites, so Reggie would have a job following them.

At the station, Vera got Sal safely booked onto a train bound for the West Country and only then did she feel as if she could breathe. Clouds of smoke hung over the platform as Daisy clung to Sal and cried like her heart was breaking.

'When will we see you again?' she sobbed.

'Come on, Daisy, put her down and let her get on the train, for pity's sake,' said Vera. 'The guard's about to blow his whistle.'

The stationmaster began to walk towards them, slamming

the carriage doors, and beckoned at Sal to board. Finally, she disentangled herself from Daisy's tearful embrace and turned to Vera with a shaky smile.

'I'll never forget what you've done for me today. You've saved my life, Vera.'

'Be on your way, love,' Vera said softly. 'And stay safe.'

'I'll try,' Sal promised chokily.

There was one last hug all round, then Sal boarded the train, and it slowly slid away from the platform.

Daisy waved furiously, but Vera simply stood and watched as it vanished from sight, taking Sal far away from the East End and to her children, where she truly belonged. When at last the train was nothing but smoke in the distance, Daisy broke down with an anguished wail. Vera put her arm round Daisy and led her towards the exit.

'Come on,' she sighed. 'I think you have some explaining to do.'

By the time they had walked the six miles back to Bethnal Green, Vera knew the whole story of Daisy and Robert's brief, ill-fated love affair.

Vera was overwhelmed with sadness at her little sister's efforts to deceive her. But what was the point in being angry anymore? It was like crying over spilt milk. It didn't change a thing.

'Promise me this, though,' Vera said, as they walked. 'Nothing untoward happened between you and this . . . this . . . American chap.'

'Robert,' interrupted Daisy. 'His name's Robert.'

'That you did nothing you could later come to regret with Robert,' Vera added warily. The note of caution and warning in her voice did not escape her younger sister. 'You were home at an ungodly hour, after all.'

'I told you already,' Daisy protested. 'We stayed very late at the dance hall and then Robert walked me home like the gentleman he is. We wanted to make the most of our last hours together. Besides,' she muttered crossly, 'do you take me for a total fool?'

'No, of course not,' Vera replied. 'But you are a young woman, and he is a young man, and we are living in extra-ordinary times.'

'You've nothing to worry about,' Daisy muttered, squirming at the line of questioning. 'I've done nothing to bring shame on our family.'

'Very well, then,' sighed Vera. 'I believe you.'

They walked in silence the rest of the way home, but when they rounded the corner of Tavern Street, Daisy paused.

'So you're not cross?' she asked.

'No, Daisy,' sighed Vera. 'I'm disappointed that you felt the need to lie to me.'

'But how could I not?' Her eyes clouded over. 'You disapprove of everything I do.'

Vera suddenly saw her reflection in her little sister's eyes. Her lips were pursed and her eyes dark with condemnation. She had tried, God knows she had tried, to raise her sister the way their mother would have wanted, but this war was making life impossible. Keeping Daisy on the straight and narrow was like trying to nail jelly to the ceiling. If she kept on this way, she risked pushing her away altogether.

Vera took a deep breath and smiled gently. 'Very well. I'll promise not to judge you if you promise not to lie to me in the future. Aside from anything, you could have put yourself in grave danger staying out so late with a man you scarcely know.'

'Oh, Robert's not a danger,' Daisy gushed. 'He's the most amazing man I've ever met, and as soon as the war's over, he's going to take me back to America with him and we're going to start a new life together.'

Vera smiled sadly. 'I dare say, love,' she replied. She could have said a whole lot more besides, but what good was it shattering her youthful dreams? She had had them once, hadn't she? Instead, she straightened herself up. 'Now then, Mr Gladstone's told me what a difference your visits make to the children up at the hospital. Just because your sweet-heart's gone doesn't mean you can stop visiting them. And I like this more domesticated Daisy, so you can keep pulling your weight around the house more too.'

'On my honour,' Daisy vowed.

The rest of Sunday passed by mercifully without incident, but the following morning, as Vera and Daisy were on their way to clock in to work, a familiar figure was hanging about outside the high walls of the factory.

As Vera had feared, Reggie was waiting outside Trout's for them as they arrived. She shot a sideways glance at Daisy and saw her sister's fists had tensed into tight balls.

'How dare he show his face here after what he did to Sal?' Daisy muttered.

Vera knew her younger sister could be a hothead, but with men like Reggie you needed to stay calm. That was the last emotion she felt right now, however. Reggie was cut from the same cloth as Frank and her heart quickened in her chest as she watched the soldier's expression harden when he spotted the Shadwell sisters approaching.

'Let me deal with this,' she warned in a low voice.

'Morning, Vera, Daisy. Long time no see. How's Frank?' Reggie smiled unconvincingly.

Vera forced down her revulsion and smiled brightly. 'Oh, you know Frank,' she replied coldly. 'Surviving. As are we all.'

'I just wondered if you'd seen Sal at all,' he said casually. His voice was light, but his narrowed eyes bored into hers. 'Only, I come back on leave to surprise her and she's done a vanishing act. Apparently she works here now. Married women working . . . Whatever next, eh?'

'Sorry, Reggie, I don't know where she is,' replied Vera, refusing to be drawn into conversation. 'Now, if you'll excuse us, we're late for our shift.'

'That's right, Reggie,' chipped in Daisy testily. 'We don't know where she is right now, but even if we did, we wouldn't tell you.'

Vera silently cursed her little sister. Why could she never see fit to listen to her?

Taking Daisy's arm, Vera moved past Reggie, but as they drew level with him, he shoved his foot in the factory door and pushed Daisy hard against the wall.

'Don't give me that,' he growled. 'You two are as thick as thieves. If I find out you know where she is and you're not telling me, there'll be trouble.'

The door swung open and in a flash, Reggie was pinned face-first to the wall with his arm twisted tightly behind his back. Mr Gladstone may have been short, but he had a vice-like grip and could move like a whippet. Vera had never seen his face so overtaken with anger. This was a side of Mr Gladstone she had never witnessed before and she was floored by his courage. His usually placid face was rigid with rage, as he held firm to a wriggling Reggie. She simply had not thought Mr Gladstone had it in him to stand up to a bully like Reggie, and she had to admit she was impressed by his bravery.

'No one threatens my girls,' he said through gritted teeth. 'You're nothing but a nasty little bully, picking on defenceless women. You should be ashamed of yourself, Reggie Fowler.' He twisted Reggie's arm higher up his back and there was a yelp of pain. 'Now get outta my factory. Go on, sling your hook, and don't come back unless you want to find yourself wearing your guts as a necktie.' With that, he pushed Reggie hard into the road. Stumbling, Reggie glared back at the group but moved on without saying another word. With a shaking hand, Mr Gladstone pulled a hanky from his pocket and mopped his brow.

'Come on, ladies, let's get you inside,' he said, opening the door for them.

Vera stared dumbstruck at the foreman. He returned her gaze. The outraged look of moments earlier had now melted into concern. Vera felt a sudden tug at her heart. Her head teemed with a cacophony of strange new thoughts and feelings . . . feelings she thought she had long since buried.

'Thanks, Archie,' she whispered when she finally found her voice. His head snapped up in surprise at the sound of his Christian name leaving her lips for the first time.

'You're welcome, Vera,' he blushed, and together they made their way back inside the safety of the factory.

Daisy followed close behind, a knowing smile playing on her lips.

Once inside the factory, Vera hastily filled Archie in on the disturbing events of the weekend. The foreman was as sympathetic to Sal's plight as she had known he would be.

'That man wants his neck wringing,' he spat. 'But don't worry, Vera – we'll sort it. The main thing is Sal's safe.'

After working out a plan, Archie called Poppy into his office and closed the door at Vera's request.

As Poppy sat down, Vera noticed she had paled to the colour of flour.

'It's all right, Poppy,' she soothed. 'You're not in trouble.'

'I . . . Oh . . . very well. Where's Sal?'

'Late on Saturday night, Sal's husband arrived home on leave, and well, let's just say it wasn't a pretty scene.' Vera sighed.

Poppy's jaw dropped open. 'But . . . Sal,' she said frantically. 'She is all right, isn't she? She told me her husband was a bad lot. I need to see her. Where is she?'

'Slow down,' replied Vera, taken aback at Poppy's nervous reaction. 'She will be fine. But she has some very nasty cuts and bruises.'

'Now, Poppy, please listen to what Vera has to say, as this affects you,' piped up Archie.

Vera nodded gratefully at her boss before continuing. 'Sal has gone to stay with her boys in the countryside until Reggie's leave is up and he returns to the front line. He has no idea where the boys are billeted, and nor for that matter do I. It's safer that way. In the meantime, we will need to cover her workload, and as you and Daisy are her closest friends at Trout's, we thought it could fall to you. The war effort can't be halted just because we're one down.'

'Of course, Mrs Shadwell,' replied Poppy eagerly. 'I'd be happy to help. I'll work extra shifts. Night shifts too if you need me.'

'That's the ticket, Poppy.' Mr Gladstone smiled. 'It's imperative we keep the real reason for Sal's absence confined only to the people in this room, and Daisy of course. We don't want anyone getting wind of this, much less Pat Doggan. I'll be telling the girls that one of Sal's boys is seriously ill and she's had to go for an emergency visit. The fewer people that know about this, the better, so keep this zipped,' said Mr Gladstone, pointing to his mouth. 'Those girls are notorious gossips, and if they get wind, it will be all round Bethnal Green by dinnertime.'

Poppy nodded. 'You can rely on me.'

'Now, hop to it,' he said briskly. 'Them uniforms won't sew themselves. And remember, as Churchill himself said, careless talk costs lives, so mum's the word. And should you come across Reggie Fowler, do not speak to him on any account, you hear me? He's a dangerous man.'

Once Poppy had left the office, Vera let out a long, slow breath and tried to calm her pounding heart. First Reggie's ambush, and now her sister's secret trysts . . . Events were moving at a rapid pace and she prayed that the future held no more disturbing revelations. But a nagging voice told her that trouble always comes in threes.

Thirteen

It had been two weeks since Sal's sudden departure to the countryside and Poppy missed her dearly. Her bright red hair and saucy banter had certainly helped to cheer up the factory no end. The drudgery of the war seemed to be grinding all the women down, especially without Sal's infectious spark of energy among them.

Reggie had not dared to show his face at the factory again, but a few of the Singer Girls had spotted him out and about in Bethnal Green, and the sightings alone had been enough to put Vera off summoning Sal home. So her workload was still left to Daisy and Poppy, and this past fortnight they had both come to feel as if they were living at the factory, they were putting in that many hours. Neither of them had dared utter a murmur of complaint, though: they knew Sal would stick her neck out for them if the shoe were on the other foot.

Nevertheless, Poppy had to confess to herself that the extra workload was exhausting. Her fingers throbbed and her back ached from the long hours seated behind a machine. She swore her foot even pumped an invisible treadle in her sleep.

Every time Poppy closed her eyes, she could picture Sal's scarred legs so vividly in her mind's eye. Sal had trusted her enough to reveal her secrets that dark night in the factory and yet Poppy still had not found the strength to spill hers. It had proved one thing to her: she truly was a coward, and sewing silly letters into seams and bandages was nothing but the actions of a girl too scared to grip life with both hands. No, it really was time to draw a veil over her furtive behaviour.

Only Vera seemed to be full of high spirits, which she attributed to Frank's increasing absences from Tavern Street. Vera had confided in her that he had picked up a new delivery job that meant he would be away for longer periods of time. Vera had not the faintest idea what this job was, but if it meant her vile father wasn't hanging around, then so much the better. Poppy also had a sneaking suspicion that Vera was thrilled her little sister was now forced to work every hour, as it meant she could keep a close watch on her. Or maybe the twinkle in Vera's eye was down to matters of a different nature? Poppy had noticed a growing closeness between her and Mr Gladstone this past two weeks, and she was glad of it.

With Frank increasingly away from the home, it meant Poppy and Vera had both felt content to spend many a cosy evening in front of a warm fire, knitting and setting the world to rights, and it wasn't unusual to find a parcel of food – a home-baked pie, a bread-and-butter pudding or a little bit of dripping – neatly wrapped up in brown paper and left on Poppy's workbench. Vera didn't show affection through words but through actions, and every food parcel and each hour spent by the fireside *showed* to Poppy that she mattered, at least to her new friend. She just wished

Daisy could realize how lucky she was to have a big sister like Vera.

The door to Mr Gladstone's office opened and the factory foreman called all the girls to attention, providing Poppy with a welcome respite from her own tumbling thoughts.

'All right, girls,' he called over the rumble of the machines. 'Shut down a minute, would you, and listen to what I've got to say.'

Thirty Singer sewing machines grumbled to a halt, and conversations stopped short.

'Vera and I have had a great idea. Well, actually, I can't take the credit for it – it was all down to Vera.' He glanced over at his forelady and smiled proudly. Their eyes locked briefly before Vera quickly looked away. Was it Poppy's imagination or was Vera blushing?

'As you all know, traditionally at the end of June, Trout's has its annual beano down to the coast.'

'Beano?' murmured Poppy.

'A day trip to the seaside,' Kathy explained. 'We haven't had one since war broke out.'

'I know you all miss it,' Archie went on.

'Yeah, especially Pat,' muttered Kathy under her breath, so the older woman couldn't hear. 'She'd be piddled before the charabanc had even pulled off from the kerb.'

'Churchill may have instructed us to tighten our belts, but I'd like to show my appreciation of all your hard work. So instead of a beano, I'm going to throw us a little party down the Dog and Duck. Show that bloody Adolf he can't stop us East Enders having a knees-up. I want everyone to dress up in the colours of the Union Jack. I'd also like us to go up to the hospital and visit the kids that day – take 'em some flags and sing 'em a few tunes. Wotcha think, then?' He grinned, looking around expectantly at the women.

'What's to celebrate, Mr Gladstone?' piped up Daisy morosely. 'We're still fighting this war, aren't we?'

'What's to celebrate? *What's to celebrate?*' he spluttered, turning such an uncomfortable shade of red Poppy thought he might burst on the spot. 'We are *British*.' His chest swelled with indignation. 'We are celebrating our Britishness. Our men are fighting and sacrificing their lives on foreign shores, and for what? Our liberty, that's what.'

A murmur of agreement rippled over the floor.

'Back to work now, ladies,' chivvied Vera, and everyone started to chatter excitedly.

At the end of the shift, as the night workers were clocking on, Daisy and Poppy pulled down the blackout blinds and stayed on longer to cover off Sal's bundles. They worked in exhausted silence, feeding through strips of material, snipping and sewing, both of them lost in their own thoughts. By ten o'clock, after a fourteen-hour day, both girls were fit to drop.

'Come on, Poppy,' yawned Daisy, tugging on her coat. 'Let's head home to bed. At this rate, it'll be time to turn round and come back the minute we get there. Every time I close my eyes I see little flickering sewing needles.'

'Me too,' Poppy giggled, her laughter quickly dissolving into a yawn.

Together the two young women bundled on their coats and hats, linked arms and wearily walked in the direction of the bus stop.

'Not much to look forward to, is there?' Daisy's voice was flat in the darkness.

'Are you not excited about the party?' Poppy asked. 'Bet the children can't wait to see you on the wards again.'

'I dare say,' she mumbled. Suddenly, Daisy halted in the street and the full moon illuminated her emerald eyes as she gazed at Poppy. There was no mistaking the heartbreak staring back at her.

'Oh, Poppy, I've had a letter from Robert,' she choked, reaching down and pulling a crumpled piece of paper from inside her bra. 'His unit's already been posted elsewhere, and after that he'll probably be shipped out. I don't know if I shall ever see him again. I met my soulmate and he's come in and out my life so fast I worry I may have imagined it all, except for . . .' Her slight fingers began nervously to play with the heart necklace round her neck, and Poppy noticed she had bitten her usually immaculate nails to the quick. 'Oh, Poppy,' she blurted, 'I'm afraid I might be in the most dreadful trouble.'

'Come now, Daisy,' Poppy smiled, rubbing her arm. 'Whatever it is, it can't be that bad. A problem shared is a problem halved. That's what Sal told me.'

'Hello, girls.' A gruff voice rang out through the night, and both Poppy and Daisy froze.

Poppy couldn't place the voice standing directly behind them, but Daisy obviously did, as she whipped round in a heartbeat.

'Hello, Reggie. Well, look what crawled out the gutter,' she spat, showing more bravado than Poppy felt at that precise moment.

'Well, if it ain't my dear wife's oldest friend,' he said. 'I blame you Shadwell sisters for turning her head with all this silly job nonsense. We was doing just fine until you came along and filled her brain with all sorts.'

'Poppycock. If you hadn't been so handy with your fists, your wife might be at home now instead of in hiding.'

'Daisy,' urged Poppy, tugging her sleeve as she flicked a nervous look up the deserted street, 'you heard what Mr Gladstone said – let's be on our way.'

'Don't worry,' Reggie replied. 'I ain't stopping. I'm getting shipped out again tomorrow, back to the front. That's what real men do, see? They don't hang around a gaggle of women in a clothes factory; they're on the front line fighting the Huns, getting their hands dirty.'

'Oh yes, Reggie,' sneered Daisy. 'We all know how you like to fight.'

The change in mood was like the flick of a switch.

'*Shut up!*' he thundered back. His hand shot out and gripped Daisy's beautiful face hard. 'Or else I'll give you a good hiding and all, Daisy Shadwell. You're too mouthy by half. Always have been. I came here so you could pass a message on to my wife.'

He squeezed her face harder as he spoke. Even through her fear, Daisy refused to break eye contact and glared back at him.

'You tell her from me that when this war ends, life will go back to *exactly* how it was before. Nothing will change, and she better be waiting for me, so help me God, or next time she won't be so lucky. I'm 'er husband and that earns me rights, see. She needs to know her place, and if she needs a little reminding, I'll gladly bring her down a peg or two.'

He released Daisy and gave her cheek a little tap before pulling a roll-up from behind his ear and calmly lighting it.

'Ta-ta, girls,' he called over his shoulder. 'You be sure to pass my message on to Sal.'

'Come on,' Poppy urged. 'Let's get out of here.'

But Daisy was rooted to the spot, staring after Reggie as he retreated into the darkness. A look of such despair was etched over her face, and soon she began to cry – fierce, hard, angry tears.

'What hope have women like us got, eh, Poppy?' she choked. 'What bleedin' hope when men like Reggie Fowler walk the streets? I thought this war was about fighting the wrongdoing men overseas. What are you supposed to do when the enemy is your own husband?'

They walked the remainder of the journey in silence, and only once she sank exhausted into bed later did it occur to Poppy that, thanks to Reggie, she never did get to the bottom of what was troubling Daisy so.

Fourteen

As soon as Daisy and Poppy had told Vera about Reggie's visit and she was reassured he *really* had left Bethnal Green, Vera had wasted no time in hastily summoning Sal back to the East End.

Poppy was, of course, thrilled to see her friend safely home again, but also secretly a bit relieved. Covering Sal's workload as well as her own had been an exhausting experience, so much so that when the party rolled around two weeks later, Poppy didn't want to celebrate; she just wanted to curl up in her bed and sleep.

The other Singer Girls, however, had no such intention, and by the time they were all gathered in the pub after their shift and the sing-song at the hospital, everyone was eager to let their hair down.

One hour after the first record had been placed on the gramophone, the bash was in full swing, and never let it be said, thought Poppy, that her fellow factory workers didn't know how to have a jolly good knees-up.

The back room of the Dog and Duck had been converted into a makeshift dance floor, and no matter that it was a little short on male dance partners, all the women were dancing to the old-time classics. Pat Doggan was leading an enthusiastic rendition of 'Knees Up, Mother Brown', revealing a pair of greying bloomers every time she high-kicked her legs. Every single one of the Singer Girls was dressed in red, white and blue, and the whole dance floor looked like a Union Jack moving in the wind. Poppy smiled in awe. The Singer Girls were an uproarious tribe of women, bonded by long hours spent toiling in a factory, but for these few short hours they were determined to put all serious thought of war and work aside.

In a darkened corner, Vera and Mr Gladstone sat at a table, deep in conversation. Vera was straight-backed as always, her thick lisle-stockinged legs crossed neatly at the ankle and her blouse buttoned up to the throat. Mr Gladstone wore a paper hat at a jaunty angle and a doe–eyed expression.

Poppy smiled self–consciously and listened as the stamping of feet grew so loud she half wondered if the floor wouldn't cave in. But best of all, there, bobbing about in the middle of the dance floor, her red curls bouncing along in time to the music, was her dear friend Sal.

Sal looked up and caught Poppy watching her. She stuck her tongue out mischievously and winked.

'Come on, Poppy,' she called through the crowds. 'Come and kick your heels up, girl.'

Poppy smiled back, blushing. 'In a minute.' She preferred to stand on the sidelines and watch her friends enjoy them-selves. Since Sal had returned from the countryside, she looked like her old self again. She had the same vivid red hair, infectious gappy grin and quick mouth, but Poppy noticed that some of her sparkle had dulled, like a silver teapot that no one had cared enough to shine. She put on a good front all right, but Poppy wasn't fooled. She suspected that as long as Reggie was alive, she would never again get a glimpse of the old Sal.

Sal weaved her way through the crowded dance floor until she reached Poppy's side.

'Blimey, it's like a Wild West saloon in here,' she joked, fanning herself with her hand. 'My heart's banging like a barn door in a hurricane. After the peace of the countryside, I forgot how noisy this lot is.'

Poppy smiled back tenderly and patted her arm. 'We missed you. Trout's just wasn't the same without you. Did I tell you that already?'

'Once or twice,' she grinned. 'But I can't tell you how good it was to see my boys. Proper little rascals, they are. They're causing mayhem, scrumping every bit of windfall fruit within a five-mile radius.'

'Were you not tempted to bring them home with you?' Poppy asked.

'Of course,' Sal replied. 'But how can I? Reggie turning up like that proved it's just not safe here. They're best off there for the duration of the war, or at least until I can take stock and work out what to do next.' She looked about her before lowering her voice. 'Anyway, less about me. Has anyone responded to your letters?'

'No,' Poppy said miserably. 'I don't think I shall write any more. They must be terribly dull.'

'Phooey,' scoffed Sal. 'What rot. Any man serving abroad would be cock-a-hoop to have a pretty girl like you to write to. Do you know what I always say, Poppy?' She tilted her head and flashed Poppy a smile. 'Success is not final; failure is not fatal; it is the courage to continue that counts.'

Poppy couldn't help herself and started to laugh. 'Oh, Sal, you really are shameless,' she giggled. 'Churchill said that!'

'I let him have that one, then.' She winked back. 'Anyway, made you smile, didn't it? Now, where's Daisy got to?'

Poppy scanned the room, baffled. Daisy had excused herself saying she was just nipping out for some fresh air, but that was half an hour ago and still there was no sign of her.

'Hmm.' The smile vanished from Sal's face. 'I'm going to take a look. She's not been right since that GI left. I said it would end in heartache, didn't I? Be a good girl and tell Vera where I've gone.'

Poppy nodded her head as her friend marched from the pub.

By the end of the party there was still no sign of either Sal or Daisy, and the bash was just winding up when Vera touched her lightly on the arm.

'Daisy seems to have clean vanished. Have you seen her?'

'Sal's gone to look for her,' Poppy replied.

'I know Reggie's gone now, but I still don't like the idea of either of them walking around on their own.' Vera frowned. 'I'm going straight home to see if she's there.'

'I'll come with you, Vera,' interrupted Mr Gladstone. 'I don't want you walking around after dark on your own either.'

'I'll be fine, Archie,' tutted Vera. 'Don't take on so.'

'I won't hear of it,' he insisted, extending his arm for her to take. 'I dare say Daisy's at home safe and sound, but I think we'd best check all the same.'

Fumbling for her bag, Vera then quickly pinned on her

hat and took Mr Gladstone's arm. 'Very well, then, let's not waste any more time.'

They headed for the door, but not before Vera turned and popped a sixpence into Poppy's pocket.

'The bus stop's right outside. Make sure you take the first bus home, dear, and I'll see you in the morning.'

'Thanks ever so.' Poppy smiled back. 'I offered to stay on a bit and help clear up.'

'All right, but just mind you don't stay late,' Vera ordered, smoothing down Poppy's collar. 'You look peaky, and you've worked ever such long hours recently.'

'Stop fussing over her,' ordered Archie. 'You sound like the poor girl's mother.'

Poppy smiled shyly at Vera. 'I don't mind, Mr Gladstone,' she said sweetly.

Once everyone had taken their leave, Poppy finished clearing up the function room, before popping her head through to the main saloon bar.

'Night, Alfie,' she called. 'I'm off now.'

'Ta-ta, sweetheart,' he called back. 'Mind how you go.'

Fifteen minutes later, she was back behind her workbench at the factory.

There was a night shift of women just clocking on who were not in the least bit surprised to see Poppy return. She had put that many shifts in of late covering for Sal she was almost part of the furniture.

'Just finishing up a bundle I should have done earlier,' she explained to a few of them.

'Blimey, girl, don't you have a home to go to?' one smiled back.

Taking a small scrap of used paper, she turned it over

and scribbled a fresh note. Her last two letters had been so dreary and self-deprecating it was little wonder no one had bothered to reply, and if Sal were to be believed and half the girls on the factory floor were sewing secret notes, she would have to be a little more forthright in her letters if she were ever to attract the attentions of a soldier.

My name is Poppy Percival and I would so dearly love a friend to write to, she began. She nibbled her bottom lip before boldly adding:

Maybe even a sweetheart.

I am sixteen and a hard-working girl, even pretty, so my friends assure me, but perhaps I shall let you be the judge of that. I work as a machinist in a factory in the East End. It's hard work, but we content ourselves with knowing we are doing our bit for the war effort.

I have decided to be terribly brave and bare my soul to you. I have never had a sweetheart or courted before, and I'm tired of stumbling my way through life, achieving only the smallest measure of happiness. I have my dreams and I search for them each night like the stars. I imagine myself living on a lush green farm in the countryside when this dreadful war is over, raising my children in the fresh air. Nothing grand, mind you, just a little cottage. Fruit orchards and a secret wooden door in the yew hedge that leads to a wild flower-filled meadow beyond. I'll have beehives to make my own honey, and a few cows. I thought maybe, as a soldier fighting so bravely, you might have your own dreams to see you through some dark days. Perhaps we

can share dreams? I would so dearly love to hear them.
You can correspond with me here, at Trout's factory in
the East End.

Keep up the good work. We are all relying on you to
beat the Jerries.

God bless you, and goodnight from the East End. x

Impulsively, she added a little kiss to the end of the letter,
before deftly folding it. She shot a furtive glance around
the room and, once assured no one was watching, neatly
tucked it within a bandage.

Quickly, she sewed down the edges and popped it in the
box under her station. There now, she had poured her heart
and soul into that letter, and if no one wrote back, well,
then it simply wasn't meant to be and that would be an end
to the whole silly business.

*

Daisy fell back on her bed with a heavy sigh. As she lay
staring at the damp seeping up the faded wall, a chill of
despair rose inside her chest. The truth was inescapable.
Her period was weeks late now and she was usually as regular
as clockwork. Added to which, her breasts were tender, and
she was overcome with sickness.

At first, she had thought her nausea was some form of
lovesickness from missing Robert so much, and then as the
weeks went on and there was only one letter from him, her
misery had deepened. But now barely a day passed without

feeling the urge to be sick. The truth had to be faced. She was with child. Robert's child.

She had been so utterly seduced by the dream of a life abroad with her handsome GI that she must have taken leave of her senses. She had convinced herself that you couldn't fall on your first time, but the truth was, she had not been thinking straight at all that night. She had selfishly decided to throw caution to the wind and now she was paying a high price for her naivety.

'You silly, wretched fool, Daisy,' she sobbed out loud.

Earlier at the pub, she had watched the rest of the Singer Girls enjoying themselves with a deep sense of dread growing in her chest. Goodness only knew what the likes of Pat, Ivy and Doris would say when they found out she was pregnant with an illegitimate baby, and a coloured man's baby at that. The women of Bethnal Green, and in particular Trout's, were deeply moralistic in lots of ways. In their eyes, she had committed a mortal sin.

Waves of panic crashed over Daisy as the full enormity of her situation sank in. She would have to be seen to repent her sins or be shunned and ridiculed forever. She would never survive the scandal. And Vera? She would have a blue fit. They were only just about on speaking terms again, and Daisy had promised her sister that nothing untoward had happened. Now, the shame and scandal would destroy them both. Vera would turn her out of the house, send her away to some awful home for unmarried mothers, and her life as she knew it would be over. No ship bound for America. Not even a semi in Dagenham. Her life would be over before it had even really begun. All her high hopes and fanciful dreams vanished, and Daisy felt as if the ground beneath her was falling away.

Groaning, Daisy rose to her feet and on unsteady legs staggered to the open window. Waves of sickness crashed over her as she poked her head out, trying to gasp great lungfuls of fresh air, but the air was thick and dusty. The sky was filled with burning from the nearby factories. Even the clouds looked like they were on fire.

Daisy wanted so desperately to keep her baby. She loved Robert and the desire to keep her child – their child – was primitive, visceral even, but Daisy was also a realist. Her father would sooner skin her alive than allow her to give birth to and keep a black man's baby under his roof. She loved her father dearly, but he would be filled with fury when he discovered she was with child. Her father, in common with so many other East End men of his genera-tion, had a deep distrust of the Yanks, envying them their smart uniforms, better wages and laid-back charm. But Daisy suspected the real reason he disliked the Americans was simply because they were different.

Although in truth, it made no real odds whether she were pregnant to a soldier or the King of England. She was pregnant out of wedlock, and for that, Frank would be mocked in every pub in the manor for having such a sinful, wayward daughter. He would even be seen as less of a man for not keeping a tighter grip over his household.

'You're done for,' she murmured out loud.

'Who's done for?' rang out a voice from the doorway. Daisy's head whipped round. She had been so absorbed in her own misery she had failed to hear Sal calling out her name as she walked up the stairs.

'I came to find you,' she said warily. 'I was worried when you just disappeared from the pub like that. Oh, Dais, whatever's wrong? You've not been yourself since I got back from the country.'

On seeing her friend's concerned face, Daisy's shoulders slumped, exhausted tears streaming down her face.

'Oh, Sal,' she wept. 'My father and Vera are going to kill me. There'll be hell to pay if this gets out.'

'Whatever it is, it can't be that bad, sweetheart,' Sal soothed, sitting down on Daisy's single bed and patting the space next to her.

Daisy sank down with a heavy sigh. 'Oh, but it is, Sal,' she replied, lifting her terrified gaze to meet her friend's. 'I've fallen . . . I'm pregnant.'

Sal closed her eyes and Daisy imagined her friend was frantically searching her mind for some words of comfort. The silence seemed to stretch on forever before Sal finally broke it.

'Are you quite sure?' she asked in a faltering voice. 'You could just be late. My monthlies have been all over the place since this bloody war started. Could just be pains from the curse?'

'Quite sure,' Daisy nodded miserably.

'Oh, Dais,' Sal said. 'Why didn't you tell me you'd lost your virginity to Robert?'

'Believe me, I wish I hadn't done it, Sal,' she groaned. 'It was on Robert's last night in London. I just got caught up in it all and I couldn't bear to think of him going. It was the same night Reggie arrived home on leave, and after everything you went through, it didn't feel right to tell you the next morning. Please don't hate me.'

'I don't hate you.' Sal sighed, casting her mind back to the events of that fateful night. 'You won't be the first woman to be swept up in the moment and get caught out later. There must have been madness in the air that Saturday night. But whatever are you going to do now, Dais?' she asked, a tremor in her voice.

'There's only one possible thing I can do,' Daisy replied, gripping the edge of the bedframe for support.

'Oh, Daisy, no,' Sal cried, fear bleaching her face. 'You can't. Not that. You can't . . .'

'What, get rid of it?' Daisy sobbed, feeling hysteria rising in her chest. 'Don't you understand, Sal? I have no other choice.'

'I'll help you find another way,' Sal pledged firmly. 'We will come up with a solution together. Just promise me you won't do anything rash. I couldn't bear to think of you doing something you may later regret.'

'But don't you get it?' Daisy cried in despair. 'Unless Robert comes back and marries me tomorrow, my child's life is already destroyed. Can you imagine me pushing a pram with an illegitimate black child up Green Street Market? I'll have committed him to a life as a destitute bastard. I'm going to be hung, drawn and quartered for this.

'You had a husband when you had your babies, Sal,' she wept bitterly. 'No matter that he's a no-good bastard, and a rotten father and husband, you at least had a ring on your finger. In folk's eyes, that makes you respectable and me the fallen woman. I will be a social pariah, the lowest of the low. The whole of Bethnal Green will shun me.'

Sal sighed heavily. 'I understand what you're saying, but

promise me you won't do anything stupid, not until you've given me a chance to think things through. Perhaps we could both leave the East End,' she said, a glimmer of hope surfacing in her eyes. 'Start up a new life somewhere nobody else knows us. I can get away from Reggie, and you get to keep your baby. Just think . . .'

Daisy felt her face soften at her friend's attempts to help. 'You're a loyal friend, Sal,' she said sadly, 'but leaving the East End won't solve a thing. Our troubles will only follow us. Reggie will find you, and I'll just have a new lot of neighbours to judge me.'

The sound of the front door thudding open made them both sit bolt upright.

'Frank?' gasped Sal.

'I shouldn't think so,' Daisy answered. 'He's working away at the moment.'

Just then the bedroom door swung open and there stood a breathless Vera, accompanied by Mr Gladstone.

'Whatever were you thinking, leaving the party like that without telling anyone where you were going? Have you taken leave of your senses?' Vera snapped.

'I'm sorry, Vera. I just didn't feel myself . . .'

'My fault,' replied Sal calmly, getting to her feet. 'I came to find her and she was all for coming back to the pub, but I kept her talking. I'm so sorry.'

'Well,' spluttered Vera, smoothing down her hair. 'A fine affair this is. I'd have thought you'd have both known better than to simply disappear like that. I was worried sick that Reggie had returned.'

'I'm ever so sorry, Vera, really I am,' said Sal sincerely.

'And you, young lady, what have you to say for yourself?'

Daisy sat mute. For the first time in her life she had absolutely nothing to say back to her big sister.

'Come on, Vera,' soothed Mr Gladstone. 'Poor Daisy looks all done in – give the girl a break. She's safe and sound, and that's all that matters, eh? Come on, Sal, I'll walk you home. Night-night, all.' He winked at Daisy as he guided Sal to the door.

His kindness made Daisy want to weep and throw herself into his arms for a cuddle. That's all she really needed right now, she realized with a sharp pang of pain: a cuddle from her mum. But who on earth could save her now?

Fifteen

Five weeks on from the party and Sal was out of her mind with worry. Since her confession, Daisy had been pretending nothing had happened. Every day that she buried her head in the sand was another day that the little life inside her grew and took shape.

Daisy had taken to making sure she was surrounded by the other girls on dinner and tea breaks, and Sal knew it was because she didn't want to discuss her problem. But she had had enough of Daisy's tactics. 'She may be choosing to ignore it, but I sure as hell won't,' she muttered angrily to herself.

It was a Saturday dinner break when she at last got the chance to corner Daisy. Sal spotted her sitting alone in the canteen, forlornly pushing a spoon round her bowl of soup.

Daisy's eyes looked up dully when she spotted Sal coming towards her.

'All right, Sal,' she murmured. 'I know these bowls of soup only cost a penny, but they're not exactly big on taste, are they? What do you reckon they put in it? Besides grey water.'

'I'm not here to discuss soup recipes with you,' said Sal firmly, sitting down in the seat opposite. She lowered her voice and glanced around the canteen to make sure no one else could overhear what she was about to say next. Fortunately, there were only a few Singer Girls about and they were huddled in a corner out of earshot.

'I'm here to ask you exactly what it is you intend to do about the fact that you are currently carrying Robert's child. If you keep on at this rate, Dais, you'll start to show and someone will spot it, and then what? You must be what by now, ten weeks? You can't side-step the issue any longer.'

Daisy refused to look at her, just carried on staring at the Formica-topped table and stirring her soup.

'Please, sweetheart, I beg of you,' Sal whispered. Her voice was firm but soft, gently entreating her friend to do the right thing. 'This problem isn't going to go away. I should know. If you don't deal with problems as soon as they surface, they only get bigger. Do you think I don't lie awake every single night regretting that I never left Reggie the day he first raised his hand to me? I'm right here by your side, Dais. I'll stay with you when you tell Vera, and that needs to be sooner rather than later.'

The silence stretched on and Sal felt her patience start to wear thin.

'Oh, for pity's sake, Daisy, put down that spoon and look me in the eye.'

Daisy lifted her huge emerald eyes and set her spoon down with a clatter. 'I'm not going to tell Vera.' She shrugged.

'But you have to,' implored Sal. 'She's going to find out.'

'She won't. I'm going to get it sorted very soon,' Daisy replied, returning to pushing her spoon round her bowl in ever decreasing circles.

Sal's head spun as she grappled with Daisy's remark.

'Sorted . . . *sorted*?' she gasped. 'Whatever do you mean by that?'

But Daisy was saved from answering by the sudden arrival at the table of Poppy and Vera.

'Excuse me.' Daisy scraped her chair back and fled from the canteen.

'Poor Daisy,' murmured Poppy. 'She's not been terribly well of late, has she?'

'Yes, Sal,' added Vera suspiciously. 'She walks around like a ghost, and she's right off her food. What is going on?'

Now it was Sal's turn to stare at the table. She couldn't abide lying to Vera, but neither was it her misery to share.

'She's missing Robert, Vera, that's all,' she replied.

'What, that GI chap? Still?' Vera shot back in surprise. 'She needs to pull her socks up and stop acting like a silly love-struck girl. She must have known there was no future in that when she met him.'

'I dare say,' Sal replied. 'But she was rather taken with him.'

'Perhaps I am being a little harsh on her,' Vera relented, recalling the conversation in which she promised not to judge her younger sister.

'Tell you what, tomorrow's a Sunday. Why don't you come over for your tea? See if we can't take her mind off that American. Archie's coming, and Poppy too.'

'But what about Frank?' asked Sal, eyeing Vera warily. 'Won't he mind us being there? He won't take kindly to us all crowding round, especially not if he's napping.'

Vera's face clouded at the mention of her father's name. 'As you know, he doesn't exactly keep me up to date with his movements, and he's something of a night owl, but for the past five weeks he's been working away, on a job down the coast, and we haven't seen hide nor hair of him. I can't pretend I'm not relieved. Except yesterday . . .' Her voice trailed off.

'Go on,' Sal urged.

'Well, yesterday two police constables were waiting on the doorstep when I got back from this place. They wouldn't tell me what it was about, but they were asking all sorts of questions about him. The hours he kept, where he worked, that sort of thing. I answered to the best of my ability, of course, but I have a nasty feeling about it all.'

Sal and Poppy said nothing, but there was no disguising the sense of fear that suddenly descended. For when it came to Frank, each and every one of them knew that whatever it was, it spelled trouble. All too soon dinner was over and they trooped back upstairs to the factory floor. Sal chewed hard on her bottom lip as she took her place behind her machine and glanced over at the ashen face of Daisy seated beside her.

'You're back, then,' she muttered. 'Don't think I'm going to forget what you said earlier. Vera's invited me over to yours for my tea tomorrow and you and I are going to talk this through properly once and for all. You have to tell Vera too, and tomorrow. In the meantime, I beg of you, don't do anything stupid.'

'Dinner break's over, Sal. There's work to tend to,' said Vera curtly, nodding at her as she swept past. The speed by which she could transform herself from friend to forelady never ceased to amaze Sal.

'Course. Sorry, Mrs Shadwell,' she mumbled, shooting a last loaded look at Daisy. Tomorrow, she would get to the bottom of this sorry mess. She just hoped she would be in time.

*

The next day, Vera stomped through the streets of Bethnal Green, glancing about as she walked. It was early on a Sunday morning and the streets were largely empty but for army personnel, and kids playing on street corners. Every shop was closed for business, their windows crisscrossed with anti-blast tape. Vera spotted three young boys squeezing through the boarded-up gap in a bombsite, and unusually she found she didn't even have the breath in her body to haul them out and chastise them.

Her thoughts were simply too preoccupied with her younger sister and her increasingly strange behaviour. Daisy had left the house even earlier than Vera had that morning, as shaky as a dog in cold water, professing to want some fresh air of all things. Daisy hadn't really been herself since this GI chap of hers had left. Thank goodness he was off the scene. Vera bristled in annoyance. What business had he breaking a young girl's heart when he knew fine well he would be off again with his unit?

Only Archie, dear sweet Archie, gave her any measure of joy at the moment. He really was a rock. He had been their knight in shining armour when Reggie had threatened them outside Trout's; he had told no one of the real reason Sal had to vanish off to the countryside; and he seemed to spend his life thinking of ways to make her and all the Singer Girls happy. They broke the mould when they made Archie Gladstone. Not that she would tell him that, mind.

So lost in her reverie was she that she had reached the steps of the children's hospital and, without realizing, nearly walked clean past it. No wonder Daisy was a daydreamer, if this was where thinking about men led you!

Vera took a cautious look left and right, and only once assured that there was no one she knew in the vicinity did she pull her hat down firmly over her head and walk quickly inside. No one knew she came here every Sunday morning, and it was imperative it remain that way too. Vera swept up the corridors on autopilot. She had walked to Matron's office that many times she could do it with her eyes closed. At the door, she knocked softly before a distant voice summoned her in. Vera found the elderly lady sitting at her desk, stirring her tea thoughtfully.

'Vera, my dear, so lovely to see you.' Matron smiled as she looked up from her cup and motioned to the seat opposite. 'Won't you sit down and have some tea with me?'

Silver threads of morning light streamed in through the window and bathed the matron in an ethereal glow, or so it seemed to Vera.

'I'd love a cup.' Vera grinned back warmly as she took her usual seat. 'With the sun coming in like that, you look like you're wearing a halo. You certainly deserve one. You're my guardian angel. I honestly don't know how you've put up with me all these years.'

'Nonsense,' Matron scoffed. 'You know I think the world of you, Vera. I always have done. Right from when they first brought you in here after the fire. Do you remember? You were such a timid little thing.'

'Do I remember?' laughed Vera, her hands instinctively moving to her chest, where she traced the outline of her scars. 'Some memories never fade. I was nothing but a girl, fifteen years old when I first arrived, and frightened out of my wits, grieving for my mother, but you looked after me all those months on the ward. And you carried on looking after me even after . . .' She felt her voice trail off as Matron's eyes looked deep into hers.

'You know, Vera, your mother would be very proud of how you've turned out,' she said softly. 'She would perhaps think that now is the time to tell the truth, unburden yourself from the secrets of the past. Things are rarely how we perceive them to be, and you might find solace in speaking freely. A lot of water has passed under the bridge . . .'

Vera shifted uncomfortably. 'Please don't,' she whispered. 'You know I can't as long as that man is alive.'

'Your father, you mean?' she replied.

'He's no father,' Vera spat back. 'He's an animal. Now he's got the police sniffing around. What he's been up to I shudder to think.'

'That's as may be, Vera, but don't you see? Once you reveal the truth, you are free of that man forever. He will hold no power over you.'

Vera could tell Matron was imploring her now, pushing her to leap over the edge, take the giant step she had always imagined to be impossible.

Slowly Matron rose to her feet and smoothed down her uniform. 'I must be on my rounds now, but please, I urge you to give some thought to what I've had to say. Perhaps it's time we looked forward now, not back. And while you're at it, won't you please put Mr Gladstone out of his misery? Once you open your heart to love, good things can happen. I bumped into him the other day while I was out doing my shopping. Did he tell you?'

'Yes, he did mention it,' Vera remarked, feeling herself flush.

'He was praising you to the very heavens above.' Matron smiled knowingly. 'He's quite smitten with you.'

'Poppycock,' Vera blustered. 'You're being presumptuous; he's just a very attentive employer. Though he is a thoroughly decent man, I'll admit.'

At the door, Matron paused and her pale eyes twinkled. 'She's very beautiful, you know, my dear. Just like you.'

On the way out of the hospital, Vera thought of nothing else. So deep in her own thoughts was she that she didn't see the slight figure of Poppy outside the door until she smacked clean into her, dropping her bag and all its contents onto the pavement.

'Oh, Vera,' burbled Poppy, getting down on her hands and knees to gather up her friend's belongings, 'I'm so sorry.'

'Poppy?' gasped Vera. 'What on earth are you doing here on a Sunday? You're not due to sing here today.'

'I, er . . . Oh gracious, I, er, was just passing,' she faltered.

Vera narrowed her eyes. 'Did you follow me, Poppy?'

She watched suspiciously as a deep flush of telltale red spread over Poppy's chest.

'Yes, I did,' Poppy blurted. 'But please don't be cross, Vera. I was just intrigued to know why you always visit on a Sunday, when we're not here. One of the little girls on the ward let it slip.'

Vera wanted to be angry, but somehow, faced with Poppy's innocent eyes, she found she couldn't summon the emotion. Despite her nerves Poppy looked deeply puzzled and Vera realized she had to provide some sort of explanation.

'Mr Gladstone asked me to deliver some bandages to the matron,' she replied as evenly as she could.

'Can we spare them?' asked Poppy. 'Mr Gladstone's always saying we can't make enough for the troops . . .' She trailed off uncomfortably. 'I'm sorry. Please forgive me. I don't mean to stick my nose in where it's not wanted.'

'Let's get back to Tavern Street, shall we?' Vera said curtly, disliking intensely the feeling that the past was nipping at her heels. 'I've a mountain of corned beef hash to make and I've not even begun.'

'Of course,' Poppy replied, relieved to be off the hook. 'I should love to help. Any sign of Frank yet?'

'No.' Vera frowned. 'He still hasn't shown his face, and I expect those police constables shall return soon as well. It really is most queer and gives me a very unsettled feeling.'

'I can well imagine,' agreed Poppy.

They were still turning it over when they arrived at the doorway to 24 Tavern Street.

Coming from the other way and whistling a merry tune to himself was Archie, accompanied by Sal.

'Well, there,' he beamed when he spotted them. 'If it isn't a sight to warm the cockles of my heart. You are both looking lovely today, ladies, if I might be so bold as to say. I found this young lady on my way and thought I'd do the gentlemanly thing and escort her here.'

'Hello, girls,' Sal chirruped. 'Our Archie's been busy.'

From behind his back Mr Gladstone produced a brace of rabbits with a flourish.

'Well, I'll be, Archie,' Vera whistled. 'Wherever did you get your hands on those?'

'I had to queue for two hours yesterday evening up at

the market.' He grinned proudly. 'I didn't even know what I was queuing for until I reached the front, but I had it in my mind it might be something you would like, Vera. I hope you're not disappointed. I know you can knock something smashing up with these.'

Vera stared at Archie's hopeful face and felt her heart soften at the gesture. Perhaps Matron was right.

Vera turned the door handle, but the door wouldn't budge. She rattled it again, but still it wouldn't shift. How strange. She hadn't left it locked when she had set out to the hospital that morning; she never did.

'Whatever's wrong with this door?' she muttered crossly.

'Allow me,' said Archie, handing her the rabbits. Pushing his body against the door, he shoved with all his might.

'I think there's something blocking it the other side,' he puffed.

An uncomfortable feeling prickled up Vera's spine and acting on instinct, she pushed open the letterbox and peered through into the gloom of the dingy hallway. What she saw made the blood in her veins turn to ice. Daisy's long black hair was fanned out over the wooden floorboards, her beautiful face pale, her dress soaked in blood.

'It's Daisy,' she screamed. 'She's on the floor, and oh my goodness, there's blood.'

In a flash, Archie was sprinting up the road. 'I'm going to scale the back wall and get in through the scullery. Wait there,' he yelled over his shoulder as he ran.

Vera felt hysteria rising inside her chest as she waited. After what felt like an eternity, Archie opened the door.

Sinking to her knees and gathering Daisy in her arms, time seemed to freeze and images came to her like snapshots.

Daisy's delicate face was so drained of blood she was almost translucent. Her breath was so faint Vera could scarcely see her chest rise. What on earth had happened? Her stomach lurched with the possibilities. Had Frank returned and hurt her in some way?

Poppy, Archie and Sal stood frozen over them, their faces paralysed with fear.

'What you waiting for?' Vera shouted. 'Get a doctor!'

'I'll go,' Archie said. 'Poppy, you run to the factory. Get as many bandages as you can gather. Sal, you wait here and look after Vera.'

And then they were gone, and Vera and Sal were left alone with Daisy.

Fearful, Vera touched Daisy's cheek. It was deathly cold. 'Oh, sweetheart,' she sobbed, drawing her into her arms.

Vera was so intent on cradling her little sister's limp body that she hadn't noticed the awful pallor that had crept over Sal's stricken face.

Oh, Daisy, Sal thought desperately, what have you done?

Finding an ambulance in wartime was a lengthy exercise and so it was that the local doctor reached the scene first and tended to Daisy, insisting he be left alone to treat his patient. After what felt like an eternity, he gently shut the door to Daisy's bedroom behind him and lowered his voice as he turned to face Vera in the narrow passage outside.

'Whoever did this wants locking up, and I for one would throw away the key,' he said gravely.

'What do you mean, Doctor? Did someone harm my sister?' implored Vera.

'It's not good, Miss Shadwell, but your sister has regained

consciousness and informed me of her pregnancy. She's lost a lot of blood, but she'll survive. I'm not sure about the baby, though.'

His words hit Vera like a leaden hammer straight in the chest.

'Pregnant?' she whispered, aghast. 'She can't be.'

The doctor cleared his throat and shifted uncomfortably. 'I can assure you she is most definitely with child, despite the best efforts of whatever abortionist she visited earlier today. It was either Hatpin Bella or Mrs Black. I can usually tell by their handiwork.' He spat the words out, and Vera saw his chest swell in rage.

'I know these women see themselves as providing a valuable service to the community, but I'm afraid I don't see it that way. I've tended to too many women who have nearly paid for their sloppy services with their life.'

Vera felt the blood drain from her head and held on to the wall to steady herself as she attempted to take it all in. The passage seemed to close in on her as she recalled her terrible fear that Daisy might do something reckless in her bid to escape her family and the East End. It seemed her awful premonition had come true.

The doctor sighed heavily and shook his head. 'The next forty-eight hours are critical. As long as she doesn't get an infection or any complications, she should make a full recovery. The bleeding has stopped now, and she is sleeping. Make sure she has plenty of fluids to drink and ensure she takes these.' He scrawled a prescription and thrust it into her hands.

Vera took it and, feeling utterly numb, looked from the paper to the doctor. 'I really can't thank you enough for coming so fast, Doctor,' she whispered. 'I'll come and settle what I owe you next week. But will you have to inform the police? And . . .' Vera's voice broke off hesitantly. 'My father, Frank, will you be telling him?'

He looked on Vera with compassion. 'I've known your family a long time, Miss Shadwell, in particular your mother, and I have no desire to bring shame on your house. I can see you are a decent woman and there is a war on. Goodness knows we are all suffering enough as it is, so in this case I shan't be filing a report to the police or telling your father, but I suggest you keep a close eye on your younger sister. Something about this blasted war is relaxing the moral code that used to govern these streets. I shall return tomorrow to check on her progress, and she will of course, need to register with the midwife as soon as she recovers.'

'Rest assured I will watch over her, Doctor,' Vera replied gratefully. After showing him to the door, she returned to the kitchen, where Sal, Archie and Poppy were seated round the table, gripping cups of tea that had long turned cold and staring at Archie's brace of untouched rabbits. They rose to their feet when she walked in.

'I may as well be honest with you all. Daisy is pregnant,' she announced. 'The silly, silly girl. I warned her, told her until I was blue in the face about the consequences of reckless actions, and now she will be forced to pay the price.'

Slowly, Vera swept her gaze across the table and noticed that only Sal could not meet her eyes. 'Did anyone know about this?' she questioned.

'I did,' replied Sal miserably. She looked up sharply and Vera was struck by the frustration in her eyes. 'I did, Vera,' she repeated. 'But you have to believe me – I had no idea where she was going this morning. I would have locked her in had I known. I've been trying to persuade her to talk to you about it for weeks, Vera, to come clean. I'm a mother myself. I could never encourage her to get rid of her own child. How could I? I tried to dissuade her from this whole fling, honestly I did, but she wouldn't listen to me.'

'Don't worry, Sal. I believe you,' Vera replied. 'I know how stubborn Daisy can be and when she gets a notion in her head, there's no stopping her. Well, as much as it pains me to say, now she will have to learn the hard way.' Vera shook her head in despair. 'Whatever will become of her and the baby? If the community gets wind of this, her reputation will never recover.'

Without saying a word Archie rose and moved across the room towards Vera, drawing her into his arms. Feeling too weak to protest, she allowed herself to be swallowed into his strong embrace. The events of the past few hours had left her bewildered and shaken. Daisy pregnant? How had she not suspected? She of all people should have seen this coming, and in truth she knew she could only partly blame Daisy. She had come down on her so hard she had succeeded in driving her away altogether.

'We'll leave you in peace now, Vera,' Archie said softly. 'Young Daisy needs you. This stays between Poppy, Sal and me until you work out what you're going to do.'

Poppy nodded furiously, her blue eyes brimming over with tears. 'That's right, Vera. I'm so desperately sorry.'

Vera closed her eyes and sighed heavily. 'Thank you, Archie. I don't know what I'd do without you, and you, Poppy and Sal.'

Then she showed them all to the door and, with a heavy heart, climbed back up the stairs.

Vera lost all sense of time as she sat by Daisy's bed, gently dabbing her fevered brow with a cold compress. Hours slipped by like minutes and it was only when the sky outside bruised to purple that she realized it was twilight.

Staring deep into the dying embers of the coal fire she had lit in the grate in Daisy's bedroom, she stood and wearily picked up the poker to prod a little life back into it. When she turned back round, Daisy's eyes were open.

It was a few moments before Daisy adjusted to her surroundings. But then an avalanche of fear washed over her face.

'The baby . . . ?' she rasped, struggling to sit up.

Vera sat slowly and took Daisy's hand gently in hers. 'We don't know yet, but the doctor is hopeful the baby will survive.'

Daisy's eyes closed and she collapsed back down on the pillows. 'I'm so sorry, Vera,' she murmured. 'I know you hate me, but trust me, you can't hate me more than I do myself right now. I didn't know what else to do, where else to turn. I just felt so alone.'

Vera bent down and planted the softest kiss on her forehead. 'It's me who should be saying sorry.'

Daisy couldn't keep the shock from her voice. 'Y-you're not cross with me?' she stuttered.

'No, Daisy, I'm not cross with you,' she replied. 'I'm cross with myself. I've been too stern with you over the years. Those things you said at the pub that night, about me making your childhood miserable . . .'

'I didn't mean them, Vera,' insisted Daisy. 'I was angry at life, angry at Mum dying.'

'All the same,' Vera said firmly, 'I should never have been so harsh or judgemental. I should have shown you more love and affection. If I had, maybe you wouldn't . . .' Her voice cracked, but she was determined to finish. 'Maybe you wouldn't have resorted to this, or maybe at least you would have come to me first and we could have found another way. Please forgive me. I promise from now on I'm going to be the big sister you always wanted, not the one I felt you needed.'

Daisy's pale face registered nothing except shock, but Vera wasn't done yet.

'Do you want this baby . . . Robert's baby?'

Tears welled in Daisy's green eyes. 'More than anything, Vera,' she cried.

'But does Robert know?' Vera asked cautiously.

Daisy shook her head in shame. 'Not yet, but I know I need to write and tell him. If the baby survives, that is.' Fresh tears flooded her face. 'Oh, what a mess I've got myself into. I've been out of my mind with confusion and fear. But I am sure of one thing, Vera. I love Robert, and I will love our baby come what may.'

'I have no doubt you will,' replied Vera sadly. 'But the fact remains you will have to give this baby up. I will help you, of course. Together we will come up with a plan.'

'Give the baby up? I can't do that. Please don't make me,' Daisy begged. 'I could never survive that.'

'You can and you will,' Vera said softly but firmly. 'It's the right thing to do. In time you will come to see that.'

Daisy retorted angrily, 'You have no idea how wretched

I'm feeling. What can you possibly know about my heart-ache?'

'Much more than you think,' Vera replied. 'I was pregnant once, you see. My baby was taken from me.'

Daisy gasped and her hand flew to her mouth.

Vera reached for the glass of water by Daisy's bed and took a shaky sip before going on.

'I was sixteen. It was after Mum died in the fire. I was a confused, vulnerable girl, recovering on the wards at the hospital.'

'What, the one where we perform?'

'That's the one.' Vera nodded. 'I was in there because I was so badly burned in the fire trying to get Mum out. Dad had gone to get help, he said. Done a runner more like. Leaving us in the fire. To this day, I can't remember much about it. Just the heat of the flames and Mum's screams. When I came to, I was in a hospital ward. My burns were so bad I had to stay there for a whole year. Matron took me under her wing, became like a mother to me, easing my grief, helping to fill the void Mum's death left in my life. I missed her so much the pain of that was far worse than the burns. I was convinced Mum was magic, you see. She could produce anything out of that tiny kitchen downstairs.' Vera felt herself smiling in spite of the trauma of reliving the terrible blaze. 'Toffee apples, pies and roast dinners to die for, all made with love. I used to sit on the step and wait for the Sunday-roast bone to chew on or the custard pot to lick. I couldn't pass her by without her reaching out and folding me into her pinny for a cuddle.'

Vera chuckled and shook her head as Daisy sat spell-bound. 'Mum could never get enough of giving kisses and cuddles. I used to pull faces and wriggle away. Looking back, I wish I'd stuck around more, but hindsight is a wonderful thing.'

She turned to Daisy, imploring her to understand what she was about to say next. 'But despite Matron's close care of me, I was still vulnerable, which is why I think I fell prey to what happened next.'

Daisy took a long, steady breath as she tried to digest the first memories of their mother that Vera had ever shared with her. 'And what exactly did happen?' she asked cautiously.

'I fell in love with a young married doctor. Dr Charles Henderson. He worked at the hospital and we became friendly. I think he took pity on me at first, but as my burns began to heal, he took me out on his daily rounds. Sitting next to him on a dicky seat on his pony and trap, I felt ten foot tall.' Vera felt herself straighten up as she recalled the memory.

'Oh, but he was handsome and so kind,' she murmured, her eyes misting over. 'And clever too. He taught me poetry, how to speak properly, how to pronounce my words, and he read me books. I was sixteen, you see, not that much younger than you are today. My brain was hungry for education. Even fancied myself as a typist up West. I was desperate to broaden my horizons. Sound familiar?'

Daisy nodded and hung her head.

'I fell in love with him. I was totally entranced. I felt as if he'd saved me somehow, or rather, I hoped he would save me. Between visits we used to go out to a daisy meadow in Chingford, have our dinner in the fields. He saw past my scars and my rough accent. He really saw *me*, the person I was on the threshold of becoming, the promise within.

Which I suppose is why I gave him my virginity. I never knew such happiness as those months with that man; I would have given him anything I was that grateful to him.'

'So what happened?' begged Daisy impatiently. 'Where did it go wrong? Did Matron not disapprove of your relationship? He was married, after all.'

'She never knew.' Vera shrugged. 'Until I realized I was pregnant, that is, and I had to tell her. I was sixteen, pregnant by a married twenty-eight-year-old doctor. The scandal would have been huge. She had no choice but to call Dad and have me discharged. I was nearly recovered from my injuries anyway, and so he came to fetch me.'

Vera's voice took on a brittle edge. 'I was forced to accept the reality of my situation. Someone had to take care of the family now that Mum was dead – someone had to do the cooking and the cleaning and look after him, and so I returned with a better vocabulary and a head full of dreams. All those fanciful notions of becoming a typist just crumbled to dust.'

'So what did Dad do when he discovered you were pregnant?'

'He was furious, of course,' Vera replied. 'But you know, I think he was actually angrier that I no longer spoke like him. I suppose I made him feel stupid in his own home. He said, "Fancy yourself well spoken, do you, my girl?"' Vera snorted. 'The only language that man understands is violence. I told him the doctor was more of a man than he'd ever be.'

'And?' asked Daisy fearfully.

Vera started to sob. 'He kicked the life out of me. Kicked me to a pulp in his steel-capped boots. Retribution, he called it, but it was murder. The baby didn't survive. How on earth could it, poor mite? When he finished, he told me he ought to throw me on the fire, watch me burn to death like our mother had.'

The tears were streaming down her cheeks by now, but she had neither the energy nor inclination to wipe them away. The effort of recounting her story had taken what little strength she had left.

'So you see, Daisy,' said Vera shakily, 'I think I do understand a little of how you're feeling. I want you to have the gift of motherhood that I never got the chance to experience, but I fear for you, and for what the future holds.'

Daisy sank back against the pillows. 'Please, Vera, will you hold me?' she whispered. 'I'm scared. What if Dad finds out about me and does the same?'

Without saying a word, Vera lay back against the tiny bed and gathered her little sister into her arms. They lay that way for a long time without moving, drawing comfort from the warmth of each other's embrace and the feeling of solidarity in the half-light, both women content to stay lost in their own thoughts. By the time darkness had sneaked in over the chimney pots of Bethnal Green, Vera was no closer to working out what to do. She thought of the little life unfurling just inches away in her sister's stomach and of the fate that awaited the poor child.

Daisy was right to be scared of Frank's reaction. She would need the entire British Army at her disposal to fend him off. And he wasn't the only one Daisy need fear. The street, the factory, the East End, the whole of society would frown upon this innocent little life.

Daisy had committed a cardinal sin and her future was

now in jeopardy. And then there was Vera's position in all this. If this got out, she knew what would be expected of her. Half the women in Trout's would have no compunction at all about casting a family member out into the cold if they discovered she was pregnant out of wedlock. And though Vera would never confess such a thought to Daisy, a part of her simply could not fathom how her sister could risk bringing such a scandal on the family. Vera was a pillar of the community, a forelady, for goodness' sake, with a reputation to uphold. Her standing would suffer a terrible blow if news of Daisy's pregnancy were ever to leak out.

But the time for judgement had passed, Vera reasoned. What her little sister needed now was not condemnation but love. As for their father, all she could do was pray for divine intervention.

It was the Monday morning after Daisy's collapse and Vera hadn't slept so much as a wink. She had been terrified her father would return, so had dragged the easy chair upstairs and placed it outside Daisy's bedroom, where she had sat like a centurion on guard.

Daisy had fallen into an exhausted, fitful sleep, and Vera had been filled with mixed emotions. If, and it was a big if, Daisy's baby survived the botched procedure, there were still a thousand unanswered questions to tend to. The biggest of which was what on earth was Daisy to do? Vera knew that there was only one possible option open to her if her younger sister wanted to retain her reputation, but telling her that she would have to give up her precious baby had still broken Vera's heart.

A sharp knock on the door startled her. It was early. Who on earth could be calling at such an hour?

Vera flung open the door to find the same two police constables she had previously talked to about Frank. One looked to be well into his fifties, with silver-streaked hair and the look of a man for whom delivering bad news was second nature; the other constable was not much older than she was. She shifted warily and cast a sideways glance up and down the street. Fear drummed in her chest.

'Yes. How may I help you?' she asked politely.

'It's about your father, Miss Shadwell. May we come in?'

'By all means,' she said, feeling a dark cloud descend as she ushered them over the threshold and into the kitchen.

'Your father, among others, was wanted for questioning in connection with a spate of thefts,' the older officer said gravely.

Vera sank down heavily into a kitchen chair. 'I think you better sit down,' she said, gesturing to the chairs opposite her.

'It is our belief that your father and his associates took advantage of our weakened police force and the chaos of the war to further their criminal activities,' the other said.

'I knew it,' groaned Vera. 'Go on.'

'Frank and a gang of five other men kitted themselves out as ARP wardens and then smashed their way into shops and abandoned homes. Such is the power of the tin helmet that on a few occasions innocent passers-by were sucked into their nefarious activities and even helped to load up their cars in the belief that the goods were being removed for safe keeping. In one case, some unscrupulous villains

– of whom your father is a known associate – even disguised a getaway car as an ambulance.'

Vera shook her head in disbelief. While the rest of the East End had been pulling together to help each other, her father, typically, had been helping himself.

'Please go on,' she sighed.

'Broadly speaking, we believe your father and his gang have had a hand in everything from shop theft to looting, and dabbling in the black market. He even claimed £500 for the loss of his home and goods contained within. Have you been bombed out, Miss Shadwell?'

'No,' she replied weakly.

'Then there's the black market. Your father has been selling everything from gin to nylons. Make no mistake, miss – these crimes are costing London a fortune. Men like your father aren't just making use of the black market. They are feeding it. Shopkeepers have lost more to this sort of crime than they ever have to German bombs.'

Vera felt her anger growing as she thought of the number of times she had queued for hours to buy what precious little goods the shops contained, and how carefully she monitored and managed her ration book. Decent, honest and law-abiding citizens like her were fighting a war on all fronts, or so it seemed. It really was beyond the pale.

'They want hanging, the lot of them,' she snapped. 'Every last spiv and drone.'

'Well, quite,' replied the older constable, taken aback at the force of her anger.

'We've been building a case on this gang and their activities. We believe your father got wind of the investigation and has been keeping a low profile, but we were fortunate enough to secure his arrest yesterday.'

Vera shook her head in stunned disbelief.

'He's due to appear before Bow Street magistrates this afternoon, where he will be expected to plead and then be committed for trial at a later date. Are you willing to stand bail for your father?' the younger officer asked.

'Heavens, no,' Vera shot back quickly. 'Sorry, Officer, I don't wish to sound rude, but we're of limited means and I have neither the resources nor the inclination to stand bail.'

'Of course,' said the constable, rising to his feet. 'I believe you have a younger sister.' He checked his notebook. 'A Miss Daisy Shadwell. May we speak with her?'

'That won't be possible, Officer,' Vera replied as calmly as she could. 'She's confined to her bed and is unwell.'

'I'm sorry to hear that, Miss Shadwell. May we return if we have further questions?'

'You may indeed, and please be sure to let me know what happens in court,' she replied, and then, as an afterthought, added, 'Please, sir, if I may, my sister and I are law-abiding citizens and if what you say about my father is true, then we hold him in deep contempt.'

Vera could tell her denouncement of her father gratified both men.

'You and every right-minded person in London.' The older constable nodded approvingly. 'Good day to you, Miss Shadwell.'

Vera showed the two constables to the door, before returning to the kitchen. Trembling slightly, she bustled to the stove and prepared a fresh pot of tea. Next she lit a small fire in the hearth and lovingly prepared Daisy some bread and jam. Only when her kitchen was in order did she allow the relief to wash over her. Thank goodness her prayers had been answered and her father was, for the moment, out of their way. At least now she could safely work out a plan for Daisy and the baby.

Vera wasted no time and on her way home from work that very evening, she paid an impromptu visit to Matron at the hospital.

Matron took one look at Vera's face and ushered her inside her office.

'I'm so sorry to trouble you, especially when I only visited yesterday morning,' she began, but she couldn't finish the sentence and broke down in helpless tears. Between great sobs she told Matron the whole harrowing story, leaving out nothing: Daisy's pregnancy by the GI, her botched procedure and, finally, news of her father's arrest that very morning.

'What on earth am I to do?' she cried, throwing her hands in the air in despair. 'This transgression of hers, if it gets out . . . well, you can only imagine. How could she be so stupid as to put herself in this predicament? What was she thinking? Robert, that's the father, doesn't even know yet.'

Matron listened calmly without interrupting. 'Do not judge your sister,' she cautioned, when Vera had finished her tirade, and then, with a little more sternness in her voice, 'Let he who is without sin cast the first stone.'

The meaning of her words was not lost on Vera.

'You're right,' Vera sighed, bowing her head. 'I'm sorry . . . but what am I to do with her, Matron?'

Without saying a word, Matron started to write something

down on a sheet of paper before sliding it across the desk to Vera.

'This is the address of a home for unmarried mothers and babies near the coast in Suffolk that is run in conjunction with the local adoption agency,' she said. 'It's a quiet, respectable place, and they have experienced little in the way of bombing raids. I know the lady who runs it well. Tell her you are a friend of mine. Some of these homes are rather hard and the girls are treated as nothing short of slaves, without a shred of compassion.'

Vera could not hide her reaction.

'But don't worry, Vera,' assured Matron. 'This home will not be like that. Make no mistake – Daisy will be expected to work for the duration of her confinement, and her handling of the baby after the birth will be kept to a minimum to avoid unnecessary bonding, but the matron of the home is not entirely without feeling for stricken girls. We have all made mistakes in the past, have we not?' she added, casting a pointed look in Vera's direction.

'The home admits mothers three months prior to the birth, and then she will be expected to stay with and care for her child for six weeks after, longer if a suitable couple to adopt hasn't been found. I think you will find this place an agreeable home for Daisy.'

'Thank you, Matron,' Vera said gratefully. 'Sage advice as always. Where would I be without you?'

Vera left the hospital feeling as if a weight had been lifted from her shoulders. Now all she had to do was persuade Daisy that this home really was the safest place for her to go, because if word got out about her condition, she would be driven out of the East End anyway.

Sixteen

Since her collapse two and a half months earlier, Daisy's world had turned on its axis. Thanks to her sister's shocking confession, she not only saw Vera in a new light, but she also saw what a truly terrible man her father really was, underlined by the fact that he was currently in a prison cell awaiting trial for handling stolen goods. How had she been so blind to his wickedness?

All the while she had imagined poor Vera to be the enemy, when it was as plain as the nose on her face that it was her father who was rotten to the core. He was nothing but an illusionist, pitting sister against sister, clouding his identity with smoke and mirrors.

Daisy was still struggling to reassemble her thoughts about her life as she had always known it. She could scarcely believe that her big sister had once been in love and carried a child. Daisy couldn't imagine the torment she must have suffered in losing her baby in such a brutal fashion at their father's hands. Little wonder she harboured such bitterness towards him, and it also explained why she had always been so protective towards her. Daisy resolved to ask Vera more about her childhood and their mother in a quieter moment. Vera had revealed more tantalizing details about her mother that night than she had in eighteen years, but instinctively Daisy sensed it wouldn't do to push. Losing her only chance of motherhood had been a terrible blow to her sister and Daisy was sure she would tell her more about it in her own good time. It was enough. For now.

Her father being off the scene temporarily solved at least one of her problems, but her slightly swollen belly testified to another, significantly greater problem. Daisy looked down and gently splayed her fingers over the soft peachy skin. She had returned to work as soon as the bleeding had stopped and had since been disguising her pregnancy with bandages she had sneaked out of Trout's. But in the privacy of her bedroom, it was a blessed relief to unwrap her bindings and finally relax without fear of discovery.

Daisy had written to Robert shortly after she had returned to work and was sure the baby was going to be all right. She didn't tell him of her actions that dark and dreadful day. There was no sense in him knowing that now, and Daisy's shame and disgust meant that she couldn't bring herself even to write the words. Instead, she had penned a long letter, finally confessing that she was pregnant. Daisy had opened her heart and spilt the contents onto the page, telling Robert how much she adored him and how, even though she knew it would be hard, there surely had to be a way in which they could keep their child. If that was what he wanted . . .

Daisy had pictured Robert's handsome face as he sat in the mess hall, or on his bunk, reading her explosive letter. He would be stunned, that much she knew, but his long-term reaction? She just prayed he was as decent and honourable a man as she thought he was. But the proof of that would come from his actions. Seven weeks on and she still hadn't heard back, but she knew how long the post took to get through. He would respond. He had to. The alternative was unthinkable.

Daisy looked down at her body. *Five months pregnant.* Paying a perfect stranger to take away her baby was unthinkable now, but back then she felt she had nowhere else to turn. She had been a desperate woman, but that still did not excuse her behaviour. And even though she now knew she had her sister's support – and hopefully in time Robert's too – the cold, hard truth of the matter was that she was still a desperate woman. Bandages would only work at concealing her pregnancy for so long.

The most ridiculous thing, Daisy thought, was that, on the face of it, she had never looked so well. In fact, the bloom of pregnancy only served to make her looks more exquisite. Her complexion was dewy, and her eyes sparkled. For five months now her body had nurtured the little life growing inside her, swelling gently to accommodate it, and her arms already ached to hold her child. She couldn't wait to meet her baby, and yet she dreaded the first contraction, because this birth didn't mean a new beginning. It meant, unless Robert could somehow find a way to save her, saying goodbye. Everything was happening as nature intended but society forbade.

The hollow pain of her predicament left her breathless. She would rather tear a limb from her body than sign a piece of paper giving ownership of her child to a stranger. Again and again Vera had gently tried broaching the subject of visiting an unmarried mothers' home, of discussing that most unthinkable of options – adoption – but Daisy had cut her off mid-sentence, begging for more time. At the sight of such a torrent of tears, Vera had backed off, for now, but Daisy knew that eventually her hand would be forced. She knew it would be impossible to keep her baby, and yet, *and yet* her heart longed to raise the little life inside her as her own. This baby was conceived in love, and could be raised with love.

Daisy also clung to the more powerful hope that Robert would return, that one day she would open the door to find his handsome face smiling back at her from the doorstep, clutching her letter in his hand. She heard his words from that last night in the West End hotel echo through her mind. *On my honour, if I can find a way back to you, I will.* Now her honour depended on him finding such a way.

Daisy got up to dress. As she carefully wound the bandages round her tummy, never had her desire to leave the East End been so strong.

There was a gentle knock at her bedroom door and Vera's concerned face appeared.

'Allow me,' she said, coming up behind her and gently winding the bandage round her sister's back before securing it with a safety pin. When she finished, Vera sighed, and even though Daisy could not see her face, she knew what was coming next.

'These bandages will only work in concealing your pregnancy for so long, Daisy,' she warned softly in her ear. 'We need to talk and make a plan. We must pay a visit to this home and see the place for ourselves. I know every fibre of your being is against giving the baby away, but I really cannot see any other option. Frank's trial is next week and unless they lock him up and throw away the key, he will return, and then what?'

Daisy drew back and jutted out her neat chin. 'I've written to Robert, telling him about the baby.'

'And . . . ?' Vera replied.

'It's all right, Vera. He'll write back in time, I'm sure of it.'

Vera gently spun her sister round to face her. 'I wish that were true, love, honestly I do, but you have to start preparing yourself for some uncomfortable truths. Even *if* Robert does return and you somehow find a way to get married, it will be clear to all that your baby was conceived out of wedlock, and that's before you even begin to consider the issue of the baby's colour. A half-caste baby in Bethnal Green?' Vera shuddered. 'Can you even imagine what the likes of Pat Doggan would have to say about that? Your life and the baby's life will be made intolerable.

'Besides, these Americans, well, they're here to fight a war, not start families. Have you considered that may be the reason why he hasn't responded to your letter? I dare say flings like that are frowned upon by his superiors.'

'It wasn't a fling,' Daisy protested, her green eyes at once filling with tears.

Vera sighed and quickly changed tack. 'I'm sorry, love. I don't mean to sound harsh, but we're running out of time. I am simply trying to be the voice of reason.' She reached down and lightly touched her sister's tummy. 'This baby is relying on you to do what's right. It's not fair on him or her to ignore this situation for a moment longer. You had a wonderful and exciting romance with your American, but you're not living in a Hollywood film. There is no fairy-tale ending to this story.'

By the time Vera had finished her little speech, Daisy knew it was futile to argue any more. Her head told her that Vera was right, but her heart wasn't ready to listen.

'Just give me more time, please?' she pleaded.

The sisters had reached a stalemate.

'Time is the one thing we don't have,' Vera replied abruptly. 'We'll discuss this again later. Now, let's get going. Those bandages and uniforms won't sew themselves.'

*

Half a mile away, Poppy was also steeling herself to leave her lodgings and face the journey to work. She was glad to leave her stuffy room, and as it was already promising to be a warm day, she had sensibly left enough time to walk to the factory. For the next twelve-hour shift she would be cooped up inside.

Outside on the streets, she was grateful for the fresh air in her lungs – well, as fresh as London air could ever be compared to the sweet air of Norfolk. Not that she missed it, mind you. Poppy had been in the East End for nearly six months now with still no word from her mother, so had no idea if the village was talking about the scandal or if it had all been swept under the carpet.

Her mother's rejection of her cut just as harshly as it always did. All she had ever done in her life was work hard and try to please everyone, and yet the one woman who was supposed to love Poppy unconditionally had turned her back on her.

If only someone would respond to her secret letters, then life would certainly look a lot rosier. True to her word, Poppy had stitched no more letters since the last one, sewn on the night of the party. That had been ages ago, and to her disappointment, there had not been a single response. She had poured her heart and soul into that letter and couldn't stand to think of a soldier finding it and perhaps even laughing over it with his comrades. 'You're a silly fool,' she scolded herself as she walked.

Suddenly, her thoughts turned to the private battle that Daisy was fighting. Her own troubles paled into comparison against hers. Pregnant! Poppy still could hardly believe it. True to their word, she, Archie and Sal hadn't breathed so much as one word of Daisy's predicament, but as every day passed, Poppy feared for her friend's future.

As the factory came into sight, Poppy spotted Daisy trailing glumly up the road after her sister, her shoulders hunched, her beautiful face a mask of misery. She was a far cry from the glamorous, self-assured girl Poppy had first met all those months ago. Quickening her pace, Poppy hurried to catch her.

'How are you feeling, Daisy?' she whispered, catching hold of her sleeve and gently tugging her back. 'Have you worked out what you're going to do yet? We'll all support you.'

Daisy's expression was thunderous. 'Oh, please, Poppy. Not you as well. I've had Vera bending my ear all morning.'

With that she swept up the narrow staircase, leaving Vera to send Poppy a despairing look. She glanced around to check no one was coming before confiding, 'I'm at my wits' end, Poppy. She simply won't listen to reason.'

'Would it help if I spoke to her?' Poppy asked.

'I doubt it, my dear,' said Vera. 'Short of putting a bomb under her, I can't seem to shake her out of this terrible inertia. The problem is, she can't seem to rid herself of the silly notion that this Robert chap is going to return, wave a magic wand and make everything all right again.'

There were no more words to be said and they followed Daisy up the stairs to where the day's work was waiting.

*

Vera had no sooner stepped foot onto the factory floor than Archie was marching towards her.

'A quick word in my office, Vera, and you too, Daisy, if you please.'

The two women walked through the door and sat down. A gale of laughter and song echoed in from the factory floor, but there was no disguising the feeling of dread in the room.

Archie's face softened with concern as he looked at Daisy. 'How you feeling, Daisy love?'

'All right, Mr Gladstone. You know . . . bearing up,' she replied guardedly.

'Is there something the matter, Archie?' asked Vera.

Archie shifted uncomfortably in his seat and steepled his fingers as he regarded them both.

'Please spit it out, Archie,' Vera urged.

He jerked a thumb in the direction of the factory floor and wiped a hand over the crown of his bald head, a habit Vera had long ago worked out meant he was anxious.

'The rumour mill has gone into overdrive. You know what

those lot outside are like when they get going, and, well, I don't quite know how to put this,' he blustered.

'Please just tell us straight,' Daisy pleaded.

'Pat's sister spotted you coming out of Mrs Black's house that Sunday morning when you . . . well, you know.' He trailed off uncomfortably.

'But that was months ago,' Daisy spluttered.

'I know, but then she got talking to another friend down the market last night who apparently saw you dancing and kissing with your Yank chap outside the Tube. They've put two and two together, and, well, you know how people talk. Folk don't like it when our girls hang out with foreign soldiers, and they like it even less when you visit a certain well-known abortionist, and Mrs Black is certainly notorious round these parts. I'm sorry to break the bad news, Daisy, but you know how it is round here. You can't even get a new coat without the whole road turning out for a look. Gossip spreads like wildfire. The streets are full of it, with the number of illegitimate babies popping up. You can't ever keep anything secret for long in the East End.'

Archie held his hands up in defeat and the colour flooded from Daisy's cheeks. The suffocating conformity of life in Bethnal Green was one of the things Daisy had always resented most . . . and now it looked as if it were to be her undoing.

'Well, I'm done for, then,' she said in a hollow voice.

Archie looked to Vera. 'I think under the circumstances it's better if Daisy keeps a low profile from now on, wouldn't you agree, Vera? Speculation will continue to mount and Daisy's situation here will become untenable, as will yours, Vera, if you allow this to persist. In any case, I will need to find a suitable replacement for Daisy, be that now or three months down the line.'

Vera nodded slowly. 'I agree, and we are both deeply sorry to have placed you in a difficult situation. Plans have to be made, and not tomorrow or next week but right now. Don't you see?' she pleaded, turning to Daisy with a shake in her voice.

Daisy sat mute.

'I know you didn't want it this way,' Vera went on, 'but you can't keep working here in your state. I'm sorry, love, but I am going to have to start laying down the law now. You will leave for the mother and baby home as soon as I have made the necessary arrangements. I wish there was somewhere else you could go for the remainder of your pregnancy, but the simple fact is, we don't know anyone outside of the East End. And even if we did, who could manage an extra mouth to feed during the war? No, we shall just have to play the hand that life has dealt us.'

Without waiting for Daisy to respond, she went on. 'You will gather your things and leave the factory floor today. And please be sure to thank Mr Gladstone – he's shown you a level of courtesy and consideration that I'm quite sure not many other bosses would have.'

Daisy shook her head, dazed at Vera's brusque handling of the situation, and blinked back tears. She was utterly crushed.

'Of course,' she mumbled, rising unsteadily to her feet. 'And thank you, Mr Gladstone, for everything. I'm awfully sorry for putting you in this situation.'

'Not at all, Daisy,' replied Archie, with a slight catch in his voice. 'You know I think the world of you.'

Vera rose to her feet, her back ramrod straight. Daisy might as well have painted herself with tar and stuck the feathers on too. She would be an easy target for the prejudices of the East End community.

'Come on, Daisy,' Vera ordered. 'Now's the time to show your mettle.'

At the door, Daisy turned to Archie and said something that made Vera's heart break afresh.

'Robert's going to come back for me and make an honest woman of me,' she whispered. 'You wait and see. Then everything will be all right, won't it?'

Archie smiled softly and nodded. 'I hope so, love, I truly do.'

Out on the floor, the women were giving it everything they had, ensuring that poor Daisy was literally being made to face the music, Vera thought with bitter irony. Their song reached a crescendo as the Shadwell sisters exited Archie's office and made their way to their workbenches.

Pat's voice was easily the loudest in the room, but every woman bar Poppy and Sal sang along: '*All the nice girls love a sailor . . .*'

As Daisy drew level with the first bank of machines, Pat pointedly turned her back on her and carried on singing.

'*Well, you know what sailors are,*' her brazen voice rang out as loud and clear as a horn in fog.

'All right, Pat?' ventured Daisy. 'You keeping well?'

It was a brave move, thought Vera, but her sister's efforts were shot down.

Without even turning round, Pat spat back her reply over her shoulder. 'You reap what you sow, Daisy.'

Vera watched as Daisy's face crumpled. She opened her

mouth to defend herself, but no words came. Instead, she turned and slowly carried on walking along the bank of machines. Every woman she passed made a show of slowly and deliberately turning her chair away from Daisy. One by one they glared at her before showing her their backs. It was as public and humiliating a snub as was possible.

By the time Daisy reached her workbench, the desolation of rejection was hers to savour. Her downfall was complete.

'All right, ladies, you've had your fun. Now back to work,' Vera warned.

With a shaking hand, Daisy started to pack what few possessions she had into her handbag. She didn't even bother to remove her light summer coat. Bravely, Sal rose to her feet and, without saying a word, started to help her friend.

'Didn't I say no good would come from mixing with them Yanks,' Pat said loudly, as she threaded cotton through her needle.

The door to Mr Gladstone's office nearly came clean off its hinges as the factory foreman burst out, his face puce with rage.

'That's enough!' he roared to the sea of stunned workers. 'I won't have it in my factory, you hear me?'

No one breathed a word. Even Vera felt herself staring stunned at their normally convivial boss. How many other men would stick their neck out like that?

'It's all right, Mr Gladstone,' said Daisy, bravely blinking back her tears. 'Don't worry. I understand why they're saying it. Probably would have said the same myself a few months ago.'

As she walked shakily down the stairs, she passed a telegram boy, so young he was barely out of short trousers, heading for the factory floor. He took in her anguished face and smiled sympathetically. 'Cheer up, miss,' he said. 'It might never happen.'

Daisy stifled a sob and silently fled the stairwell as fast as her feet would carry her. Only once she was outside on the street and alone did she allow the tears to really come, streaming unchecked down her face. She was out of a job now, her reputation tarnished. The sun beat down mercilessly on her face as she looked up to the heavens above.

Suddenly, an ear-shattering scream pierced the air, a noise the likes of which Daisy had never before heard. Her stomach turned painfully, for she guessed instantly to whom the voice belonged, and more horrifyingly yet, that she couldn't go to her and comfort her like a friend should.

*

Five floors up, Sal gripped the freshly delivered telegram in her hand. She was aware that the whole floor had turned to stare at her, aware too that the strangest of noises had just escaped her body, halfway between a scream and a moan, but she was powerless. She felt as if she were somewhere up on the ceiling looking down at herself. For this was a moment she had longed for, even prayed for night after night, and yet, somehow, now the moment was here, she felt nothing but a deep well of pain and shock.

'Sal, Sal, whatever is it?' The voice brought her back to the present.

She stared up at Vera's face before handing her the telegram. 'It's over . . .' she mumbled.

Vera read, her eyes widening in surprise.

Mrs S Fowler, Bethnal Green. Deeply regret to report death of your husband R Fowler c/JX 28846 on war service. Letter follows.

*

At the end of the strangest day Poppy had experienced during her time in Bethnal Green, they all gathered back at Tavern Street to take stock of the dramatic events.

After she had received the telegram informing her of her husband's death, Sal had been allowed to leave early on compassionate grounds, provided she make the work up the next day. In deep shock, Sal simply hadn't been able to face going home alone and so had gone straight to Daisy and Vera's house, where Daisy had been waiting. By the time Poppy and Vera had returned at the end of their shift to join them, it was hard to say who looked more shaken.

Nursing cups of hot, sweet tea, they all sat round the kitchen table in a state of disbelief.

'I just can't believe he's really dead,' Sal said again in a flat tone. 'When will it hit me?'

'Not for a long time, love, I shouldn't think,' replied Vera. 'You have lived in fear for so many years – your body and mind will take some time to adjust.' Vera's hand reached across the table and her fingers laced through Sal's. 'I know death is no cause to celebrate, my dear, but at least this means you are finally free of that man,' she whispered.

'I suppose so,' Sal replied shakily. 'There's so much to think about now, though. Like whether to bring the boys home, and if so, do I give up work? But I'm loath to. Work is the one thing that has helped define who I am these past two years. It gave me a sense of identity after Reggie stripped it from me. What will I be without my life at Trout's? I'm proud of my job.'

'One step at a time, love,' counselled Vera. 'You don't even have the official letter from the army yet. And don't forget, you can depend on us all for help and support.'

'That's right,' Poppy smiled gently. 'If you need me to cover any shifts for you while you sort things out, I'd be happy to help.'

'That's so kind of you all, girls,' Sal said, smiling at last. 'Where would I be without you, and work, of course?'

'We're all here to help you too, Daisy,' Poppy said.

'You are sweet, Poppy, but life couldn't look any more bleak right now,' Daisy replied. With that she scraped her chair back from the table and fled sobbing to her bedroom. Her footsteps clattered up the wooden steps. The walls were so fragile they could hear her heartbroken cries drift down from the bedroom above.

Sal got up to follow, but Vera placed a cautionary hand on her arm. 'Leave her be, Sal,' she said. 'She still has it in her head this Robert chap will return for her, and when the truth finally hits home that that is never going to happen, it will break her heart all over again. Her life will change irrevocably over the coming months and all we can do is hope she finds the fortitude to survive the scandal and move on.'

'What will you do now, Vera?' asked Sal nervously.

'The only thing I possibly can do under the circumstances,' she sighed. 'There's a mother and baby home far away from here, in Suffolk, that will house Daisy for the duration of her confinement. She will give birth there and they will arrange the adoption. I just need to let them know she is coming, sooner than perhaps we all expected.'

'So you really are sending her away?' Poppy asked.

'I have no choice, Poppy dear,' stated Vera crisply. 'She cannot raise this child on her own or provide it with any kind of a life. It's for the best.'

A heavy silence fell over the table as they digested what it would mean to Daisy to be forced to give away her baby.

'I suppose we should count our blessings for one thing, though,' Vera said, breaking the silence.

'What's that?' asked Sal.

'Frank's trial is next week. Mercifully he knows nothing of this.'

'Will you go?' asked Poppy.

'No, I shall stay away. The police will inform me of his prison term if he's convicted. I doubt very much they shall lock him up and throw away the key. Apparently, they are dealing with lots of cases like this, and thanks to the war, the prisons are understaffed. Let's hope he at least gets locked up until after Daisy's baby is born and safely away from here.'

Poppy drained her tea and rose to leave. 'The longer he gets, the better,' she said, knowing full well what it would mean to Vera to have her dreadful father finally off the scene, especially during these trying times. 'If you'll excuse me, I best be off. After today I'm fit to drop and my bed is calling.'

'Of course, my dear,' smiled Vera, showing her to the door. 'Goodnight.'

Poppy felt desperately for her friends and had vowed to be there and support them all during their hours of need, but tonight, she also had something else on her mind.

Poppy dug her fingers deep into her pocket and, on feeling the sliver of paper there, allowed a little burst of delight to run through her. She had buried her excitement all day, as it hadn't seemed right to indulge herself when her friends were having such a trying time, but ever since she had opened the letter that had been delivered at the same time as Sal's telegram, she had been secretly thrilled.

Joy of joys! At last someone had actually replied to one of her letters. Poppy had felt so choked that Sal's telegram contained such sadness that she had kept her own letter a secret from her, hastily reading it on her dinner break in the privacy of a toilet cubicle. It had been burning a hole in her pocket ever since.

Letting herself into her lodgings, she breathlessly pulled it out and, without even taking off her coat, sat down at her small table and carefully smoothed out the paper. Impulsively she held the letter up to her face and breathed in deeply, as if trying to prove to herself it really existed and wasn't just a figment of her imagination.

Good day to you, Poppy Percival, wrote Private Freddie Beecroft. His handwriting was neat and small, with perfectly spaced loops.

> *Well, where to start? Firstly I would be simply chuffed to bits to have you as a confidante. You sound like a lovely, hard-working girl, the sort that any man could count himself proud to know.*
>
> *I am currently in a military hospital located close to the front with shrapnel wounds to my leg, and no idea when, or indeed if, I will be declared fit for service again. Imagine mine and the nurse's surprise when she*

came to dress my wounds this morning and your letter dropped out of the fresh bandage as she ripped it open. Talk about pennies from heaven. I dare say there wasn't a happier invalid that morning!

I too am a country lad at heart. My comrades like to take the mickey out of me something rotten and my nickname is Private Bumpkin. I'm afraid to say I'm most dreadfully shy, so this good-natured teasing has the effect of turning me quite the strangest shade of red, which seems to amuse them even further, but I don't mind a bit. Laughter is so important to morale, don't you think, Poppy?

Born and bred down in Devon, it was quite a shock to me when I first arrived in the battlefields. I almost laugh when I look back and think how naive I was when I signed up to fight. I was so green. I lived on a farm with parents who loved me. I was proud of my animal-husbandry skills, honed over the years (I was so happy to read you love animals too), but I wanted to make my mark and do my bit for my country. I couldn't bear to think of the Nazis getting their hands on our green and civil land.

I don't have children. Well, to be honest with you, Poppy, I don't even have a sweetheart and never have, but I live in hope. One day, I so wish to have a family of my own, and I couldn't bear to think of them being brainwashed by the Nazis, so off I marched to war in my squeaky-clean boots. To this day, Poppy, I don't regret that, but I wish I had not seen some of the things that I have. War is a terrible thing. You see, you cannot undo what you have done. I have seen my comrades die next to me in the most terrible ways imaginable. When you look at them, you can't help but think, Why are they dead? Just a year or so ago, they were going to school, working, getting married . . . Many had ambition; all looked forward to the future and talked constantly of what they planned to do once this dreadful war is over. Now they're gone. Those ambitions will never be realized. I suppose what I'm saying, Poppy, is that war has made me realize what is truly important in life.

You talked of dreams in your letter and that is what compelled me to write back to you. For I have so many dreams I fear I might burst with them. I just hope I get the chance to fulfil them. Goodness but this letter is taking on a maudlin edge. Sorry – I shall talk no more of this, but it feels so good to be able to speak freely. I cannot write of these things to my mother, you see, as she worries about me dreadfully. But mainly, Poppy, I would love someone to share dreams with.

I'd like to finish this missive by paying tribute to the courage of you ladies back home in the land I love. We have heard such terrible stories of what you are all enduring on the home front. It is one thing to stare the enemy in the face, but facing the unseen enemy of uncertainty, hardship and poverty is another. You ended your letter with blessings from the East End, and I end mine by taking my hat off to you, Poppy Percival. Here's to the sharing of dreams.

I await your response eagerly.

Yours,

Freddie

When she had finished reading, Poppy let out a deep sigh and held the letter to her heart. In all her days she could never have hoped to have a more perfect, sensitive and intelligent man write back to her. Taking out her pencil and paper, she began to compose a reply.

Dear Freddie,

I can't even begin to tell you how thrilled your response made me. Not that you're in hospital, I mean, but that you wrote back. Nothing would make me happier than to be your friend. I nearly cried reading your sweet comments about all that we are enduring on the home front. But in reality we are just getting on with the business of work. It is you soldiers risking your lives for our freedom who really deserve the cheers.

Tell me about the hospital. Are there nice VAD nurses looking after you? What do they call them? Very Adorable Darlings? It's so important to have people to look out for you, after all. I have three wonderful friends looking out for me here in Bethnal Green. They're all as different as chalk and cheese, but I'm fairly certain I wouldn't have survived the move to London were it not for them.

My eyes were truly opened to the hideous effect this war is having when I moved to the East End. So many

*people were killed in the Blitz, and those who did
escape with their lives more often than not had their
homes bombed from under them. But they never seem to
stop smiling . . . or singing. Did I tell you the women in
the factory where I work are nicknamed the 'Singer
Girls'?*

*I don't think I sang one word when I was a scullery
maid; now I feel like I'm in a music hall we sing that
much, but it's wonderful. They're wonderful. I'd love
you to meet my friends one day.*

*But for all that the East End has given me, my heart
still belongs out in the countryside. Simple dreams,
really, but I'm a simple girl at heart. Please tell me
what you hope to do when this war is over. I would so
love to hear.*

Yours in anticipation,

Poppy Percival

Poppy looked at her small and deeply treasured bottle of
Ashes of Violet on the sideboard. She knew Betty would
have given the letter a liberal coating of perfume, but she
decided against it. It wasn't really her style. Instead, she
gave the envelope a breathless little kiss and hurried off out
through the door to post the letter to her new friend.

Seventeen

It was the Sunday after Daisy had found herself suddenly without her job, and Vera and Archie had summoned her downstairs, to discuss her future.

'Don't look so worried, love,' said Archie, as Daisy gripped her lower back and eased herself down into a chair.

Clutching her tummy protectively, Daisy eyed Vera and Archie nervously over the kitchen table.

'We need to make a plan of action,' said Vera softly. 'I invited Archie here today as he's pledged to help us in any way he can, and from where I'm sitting, we could do with all the help we can get right now.'

'Really?' snapped Daisy. 'Because from where I'm sitting, it looks like a council of war.'

'All Vera wants is to make sure that when the time comes for the little 'un to be born, you're in a place of safety and comfort,' said Archie.

'Sorry,' mumbled Daisy, contrite. 'It's just that, well, I'm scared.'

'I know you are, love,' soothed Vera. 'That's why Archie's kindly agreed to use up his fuel allowance and drive us both to the home next Sunday. I've telephoned the matron there and she has agreed to admit you a little early. She sounds nice, and look at the positives. At least you'll be in the peace of the countryside, surrounded by other young women in the same position as you, with no one judging or whispering.'

Daisy nodded and slowly rose to her feet. 'I suppose I better start packing, then,' she said in a hollow voice.

Upstairs in her bedroom, Daisy lay on the bed and stared up at the ceiling. She knew Vera and Archie were both acting with the best of intentions, but right now she felt so helpless, as if her whole life were hurtling out of control and there was not the slightest thing she could do about it. The die was cast. Her baby would be taken from her. The realization made every cell in her body thrum with despair and agony.

This child was *her* flesh and blood. *Hers and Robert's* . . .

Pulling her candlewick bedspread over her head, she wished she were dead.

The muffled din from downstairs was distant to begin with, but grew gradually louder. Footsteps pounded up the stairs and in alarm Daisy realized the voices were raised in anger. Vera's suddenly rang out in distress.

'You can't go in there!'

Daisy sat bolt upright, gripped with fear, and frantically looked around the room for something to defend herself with. Oh, please, God, no, don't let it be her father. Had he got out of prison somehow? She felt the blood drain from her head as the door flew open. But it wasn't her father's furious face she found herself gazing at. Sheer amazement prickled up her spine.

'Daisy?' breathed a deep male voice. 'It's me. I'm back.'

It was hard to say who was most shocked, Daisy, Vera, Archie or Robert, whose gaze was fixed firmly on Daisy's swollen stomach. It was the GI who broke the silence first.

'Daisy, are you pregnant?' he whispered.

'Well, she's hardly been overeating,' snapped Vera. She glared at Robert and looked set to give him a piece of her mind when Archie took her by the arm.

'Come on, Vera, let's give them some space to talk,' he said quietly.

'But this . . . this is ridiculous,' spluttered Vera. 'He can't be here, alone with Daisy in her bedroom. It's simply not right.'

'Vera, just give them ten minutes – that's all,' said Archie firmly. 'The lad has come a long way.'

'Ten minutes, and I shall be downstairs, so no funny business,' muttered Vera, glaring at Robert, as she shut the door reluctantly.

And then they were alone.

'Sorry about my sister,' murmured Daisy, still in a haze of disbelief. 'She's just a bit protective of me.'

'I-I got forty-eight hours' leave off base, my first leave in months. I came as soon as I could,' Robert stuttered, unable to tear his eyes away from Daisy's rounded tummy.

Daisy went to reply, but to her surprise, found she had no voice. Her heart was pounding so loudly she could scarcely hear her own thoughts. Robert sank to his knees at her bedside. She had forgotten how big he was. His shoulders alone seemed to fill the tiny room. She simply couldn't believe her eyes. His strong, chiselled face was more handsome than she remembered and her heart ached afresh.

'Robert,' she whispered eventually, 'why didn't you reply to my letter?'

'Oh, Daisy,' he cried, 'I never got any letter, I swear it. It's possible it was destroyed by the censorship office, if you maybe mentioned something you shouldn't have. Or it could have been lost in transit. We've been moved around here, there and everywhere for the last five months. The training has been so intense I forget how many bases we've even been through, but you were never out of my thoughts for a second. When I didn't get a reply to my letter, well, I thought you'd moved on with your life, but I knew I had to come and find you and see for myself, just in case.'

He gripped Daisy's face in his hands. 'You have to believe me, Daisy, please,' he pleaded. 'I'm in love with you. I knew the first moment I got leave I had to be with you. I've only got forty-eight hours. Darn it all, it's taken me twelve hours just to get here, but I don't even care.'

His words were tripping over themselves to escape. 'I don't care. I'd spend all day travelling just to see your face for five minutes . . . And, Daisy?' His giant hands gently cupped her tummy in wonderment.

'Yes,' she breathed.

'You're pregnant! I'm just so . . . so shocked,' he babbled, holding out one trembling hand. 'Look, I'm actually shaking.'

He stood back to admire her, before dropping to his knees again and kissing every inch of her swollen tummy. When at last his face gazed up at her, she saw a hundred questions sweep through his mind.

'I will take care of you, and look after you,' he promised.

The words she had waited so long to hear. Except now it was too late.

Daisy reached down and touched his cheek sadly. 'Robert,' she said fearfully, 'you have no idea what I've been through these past five months. I've been turned out of my job and shunned by the girls. I want this baby every bit as much as you, but it's impossible. You're a soldier serving in the US Army. You have to leave again soon. How can you support me when you don't even know where you'll be next week, never mind next year? I'm to be admitted to a mother and baby home, and then preparations will be made to . . .' Her voice caught as her emotions overcame her. 'Sorry . . .' she wept. 'What I'm trying to say is that I can't keep our baby.'

Robert's face fell. 'So that's that?' he blazed. 'We simply give up? You don't care enough to even try?'

She shook her head bitterly. 'Of course I care, Robert,' she said, her cheeks flushing with anger. 'I've been living and breathing this and thinking of nothing else since the moment I knew I was expecting, but don't you see? It's impossible.'

Robert rose to his feet slowly. He was such a handsome colossus of a man, but this was one battle she was pretty sure even he couldn't win.

'Well, I will still marry you, Daisy. That is my intention and I will make that clear to your sister,' he announced.

A glimmer of hope surfaced in Daisy's heart.

'When?' she blurted. 'Could we go tomorrow, before I have to leave for the home? Then they'll have to change their mind, surely?'

Robert shook his head. 'Oh, Daisy,' he groaned. 'If only it were that easy. You cannot even begin to imagine the paperwork that's involved when soldiers in the US Army marry English girls while on duty abroad. It was all explained to us when we first arrived in the UK.'

'How hard can it really be?' Daisy scoffed. 'I know heaps of people who have had the hastiest weddings ever before their sweethearts went back off to fight.'

'English soldiers, maybe,' Robert replied, shaking his head. 'But for us Americans, it's a whole lot more complicated. They wrap you up in red tape. My commanding officer will need to approve the application once it's been officially placed and then will write to the church or civil authority who will conduct the ceremony. Then we would both be questioned by an army chaplain and need to provide character references.'

Daisy's head started to spin as he went on.

'They will also run checks into any dependants I might have back in the United States to ensure I can afford to keep a family. The whole process can take as long as six months, so you see, a quick wedding before I return to base just isn't possible. Besides which,' he added, sadly, 'a part of me doesn't even dare attempt it. If they got wind that I'd got a white woman pregnant, I reckon they'd ship me out so fast my feet wouldn't touch the ground.'

'Then let's elope?' she babbled, knowing how daft the suggestion sounded before it was even out of her mouth.

'Anyone caught violating US Army procedures on marriage will be subjected to a court martial,' Robert replied.

'Well, I certainly don't want you slung in jail,' she sighed, coming down to earth with a bump. Daisy knew that even if they did find a way to cut through the red tape and get married the next day, it would be of little use anyhow. Her desperation was clouding her judgement. Daisy was so obviously pregnant that there was no wedding dress on earth big enough to disguise the unsavoury truth. It was simply too late. In a little over three months her baby would be born illegitimate, a dirty, disgraceful secret, at least in society's eyes.

'We're out of options and time.' Daisy sighed heavily, feeling like a condemned woman. 'First comes love, then comes marriage, then comes the baby in a carriage. We've gone about things the wrong way, Robert.'

'I guess so,' he replied miserably. 'But hear this, Daisy. I love you and I am going to marry you one day. I promise you we will be together.'

With that he sat back down on the bed and took her hand in his.

She marvelled at the sight of her slight white fingers entwined in his strong brown ones.

'Half-caste children will be harder to adopt, they say. So the longer I stay in the home can only be a good thing surely,' she reasoned. 'It could take months for them to find potential parents to adopt. I can work there, in the laundry, in return for my keep. Perhaps by then the war will be over and we may get permission to wed. That's our only hope.'

Robert shook his head. 'I wouldn't bank on a swift end to this war, Daisy. Trust me, Hitler's not going to be throwing in the towel anytime soon. But I do know this: I want to be in your life and the baby's,' he answered. 'It might seem impossible, but it doesn't mean we can't keep trying.'

Daisy nodded, suddenly feeling quite overcome with exhaustion.

'It means the world to at least know you do care for me

and feel the way I do. I knew I wasn't imagining it. It will give me something to cling to when the time comes to—' Daisy broke off.

Robert's chocolate-brown eyes flashed with love. 'I got you into this mess and I will get you out of it somehow,' he vowed.

He wrapped Daisy and their unborn baby into his big, warm wool coat and planted a soft kiss on the top of her head. Snuggled safely in his arms, Daisy prayed he was right. In just a short while Robert would be gone again, she would enter the home, and then what? Who knew what the future held for their ill-fated love affair? She was fast running out of options and time.

They stayed wrapped in each other's arms, neither daring to utter a word. What was the point? Every conversation just seemed to lead them down a dead end, and there were more questions than answers.

A sharp knock at the door startled them.

'I think it's time Robert was leaving now,' Vera called stiffly from the other side of the door.

'You better go,' wept Daisy. 'Vera will be having kittens at the thought of you in here.'

'All right,' he sighed, reluctantly pulling back from Daisy's embrace and planting a gentle hand on her tummy. 'But never forget me, dear Daisy. Wherever I end up, I shall never forget you, or our baby.'

Eighteen

Sunday morning in the children's hospital and Vera was enjoying what was always the highlight of her week. A pot of tea and some time spent with the woman whose wise counsel she valued above all. It had been two weeks now since she and Archie had taken Daisy to the home in Suffolk, and Vera was still haunted by the memory.

'I feel so guilty,' Vera confided to Matron. 'You should have seen her face when we pulled off and left her there. Didn't help that GI turning up like that at the last minute and unsettling her with promises he can't possibly hope to keep.'

'You must have felt wretched, Vera,' replied Matron sympathetically. 'But it was the right thing to do. You have spared her a scandal, and when she returns, she can start to pick up the pieces of her life.'

'I dare say,' Vera sighed. 'I just hope she doesn't end up hating me for it.'

'How could she possibly when you were acting with her best interests? And now tell me, my dear, what news of the man in *your* life?' she enquired, raising her eyebrow a fraction as she sipped her tea.

Vera knew she was referring to Archie, but she deliberately chose to misconstrue the question.

'My father, you mean?' she asked. 'I heard from the police that he received a six-month prison term for handling stolen goods. He isn't due for release until next April. Daisy's baby is expected in the middle of February, so that gives us a little breathing space to make sure things are dealt with by the time he returns. Hopefully, the rumour-mongering will have died down by then, but I have to figure out a story to feed my father should the gossip ever reach his ears, and I better make it a good one. Goodness only knows what he'd do if he discovered his younger daughter had an illegitimate child in his absence.' Vera's face paled. 'Can you ever imagine?'

'On this matter, have you given any thought to what we discussed before?' asked Matron. 'Your father may temporarily be out of your life, but your problems are not quite dead and buried. He will come out of prison an angrier man than he went in, and then what?'

Vera shuddered at the thought of how much more twisted her father could grow behind bars. 'I'll worry about that later,' she replied quickly.

Matron smiled softly, undeterred. 'The past may dictate who we are, my dear, but we get to determine who we become.'

Matron's comment was left hanging in the air and Vera swiftly changed the subject.

A very happy half-hour was spent setting the world to rights before Matron rose to her feet. 'I must be on my rounds now.'

'Of course,' Vera replied, meeting the elderly woman's smile with warmth and affection. 'I must go too. I have Poppy, Archie and Sal coming over for their dinner.'

Vera left, safe in the knowledge that no matter what secrets lurked in her past, they would always be safe with Matron, for she alone knew the *whole* truth and would take it with her to the grave.

An hour later, Vera was busy preparing dinner when Poppy, Sal and Archie arrived. Since Frank's arrest, Sunday dinner at 24 Tavern Street had become a bit of a ritual. The girls and Archie always brought what modest provisions they could find, and by teaming up their rations, they could usually put together something quite passable to eat.

'Vera, that stew smells out of this world,' grinned Archie, pouring himself a glass of frothy brown stout.

Sal cleared her throat nervously. 'Please listen, everyone,' she said. 'I have some news. I finally got the letter informing me what happened to Reggie.'

'And?' Vera whirled round, dropping her potato peeler into the sink with a clatter.

'Yes, do tell, Sal,' urged Poppy.

Sal took a deep breath. 'Well . . . apparently he was working as a fly driver, transporting jerrycans of fuel, when a long-range struck one of the cans and it ignited. He tried to throw the burning cans from the lorry, but the fire spread and the lorry blew up. He burned to death.'

The room fell silent. Vera said nothing, but she was certain the irony of his death escaped no one. He had burned and branded Sal in the worst possible way and now God had punished him.

'So will you think about bringing your boys home now?' Poppy asked.

Sal's face lit up. 'Well, that's what I was thinking,' she admitted.

'But is it the right time to be thinking of bringing them home to the East End?' Vera interjected. 'There may be fewer bombs now, but it's still not safe.'

'I know, and I've pondered the wisdom of it long and hard,' said Sal. 'But I'm the only parent they've got now, and when Reggie was alive, I was so petrified I was never a proper mum, not like they deserved. The guilt will never leave me.'

'Oh, poppycock,' scoffed Vera. 'You've always loved the bones of your lads, as well they know.'

'No, Vera,' Sal insisted, her voice thick with passion. 'You don't understand. I wasn't the mother they should have had: fear knocked the stuffing out of me. I was there, but never *really* there for them. I've got a lot of making up to do, and it might sound selfish, but I need them near me, now more than ever. I'm going to write to the postmistress they're billeted with and send her the train fare so they can return.'

Archie had remained silent up until now. 'Sal,' he said warily, 'I'm thrilled for you, love, that your life seems to be getting back on track, but what about work? Who's going to look after your boys? I need full-time workers right now.'

'Already looked into it, Mr Gladstone,' she replied. 'I've enrolled them both in the local primary school.'

Archie frowned. 'And if the school closes or gets bombed out? You know what the schools are like round here, Sal, there just aren't enough teachers to keep 'em open.'

'Then I'll go down the town hall and see what *can* be done,' she replied firmly. 'I heard on the wireless that the government's setting up hundreds of wartime day nurseries around the country providing childcare to free women like me up for war work. Why, there's one opening up right here in Bethnal Green! Tell me why I can't be a mum and work? Us women workers are the backbone of the home front, or so the government keep telling us.'

'Two lads and a job, though, Sal? It's a lot to cope with on your own,' he warned.

'She's not on her own, though, is she?' Poppy blurted, to everyone's surprise. 'We're all here, and we can help out with the boys. Vera's been feeding me since I arrived in the East End, and I'm sure she won't let Sal's boys go hungry. I'm happy to help out with caring for them. As long as we all pull our weight, Sal will manage. The East End looks out for its own – isn't that what you always say? Those lads mightn't have a dad anymore, but they've got a mum who loves them and two aunties on standby. Three when Daisy comes home.'

Poppy's face shone with determination as she gazed around the group. 'Coming here was the best thing that's ever happened to me. I feel as if I've got a proper family for the first time ever. Don't we owe it to Sal to reunite her family?'

Sal, Vera and Archie stared at Poppy, shocked but impressed with her forthright manner.

'Well said, Poppy,' Vera breathed admiringly. 'That's settled, then. They're coming home.'

'Thank you, girls,' Sal said gratefully. 'I just can't bear to be apart from my boys any longer.'

'Good, now please be seated for dinner,' Vera ordered. 'This stew's going cold.'

After Archie had said grace, he held his glass aloft. 'A toast, if I may, to Sal. I'm truly happy you're getting your family back, love. If anyone deserves some happiness, it's you.'

As everyone clinked glasses, Vera smiled along too, but she found her gaze drifting to the empty chair where Daisy usually sat. Poor Daisy. Just as Sal was making plans to be reunited with her children, Vera's sister was about to be wrenched apart from hers. It was all unutterably sad, and she prayed Daisy would find the strength to survive the heartache that lay ahead. For no one knew better than she the true price of such a selfless act.

*

Poppy had wolfed down her stew and couldn't wait to get back to the sanctuary of her digs. As wonderful as it was to see Sal making plans to rebuild her life, she was dying to get home so she could write another reply to Freddie. It was all she had been able to think of that day.

She had received his reply to her second letter yesterday, and already she had managed to read it so many times the pages were well thumbed. Sitting on the back of the bus as it trundled its way through Bethnal Green, she couldn't even wait to get home before fishing it out again for another look.

Well, I'll be. The Singer Girls indeed, he'd written in the same immaculate handwriting as his last letter, which was neatly folded on Poppy's bedside table.

> *That put a rare smile on my face. I imagine you all to look like nightingales now. I expect you're very pretty, Poppy, I'd love to see a photo if you could see your way to sending one. I hope I don't sound too forward when I say I love a curvier lady. Skinny girls with no meat on their bones wouldn't last two minutes out in the countryside. Rakes are for hoeing. Least, that's what Mother says.*

Poppy giggled, sighed dreamily and rested her head against the bus window before reading on.

> *Sitting here waiting for my leg to heal is so dreary. The nurses are super and all, but lying on your back staring at bare plasterboard is achingly dull. If I had your face to look at, life would look up no end. I can't believe my luck that I have you, such a lovely young lady with such similar interests to my own to write to. No one's ever written to me before and I think about you all the time. I'd truly love to be able to put a face to my thoughts.*

A deep flush spread over Poppy's cheeks at the thought of her face being pinned to a soldier's bedpost. Happen there was no harm in sending a photo, was there? There was a shop near the factory where she could get one done for a couple of pence. It's where all the girls went to have photos taken for their serving sweethearts. Chewing her lip slightly at the thought of what to wear, she read on.

> *In your letter, Poppy, you asked what I should like to do with my life once this war's over. Well, it looks as if I'll be demobbed as soon as I've healed. Not much call for crippled soldiers on the front line, I'm afraid. I've been told I'll most probably always walk with a limp now. I feel like such a coward, as if I'm abandoning the men I've served with from the start. I'm to be put on clerical duties in London for the remainder of the war. Not really something to boast about, but I suppose I should be thankful I am alive. It also means I can concentrate on finding myself a wife. Someone who preferably doesn't mind mud and would be happy living in the middle of*

nowhere. *Gracious, but I don't make it sound very enticing, do I? Perhaps I should take some tips from some of the silver-tongued GIs on the wards here. They seem to have a way with words and have the nurses eating right out of their hands.*

Righty-ho, well, I suspect I am waffling now. I await with much excitement your reply. Your letter really did make me most happy, Poppy Percival.

Yours gratefully,

Freddie xx

When the bus reached her stop, Poppy virtually floated off and ran all the way back along Burnham Street to her lodgings. Inside her room, she breathlessly removed the new writing pad she had purchased with what little money she had left from her wages and began to write, the words flying over the page in her haste to put them down on paper. Why was it, she mused, that she found it so much easier to express herself on paper than in person?

She wrote back with a little smile on her flushed face:

All right, then, Freddie, I'll get a photo taken, if that's what you really want. Though I think it's only fair to warn you I'm as plain as a pikestaff. Nowhere near as pretty as my good friend Daisy – she's the spit of Vivien Leigh. You'd fall in love with her if you saw her: men usually do; they fall at her feet.

Then there's Sal. I was scared of her when I first arrived in the East End. She's a force to be reckoned with, our Sal, though now I know her, I see she has a heart as soft as butter. She's potty about her two boys as well. She had them evacuated at the outbreak of the war, but now things have quietened down in the East End a little, she's making plans to have them returned. I can't wait to meet the little poppets. I do so hope I get the honour of bringing a child into the world. Could there be a bigger privilege? It's my dearest wish, and I hope to high heaven it will happen one day.

Poppy hesitated and nibbled the end of her pencil. There was more, of course, so much more. She wanted to tell him everything. The truth about why she had been banished to the East End, the real reason why the mere mention of her name probably still raised eyebrows in Little Framshalton, but she did not dare. She could spill all her secrets onto this page and, in doing so, free a little part of her soul forever, but she knew that would be utterly foolish if she wanted this fledgling romance to continue. Freddie seemed like a decent, upstanding chap. She would never hear from him again if she told him the dreadful truth about what really happened that night. So she tried her hardest to bury the past as always and keep her tone light and chatty.

Once I move back to the countryside, I suppose there will be plenty to keep me busy. Vera says I'm quite the seamstress now, so perhaps I shall get a job teaching needlework. There, now. That's another dream to cling to.

I do so hope you are away from danger now that you're in hospital. I await your next letter and, in the

*meantime, shall busy myself with getting a photo taken,
though please don't get your hopes up.*

Yours faithfully,

Poppy xx

Ever so carefully she folded the letter, planted a delicate
kiss on the seal and popped it in her bag ready to post the
following day. Next, she undressed and changed into her
white nightgown before snuggling down under the eiderdown and flicking off the little oil lamp by her bed.

In the darkness, her thoughts uncontrollably strayed, as
they always did, back to Norfolk. With her sense of sight
cut out, her imagination burst into life. She could see the
old kitchens back at Framshalton Hall as vividly as the day
she left over six months ago.

There was Cook's harassed voice ordering her to season
the dishes, the flash of copper pans through the steam and
the distant chiming of a gong. Then her thoughts turned
inevitably to the scullery. That hateful small, dark, window-
less room, a few feet lower than the kitchen so it was always
colder in there. Poppy shivered and pulled the covers a little
tighter, but it was no good. She felt it again, hot breath on
her neck, hands encircling her waist . . .

Gasping for breath, Poppy sat bolt upright in bed. What
on earth was she playing at with this Freddie chap? Had
experience taught her nothing? No good could come from
this liaison, and yet she knew that when tomorrow dawned,
she would post the letter.

Nineteen

It was Christmas Eve on the factory floor and Sal was tingling all over with excitement, for today was the day her boys were coming home to the East End at last. It had been a little over a month since she had written to the postmistress requesting their return, but it had been decided best all round that they be allowed to finish their term at the local village school and then arrive home in the holidays.

Sal had not dared to complain. She had waited so long anyway, what were a few extra weeks? Now, she stared out of the high factory windows at the soft snowflakes drifting down from the white skies and settling on the chimney pots outside. She sighed contentedly. At seven o'clock that evening, when she collected them from Paddington Station, she would be a proper mum again and she had years of love and cuddles to make up for. Reggie was gone for good. The dark spectre of his return no longer hung over her and for the first time in years, she felt free.

Sal's happiness was infectious and all the women were in high spirits, belting out a tuneful chorus of Bing Crosby's 'White Christmas' as it crackled out from the wireless tuned to *Music While You Work*. There were many other festive songs around, but that one was the Christmas favourite this year.

Archie had agreed to let everyone off work early if they finished their bundles, so the sounds of humming machines, laughter and song filled the air. The floor was a hive of industry and excitement. Even Vera sang along, exchanging a little smile with Archie as he passed by her desk. Sal chuckled to herself. There was no mistaking the look of pure adoration that took over her face.

Vera's whole persona was changing; her green eyes were softer, and even her scars seemed to have faded a little. It was obvious to everyone but Vera that she was in love. Why could she not see that Archie was a diamond in the rough?

'Sing as you sew, girls. Sing as you sew!' hollered Ivy from behind her machine.

Sal laughed along with the rest of the Singer Girls. They were all facing their fourth Christmas in wartime, and rationing was escalating something savage, but nothing could stop them from celebrating with a brave face.

Paper chains recycled from old bandage boxes were painted in bright colours and slung from the ceiling, and some wag had drawn a picture of Hitler and his cronies as donkeys, where at dinnertime a raucous game of pin the tail on the donkey would ensue. The war may have been grinding the nation down, but at Trout's everyone was working hard to bring back the magic and sparkle of Christmas.

There was just one person not joining in the festive fun. Sal glanced over at Poppy. Her young friend was lost in her own thoughts. Abruptly, Poppy put her arm up and requested a toilet break. When Vera granted it, she hurried from the floor, chewing her lip nervously as she went.

Poppy had received the letter from Freddie the previous evening, and after reading it, she knew she had no choice but to end their relationship without delay. The contents had sent her into spasms of anxiety all morning.

Hurrying across the yard, she gasped as the sharp December air hit the back of her throat like needles. Slamming the toilet door closed behind her, Poppy breathed hot air into her frozen hands and, with chattering teeth, fished the letter from her pocket.

Poppy, I'm afraid I must accuse you of being the most dreadful fibber. I received your letter and photo today, and well, I'm not one for smooth talk, as you must know by now, but you're right. You aren't pretty. You're beautiful! I simply can't believe you don't have a sweetheart and haven't been snapped up by some other lucky lad. You are just about all a man could want in a woman. You're funny, beautiful, loyal to your friends and kind of heart.

I hope you don't think me too forward – maybe it's all the morphine I'm on for my leg at the moment – but I do believe I'm falling for you, Poppy Percival. I'm most definitely not sending you a photo of myself or I fear I'll never hear from you again. Perhaps I'll send you a cut-out of that handsome actor chap – what's his name, Cary Grant? All the nurses gush about him here. Though I suppose I should send one of myself really, otherwise how on earth will you recognize me when we finally get to meet in the flesh? Yes, Poppy, that's right. At long last I have been told I am due to be discharged and flown home in March. March, Poppy, can you believe it? Just three months away. I'm beside myself with excitement. Nothing on earth would bring me more happiness than to meet you.

Letters are all well and good, but they are no replacement for the sound of your voice and to have the unending honour of meeting you. My heart beats fast at the very thought. I do so hope that is your wish also, and I am not being too forward in this suggestion.

Poppy stared down at the letter in her hand like it was a loaded grenade. This game was getting out of hand. She was toying with Freddie's emotions, for she'd had no intention whatsoever of meeting him in person. Hadn't she? That hadn't been her intention when she started writing letters. Or had it? Her brain started to spin with the repercussions of what she had instigated, but it always came back to the same point. She was simply too scared to meet him in the flesh. He had written that the thought of meeting her made his heat beat faster. It made Poppy shake in fear. With a soft moan of despair, she crumpled the letter into a ball in her fist and exited the toilet.

In her rush to get inside to the warmth of the factory, she didn't notice Sal and bumped straight into her. The note was knocked clean from her hands.

'What's this?' smiled Sal, reaching down to pick it up and uncreasing it. 'You got yourself a sweetheart? Fancy that! You told me at the party that no one had replied. Good thing I followed you out here. Spill the beans.'

'No one had replied back then,' Poppy whispered glumly. 'But then I wrote one more note and someone did reply. Ever such a lovely chap. Private Freddie Beecroft is his name. He's shy and sweet, a farmer's lad from Devon. He found my letter when he arrived injured at a hospital near the front.'

'Why, that's wonderful news,' gushed Sal brightly. 'I couldn't be happier for you. With any luck he'll get leave soon and then you'll get to meet him.'

'He's home in March. He wants to come to Bethnal Green and meet me.'

'But that's marvellous, surely?' said Sal.

'You don't understand, Sal. I can't meet him,' Poppy said.

'But why ever not?' she gasped. 'Especially if he's half the man you say he is. He sounds perfect for you. You deserve a little happiness, sweetheart.'

'I'm shy, Sal, you know that,' Poppy muttered, stamping at a little drift of snow on the yard floor.

Sal stared at her curiously, then took Poppy's chin in her hands and gently tilted her face so she was looking up at her. Snowflakes drifted down and settled on Poppy's lashes, framing blue eyes that shone with unshed tears. Sal longed to shake her secrets out of her.

'But it's not just that, is it, sweetheart? You can't pull the wool over my eyes. Do you remember all those months ago when I discovered you here alone sewing notes in bandages?'

Poppy blinked nervously but said nothing.

'Well, I do,' Sal said softly. 'You told me you were scared and I told you I was too. Even showed you my scars and confided in you about Reggie. You can tell me *anything*,

Poppy, and I will never stand in judgement over you,' she urged. 'Please tell me one good reason why you can't meet this Freddie chap and see if he isn't the one to sweep you off your feet.'

At Sal's show of kindness, Poppy choked back a sudden sob. 'I can't tell you, Sal,' she wept. Poppy suddenly felt suffocated by the power of her emotions; she longed to reach out and confide in Sal, the way she had in her, but all that came were tears, not truths.

Poppy started to shiver, the cold December air working its way into her bones, and Sal reached out and hugged her so tightly she felt the breath leave her body.

'I just hope one day you'll trust me enough to tell me what's really running through that head of yours,' she urged.

Pulling back from her embrace, Sal fixed a bright smile on her face. 'Look here, why don't you come with me to collect the boys later? That'll cheer you up.'

Poppy smiled for the first time since opening Freddie's letter. 'Oh, I should like that,' she replied, feeling a little brighter at the prospect.

When the final end-of-shift bell sounded, a loud cheer rang out through the floor as the Singer Girls downed tools and exchanged hugs and season's greetings. They only had Christmas Day off, but everyone was determined to enjoy it, and most of the workers were already heading to the door in a rabble of excited chatter.

'Now remember, girls,' said Vera, turning to Poppy and Sal, 'as soon as you've collected the boys, you're to come straight to mine.'

'You better had,' piped up Archie, as he went round

lovingly oiling all the sewing machines, like he did at the end of every shift. 'Vera's cooked enough food to sink a battleship.'

'Behave, Archie,' Vera said, but she couldn't stop herself from laughing. 'I just thought it'd be nice for the boys to get a good meal in their tummies after their long journey, and besides, I'm dying to see them.'

'Don't worry, Vera,' Sal smiled. 'We'll be there in a jiffy.' With that, she threaded her arm through Poppy's. 'Now come on, let's get going to the bus stop. Don't want to be late. I'm so excited my stomach feels like a bag of ferrets.'

Out in the street, Poppy and Sal weaved their way by the little row of local shops that had piled-up carrots in their windows in place of fruit in an effort to look decorative, past the local ARP centre, where the hopeful wardens had stuck mistletoe to the front of their helmets, and smiled cheerily at the bedraggled group of Salvation Army carol singers bravely facing the cold to bring a little festive cheer.

By the time they reached Paddington Station, the crowds had intensified, as hundreds of war-weary souls battled to make their way home for Christmas.

Poppy gazed about the steamy station concourse curiously. The last time she had been at a big station like this was after her arrival at St Pancras. How different a person she felt now compared to then.

Suddenly, a flash of blond hair and a shriek jolted her out of her reverie. A lump caught in Poppy's throat for there, tearing down the station platform out of the steam, were two freckle-faced, sandy-haired boys she recognized only from Sal's photos.

Sal collapsed to her knees and the boys flung themselves

into her outstretched arms like cannonballs, their faces ablaze with love and mischief.

Sal drew Billy and Joey into her and hugged them fiercely as her tears flowed freely.

'Oh, my darlings, I cannot tell you how much I've missed you,' Sal sobbed, kissing them over and over.

'Hi, Mum,' grinned Billy. 'Guess what? Joey ate all his sandwiches before we'd even pulled out of the station, so we're starving.'

'Just as well your auntie Vera's cooked up a feast,' she chuckled. 'Come on, let's get you back to Bethnal Green.'

*

By the time they made it to Tavern Street, Sal's happiness was complete, and they all trooped over the doorstep, grateful to be in the warmth of the welcoming little terrace.

'Hello, boys,' boomed Archie from the fireside. 'Remember me?'

'Course! Hello, Uncle Archie,' said Joey.

'You two still love them penny blocks of lemon ice?' he asked.

Two little heads nodded furiously.

'Come on, then, let's go up the corner shop and I'll treat you.' Archie smiled, holding out his hand to them.

Once they had left, Sal looked to Vera curiously.

'Sorry, Sal. It's lovely to have the boys back, but I wanted to have a moment alone with you two,' Vera explained. 'I've just received word that Daisy has given birth prematurely.' Vera held a letter aloft in her hand. 'It's from the matron of the mother and baby home. It was waiting for me when I got back from the factory.'

Poppy and Sal both gasped as one.

'Is she all right?' babbled Sal. 'What else does it say?'

'She's fine, and the baby's fine,' Vera reassured them. 'A little girl, called Hope, five pounds.'

'That's an unusual name,' Sal said.

'Certainly is,' agreed Poppy in excitement. 'But very pretty. Oh, I bet she's a little smasher. When do you think we can visit, Vera?'

Vera shook her head sadly. 'I'm afraid that's out of the question, Poppy. Daisy will stay at the home until Hope puts on weight and the midwife declares her well enough to be adopted. Then Daisy will return to Bethnal Green.'

'And then what?' asked Sal sadly.

'Well, she can't return to Trout's, of course,' said Vera. 'But Archie has a friend who owns a factory who will take her on. And life continues.'

'As if nothing ever happened?' Poppy said in dismay. 'Oh, poor Daisy. It's all just so dreadfully unfair. If only the American Army would give them permission to wed, then she need never suffer.'

'It's not just the American authorities, though, is it, Poppy?' Vera pointed out. 'Even if they did get permission to marry, Robert's colour is a huge issue. She and the baby will be treated as pariahs, and then there's the fact that Robert is to be sent off to fight, with no guarantees for his future. That's no life for an innocent child.'

'I'm sorry, Vera. I didn't mean to sound impertinent,' replied Poppy meekly. 'I think I might skip tea, I suddenly don't feel very well.'

With that, she turned on her heel and fled up the dark street.

'What on earth is wrong with Poppy?' asked Archie, coming the other way with Joey and Billy. 'I just called out to her, but she was in a right state, as skittery as a paper bag in the breeze.'

'It's Daisy's predicament,' Vera said sadly, as she stared up the street after Poppy. 'It's upset her more than I think any of us realize.'

*

Back at Burnham Street, Poppy didn't even take off her coat before she reached for her notepad. Without pausing to think, she picked up her pencil and began to write, her words tumbling out like tears. Life was so precious, she realized, and with all their worlds hurtling out of control, she needed to reach out to the one person with whom she felt she really connected.

Oh, Freddie, where can I even start? I've been the most dreadful fool. I started this relationship with you under false pretences. I love you too. Truly, deeply and with all my heart. I believe you can love a person you've never met before. I spend every second of every day thinking about you, imagining the happy life we could dream of together, but I am not the person you think I am.

I will meet you, dear Freddie, when you return to England, but only so I can tell you the whole story and at last be truthful to someone. I have no doubts you will

*walk away when you hear who, or rather what, I am.
I owe it to you and to myself to at last tell the truth.*

Yours, with foreboding,

Poppy xx

Poppy folded the sheet of paper and stuffed it into an envelope ready to post. It was time. He had to know the truth.

Twenty

The war raged on across the globe and by the time the freezing winter rolled around to a milder February, world events were taking a dramatic turn. Vera had listened, gripped, along with the rest of the nation as the German 6th Army surrendered at Stalingrad, the first defeat the Nazis acknowledged; British fleets and air forces advanced on the enemy in the Mediterranean; and Germany suffered heavy bombing. Vera had felt a sense of cautious optimism prevail in the factory and had smiled as she watched Sal lead a rousing rendition of 'When the Poppies Bloom Again'.

Seeing the blossoming of Sal from a scarred wife who lived in terror of her husband's return to a confident and happy mother was a joy to behold. Fortunately, for Sal at least, her suffering was over.

The matron of the home had written to Vera to tell her that Hope was doing well for a baby born so small, and that she was trying her hardest to secure a suitable couple to adopt. Vera prayed this would happen soon. Then at least Daisy could return to the East End and they could begin to put this nightmare behind them.

Vera found herself discussing it with Sal and Poppy over their dinner break one Saturday.

'I had a letter from Daisy yesterday,' Sal admitted.

'And?' said Vera warily.

Sal pulled the letter from her pocket and smiled reassuringly at Vera before she began to read.

Every day rolls out with the same routine here. We feed our babies before settling them back down in the nursery and go about our chores. Matron has it in for me. She's got me milking the cows. Me? I ask you. A girl from the East End who wouldn't know one end of a cow from another! If only you could see me, Sal, you wouldn't recognize me. Victory rolls and dances are a thing of the past. I've changed. I'm not the girl I once was, and that's down to Hope.

Oh, Sal, where do I even start? I might be biased, but she's the most beautiful, bonny baby ever. The midwife who visits every few days told me she is doing splendidly for a baby born so small and that's because of me and my care of her in the days after she was born. That's some comfort to me, because our contact with the babies is now limited to feed and nappy changes only. It's to prevent unnecessary bonding apparently. It's a little late for that, I fear.

The rest of the time, they're placed in a row of cots in the baby nursery, in a little line like soldiers. It's the most pitiful sight, Sal. Only the other day, a girl who I had grown quite fond of had to leave after her baby was handed over to a couple from Norfolk. You should have seen her. Broken, she was. Signing away all rights to her baby, well, it destroyed her. The night before the adoption, she sobbed non-stop into her pillow. It was heart-wrenching. I couldn't stand to hear her cries any longer, so I sneaked down into the nursery and just spent the whole night gazing down at Hope as she slept, relishing every second. Matron would have had my guts for garters if she'd found me, but I had to do it. She has Robert's eyes, you know, big and brown, and my chin. When I hold her in my arms to feed, it's like I'm holding a little piece of me. Does that make sense?

I don't know that I shall survive giving her up. The only saving grace is that I think it will take longer to find suitable adoptive parents for her because she's a chocolate baby. Hope's the 'wrong skin colour' apparently. Well, that suits me fine, and I'm just trying to live day to day. Although already I know time is running out.

Robert has written me many letters and is being very sweet, still insisting that he's going to marry me, but the reality is, there is nothing he can do for me and Hope right now. He's been posted to the south coast. I cling to the dream that I will see him again and that a solution will present itself to my predicament, but I suppose I need to start facing my problems head on, as Vera is so fond of saying. On the subject of which, please tell her I don't blame her for this, none of it. I know she was acting with my best interests at heart when she admitted me here. That night in the hotel, I know in my heart it was madness, and yet from it came Hope. The most incredible thing I've ever achieved in my life.

You're a mother, Sal; that's why I'm telling all this to you and not Vera, because I know you'll understand. I beg of you this – when I return to the East End, please don't treat me with pity, for I really don't think I shall be able to bear it.

Until then. Your friend,

Daisy x

When Sal finished reading, you could have heard a pin drop at the table.

'I don't wish to betray Daisy's confidence,' Sal said, 'but I read you that, Vera, because I thought you needed to hear it in order to understand how to treat her when she returns.'

Vera nodded. 'And I thank you for it, Sal. Sounds like she's grown up more in the past few months than the whole of her eighteen years.'

She drained her mug of tea and rose from the table shakily.

'And now, if you'll excuse me, I have urgent work to attend to. Only five minutes left of dinner break, girls. Mind you're not late back.'

After Vera exited the canteen, Sal shook her head and sighed.

'Dear old Vera. She's never been very comfortable with talking about her feelings, has she? She's a real East Ender in that respect.'

Poppy nodded. 'This must be terribly hard for her too,

though. She must be aware that Pat and the others are constantly talking about it behind her back.'

'Stuff 'em all,' announced Sal defiantly. 'The best way to deal with gossips is to ignore 'em. A fool's tongue will run before his feet. Now then, I hope you don't think I'm probing, Poppy, but I have to know. Have you come to any decision on whether to meet Freddie when he returns next month?'

Poppy looked up at her hesitantly.

'Well, yes, actually. I wrote back to him and . . .'

'Go on,' urged Sal.

'I told him I *would* meet him when he returns.'

'But that's wonderful news, Poppy,' grinned Sal, with a blazing smile.

'What if he doesn't like what he sees?' Poppy replied.

'How on earth could he not?' she protested. 'Look at you, you're everything a fella could want in a girl. You're going to make a smashing wife to some lucky chap.'

'If you say so, Sal,' replied Poppy, unsure. A shrill bell sounded through the canteen. 'Uh-oh, dinner break's over,' said Poppy, relieved to be ending the conversation.

'Very well, we'll leave it. For now,' Sal replied. 'But just remember, Poppy, secrets can be your jailor.'

*

Later that night, Vera heard the rap on the door and smiled nervously to herself as she quickly checked her appearance in the mirror.

'Stop acting like a silly little girl,' she scolded her reflection. 'It's only Archie.'

It was a Saturday night, and at long last, Vera had relented and agreed to allow Archie to escort her to the picture house.

On impulse, Vera had even dressed herself up a little bit. And now here he was, on the dot of eight thirty.

Vera opened the door and smiled.

'Good evening,' he said, his eyes twinkling with excitement as he held aloft two ticket stubs. 'Two tickets to see *Casablanca* at the Troxy. It's got that Ingrid Bergman in it. I think she looks a bit like you, Vera, though not quite as classy.'

'Get in, you daft beggar,' she chuckled, ushering him in. 'Let me just get my bag. I'll be one minute.'

Once the front door shut behind him and Archie's eyes adjusted to the light in the passage, his mouth fell open.

'Oh, Vera,' he breathed. 'You look absolutely beautiful. The green in that dress really brings out the colour in your eyes. It's a smashing rig-out.'

Vera blushed and fiddled with the clasp on her handbag. 'Behave, Archie. It's an old dress I made out of a pair of curtains twice remodelled, my hat's seen five summers, and these shoes have had more patch-ups than a Spitfire. It's nothing special.'

Archie smiled like a small child whose wish had finally been granted by Aladdin, and held out his arm to Vera. 'Well, I happen to think *you're* rather special. Let's step out, shall we?'

Vera had the most glorious evening and Archie was the perfect gentleman, even stopping on the way back to buy her a cup of tea and a sticky bun before walking her home. At the darkened doorstep, Vera hesitated.

'I'd invite you in, Archie, but I think this house has seen enough scandal. I don't want the neighbours to talk.'

'That's all right.' He smiled tenderly. 'I understand. Your happiness is so important to me, you see . . .' He hesitated and his craggy little face shone with sincerity. 'It's like this . . . Oh come on, Archie, you fool. What I'm trying to say, Vera, in a cack-handed way, is that I'd like to spend the rest of my days making you happy.'

Vera felt herself blushing for the second time in an evening, but then she spotted something that made her stare straight past Archie up the darkened street, her cheeks turning cold.

'Hush, Archie,' she ordered, gazing into the gloom. 'Is that a policeman?'

Archie's voice trailed off and he swung round to where Vera was looking.

Vera's heart sank as the officer drew closer and she recognized the same older police constable who had informed her of Frank's arrest.

'Good evening, Miss Shadwell,' said the constable. 'Apologies for disturbing you at this late hour, but may I come inside?'

Once indoors, Archie stuck protectively by Vera's side.

'I have some news regarding your father,' said the constable. 'He's due for release on 3 March.'

Vera could scarcely believe what she was hearing. 'But I thought he wasn't due out until April,' she gasped.

The police constable sighed in resignation. 'Like everywhere, the prisons are overstretched at the moment,' he explained. 'There simply isn't the manpower to staff them adequately with so many wardens conscripted, and as your father doesn't pose a *serious* threat to public safety, he is being released early. I thought you might like to be fore-warned.'

Vera was speechless as her brain attempted to digest the news.

'We appreciate you taking the time to let us know, Officer,' said Archie.

'Not at all,' he replied. 'I was passing on my beat anyway.'

After Archie had shown the constable out, he returned to find Vera pacing the kitchen, the smile from their pleasant evening replaced by a dark shadow of worry.

'Daisy,' she blurted fearfully, 'we have to get her home before Frank returns.'

With that her face paled. 'Oh dear God, he's coming home.'

'Calm down, Vera,' said Archie. 'You can use the telephone in my office tomorrow to call Matron and explain your predicament. I'm sure she'll understand and authorize Daisy to be discharged.'

Vera's heart started to beat fiercely in her chest.

'Well, she has to,' she replied shakily. 'Because if Frank discovers where she is, he'll go there himself and kill her with his bare hands. There is no time to lose.'

*

It was mid-morning on a Sunday, and after a visiting chap-lain had been to pray with the girls, Daisy had made to return to the common room when one of the domestic staff tapped her on the shoulder.

'Matron would like a word with you in her office, Daisy.'

Daisy felt her heart quicken as she hurried down the long corridor. She hoped and prayed her being summoned here this morning didn't mean that prospective adoptive parents had been found for Hope. Daisy took a deep breath before knocking.

'Enter!' called back a shrill voice.

Matron gestured to the seat opposite her desk and Daisy perched nervously on the edge of her chair, while the older woman consulted the manila files laid out before her.

'Hope is eight weeks old and thriving. We are satisfied with her weight and she is now as healthy as any other baby born at full term.'

Daisy's heart started to race as she waited for Matron to deliver the crushing blow.

'However, despite our best efforts, we haven't so far been able to secure a suitable couple to adopt her. No one has yet come forward. I warned you before her delivery that it is difficult enough during these trying times to find adoptive parents for any child, much less one of a coloured persuasion.

'Since you are not in a position to be able to offer a respectable home to this child, it falls to me to make suitable arrangements. I am not alone in this conundrum. One hears stories of other coloured illegitimate children with no one to take responsibility for their welfare. I can only hope that this serves as a valuable lesson to you on the repercussions of immoral behaviour.'

Daisy felt her face flush a furious red. She didn't view her romance with Robert as immoral. But Matron wasn't done with her yet.

'I have written to the general secretary of the Church of

England Moral Welfare Council, who advised me that Hope should be placed within a local authority home. One can only hope in time that mixed-race children will be viewed as casualties of war and perhaps sent back to their father's country of origin, where they might receive a better start in life.'

'Hope will be shipped to America?' blurted Daisy, unable to hide the horror in her voice.

'Her long-term future is not certain,' Matron replied tersely. 'All we know is that shortly she will be transferred to a local home and cared for there until the government decides what to do with these children. You, in the meantime, shall leave tomorrow.'

Matron carried on talking, but Daisy had stopped listening. She was drowning in misery and disbelief. After she was dismissed, she left the office in a trance and went straight to the baby nursery. She would be in line for a roasting if any of the staff spotted her coming in here outside of feed times, but what did it matter? As of tomorrow, her life was over anyway.

There was Hope in her cot, ready to be packed off to some godforsaken home where she would be treated like an orphan. Now, as always, her beauty and innocence took Daisy's breath away.

Daisy crept to her cot feeling like a fugitive and gripped the iron bars for support. For once, Hope wasn't asleep. Her deep brown eyes were wide open, her chubby legs kicking out against her nest of blankets as she gazed about her surroundings looking for Daisy's face.

Hope had only been in this world eight weeks and already Daisy could not imagine a life without her. Her daughter was exquisite and had utterly beguiled her. From her tiny rosebud lips to the minuscule fingernails that topped each delicate finger, she was perfection.

The centre of Daisy's universe had shifted. Nothing came close to touching the love she felt for her child. Not the distant memory of her mother, or even the passion in her heart for Robert.

How could she part with this little girl? How? It was just one more unfathomable cruelty in this whole senseless chapter of her life.

Stifling a sob, she plucked Hope from her cot and lifted her reverently to her face, gently nuzzling her with her nose, kissing her soft, downy head over and over, as if trying to drink in the smell of her.

At the feel of Hope's velvet soft skin against hers, Daisy could no longer stem the flow of hot tears that trickled down her cheeks, but she angrily brushed them away. Nothing would obscure her view; she wanted to commit every last inch of Hope to memory.

Searing agony ripped through Daisy's heart.

'Mummy has to leave tomorrow. I'm so sorry,' she sobbed. 'If there was any other way, my darling . . . I hope one day you'll understand and forgive me.'

The next day, Daisy took her leave of the home for unmarried mothers and felt as if she had been cut open. A little piece of her soul would now be missing forever.

Twenty-One

Two weeks later, Frank Shadwell was released from his confinement. A sulphurous spring rain drummed on the cobbles as Vera opened the door to find her father standing on the doorstep, a satisfied grin stretched over his face.

Vera's first thought was that his incarceration had physically done him good. Daisy's spell in the unmarried mothers' home had left her paler and thinner than Vera had ever seen her. In the two weeks since she had arrived home, she had drifted about the place like a ghost, barely eating or drinking. In the mornings, she went to work at the new factory and returned home each night to shut herself away in her room with scarcely a word passing her lips.

In stark contrast, Frank's time at His Majesty's pleasure had left him with more meat on his bones. His face was fuller, and he was squeaky clean from regular washing in the prison yard, but when he opened his mouth, Vera realized that he was still the same old Frank on the inside.

'Bleedin' hell,' he growled, pushing past Vera. 'I must have the luck of nine blind bastards to have to come home to a face like that.'

In the kitchen, Daisy looked up in terror. 'Hi, Dad,' she said weakly.

'Look at the state of you,' he mocked, when he set his eyes on his younger daughter. 'You're a bag of bones. Vera not been feeding you?'

'Just been working hard,' she replied quietly.

'Good. Well, I'm home now and I'm going to be keeping close tabs on the both of you. I'm laying down the law as from now. This is my house and I'm your father and I demand respect,' he hissed. 'And I don't want that busy-body Archie from the factory trying to get his feet under my table neither. He's banned from this house from now on. Understood?'

Vera nodded miserably.

'Good,' he said. 'Now, fetch me some breakfast. I'm starving.'

As Vera walked to the range and set about preparing her father's breakfast, a terrible, haunting fear unfurled in her heart. Just what would she have to do to end that man's reign of cruelty? For the last few months she had been given a tantalizing glimpse of what her future could be like. A life lived away from her father's terrifying control. Her hidden feelings for Archie, her sister's illegitimate child, the legacy of her past . . . all were secrets that her brutal father would surely unearth over time. Their home would become a toxic melting pot of fear, secrets and recrimination, and she had to find a way to get her and Daisy away from it. Their very lives depended upon it.

*

Across town, Poppy was also waking up to a sharp realization. It was Wednesday 3 March. The day had finally dawned. The day when she was due to meet Private Freddie Beecroft in the flesh. By five that morning, she had tired of trying to sleep and had leaped out of bed and ripped down the blackout blinds.

Sal was right. Poppy had indeed been a prisoner to her own thoughts, and though a part of her longed to live a normal life, she knew she was a long way from what could ever be described as normal. Freddie was sure to see that the moment he set eyes on her. His new life back on British soil was just beginning, just as hers felt like it was about to self-destruct.

Sighing, she fixed herself a weak cup of tea, scraped a bit of butter over a slice of wholemeal bread and pulled out his last letter.

My dearest Poppy,

I implore you, whatever it is you have to tell me surely cannot be that bad. You say you are not who you seem, but in your letters you are the sweetest girl I can imagine. It is only the image of your lovely face that has sustained me in my hospital bed. I simply don't care what it is you are hiding, for I know I can forgive you just about anything. On 3 March, I will be in London to find out which administrative office I am to be stationed at for the duration of the war. I would like to suggest meeting outside the entrance to Bethnal Green Tube Station at 8 p.m. I know what you look like, but alas, you don't know what I look like, so I will be carrying a red flower. I still walk with a slight limp.

*I cannot wait to meet the girl I have fallen in love
with. The girl of my dreams. You, Poppy Percival.
Please show up. I will be waiting, all night if need
be, and together we can find a way out of your
unhappiness.*

Yours with anticipation,

Freddie xx

Poppy's stomach lurched and she pushed away her meagre
breakfast. She was almost sick with fear at the thought of
meeting Freddie. She must have been out of her mind to
start stitching secret letters to soldiers in bandages with no
thought as to where it could lead. No. She would not go to
the Tube station that evening. He could wait all night, for
she would not show up. She had locked her pain away and
no one, not even someone as wonderful as Freddie, could
touch it.

*

Sal found herself first on shift that morning. The factory
floor was still near deserted when Poppy walked in.

'Hello, ducks. How's yourself?' she chirped. 'I saw a
clump of gorgeous golden crocuses sprouting out of a bombsite of all places. I picked them for you.' With a flourish,
she produced the cheerful yellow flowers from behind her
back. 'Ta-da!' she grinned. 'When I saw these things nodding
in the wind, I says to myself, It's a sign. We're going to win
this war.'

Poppy smiled weakly. 'Thanks,' she mumbled. 'You shouldn't have.'

Determined to elicit more of a response, Sal pressed on. 'Did you hear the news? Our boys bombed Berlin two nights ago. Means we'll cop it tonight I shouldn't wonder. If the sirens go off tonight, don't shelter with that awful landlady of yours – make sure you come with me and the boys down Bethnal Green Tube. Shouldn't think we can persuade Vera and Daisy to join us, but I'll give it a go. It'll be heaving at the Tube, but if we sing loud enough, we should be able to drown out the bombs.'

Poppy's face paled. 'I . . . I can't go there,' she whimpered. Before Sal had a chance to ask her why, Poppy turned and ran across the factory floor towards the stairs.

Sal walked to the window and stared in astonishment as Poppy fled through the yard to the toilet block. 'Oh, for pity's sake,' she muttered under her breath. 'I've had enough of this.' Sal took the stairs two at a time and flew across the yard into the lavatory. She pushed the door open with a clatter.

The retching sounds from the locked cubicle stopped her in her tracks. 'Poppy,' she called. 'Are you being sick?'

It was a full five minutes before Poppy shakily emerged from the toilet. When Sal set eyes upon her, her hand flew to her mouth. Poppy was a wretched sight. Her eyelids were ringed with red dots, and her blue eyes seemed lost in the pallor of her face.

'Poppy, you look terrible,' she gasped.

'I must have a stomach bug,' she muttered, carefully wiping her face on the edge of a roller towel.

Taking a deep breath, Sal looked her in the eye. 'I didn't

come down in the last shower, you know, Poppy,' she said firmly. 'I'm not moving from this spot until you tell me what's wrong, and don't try fobbing me off either. I recognize fear when I see it. I've known something was wrong ever since I caught you sewing notes into bandages that night. This problem of yours isn't going to go away, is it?'

Sal's words were rapid as she urged Poppy to spill her secrets. 'Please, Poppy, just tell me,' she begged. 'No woman is a blank page.'

Poppy leaned back heavily against the white tiled wall and closed her eyes. 'All right,' she groaned eventually. 'I will tell you. Tonight's the night I'm supposed to be meeting Freddie, but it's impossible, you see, because . . .'

Sal scarcely dared breathe for fear of interrupting her. Only the dripping of a leaky tap echoed throughout the toilets. Instinct told her she wasn't going to like what her young friend was about to tell her, but there was no way out of here for either of them now.

'Well, because . . . my mother didn't really send me here to see another way of life,' Poppy said, staring hard at the floor. 'She sent me away because I brought shame on her and Lord Framshalton's whole family. I did something awful, Sal.'

Nervously, Poppy started to pick at a loose tag of skin by her chewed thumbnail, and a solitary tear slid down her cheek.

'Whatever it is, darling, it can't be that bad,' soothed Sal.

'Oh, but it is, Sal. Much worse than you can ever imagine,' Poppy replied.

The silence stretched on forever, but Sal knew better

than to break it. If she put the slightest pressure on her timid friend, she would bolt.

'I was working late one night, washing up in the scullery,' she whispered at last. 'His Lordship had been entertaining after one of his shooting parties and there was no end of dishes to be done. It sounded like they were having a gay old time. I could hear the laughter drifting down from the dining room even as far as the scullery. That's why I didn't hear him behind me until he was nearly on top of me.'

Poppy's chest heaved and Sal half wondered if she wasn't about to be sick again. Instead, she carried on picking at the wretched bit of skin, her slight fingers trembling as she burrowed compulsively into the flesh.

'He pushed me back against the wall . . . He . . . he put one hand over my mouth. His breath smelt of brandy and cigars. I couldn't breathe,' she gasped, frantic now with panic. 'I couldn't breathe.'

'Who was he, Poppy?' Sal urged. 'What happened?'

'His Lordship's son and heir, Edward Framshalton. He was strong. Too strong. I didn't struggle. He told me . . .' She broke off and more tears flooded her cheeks.

'Go on,' Sal whispered.

'He told me he'd seen me about the place, that I was lucky to have caught his eye. Then he ripped up my skirt.' She closed her eyes. 'He forced himself on me.'

By now Poppy was weeping unashamedly, trembling in terror as she held on to the wall for support.

In horror, Sal realized Poppy was reliving the moment. She was no longer with Sal in the toilets but back there in the gloom of the Norfolk scullery.

'I closed my eyes and prayed for it to be over,' she

whispered. 'All I could smell was the distemper on the walls, such a queer smell, fetid and rank. I can smell it now, you know. It's my abiding memory.'

Sal fought the urge to scream as she pictured Poppy's sweet apple cheeks forced up against a damp scullery wall. In that split second she felt as if she might melt right into a puddle on the floor. Little Poppy Percival was the sweetest, most lovable person she had ever come across. That something so evil and poisonous should happen to her was beyond all imagining.

'When . . . when he was finished, he told me I was a silly little girl for leading him on and he was only taking what was his by right. Except when he walked out, he bumped into the hall boy.'

'But surely he heard. Didn't he do anything?' cried Sal in frustration.

'But that's just it, Sal,' wept Poppy. 'Heard what? I never screamed. I didn't make so much as a murmur. I saw His Lordship through the crack in the door. He winked and nudged the hall boy, told him we'd been having a bit of fun, but that it was to go no further. He even tucked a pound note into the hall boy's pocket and told him he was sure he could trust him to keep our affair secret. Man to man.

'Course, servants being what they are, the news was all over the servants' hall by noon the next day. I was dismissed by evening service and my mother notified. She told me she'd never be able to forgive me for my scandalous conduct, or for jeopardizing her position as Her Ladyship's maid, and I had left her no choice but to be sent away. My feet barely touched the ground. She's not written to me once in all this time.'

Sal shook her head and felt disgust and anger crawl over her.

'He took advantage of you. He forced himself on you. You are sixteen, for pity's sake. That was no affair, and as for your mother . . .' Sal's voice trailed off in disgust.

Poppy looked up despairingly. 'But don't you get it, Sal? It is my fault. I led him on. He told me so himself.'

'Of course he would, the rotten swine!' yelled Sal, feeling a steady rage build in her chest. 'He'd have done anything to defend his position. He's an animal.'

'And besides,' Poppy added sadly, as though Sal hadn't even spoken, 'I did nothing to stop it, did I? I never even cried for help. Maybe, maybe that means I did ask for it.'

'Oh, Poppy,' Sal moaned, closing her fist and punching it against the wall, 'don't you see? This isn't your fault. That man should have been prosecuted for what he did to you. Bloody gentry, forcing himself on you and telling you it was his right. He probably believed it himself, the over-privileged fool. You never made a sound because you were paralysed with fright. That's what fear does to you, Poppy – it knocks the stuffing out of you. You know the times I've looked back and wondered why I never fought back against my Reggie when he gave me a hiding? Because I was rigid with fear. I couldn't have moved if I wanted to.'

'It doesn't matter now,' replied Poppy sadly. 'I'm tainted. So you see why I can't meet Freddie tonight? Once he sees how damaged I am, he'll know me for the fraud I really am.'

'Well, that makes me a fraud too in that case,' Sal replied, gazing deep into Poppy's eyes. 'Except I don't really see it that way. I'm not damaged, you see. I survived.'

'What . . . what do you mean, you too?' Poppy asked incredulously.

Sal nodded. 'My Reggie repeatedly forced me against my will during our marriage. I survived, just as you have, and I reckon that makes us pretty tough.'

'I suppose,' Poppy nodded. 'I never really saw it that way before.'

By the time Sal got the rest of the truth out of Poppy about the rendezvous outside Bethnal Green Tube, she was certain of one thing.

'You are meeting Freddie tonight, Poppy,' she stated firmly. 'That posh animal may have stolen something precious from you, but don't let him steal your future.' Digging out a hanky, she handed it to Poppy. 'Dry your eyes, sweet girl. I know you're hurting right now, but trust me on this. What men inflict on you is never your fault. The devil has many guises. This Freddie could be one of the good ones. I promise I'll be right there with you to make sure of it.'

'You'll come too?' asked Poppy, a glimmer of hope shining in her eyes for the first time.

'I'll walk with you, then wait and watch at a safe distance. If you feel panicked, just give me a signal – touch your ear or something – and I'll be right there by your side.'

'I'm not sure.' Poppy sighed.

'I care deeply about you, we all do, and we just want to see you happy,' said Sal softly. She hesitated before placing a gentle arm around Poppy's trembling shoulders.

'Thank you, Sal,' Poppy replied in a tiny voice. 'You know, I always used to feel like I was on the outside looking in when I was around you all, but I don't think I shall feel like that anymore.'

Sal smiled and brushed away her tears. 'Good. Now come on, best get going. Vera's probably clocked on by now and you can guarantee she'll notice we're gone. And your secret's safe with me. Us survivors got to stick together.'

*

Poppy had thought the day would never end, but at last the final shift bell sounded. She jumped from her seat, her nerves jangling nearly as loudly as the bell.

Sal appeared by her side. 'Ready?' she smiled reassuringly.

'No,' Poppy muttered.

'Come here,' Sal smiled, pulling out a comb from her handbag and gently brushing out Poppy's fine brown hair. 'Let's see if we can't make this Freddie chap fall a bit more in love with you.'

The gesture was so comforting that Poppy felt her nerves subside.

'But what about your boys?' she asked, suddenly remembering that Sal usually tore out of the factory like her heels were on fire to get home to them.

'Don't worry – I've thought of that,' she soothed, and then, turning to where Vera was fastening her coat, she called out, 'Vera, would you fetch the boys and take them home with you? There's an urgent errand I have to run, but I shan't be long.'

'Course, Sal, but mind you're not. There's talk of a raid tonight.'

'Indeed there is,' piped up Archie, who was listening in.

'There's bound to be reprisals over us bombing Berlin. I might head down the Tube now, secure a bunk. Vera, you sure you won't come?'

'You know how I feel about being underground, Archie,' she replied. 'Me and Daisy will take our chances under the stairs.'

Poppy could see she was in a chippy mood. She knew that Frank had been released from prison that very morning. The tension of his release hung over her head like a rain cloud, but for once Archie was in no mood to humour her.

'You're as stubborn as a mule at times, Vera,' he muttered.

'Oh, is that right, Mr Gladstone?' she said in a low warning voice.

Poppy winced. Whenever she used his full name, it usually meant he was about to get a royal ticking-off.

'Well, if I'm a mule, that must make you an ass,' she snapped back.

'Don't be so trite, woman,' Archie answered crossly. 'I hate to think of you there if the sirens go off. Doubly so now your father's out of prison. Please,' he urged. 'There's plenty of room at the Tube, and if we leave now, there'll be time to get you all a bunk.'

'Listen to me,' Vera blazed. 'In here you may be my boss, but outside of this factory, I'll decide what's best for my family. I've never needed a meddling man about the place to tell me what to do, and I certainly don't need one now.'

He glared at her despairingly. 'I'm just trying to look out for you, Vera – that's all I've ever done – but if that's the way you want it, then I give up!' he yelled, throwing his hands in the air in defeat.

'Good,' she snapped before turning her back on him.

'Good,' he mirrored angrily, picking up his coat and marching from the room. The door frame rattled as he slammed the door shut.

Sal sighed heavily. 'Those two want their heads knocking together. When will Vera see what's best for her?'

Glancing at the clock on the wall, she took Poppy's arm. 'But never mind that. It's *your* love life we should be worrying about.' She winked. 'It's five past eight already. He'll be waiting. You've got a date with destiny.'

The rain started to fall softly as they made their way down the street towards Bethnal Green Tube Station. It was a dank, dreary and wet night. Poppy could feel her freshly brushed hair turning to a sticky mess in the rain. She sighed. What did it matter? Freddie was bound to take one look at her and realize he had made a dreadful mistake anyway.

As they neared the Tube, they became aware of hordes of people all brushing against them in the dark, and all heading in the direction of the station too. The pavement chimed with the sound of wet shoes slapping against concrete. Poppy could feel hot breath billowing against her cheek.

'Blimey, lot of folk out tonight. Must all have the same idea.' Sal's voice rang out next to her.

'It is busy,' Poppy agreed. 'I probably won't be able to find him in this. I think I'll head home.'

She felt Sal's hand clamp tightly round her wrist. 'You'll do no such thing, young lady. You're meeting him, if only to say hello. He's come a long way to see you.'

Poppy sighed and kept walking, resigned to her fate now. The rumbling of buses pulling to a stop nearby told

Poppy they had arrived at the Tube. She felt her legs go weak and nearly buckle beneath her.

'I'll try and stay close so I can see you, check you're all right. Now go, and good luck,' urged Sal's voice through the darkness.

At the Tube entrance, Poppy deftly stepped to one side to avoid being sucked into the slipstream of people heading down into the darkness. Gazing around the crowded entrance to the Tube, she felt uneasy. Nineteen slippery steps led down to a small landing, fifteen by eleven feet, which was lit by a dim twenty-five-watt bulb, partially painted black to comply with the blackout rules. It was a gloomy and forbidding stairway. Sal and the other girls at the factory were forever on about what a danger it was, what with the sheer weight of people who made their way down those steps night after night to shelter.

What a ridiculous place to arrange a meet. Why hadn't she written and arranged another place to rendezvous, or better yet, called it off altogether?

A fug of heat and that peculiar acrid smell of hundreds of damp unwashed bodies all pressed together drifted up the narrow stairwell to greet her. Sal had said there were bunks for 5,000 down there, and she had heard tell the tunnel had no tracks as it wasn't yet a working Tube station, just row upon row of triple bunks, chemical loos and even a library. By the loud swell of cockney chatter that seemed to rise up from the very bowels of the earth, she didn't doubt it. It barely seemed credible that such a tiny entrance could be the solitary gateway to a small subterranean town.

Chewing her lip hard, she scanned each face as it loomed out of the dark, looking for any glimmer of recognition from the passer-by, but every face was too preoccupied, gazing down at the rain-spattered ground so as not to lose their footing and fall. There was no central handrail, so people were forced to rely on sight alone to feel their way down into the inky darkness.

Suddenly, a voice rang out, unfamiliar, with the soft, lilting tones of a West Country accent. 'P-Poppy? Is that you?'

The hesitant voice emerged from the gloom and suddenly, there he was, standing just inches in front of her. Poppy felt her heart turn to water.

'Freddie?' she breathed. 'Is that really you?'

'Poppy?' He smiled back shyly. And all at once, Poppy was overcome with a rush of emotion so powerful she couldn't put a name to it. Not fear, not panic, just a blissful feeling of reassurance. She didn't know how, but instinctively she was sure this was a man with whom she could feel safe.

'You came,' he smiled, gingerly holding out a red flower. 'For you,' he added, and Poppy noticed his hands were trembling as he handed it to her. Her heart went out to him. He was right. He wasn't handsome, not in the traditional sense at least. A thick head of dark hair had plastered itself to his face in the damp air, and his spectacles were steamed up, giving him a strange vulnerable quality. A deep red flush was creeping up his neck as he gazed at her adoringly.

'I look like a drowned rat,' she giggled.

'Me too,' he laughed, adding hastily, 'That is to say, you don't look anything like a rat, drowned or otherwise. You're, well, you're just as beautiful as in my dreams . . . Gosh, that sounds corny.'

'Your leg?' she asked, suddenly remembering his injury. 'Are you in pain?'

'This old thing?' he laughed, tapping his leg. 'Not really. Got another one. I'm such a clod it was bound to happen . . .' His voice trailed off. 'I'm frightfully nervous.'

'That's all right.' Poppy smiled back warmly. 'So am I. Come on, shall we get out of here? It's awfully crushed.'

'Yes, let's,' Freddie agreed. Turning, they tried to push their way against the crowd of people, back down the street.

At that moment, the low wail of a siren went off.

'Oh no,' gasped Poppy.

Freddie grasped her hand. 'Where shall we shelter?' he asked. 'Down there, or somewhere else?'

'Sal, where's Sal?' she babbled. 'I have to find her before we go anywhere.'

He looked at her, confused. 'Who's Sal?'

'She's my friend. Remember, I told you about her in my letters? She was waiting here to make sure that everything was all right. We can't go without her. Let's just wait. She'll be here any second.'

'All right, Poppy,' he agreed cautiously. 'But not too long, I should like to get you to safety.'

Poppy's foot tapped the pavement impatiently as the siren wailed on relentlessly. 'Come on,' she muttered, scanning the street frantically. 'Show yourself, Sal.'

At that moment, three buses stopped at once and the already crowded pavement was flooded with sticky bodies clutching bundles, all bumping and jostling to get underground.

'Oh no,' Poppy panicked. 'She'll never be able to see us now.'

A mother rushed past Poppy clutching a wailing baby and a bundle of bedding. As Poppy gazed on the baby's face, a strange thing happened. Out of nowhere a prickle of fear ran up her spine. Shuddering, she felt as if someone had just walked over her grave. She had the most terrible premonition.

'Poppy,' urged Freddie, 'I really think we ought to—'

He never finished his sentence.

The whoosh rippled through the station at the speed of sound and the very earth beneath their feet shook. The force and penetrating noise seemed to lift Poppy's hair clean off her scalp and she felt as if her eyes were being sucked from their sockets. She reached out to clutch Freddie's chest and steady herself while her ringing ears adjusted. What on earth was that? It sounded like hundreds of rockets whistling down to earth.

Out of the dark sky, heavy metal pipes rained down like confetti, pinging on the pavement around them. The crowd froze as one and there was a sickening moment of horror.

Poppy stared up at Freddie. He stood stunned and blinked wildly through the cracked lenses in his glasses.

'It's a bomb,' shouted a woman nearby.

'We're under fire,' shouted another.

The crowd surged forward as one, frantic to get underground to safety.

Poppy and Freddie found themselves lifted clean off the ground by the sheer weight of human traffic. Frantically, Poppy wriggled and struggled to free herself, but the wall of bodies heading down to the stairs was solid as a rock. They were trapped. The force was too immense, and as they reached the top of the gloomy stairwell and Poppy saw the unfolding scene, a scream caught in her throat. Freddie saw it at the same time as her and his face froze. It was the very image of hell.

The woman and her baby who had passed by Poppy not one minute before had tripped at the bottom of the flight of stairs and were sprawled in the stairwell. Before they could get up, others were falling over them. The stairway was soon a seething mass of screaming men, women and children. The pile-up caused a human-domino effect all the way back up the narrow stairwell. Down they went, one by one.

A crush of people desperate to get downstairs just added to the scenes of despair. In horror, Poppy realized Freddie was getting sucked down faster, his body moving away from her.

'Poppy!' he gasped. Reaching his hand out over the bodies, his fingers made a grab for her. Thanks to his cracked spectacles he'd partially lost his vision, but his grip was strong and his fingers laced through hers and held on tight.

'I'm not letting go!' he shouted above the roar.

As they moved forwards, everything seemed to go into slow motion. Poppy had the strangest sensation she was drifting along a river that was about to cascade into a water-fall. And then she tipped over the edge and found herself sucked helplessly into the seething pit of flailing bodies.

It could have been minutes; it could have been hours. Time lost all meaning as she drifted in and out of consciousness. She was aware of nothing. Not the great crush of people, the tangle of twisted limbs or the immovable weight pinning her to the stairwell. Just the muffled groans of strangers clinging to life, attempting to claw their way out of the hell. Chaos swirled as desperate cries for help pierced the air.

Curled into the foetal position, Poppy found she had a small pocket of air from which to breathe and gratefully gulped in, but as she lifted her head an inch off the floor, she quickly realized it was futile. This narrow corridor was turning into a charnel house before her eyes. The faces squashed around her bulged in terror, slowly turning lilac as the air was forced from their lungs; protective arms thrown around loved ones were now squeezing the life out of them. Blood-curdling screams turned to groans, then silence. The interlaced mass of bodies was five, six or more deep. They were all trapped. It was too terrifying for words. Poppy could stand to watch no longer and closed her eyes, waiting for the merciful moment death would claim her.

How poignant, she thought as the oxygen slowly left her brain, that in the very moment she should find the love of her life, she should lose him again. Love and loss all wrapped up in the same haunting heartbeat.

A tugging at her hand roused her and her eyelids, swollen and thick with grime, opened a crack. The tugging grew stronger. Her foggy brain struggled to make sense of what was happening. And then she was moving. Was she alive or dead? Strong arms were hooked under her armpits and she was being hauled up and out. Up, higher and higher over the bodies. Then hands were gripping her waist, encircling her, and she was swooped up into the air.

'Poppy,' chimed a distant voice, 'hold tight. I've got you. You're safe.'

Blearily she came to in Freddie's arms. His face gazed down at her, full of love and relief.

'I thought I was going to die,' she croaked.

Tears coursed down his cheeks as he walked away from the crush, deeper into the Underground station, holding on to her for dear life.

'I couldn't let that happen,' he sobbed. 'I've only just found you. I wasn't going to lose you so soon, Poppy Percival.'

At last, they found a spot by the ticket hall and gently he laid her down. In stunned silence they watched the scenes.

Frantically, rescuers attempted to pull free those trapped at the bottom of the crush. Poppy recognized a local warden by the name of Mrs Chumbley forcibly wrenching children and babies free with her bare hands. It was unbridled pandemonium. Poppy squeezed her eyes shut in horror against the image.

'Are you feeling all right now, Poppy?' he asked. 'It's just that if you are . . .'

Their thoughts were the same.

'Go,' she urged. 'You must go and help the others.'

She watched as Freddie, her hero, ran as fast as he could on his crippled leg back across the hallway in the direction of the crush and joined the rescuers.

Twenty-Two

Sal watched the unfolding scene in total disbelief. Her brain felt as if it were still rattling in her head from the noise of the blast. She had spied from the shadows as Archie, then Ivy and Betty from Trout's had hurried in the direction of the Tube with their bundles of bedding and pillows.

It had taken every ounce of self-restraint not to go to Poppy and comfort her when she had spotted her looking panicked. Then at last Freddie had arrived. Watching them lock eyes and smile at one another, Sal had known in a heartbeat that Poppy was safe with him. Except now she was in peril.

Suddenly, her body was galvanized into action.

'Out of my way!' she screamed, pushing her way to the mouth of the Tube. 'My friends are in there. I've got to help.'

But it was useless, with the weight of people forcing her back. It was bedlam: there must have been nearly three hundred people crushed in the stairwell and clamouring outside the entrance. The distant clanging of ambulance and fire-engine bells arriving on the scene mingled with deafening screams.

In all her days, Sal had never witnessed scenes like it. Desperate men dived into the crowds to pull free their loved ones; shoes flew through the air; bodies lay tangled and jumbled. She even saw a leg poking out of the crush, twisted round at an absurd ninety-degree angle. Others had climbed to the very top of the pile of bodies and were attempting to extricate loved ones from the tangle of limbs and torsos.

Rescuers formed a human chain that started at the entrance to the Tube and snaked back along the pavement, in an organized bid to free people from the crush. Every now and again, a person would be wrenched from the pile with such force their shoes would be left behind. There was no time even to take pulses, and bodies were being laid out by the railings to Barmy Park on Green Street, dead or alive.

'Go home, lady,' ordered a fireman, as he rushed past Sal. 'This is no place for a woman.'

'Go home? Not bloody likely,' she muttered. Sal hadn't survived the Blitz and a marriage to Reggie to come over all faint at a time like this. 'I'm helping and that's that.'

Gripping the arm of a passing ARP warden, she stopped him in his tracks. 'I'm here to help. What can I do?' she asked breathlessly.

'We need transport to get people to hospital. Gather whatever you can find,' he urged.

And so for the next two hours, Sal worked tirelessly in the dank darkness, flagging down cars, trucks, whatever means and method she could, to help to transport the dead and injured to hospital. As the human chain of rescuers piled up the bodies against the railings, two things quickly became apparent. Firstly, no one knew if they were dead or alive. Their faces were so swollen and disfigured and their breathing so shallow it was almost impossible to tell. And secondly, the body count far exceeded the transport available. In no time at all, there was a line of bodies snaking along the road by the park. Sal watched in growing panic. If they hadn't already died of their injuries, hypothermia from lying on a cold, wet pavement would finish them off.

'Quick,' she urged, leaping into the road and hammering on a passing car window. 'You have to help get these people to hospital. Bethnal Green Hospital or the children's hospital.'

Sal did what she could, running to nearby rest centres and banging on strangers' doors to gather as many blankets and as much water as she could find to tend to the survivors. Despite the atrocities she was witnessing, a guilty feeling of relief nagged at the back of her brain. Thank goodness her boys were home safe with Vera. If she had not insisted on accompanying Poppy, the chances were that they would all have been stuck down there in the crush of bodies. As for Poppy, Freddie, Archie, Ivy and Betty, she just prayed they had escaped in time and that the next dead body she saw would not be one of theirs.

More and more people had come from their homes and were trying to help. It was all hands to the pump. Men and women ran down the middle of the street dodging cars, pulling handcarts and pushing barrows to load bodies onto. ARP wardens in tin hats worked alongside housewives in aprons. Heartbreakingly, even children had pitched in to help, and Sal gasped when she saw two Boy Scouts barely older than her Billy helping injured children onto barrows and running at full pelt with them in the direction of the hospital. Ambulance men, wardens and a lone doctor darted between the injured trying to do what they could. Those that survived sat white-faced and dazed, shivering from cold and shock. They had no broken bones, but Sal was sure their mental scars would cripple them for years and she tenderly covered them in what blankets she could find.

Bethnal Green was tending to its own, as she realized when the fireman working next to her issued a broken-hearted wail.

'My Lil!' he cried in sheer anguish as he pulled a body free from the crush. In that moment, he transformed from a tough fireman who'd battled a thousand Blitz fires to a heartbroken husband as he hugged the body of his wife to his chest and rocked her in his arms.

'No, no, no,' he sobbed. Sal lost sight of the poor fella as he loaded his wife onto a stretcher.

One scene that felled her clean to her knees was a mother running along the line of bodies screaming for her daughter.

'My Sarah, I got separated from her!' she screamed to anyone who'd listen. 'I've got to find her. Help me!'

'Come with me,' said Sal, taking her hand and leading her up the line. Checking the bodies of children, the lady found the girl she believed to be hers, but identifying her bruised face was too traumatic, until at last she examined her clothes.

'It's her,' she breathed, gripping her face in shock. 'She ripped her cardigan on the way to school this morning and there's the hole, look. Oh my days, I tore a strip off her for that. My baby girl, I'm sorry. I'm so sorry.'

The woman let out a tortured wail as Sal drew her into her arms to give her what little comfort she could.

'That's my baby. Oh, however shall I live without her? I'll never forgive myself,' she wept. She wrenched herself from Sal's embrace and threw herself back on her daughter's body, weeping inconsolably until at last her husband appeared and pulled her back.

'She's gone, gal,' he whispered. 'She's gone.'

Sal gently closed the little girl's eyes and drew back the sheet to cover her face. She shared that poor mother's grief and swallowed back sobs, all the while offering up a silent prayer of thanks that her two boys were safe.

By eleven forty that night, most of the dead and injured had been removed, either rushed to nearby hospitals or to the crypts of two local churches. Sal still hadn't spotted Poppy, Archie, Ivy, Betty or Freddie, but knew enough not to draw conclusions. They could be anywhere.

'Word has come back there's no more room at hospitals and they're piling up the dead in the corridors,' shouted a passing ambulance man. 'Where shall we start taking people now?'

'Take 'em to the crypt of St John's over the road,' a fireman called back wearily.

On instinct, Sal started walking towards the crypt of St John's. She could walk there with her eyes shut: she had gone there often at night during the Blitz to shelter and had spent many an hour singing underground. But once inside, she realized it was a very different place. Gone was the joyful camaraderie, in its place silent despair. Rows of bodies were laid out in the freezing gloom of the crypt.

A tea urn had been set up and the WVS were gingerly picking their way around the room serving up hot tea to shaken survivors. On one side of a room, someone was busy erecting a makeshift curtain to separate the bodies until they could be claimed.

Sal's stomach lurched when she realized that now was

the time she would have to start looking for Poppy, Freddie, Archie, Ivy and Betty. Pausing, she spotted the slight figure of a woman she recognized hunched over a body, her shoulders shaking from the force of her sobs. She touched the woman lightly and she whirled round. It was Betty's mother.

'It's not, is it?' Sal asked, already knowing the answer.

'It's my Betty,' her mother whispered, trembling. 'I got separated from her. Breaks me apart to know she died alone. Do you know what she used to call me, Sal? The Duchess. She used to say that nothing bad could ever happen to her while I was by her side . . .' Her voice trailed off.

'I'm so sorry,' Sal replied, tormented that the tragedy had claimed its first Singer Girl.

The woman shook her head and motioned to a body a few feet away. 'And that's Ivy.'

'And Poppy, and Archie?' Sal ventured, hardly daring to ask the question.

'I haven't seen them,' she replied, stroking her daughter's cold cheek over and over.

Sal gently touched her on the back and instinctively left the grieving mother to be alone with her daughter.

Tears blinding her eyes, she stumbled back outside onto the street.

'Excuse me, love,' said a fireman, with his arm around an elderly lady. 'I got walking wounded coming through.'

At that moment, a movement just past his head caught her attention. In astonishment, she realized it was Vera. She was running full pelt down the road towards her, no coat. When she drew nearer, Sal realized that tears were pouring down her face. It was the first time she had ever seen the older woman cry, she realized with a jolt.

'Billy and Joey?' Sal gasped.

'Safe at home with Daisy. I came as soon as I heard, Sal. Where is he? Just tell me where – I have to see him!' she babbled hysterically.

'Calm down, Vera,' she soothed, gripping her arm. 'Who?'

'Archie, of course!' she yelled. 'Now just tell me where he is so I can go to him. He'll need me.'

Sal closed her eyes and gulped deep in her throat.

'I don't know, Vera. I last saw him going down the Tube and I haven't seen him since.'

The blood drained from Vera's face. 'Oh no, not Archie,' she cried, and then she was off, belting towards the Tube.

Sal caught up with her just in time. 'You can't go down there, Vera,' she panted. 'Anyone still left down there is bound to be dead by now.'

'But you don't understand, Sal,' Vera wept bitterly. 'I argued with him, told him I didn't need him in my life. Such horrible words. I have to be with him, tell him I meant none of it.'

'No, Vera.' Sal wept helplessly. 'You can't go down there.'

Eventually, Vera's body slumped in her arms and Sal released her grip. Vera was a broken woman.

'I love him, Sal, and now it's too late to tell him.'

There was nothing Sal could say or do to ease her torment, and though she didn't like to admit it, after what she had witnessed tonight, Vera was probably right. All Sal could do was lead her home. It was nearly midnight and she was bone-weary and sick of heart. There was nothing more any of them could do now, except wait.

Twenty-Three

Vera glanced at the clock over the mantel. Five thirty in the morning. Sal had called the doctor out last night and he had given her a sleeping draught, but it hadn't worked. Regret had stolen any chance of sleep. Nothing could calm the savage sense of guilt that had burrowed into her head and heart.

One thought worked its way repeatedly through her mind.

'You told him you didn't want him in your life,' she whispered to herself. 'And now God's punishing you. You brought this on yourself.'

Gingerly, she pulled on her coat and peeked her head round the parlour door. Sal was fast asleep on her makeshift bed where she had fallen in exhaustion when they got in the night before, her face black with grime and her arms clamped protectively around her two boys. Thank heavens they were unharmed. Daisy was asleep upstairs, and as for their father's whereabouts, goodness only knew. Vera hadn't seen him since she had left for work yesterday morning and he hadn't come home last night.

Taking care not to wake anyone, she crept silently from the house and began to walk in the direction of the Tube.

She had no idea why she was going there, but it felt necessary in order to make sense of Archie's death.

As the first light of dawn tinged the sky, she stopped in front of the scene of the disaster and drew a long, shaky breath. Sal had described the horrific events of the previous evening and yet this morning it seemed barely credible that it was the same place. In the grey half-light, all was still and quiet. No bodies, no emergency services, no noise. Nothing. The only way you could tell that so many poor souls had perished there was the small pile of wet shoes neatly stacked by the entrance and a broken pram that lay discarded by the railings.

Vera pressed her knuckles into her mouth to prevent a sob escaping. Such a senseless loss of life. Over a hundred people killed in the crush, the doctor had told them, and that death toll rapidly rising. Word had already filtered back that the loud explosion had been some sort of new anti-aircraft rocket they had been testing from nearby Victoria Park. No enemy aircraft had even been spotted in the immediate area. All that fear and confusion, and it hadn't even been the Germans. Two of the Singer Girls dead and a third still missing, believed dead. She wanted to howl at the thought of sweet, innocent Poppy lying alone and in pain or worse . . .

For the past year all Archie had done was show her his undying love and support through his everyday actions. He was just an ordinary man with an extraordinary capacity for love. His heart was made of pure gold and she had trampled all over it.

Staring at the broken pram by the railings, she hugged her arms around herself and started to cry.

'Now, whatever are you crying for, woman?' said a familiar gruff voice from behind.

Vera whirled round and gaped in astonishment. There, as black as night, with his clothes hanging off him and looking fit to drop, was Archie. She flew at him, nearly knocking him off his feet, and clung to his chest.

'Blimey,' he gasped. 'Steady on, girl.'

'I thought you were dead,' she breathed, gripping his arms as if he might just suddenly melt under her touch.

'No,' he said wearily. 'But I do feel like I've come back from the dead. I've been up at the churches all night – St John's first, then St James the Less – helping get the survivors sorted.'

'Of course you have,' Vera said, shaking her head. Knowing the man as she did, why had she not thought to look there?

'So many people in shock. I saw one woman's hair turn from brown to grey overnight, I swear, but I guess they're the lucky ones. They escaped with their lives.'

Vera nearly couldn't speak for the lump in her throat, but she had to ask.

'Did you hear, about Ivy and Betty?' she asked.

His face darkened as he regarded the pavement. 'I did, and I take it as a personal failure. They were my girls and I should have saved them. I let them down. I've let all the Singer Girls down.'

'And Poppy?' she asked haltingly.

He shook his head in sadness. 'No, Vera, I haven't seen her, and I looked everywhere, believe you me. I'm so sorry. I should have got all my girls out.'

'Oh, Archie,' she wept, feeling as if her heart might just

burst out of her chest. 'If only you knew how we all feel about you.'

He fixed his gentle eyes on her, and there it was, that look of admiration and adoration.

'There's only one person whose feelings I hold above all others, and I think you know who that person is, Vera.' Tears formed rivulets of grime down his gnarled cheeks. 'After the night I've had, I may as well lay myself bare,' he stuttered. 'I've . . . I've loved you from the moment I set eyes on you.'

'But why?' she spluttered, genuinely mystified. 'Look at me.' Slowly she pulled down her top to reveal the scars snaking over her chest. 'Really look at me. I'm ugly. I'm prematurely old. I'm covered in scars.'

Archie took her hand in his and raised it to his lips. 'They're battle scars, and they're part of you, Vera, so of course I love them. I hope one day you'll open up to me about your past, but more than anything I want a future with you. After all the suffering and loss I witnessed last night, I need something good to cling to.'

He hesitated and then dropped to one knee. 'I want to make old bones with you. Marry me?'

Vera knew her father would kill her, but she may never get this opportunity again. If the last night had showed her anything, it was that she couldn't live her life without Archie in it, and second chances like this rarely came around.

She didn't know whether to laugh or cry.

'Get off the pavement, you daft sod – your knees aren't up to it,' she ordered.

Looking resigned to a knockback, he hauled himself

slowly to his feet, but his face was a picture of surprise as Vera leaned over and brushed her lips against his.

'I will.'

Relief washed over her and she leaned her head against his solid chest. She could have stayed that way all day except for the lights of the station flickering on.

They both watched flabbergasted as a stream of weary shelterers stumbled out onto the street, yawning and blinking into the half-light.

'All right, Archie,' called a man Vera recognized from the market. 'You haven't seen my brother, Ron, have you? He was supposed to join us down in the shelter last night.'

'Oh no,' moaned Archie under his breath. 'They don't know yet.'

'What do you mean?' she asked quizzically.

'They've been shut away down in the tunnel, oblivious to what was happening over their heads. The wardens probably hushed it up, as the last thing they would have wanted was folk running up and causing more mayhem.'

Vera closed her eyes and leaned back against the railings. 'You go and break the news to him. I'm going to head up to the hospital. See if I can't find Poppy.'

'All right, love,' he said. 'I'll see you back at yours.' He pulled her hand towards him as she went to move off. 'And thank you, Vera, for giving me something good to live for. This might sound strange, now of all times, but we are so blessed. This war seems to have no end, but with you by my side, I know we'll have the strength to see it through.'

Vera started to walk in the direction of the hospital and wearily let her eyes flicker down to the pavement. She couldn't bear to see all those confused faces spilling out of the Tube, knowing as she did the dire news that awaited them. Bethnal Green was a small place. Almost everyone who had made it to the safety of the shelter last night would know someone who hadn't.

With her eyes downcast, she didn't see Poppy coming out of the station until she bumped clean into her, and when she did raise her gaze, she felt as if she had seen the second ghost in as many minutes.

'You're alive!' she wept, feeling her legs start to shake.

'I am,' Poppy smiled weakly, plainly exhausted. 'Thanks to this man.'

Vera hadn't noticed the shy-looking man in cracked spectacles until Poppy held tightly on to his arm.

'This is Freddie. He saved my life. He's a very dear friend.'

Vera saw the secret look that passed between the two and was surprised by the affection in Poppy's eyes.

'Come on,' she said. 'Let's get back to mine. I think I need to hear this, and there'll be a couple of girls who will be extremely relieved to see you.'

Twenty-Four

Ten days after the Tube disaster, Daisy dressed carefully for the funerals of Betty and Ivy. She still could scarcely believe what had happened. The final death toll was now in. One hundred and seventy-three poor souls killed in the crush, sixty-two of them children, all dead through suffocation. The life had been literally squeezed out of them. The thought made her shudder. The biggest civilian wartime disaster, they were calling it. She supposed it really ought to put her own recent loss into perspective, but somehow it didn't.

Baby Hope was in her thoughts every single minute of every single day. Daisy supposed this must be what it felt like to experience grief. She felt almost as if she was suffocating like one of the poor souls who had perished. She couldn't eat or sleep, and her arms literally ached to hold Hope. She walked about on the periphery of life, haunted by her loss.

It had been just over three weeks now since she had left the home and she was still no closer to working out how it was she was simply supposed to forget such an utterly life-changing event. She had brought a tiny person into the world and loved her with a fierce maternal passion, and now she was supposed to just forget that she was a mother? Daisy knew that she could never truly forget her loss, but like everyone else in Bethnal Green, she would somehow have to find a way to keep moving forward.

Just then Archie poked his head round the door.

'Hello, darlin'. I got you a nice cup of tea downstairs.'

Thank goodness for Archie. Vera finally admitting her love for him was the only good thing to come out of this whole traumatic ordeal. In the ten days since their father's return from prison, on the fateful morning of the Tube disaster, he had barely been seen about the place. Vera was convinced he was up to his old tricks, and when he was home, he watched them both like a hawk. Daisy loathed their father and found herself wondering, yet again, how he managed to pull the wool over her eyes for so long.

She turned to Archie now with a grateful smile. 'Thanks, Archie. But should you be here? You know what our dad's like, and he seems to have it in for you. If he comes home and finds you here, he'll make no end of trouble.'

Archie's smile slipped. 'Your father is nothing but a nasty little bully, just like Reggie Fowler was, and the only way to treat bullies is to stand up to them. I'm not scared of him. I'm marrying your sister and I don't give a fig what your father makes of it. Now, come on downstairs and wet your whistle before your tea goes cold.'

Daisy followed Archie downstairs to find Sal and her boys and Vera sitting sombrely at the kitchen table, all dressed in black.

'All those people killed and not a single mention of it in the news or on the wireless. I should know – I've been scouring the papers every day,' snapped Sal.

'There was a small piece on it in the paper two days after, but there was no mention of where it was in the country or the true extent of the casualties,' piped up Vera.

'Simple.' Archie shrugged. 'It's been hushed up, kept under lock and key. Bad for morale, ain't it? Churchill don't want this sort of news spilling out. Imagine the propaganda. The Nazis would have a field day with it.'

'So what,' fumed Sal, 'we say nothing? Just keep our mouths shut as if nothing ever happened? Do the lives of all those poor people count for nothing?

'Do you know, the day after the disaster, some fellas from the council were down at the station painting white lines on the steps and installing handrails. A little too late for that, wouldn't you say?'

Vera nodded. 'Do they imagine they can just patch over all that death like we do a jacket filled with bullet holes?' she said.

Sal shook her head in despair. 'Well, I won't forget, or forgive.'

Without saying a word, Daisy placed her arms around her friend's trembling shoulders and a heavy silence descended on the room. She guessed that Sal was deeply traumatized by all that she had seen, but that didn't mean that every word out of her lips wasn't true. The East End was paying a heavy price for this war, and their suffering on the home front seemed destined to be forgotten.

At the funeral, each and every one of them stood ramrod straight and sang their lungs out. Betty's mother had chosen 'Jerusalem' as the hymn for her daughter's final send-off and the Singer Girls' voices soared loud and proud. They wanted God to know He had a good 'un coming His way.

Betty had been just fourteen, and a more merry-eyed scamp you'd be hard pressed to find. Daisy smiled to herself as she thought of the time Betty had written to a serviceman passing herself off as a twenty-one-year-old. Trout's wouldn't be the same without her quick tongue and infectious giggles filling the place. By the time the pallbearers got ready to transport her coffin outside for the burial, Daisy was unable to stem her tears. They weren't just for Betty but for the daughter she too had been forced to say goodbye to. Glancing over at Betty's mother as she bent down to kiss her daughter's coffin, she felt every ounce of that pain as if it were her own.

As they trooped out of the church afterwards, bowing their heads, she noticed how weary the vicar looked. Little wonder. Vera had said this was his thirteenth funeral of the day, and Ivy's was in half an hour. The group went to pay their respects to Betty's mother, who was stood on the church porch.

'God bless you, girls,' she whispered, after they had all uttered their condolences. Before they went to move away, Betty's mum called after them. 'Sal, I've been meaning to ask. Betty was wearing her favourite amber brooch. It was her nan's. But by the time I found her in the crypt, it was missing. You didn't happen to see it, did you, when you were in there? It's just that I so wanted her to be buried wearing it. I felt she should have something bright and pretty in her coffin, just like she was.'

'I'm so sorry, but no,' Sal replied. 'Try asking some of the wardens. They removed jewellery from the poor souls too bruised to be able to identify, to help their families find them. They should be able to help you.'

'Thanks, Sal. I'll do that,' she whispered.

By the time Ivy's funeral ended, Daisy felt quite drained. As the congregation spilled out once again, she spotted Poppy and her new beau, Freddie. His appearance on the scene was really quite mysterious. He was a pen pal apparently, but that was the first Daisy had heard of Poppy even having a friend in the forces. Daisy was sure Sal knew more than she was letting on; in fact, the two of them had seemed to be in cahoots ever since the night of the disaster. She had often found them huddled in mysterious little chats that tailed off whenever she came near, but no matter. At least Poppy seemed happy. In fact, it was as if there had been a light switched on in her beautiful blue eyes. She walked over to where the pair stood under an old yew tree in the graveyard, Poppy's arm linked through Freddie's, and his hand placed protectively over hers.

'Hello, you two.' Daisy smiled, extending her hand towards Freddie. 'I don't think we've been properly introduced.'

'So thrilled to meet you at last, Daisy,' he replied, shaking her hand firmly. 'Though what a pity it has to be under such sad circumstances.'

'Indeed,' she murmured. 'Just you make sure you look after this one. She's very special.'

'I promise,' Freddie vowed.

'Stop it, you two,' blushed Poppy. 'Freddie and I have only just started courting.'

But Daisy could tell by the way the young serviceman was gazing down at Poppy that he was smitten, and she could see the feeling was reciprocated. Daisy thought suddenly of her own handsome soldier, Robert, and the love she felt in her heart for him still. He would have made a terrific father, she realized with a sharp pang of loss, but society would never accept their relationship in the way it would Poppy and Freddie's. The awful fact of the matter was she didn't know whether she *could* be with Robert now, even if that were an option. Looking at Robert's face would always remind her of their daughter. She feared they had simply lost too much ever to find true and lasting happiness together. Robert had written to her again and again pledging his love, but as he had no idea when he would next get leave, the words somehow seemed meaningless.

Daisy had started at least five letters to him explaining how she felt, but somehow she couldn't seem to find the words that summed up either her searing loss or how she had changed since Hope's birth. But she owed it to him to at least try, and Daisy vowed that tomorrow she would write that letter. As for their long-term future . . . who knew? She cast her mind back to what Robert had told her when they had first met, and his words echoed in her ears: *This war is going to change the future for the likes of me and you . . . Anything is possible.* She had so desperately wanted to share in that belief, but from where she was standing right now, in a battle-weary graveyard, his prediction sounded hollow. It didn't even begin to cut through her pain.

'I believe we owe you a great deal for rescuing our Poppy,' she said, forcing herself not to dwell on her own agony.

'It was nothing really.' Freddie blushed modestly.

'Nonsense,' Daisy replied. 'Poppy's one of our own now

and we treasure her. Thank goodness you were on the scene when you were.'

'Come on, then,' said Poppy, slipping her arm through Daisy's. 'Alfie's putting on a memorial tea at the Dog and Duck. Shall we all walk together? I think Vera and Sal have gone on already to help set it up.'

Daisy nodded and they all moved off through the grave-yard, out into a dazzling spring afternoon, where shattered Bethnal Green was doing what it did best: putting one foot in front of the other and simply getting on with things. Daisy knew that few words would be said on the subject of that dreadful night, but she doubted that anyone would forget. They would carry the memories with them always in their hearts and minds. But at least love was blossoming along with the cherry trees: Poppy and Freddie courting, Vera and Archie a proper couple at last.

This time last year, she and her sister had been at logger-heads, unable to see reason or sense and both too stubborn to admit when they were in the wrong. Now her sister was experiencing the love she had hoped for herself, and Daisy felt nothing but happiness for her.

*

The memorial party at the pub had been subdued by East End standards. Poppy thought back to her first night in Bethnal Green and what a baptism of fire that had been for her. She had been scared out of her wits back then and haunted by her secrets. A lot had happened in a year, but one thing remained the same and now she was determined finally to lay her past to rest.

She reached up on her tiptoes and whispered in Freddie's ear, 'Shall we leave now?'

'Of course, Poppy.' He smiled down tenderly at her. 'I'll go and fetch your coat.'

As he rushed off, Sal, Vera and Archie exchanged knowing looks.

'Well, I'll say this, love,' remarked Vera. 'I don't know where you found him, but he's a keeper all right.'

'A proper gent,' agreed Archie. 'How did you two meet, then?'

'She sent a message in a bottle,' Sal said with a wink.

'Something like that,' Poppy giggled.

Fond farewells were exchanged before Poppy and Freddie walked out into the warm spring evening and strolled down the road that hugged the park. GIs whizzed past in jeeps and hordes of factory workers were spilling out onto the street, relieved to be outside in the fresh air. At a bench, Freddie paused.

'Shall we sit for a while?' he suggested. 'I know I should be getting you home and me back to my lodgings in Earls Court but I can't bear to leave you.'

Together they sat down and Poppy took a deep breath, but Freddie beat her to it. In dismay, she realized he was standing, and then sinking down onto the pavement on one knee.

'Freddie, whatever are you doing?' she asked, flabbergasted.

'Please, Poppy, just hear me out,' he begged. His hands were shaking as he reached forward and clutched hers. 'I know our meeting like that on the night of the Tube disaster was tragic, but it made me realize how much I truly adore you. To come so close to losing you when I'd only just met you was unthinkable, and since then, I haven't wanted to be apart from you for a moment. I believe you're my soulmate. I know you have your life here, but I hope that once this war is over, you will move back to Devon with me.

'What I'm trying to say, in the most terribly clumsy fashion, is that I love you, Poppy Percival, and I want you for my wife. So will you? Marry me, that is?'

Poppy's hands flew to her mouth in surprise. 'Oh, Freddie, nothing would make me happier! Except—' she broke off, her voice faltering. 'I need you to hear what I have to say and then I shan't mind in the slightest if you wish to retract your offer. Do you remember when I wrote to you and told you I wasn't who I seemed?'

Squeezing her eyes shut, she blurted out the whole story, of that night in the scullery, of the months of shame and guilt that had torn her apart piece by piece, her mother's rejection of her and how she honestly doubted she would have survived any of it were it not for the love and support of her new friends.

'So there you have it,' she said at last, opening her blue eyes and staring at the pavement. 'I understand that I must be a disappointment to you, and I won't blame you if you walk away right now.'

She could hardly bring herself to look at Freddie's face. She knew he would be reeling from her confession. But when at last she summoned the courage to look up, the expression he wore was not one of disgust or even pity. It was pure, undiluted love, etched with a deep compassion.

'It doesn't matter, not to me at any rate,' he said simply. 'Nothing can stop me wanting to look after you. I can't pretend it will be easy to hide my anger, not at you, but at the brute who did those terrible things, but it doesn't change my feelings towards you one bit. You are still the woman I want to end my days with. So I pledge my love to you and ask again, will you marry me?'

This time Poppy nodded, and tears of relief splashed down her face as Freddie gathered her in his arms and kissed her. His kiss was the most delicious of sensations on her lips, as soft as silk and as sweet as cherry jam. After his lips broke away from hers, she nestled into the crook of his arm and snuggled in close to her fiancé's chest. Poppy pulled Freddie's love and acceptance around her like a soft wool blanket and let out a long, slow sigh of relief. It would still take time to erase the pain of her past, but thanks to Freddie, she did at least have a future to look forward to.

Twenty-Five

The day after the funerals was a Sunday and Vera insisted that Daisy spend some time resting.

'You look exhausted, love,' she said, after they had cleared the breakfast dishes away. 'Why don't you finish your chores, then have a sit-down? I've got to pop out and see a friend. I'll see if I can't borrow some barley from her, boil it up with a little milk. That'll put the colour back in your cheeks. Tell you what, I'll even light a fire in the front parlour before I go and you can rest there.'

Daisy looked up from sprinkling Vim on a cloth. 'You must be going soft in your old age,' she smiled, as she started to scrub down the table. 'Either that or this is Archie's influence.'

'Not a bit,' Vera replied. 'I do worry about you, though, after everything you've been through.'

Daisy's eyes flickered downwards. 'Please, Vera, I can't talk about it, not yet.'

Vera nodded thoughtfully, picked up her string bag, and was just heading out through the door when Daisy called her back.

'Just one thing, though, that's been on my mind: do you think Mum would have forgiven me, for Hope, I mean?'

340

'What do you think, love?' Vera asked quietly.

Daisy shrugged. 'I honestly don't know.'

'She would have been proud of you for the dignified way you've handled it. She loved you more than words, you see.'

Daisy smiled sadly and Vera left hurriedly so she wouldn't see the emotion on her face.

As Vera stepped down her perfectly whitened front door-step, she caught sight of their father, Frank, coming from the other direction. Lowering her head, she quickly went on her way. He had scarcely been out of prison two minutes and already he was up to his old tricks again, not that Vera had been under any illusions that prison would reform her rotten father.

As she walked, the spring sunlight drenched her face and it felt good. Even Frank couldn't bring her down today. Archie had a plan up his sleeve. He had savings, and as soon as they were married, they would rent a nice house over the other side of the park, with enough room for them both and Daisy. Then Frank could have the run of his house and they need never see him again. Vera's only regret was that she had been too stubborn to accept Archie's love for so long. She knew now and that was what mattered. A fresh start was just what they all needed.

Vera enjoyed her customary tea break with Matron at the children's hospital, then headed back for home with a smile on her face. Seeing Matron always cheered her up, par-ticularly as Vera had such joyous news to impart about her engagement to Archie. Matron was thrilled, as Vera knew she would be. The visit had been tinged with sadness, though, as Matron had shared the harrowing details of the Tube disaster and how they had all worked tirelessly through the night to deal with casualties coming in. Vera was still mulling it all over in her mind, and wondering what, if anything, she could do to help the survivors, when she turned the corner into Tavern Street.

The explosion was as unexpected as it was ferocious. The force of it nearly blew Vera clean off her feet and instinctively she flattened herself against a doorway. A hot wind rushed over her, followed by the sensation of something raining down on her head.

'Oh, my days,' she choked. She had felt the very ground lift beneath her feet, and clouds of debris and brick dust were spewing into the air like an exploding volcano.

Although her body was shaking uncontrollably, her brain slowly kicked back into gear: that immense boom could only be one thing. She had heard enough of them, after all. A bomb!

Vera began to run, her heart thumping painfully in her ears. Broken glass crunched under her feet as all about her people coughed and screamed.

Never had the terraced street felt so long, and by the time she reached the far end of Tavern Street, she could already hear the distant clanging of a fire-engine bell.

The smoke and dust hung in the air and the sky was as black as night. Disorientated, Vera struggled to make sense of her surroundings.

'Where's my house?' she screamed, whirling round and round. But her neighbours, staggering shell-shocked out of the ash clouds, were too dazed to answer, their eyelashes and eyebrows encrusted with brick dust and blood.

A woman with a face full of glass and clearly still in

shock, with no idea of her injuries, looked at her and shrugged.

When the swirling clouds of dust settled, Vera finally got her answer.

Five or six houses had been destroyed by the blast. Dirty, bloodied people were everywhere, frantically picking through the wreckage of their homes, or sitting, completely dazed, on their settees. But Vera had no time to worry about that. There was only one home she could think about. In no time at all she had identified hers. It was easy really: she could now see straight through to the kitchen.

Number 24 Tavern Street looked like an exposed doll's house. The front had been blown clean off and only the party walls were standing. Her beloved front parlour was on show for the first time, her hearthrug lying in a crumpled, soggy heap, and her chaise longue had been blasted into the street, its stuffing spilling out onto the cobbles. The dust sheet she so diligently used to protect it was hanging off the ledge of number 28, and her net curtains were wrapped round the top of a nearby gas lamp.

Vera's heart turned to stone when she spotted the mangled fireplace. Before she had left, she had carefully lit a fire in that grate and told Daisy to rest beside it.

An unearthly howl filled the street. Vera was shocked to discover it was emanating from her.

'I'm coming, Daisy!' she screamed.

Desperate hands clung to her, attempting to pull her back.

'It's not safe,' pleaded a warden. 'The ceilings could come down at any moment. You have to stand back. *Stand back!*'

Time stood still. Images came to her like snapshots.

Two firemen picking their way through the ruins of her front parlour. A chunk of ceiling falling onto her kitchen table.

Then, through the smoking debris, came the sight she feared more than anything.

Vera felt as if she were having an out-of-body experience as she watched Daisy being loaded into the back of an ambulance on a stretcher. Her dress was covered in dust, and a film of blood streaked her face. The doors slammed shut, and in the distance she heard someone shout, 'Fetch Archie!'

Suddenly, she came to her senses. 'Wait for me!' Vera screamed, pummelling on the back of the ambulance door as it pulled away. 'My sister's in there.'

An ARP warden gently held her back. 'There's no time, Vera. Let her get to hospital. Wait for Archie.'

Trembling with fear, Vera frantically scanned the street and tried to assemble her thoughts. Just then, she heard a faint groan coming from inside the wreckage of her home. Startled, she listened over the shouts from the street, but there it was again. A soft, muffled moan of pain.

In the chaos, she slipped free and walked through the remains of her kitchen, following the noise. The groaning seemed to be coming from the yard out back. She stepped outside and gasped afresh.

The old toilet block had toppled over and the small yard was strewn with great chunks of masonry. The neat strips of newspaper she had cut up that morning and pinned to the toilet door were fluttering all over the place.

Just then a sheet of newspaper moved.

'Vera,' coughed a voice, and the paper fluttered up into the air, revealing the face of a man.

'Frank?' she gasped. 'Frank, is that you?'

It was hard to tell. His face was coated in a thick layer of grime, and his mouth was foaming with blood, opening and closing like a stranded goldfish. Small crimson bubbles of blood peppered the gashes all over his face.

'Course it's me, you stupid cow,' he rasped. 'I was on the lav and then the whole bleedin' thing collapsed. I think we've been hit.'

Vera stood rooted to the spot.

'What you waiting for?' he croaked. 'Hurry up and get me out of here.'

She shook herself and rushed to his side, frantically flinging bricks and rubble away with her bare hands. With his one free arm, Frank started to join in. Vera looked down at his gnarled old hand as, trembling, he removed the smaller bricks.

Suddenly, a vision of the future flashed into her head. With her father alive, the lies that had plagued her would be perpetuated into eternity. She should walk away, leave him here to die . . . But wait, what was she even thinking? She was no murderer.

'Vera,' Frank begged, sensing her hesitation, 'what you up to? Come on, girl – it's me, your old man.' His voice grew more desperate. 'I'm bleedin' to death 'ere. You've got to get help.' And then, resorting to the only language her father really understood, 'Get me outta here or I'll bloody kill yer, yer stupid little whore.'

Vera remained rooted to the spot, the distant clanging of

fire-engine bells and shouts ricocheting through her tired brain.

Suddenly, like a magpie, she spotted a flash of silver gleaming among the grey rubble near Frank's body. Stooping down, she picked it up and rubbed it between her thumb and forefinger. With the dust brushed off, she realized it was a piece of jewellery, an amber and silver brooch. Her brain was so foggy she couldn't make sense of it, but something was nagging deep down in her skull.

'Give that back!' Frank spat, alarmed when he spotted what was in her hand. 'That's mine.'

Her eyes widened in disbelief. *Of course.*

'This isn't yours. It's Betty's, isn't it?' she shrieked. 'Her mother told Sal at her funeral that it went missing from her body when she lay at the church.'

Vera's whole body started to tremble violently, and for a second, she thought she might be sick. She felt Betty's mother's pain in every corner of her being.

'You . . . you sneaked into the crypt and stole it from the body of a dying girl? We never saw hide nor hair of you here the night of the disaster, or the next morning. H-how could you?' she stammered eventually. 'Is there no end to your depravity?'

'Don't talk rot,' he croaked. But he didn't even have the decency to try and deny it too strenuously.

Vera searched deep into his grey eyes as they blinked back up at her from the wreckage. She was looking for something, anything that showed her there was a shred of compassion or decency there. He lay whimpering in a puddle of his own blood, growing colder and weaker by the second.

In an instant, her crippling indecision was over. It was

everything – the neglect, the lies, the beatings and now this, the ultimate betrayal – all crystallized together in a single bolt of pain and fury.

Too many women had suffered at the hands of her cruel father. It was time.

As she picked her way through the remains of the kitchen and out through the blackened shell of their front door, a passing ARP man gripped her shoulder.

'You shouldn't be here, miss,' he said in shock. 'The street's evacuated now. They're about to start sealing it off. Anyone left in there?'

She shook her head. 'No. Nothing worth saving.'

There was no avoiding it now: she had to get to the hospital and tell Daisy everything. No half-truths. She deserved to know the whole story. But was there time?

Sal was waiting at the end of the cordon with Poppy.

'Vera. Oh, thank God, there you are,' she blurted. 'We came as soon as we heard. Look at the state of you. Archie's on his way. You're to stay with him. He's been down the Salvation Army and collected some clothes for you. He's out of his mind with worry, Vera . . . Vera, are you all right? You look as if you've seen a ghost.'

'I'll survive,' she whispered. 'But I've got to get to the hospital. See Daisy. They wouldn't let me in the ambulance.'

'Of course.' Sal wept, placing her hand gently on her shoulder. 'But wait until Archie arrives. We'll get the bus up together.'

'No!' she howled, pushing her away, her green eyes wild with fear. 'There's no time. Don't you see?'

And then she was off, running away from her bomb-shattered home in the direction of Bethnal Green Hospital.

As her feet pounded against the cobbles, she prayed she wouldn't be too late.

Taking the stairs two at a time, she burst her way through the double doors and nearly knocked two nurses clean off their feet.

'Mind yourself,' one gasped, gripping on to her cap.

The reception area was brimming over with the walking wounded. The hospital was still full to bursting with survivors of the Tube disaster, so those who could wait to see a doctor were sitting stoically in the reception area.

Vera took a breath and joined the queue at reception, but there was an almighty rabble of people wanting to know how their loved ones were.

'Yes?' snapped a harassed-looking nurse when at last she reached the front of the queue.

'My sister's here and I have to see her now,' Vera pleaded.

'Name?' she barked.

'Daisy Shadwell.'

The nurse frowned as she looked down a list on her clipboard.

'Was she admitted from Tavern Street? UXB?'

Vera looked blank.

'Unexploded bomb,' she added, more softly.

'That's right. Please just tell me, is she going to be all right, Nurse?'

The nurse consulted her clipboard once more and gestured back to the waiting room. 'Take a seat over there. The doctor will be right out to see you. Next.'

Vera had a horrible sick feeling in her stomach. She had only seen Daisy briefly when they had stretchered her out of the house, but she hadn't looked in a good way. It had all happened so quickly, but Vera prayed she had escaped the worst of the blast.

Eventually, she saw a young doctor appear behind the reception desk and she watched as he was pointed over in her direction. Vera rose sharply.

'Are you Miss Shadwell's next of kin?' he asked.

'I am,' she gulped.

'Very well. Follow me,' he ordered, sweeping down the long, tiled corridor. 'I am going to allow you a few moments with your sister, but I should warn you she's in a critical condition. She took the full brunt of the roof collapsing and has suffered massive internal bleeding. We have removed her spleen and managed to stabilize her thus far, but I feel it only fair to warn you her prognosis looks bleak. If she survives the next forty-eight hours, she will be lucky.'

Vera's body seemed to move of its own accord and for a moment, she wondered if she might just pass out cold on the floor.

'Police have already informed us it was an unexploded bomb,' the doctor went on. 'Probably left over from the Blitz. Bomb-disposal units have worked tirelessly in this area since then, but I suppose they can't get them all.' His voice trailed off as he paused at the entrance to a private room. 'I'll give you some time alone, Miss . . . ?'

'Shadwell,' she replied. She could hear her own voice, yet it sounded queer to her ears. 'I'm her . . . Well, I'm her big sister, and if you don't mind, I should like to get in there now and see her.'

But once inside the room with the door closed firmly behind her, Vera knew the time for lies was over. No more

349

tiptoeing around in the past. The bomb had blown a gaping hole through her secrets.

Vera took a cautious step towards her bed. Daisy's beautiful dark hair was fanned out over the white pillow, but her face . . . Vera stifled a sob. Oh, her beautiful face. The skin was still and cold, like alabaster, and her green eyes were open, staring vacantly at the ceiling.

The awful stillness in the room turned Vera's heart over. 'Daisy, can you hear me?' she whispered, touching her cheek softly.

With an agonizing rasp, Daisy painstakingly turned her head towards Vera's.

'Vera,' she croaked, slowly stretching her fingers across the sheet and lacing them through Vera's. It seemed to take every ounce of her strength to move her hand, and her breath was painfully shallow.

Vera fixed her eyes on Daisy's, but something about the way she stared back cloaked her in dread. She was having trouble focusing, and her eyes seemed to be growing cloudier by the second.

'Please stay with me, love,' she pleaded. 'It's so important you hear what I have to say.'

There was no turning back and in that moment Vera hated herself more than she could ever have imagined.

'I've not been honest with you, Daisy, you see.' She trembled. 'I have to tell you something. I did have my baby. I had her, sweetheart. She never died. Oh, Frank tried to kick my baby from me, but he never succeeded. I should have told you, I know, but I was scared. I've been a fool, you see, a silly, scared, selfish fool all my life, and I'm not proud of the lies.'

Pausing, she scanned Daisy's face for any flicker of emotion, but there was nothing, just the dreadful rasp of her breath as her eyelids flickered opened and shut.

Cold, hard fear clamped Vera's heart. She was losing her.

'Do you understand what I'm saying?' she urged. 'Can you ever forgive me? I should have been a mother to you, not a controlling sister . . . I should have told you. All those times during the Blitz I hid away at home, I was scared of being underground with you, scared of what I might say or do if you were harmed. You're the most precious thing in my life, you see . . .'

Vera was speaking faster now, her confession reduced to a frantic jumble.

Daisy's mouth opened slowly, struggling to form words through her pale lips. Vera leaned in close.

'Hope, find her . . .'

The effort of uttering those words seemed to use up what last shred of life Daisy had left in her body. Her chest sank, and her eyelashes flickered.

'What's that, my darling?' Vera pleaded, rubbing Daisy's cold hand in hers. 'What did you say? Tell me!'

Daisy lay as still as a stone.

'Please, sweetheart, talk to me,' Vera begged. But in her heart she knew. Daisy was gone.

In a trance, Vera kicked off her shoes and gently climbed up onto the bed next to her. Scooping her cold body into her arms, she curled herself around her, and only then could she let the tears come. She wanted to take Daisy back into her body, back into her womb. Reclaim all the lost years. And there she remained, stroking and rocking Daisy's body in her arms, crying until she thought her heart might just break in two.

The door swung open and a nurse bustled in, stopping in her tracks when she spotted Vera.

'And who on earth might you be?' she spluttered.

'I'm her mother,' Vera whispered for the first time.

Vera stayed with her daughter's body until the doctor came in and gently informed her it was time for Daisy to be taken down to the morgue. Leaving Daisy behind in the hospital was the hardest thing she had ever had to do in her life. She hadn't been aware of anything going on around her. Not Archie's arrival, him gently prising her from Daisy's bedside, or her legs buckling as he led Vera back out through the packed waiting room. Nothing permeated the intense layer of grief that had settled over her.

Back at home, Archie sat Vera down in a chair and placed a strong mug of tea in front of her.

'Here you go, love,' he said softly. 'I've made myself up a bed on the living-room floor; you can have my bedroom until we can rent the new house. Landlord says next week should be fine. But there's all the time in the world to be thinking about that. We better, well . . .' His voice broke off and Vera could see he was struggling not to cry. 'We better sort Daisy's funeral out first, and I'm afraid I've more bad news . . . There's no easy way to say this, Vera, but the warden's found your father's body. He was trapped under a piece of masonry in the backyard. I shouldn't think he'd have felt much pain. The warden reckons he would have been killed outright.'

Vera shrugged.

'Don't you care?' he asked, visibly shocked. 'I know he was cruel, but he was your flesh and blood, and now he's dead.'

'There's a lot you don't know about that man,' she blazed suddenly, turning to face her confused fiancé. 'I may as well tell you. I've had a gutful of secrets and lies. That's all my life has been until now. I don't expect you shall still want to marry me after you hear what I've got to tell you, but from now on, for the memory of Daisy, I have to be honest.'

And so, between great heart-wrenching sobs, Vera found herself spilling out the whole story, about her mother's death in the fire, her father running and leaving them all to burn, and how Vera escaped, but her affair with the older married doctor left her pregnant.

Up until this point, Archie had been listening in incredulous silence, but when Vera described how her father had attempted to kick her baby from her, he shook his head and started to weep.

'No, Vera,' he cried, placing his head in his hands. 'I can't stand to think of you suffering.'

'Listen to me, Archie,' she begged. 'You need to hear this. I gave birth, aged sixteen, at a mothers' home, similar to the one Daisy stayed in, so you see, I felt every bit of Daisy's shame. I know what it's like to be judged as a so-called sinner. I was all alone in the world apart from Matron, who took me under her wing.'

'So you had the baby. But what did you do? Give her away?'

'In a manner of speaking,' Vera replied. 'I gave away the right to call myself "Mum". It was agreed, between Matron, myself and my father, that I couldn't possibly raise her as my own. Can you ever imagine the scandal? So I, or rather Frank, decided that it would be easier all round if he pretended to be her father and I her elder sister.'

Archie's mouth fell open. 'Daisy?' he gasped. 'Daisy is your daughter?

'Was,' she corrected, her voice hollow. 'Daisy was my daughter. And not a day of her eighteen years did I not long to tell her the truth.'

She fingered the gold half-heart necklace at her breast. The other half was round the neck of her daughter in the morgue.

'With the little bit of money Mum had managed to put by and left for me after her death, I bought this for me and a matching one for Daisy. I figured that if I couldn't tell the world we were connected, I could at least show it.'

'But how did he get away with it?' Archie breathed.

'It was easy really,' Vera shrugged. 'We had to move after the fire anyway. So as soon as I was discharged, we moved from Whitechapel to Bethnal Green, where nobody knew us, and Dad cobbled together some cock-and-bull story about how Daisy was a miracle baby and how Mum died in the fire shortly after having her. Why would you disbelieve it? I was so young it never crossed anyone's mind she could actually be mine.

'When we moved into Tavern Street, he even invited the neighbours round, played the part of the grieving husband to perfection. "Daisy's mother, God rest her soul, was a wonderful woman. This little girl is all I have left of her," he told them.

'"Poor soul," I heard them mutter as they left. "And his wife dying so soon after childbirth like that, a tragedy."

Watching his charade, I felt such hatred and anger towards him, and myself for going along with it. To this day, I don't think that anger has ever really left me.'

'So when did you . . . ?' Archie went to ask, but instead his voice trailed off.

'Realize it was a mistake?' she replied. 'Almost immediately. But once it was decided, it was too late to go back. I only agreed as it meant at least being able to keep Daisy near, but Frank just used it against me. He loved knowing the secret – it gave him the upper hand, and he never lost an opportunity to twist the knife. As Daisy grew up, he used it to drive a wedge between us. He got a kick out of it, I suppose.'

'Such cruelty,' Archie breathed, shaking his head in disbelief.

'But I can't let him take all the blame, you know, Archie,' she replied. 'The older Daisy got, the more I tried to control her. All I could think was that if she knew I was her mother, she'd respect me more, but she was a stubborn little thing.'

'Wonder where she got that from?' Archie smiled softly.

Vera shot him a wry look. 'I was too eaten up with bitterness and regret, and I let that infect our relationship,' she replied. 'I didn't give her the love and affection she really needed. Too busy boiling my nets and whitening the doorstep to reach out and give her a cuddle. I've stayed in touch with Matron, you know. Every Sunday without fail, I've gone up to visit her. It's the only place where I've been able to feel like me. Madness, isn't it?' She trailed off. 'I'm afraid I failed her, Archie. Miserably.'

'But don't you see?' Archie protested. 'You were looking out for her, and you came through for her when she needed you most. When she had baby Hope, you supported her like a real mother would. How many women round here would have turned her out on the street? She may not have had a mother in name, but she never wanted for the love of one.'

'I suppose so,' Vera replied. Suddenly, she felt so very, very tired. This war was savage. It had shattered her. Stripped her of everything . . . No, not quite everything.

Daisy's last words came flying back to her.

'She asked me to find Hope, you know.'

Vera looked deep into Archie's eyes, searching to see if the ramifications of Daisy's deathbed request had sunk in: that he had gleaned the full meaning of what was being asked of him.

'She wanted me to find her daughter, Archie,' she repeated. 'But I don't know that I'm strong enough, or even that it's possible, without your support, that is . . .'

Vera waited with bated breath while Archie paced the bedroom. Finally, he stopped and turned to face her, the tiny gas lamp casting shadows on his face.

'I'm an old man now, Vera – forty-five. Many would say too old to be a father to a newborn.'

'I understand.' She sighed. 'It's a lot to ask of you.'

'But since when did I care what others thought?' he replied.

Vera looked up in surprise. 'You mean . . . ?' She had never seen Archie look more determined.

'Absolutely. I know it will be a tough road to travel, what with us being older parents, Hope's colour, the question of her background . . . But hang it all, I don't see why if we marry immediately, we can't at least try. I think we owe that much to Daisy at least.'

Vera felt her blood race and tears cloud her eyes. 'Really, Archie? You'd put yourself through all that for me?' she cried in disbelief. 'After everything I've just told you?'

'Vera, I would move heaven and earth for you. Surely you must know that by now?' he said despairingly. 'I love you, and I would do anything to make you happy. I know your father destroyed your trust in men, but I will never let you down. God's honest truth. But just one thing I am adamant on, Vera,' Archie added firmly. 'We must contact Robert. I know he agreed with the decision for Hope to be given away for adoption, but his feelings may change on hearing about Daisy's death. He may even have family back in America who could raise the little girl. Besides, he has a right to know. He struck me as a decent enough fella, and he clearly thought the world of your Daisy.'

Vera wiped her eyes and sat bolt upright on the bed. 'Of course. You're right, Archie. We must.' She reached out for his hand and threaded her fingers through his. 'Thank you.'

Archie said nothing, just gently lifted Vera's hand to his lips to kiss.

'Oh, and, Archie, I will learn to trust you,' she murmured.

'Yes, you will,' he said softly. 'You can't crumble now. I'm going to be right here by your side every step of the way, but your granddaughter is relying on you.'

Hearing the word 'granddaughter' sounded so strange to Vera's ears, but somewhere deep inside, it stirred an emotion. Archie was right. It was time to bring her granddaughter home.

Twenty-Six

'This certainly is an unusual situation, Mrs Gladstone,' said the matron of the local authority orphanage. 'We've never had a baby claimed in such a manner before. Usually illegitimate children are absorbed into the extended family from birth, so as to make it as seamless as possible for all concerned.' The matron checked the files laid out before her. 'Hope is three and a half months old now,' she said. 'And what of the baby's father and his position in all this?'

Vera sat on the edge of her chair and gripped Archie's hand tightly. From the moment she had followed the matron down the long, carbolic-scented corridor, her heart had been in her mouth. That Hope, whom she had never even laid eyes on, should be so close was giving her palpitations.

'We are aware of that,' Vera replied nervously. 'But there has been a change in my circumstances. I am married now and in a position to provide a stable home for my sister's child, unlike her father, Robert. I mean that with no dis-respect to him. Robert is a GI serving here in the US Army. We have written to him and he is happy for us to assume care of Hope and will testify to that in a letter. Robert's only family is his father back in Missouri, and he won't take responsibility for Hope. Robert himself is clearly not in a position to raise his daughter, as much as I know he would want to. It's my belief that he loved Hope's mother very much and intended to marry her, but their relationship was ill fated. I will, of course, provide you with his details in order for you to be able to verify all this for yourself.'

Matron frowned as she absorbed Vera's words. 'There aren't too many aunts who would assume such a great responsibility for their niece,' she said. 'Particularly given that this adoption will come with a great stigma attached. You too will bear it. You are aware of what it means to raise a half-caste child when you are both white?'

'We are going into this with our eyes wide open, Matron,' reassured Archie. 'We know it won't be easy, but we are determined to provide a secure and loving home for this child, and personally, we are unaffected by the colour of her skin. We know society won't be as tolerant, but we feel she is better off with us, her flesh and blood, than in an institution.'

'I am inclined to agree, Mr Gladstone, but I cannot discharge this baby to your care only to have her returned a few months down the line when you've realized the enormity and gravity of your undertaking. Babies cannot simply be passed about at will.'

'We know that,' blurted Vera more sharply than she intended. She took a deep breath before continuing. 'I apologize if I sound rude, but I can assure you we have thought this through. We are well regarded within our communities. Mr Gladstone is the foreman of a large textile factory, and I will, of course, leave my position as forelady in order to be able to devote my time to Hope. We know her life will be somewhat of a struggle, but we hope in time she will be regarded as what she is, another innocent casualty of this war.'

An uneasy silence filled the room. It wasn't long before Archie broke it. 'The thing is this, Matron,' he said passionately. 'We know there were many in Bethnal Green who frowned on Daisy's transgression, but as far as we are concerned, any shame died with her. Hope cannot be made to suffer the stigma of her mother's liaison any longer. She is the innocent party in all of this, and right-minded, God-fearing folk will treat her with kindness. Any other sort of person's opinion is not something we care for. We intend to devote all our energies into giving Hope the best possible start in life. Doesn't every child deserve that?'

'They do, Mr Gladstone,' murmured Matron in agreement. 'I suppose this is wartime, and it has thrown up some extraordinary situations. Why, only the other day, I heard of a lady who lives three villages along who has had two illegitimate children to a deserter. Her husband home on leave has not only forgiven her but pledged to take them on as his own.'

'He must be a saint!' gasped Archie.

'But doesn't that prove that the ability to forgive must be our guiding light?' urged Vera. 'I forgave Daisy, and in time I hope the community will. Bethnal Green has always been and always will be a place of families. Kinship counts. Nothing is more important than your flesh and blood, and Hope is *our* flesh and blood. The disaster at the Tube decimated whole families. Isn't it time we started rebuilding them?'

Matron seemed to be thinking carefully as she regarded them both closely. Vera tried to appear calm, but inside she was gripped with emotion, her grief over Daisy's sudden death mingling with her fierce determination to do right by her. It had been just four weeks since Daisy's passing, and thanks to their sympathetic local vicar, used to conducting hasty marriages in wartime, they had been able to marry just a few days after the funeral. Sal and Poppy were the only people who had attended the small, bittersweet ceremony.

As they sat waiting to discover whether they were to become a proper family, Vera's heart was in her mouth.

'I am happy to release her to your care, subject to a meeting with my superiors at the local authority and the baby's father's written consent,' said Matron at last. 'It will take a few days to draw up the adoption papers, so I suggest you return ten days from now.'

Vera felt her bones sag with relief. 'May . . . may I see her now, Matron?' she ventured.

'I see no reason why not.'

A second later, a nurse was summoned from a connecting office.

'Please bring in Hope.'

Vera shot a glance at Archie, who looked as excited and anxious as she. There was a flurry of small talk, but Vera wasn't really listening. Her eyes were trained on the door to hurry the moment she would hold her precious grand-daughter in her arms. And suddenly there she was, a little bundle cocooned in white blankets, being lowered into Vera's arms, and all the pain of the last four weeks, the dread of what the future held, all melted away. Suddenly, nothing else mattered.

'I'll give you a few minutes alone,' murmured the matron,

discreetly closing the door behind her. Neither Archie nor Vera even noticed her go; they were too busy looking down at the little girl they had just pledged to raise as their own.

Staring at Hope's face, Vera felt she could hardly breathe. If she lived to be a hundred, she would never again experience the feeling of euphoria that flooded her body. Hope was the image of Daisy, down to her rosebud lips and neat chin. Losing Daisy in such a sudden and violent way had torn Vera apart, but cradling her daughter's child in her arms allowed her to make sense of her grief. She didn't know if everything in life happened for a purpose, but saving Hope from a rootless existence in an orphanage was the only good thing to have emerged from the whole tragedy.

Nestled in her grandmother's arms, this baby was a literal symbol of hope, perfection against the wanton destruction of the past month. Hope was Vera's second chance. No more lies. No more secrets. She may not have been able to be a mother to Daisy, been too cowardly to tell her the truth until it was too late, but she wouldn't make that mistake with her granddaughter. In time, when Hope came of age and was old enough to fully understand, she would reveal the complex truth of her heritage. But for now, what this little mite needed more was stability and bundles of love.

'I hope your mummy, wherever she is, has finally escaped the East End,' Vera whispered. 'I hope she's found some fresh stockings, maybe even some silly high-heeled dancing shoes, knowing her.'

Tears coursed down her face as Archie leaned over and hugged his new family tight.

'Silly me,' she cried. 'We can't have that, now, can we? I won't let you down, sweetheart.'

And with that simple vow, Vera realized that, above all else, love was the most precious thing.

Ten days later, Mr and Mrs Gladstone returned to the orphanage, and this time they left with their new baby. To the outside world, Vera was a doting auntie, selflessly taking on her sister's illegitimate child to save her, but in Vera's heart, she knew the truth. She was Hope's grandmother, and a more perfect love she had never known.

With all the care and devotion of a proud new father, Archie placed Hope in her bassinet and tucked her snowy-white blankets around her, while Vera fumbled nervously with her bonnet strings.

'There we are, poppet,' she beamed. 'Snug as a bug in a rug. Let's get you home where you belong, shall we? There's two of my very good friends just dying to meet you.'

Archie drove them back to Bethnal Green as carefully as if he were transporting the Crown Jewels, and only once Hope was tucked up in her cot did Vera feel she could finally breathe. Their new house contained a small room off their bedroom that Archie had lovingly decorated as Hope's nursery.

Vera threw open the window, which had sweeping views over Victoria Park, and smiled to herself as a steady stream of fresh air filled the nursery. At least Hope would be able to look out over a small lake and treetops, and when this war was over, she was certain that the families, the Sunday picnickers, the fairground roundabout and the pleasure boats would all return. The sounds of war would one day be replaced by splashes and the creak of oars, of children larking about and carefree laughter. Vera couldn't wait to take Hope there, like she had Daisy when she was a nipper. Life would return to normal.

Next Vera set about carefully unpacking the small case that Matron had handed to her before they left. Contained within were the most beautiful baby clothes she had ever seen. Crocheted bonnets, matinee jackets and shawls, all knitted with love, care and attention. Vera delicately ran her hands over the soft wool and felt a lump forming in her throat as she realized she was handling the only thing Daisy had ever really been able to give her daughter.

'I know how much you loved her,' she whispered, holding a little bonnet to her cheek and closing her eyes. For the briefest moment Vera smelt Evening in Paris, Daisy's fragrance. She half wondered whether Daisy had deliberately wanted her perfume to linger on Hope's clothes so that at least the scent of her would remain.

Daisy had been just nineteen when she had been killed. Her journey through life had only just begun, but Vera held back the flood of tears she knew she could very well shed right now. She had to focus her energies elsewhere. Daisy's legacy was Hope, and in asking Vera to find her, she had bestowed upon her the greatest responsibility.

'I won't let you down,' she murmured, as she carefully started to hang up the clothes in the wardrobe. As she did so, a small white package slipped out from between the folds of a matinee jacket. It was addressed to Hope Shadwell and Vera could feel that it contained a small item, a keepsake perhaps. On instinct, Vera went to rip it open, but she stopped herself just in time. This was not her letter to open.

Contained within it were words that only Hope should read from the mother she would never know. How she would feel upon learning the truth of her heritage goodness only knew, but fortunately, those bombshells were decades away. Vera decided to keep the letter safe and give it to Hope when she came of age.

Just then, Archie walked in with two cups of tea, and Vera quietly slipped the package into her pocket.

'Made us a brew, love,' he grinned. 'How's little 'un settling in?'

'Ssh, she's asleep,' Vera whispered, smiling as he placed down their cups.

They stood in silence, their shoulders gently resting against each other as they watched Hope sleeping, marvelling at the rise and fall of her tiny chest and admiring the soft brown tendrils of hair that curled round her plump little apple cheeks.

'I know the future won't be easy, but thank you, Lord, for bringing us all home safely,' murmured Archie. 'We have to put our suffering behind us now and concentrate on giving this little angel the best life she can possibly have. For Daisy's sake.'

Vera looked from her sleeping granddaughter to her new husband and smiled softly at him before planting the gentlest of kisses on his lips.

'Amen to that.'

Epilogue

'Right!' whooped Sal. 'Let's be having you, girls. Let's make this the best street party the East End's ever seen. It's not every day you get to celebrate the end of the war, after all.' Archie stepped forward and, with a mock bow, introduced them to the rest of the partygoers. 'I give you the Singer Girls!'

Soon the whole of the street was filled with their glorious voices. As Poppy, Vera and the rest of the girls linked arms and sang 'We'll Meet Again', Sal felt her heart might burst with relief and joy. There was only one person missing, her best friend Daisy, but she lived on in little Hope. She was growing up so fast. Nearly two and a half years old, she charged after Billy and Joey, chubby little legs pumping ten to the dozen as she raced after her playmates, shrieking with excitement. Soon all three of them had ducked down under the trestle tables, which groaned with sandwiches and jelly.

Every woman in the area had done the neighbourhood proud, emptying their larders to produce a feast that would mean their ration books had taken a battering, but who cared? Today was a day of celebration. After a tremendous storm the night before, it was now a perfect, hot spring day and the sun shone brightly.

Church bells pealed all over the East End in triumph. All the women wore red, white and blue ribbons in their hair, and Sal couldn't remember a time of such gaiety. Bunting fluttered from the gas lamps, Union Jacks were plastered from every window ledge, and she knew the singing would go on long into the night.

Most of the men in the street were already sailing two sheets to the wind, all except Archie, who Sal knew would remain sober as a judge to keep a watchful eye on Hope. Looking at him now, a big besotted grin spread over his face as Hope ran giggling from under the tables straight into his outstretched arms, Sal couldn't help but feel breathless at the love of that unconventional family. Archie's hair may have turned silver, but pure gold shone in his heart for taking that little girl on as his own. You could hang your hat off Archie Gladstone.

After the sing-song, Vera, Sal and Poppy paused for refreshments.

'Do you think Daisy would have approved?' Vera asked, as Sal poured her a ginger beer.

'Why, it's a party,' she grinned back at her. 'Of course she'd have approved!'

But then, to let the older woman know she felt her ache of pain, she raised her glass in a toast and slid her other arm around Vera's shoulder.

'To Daisy, the girl with big ambitions.'

'To Daisy,' they chorused back.

They fell into a respectful silence, each of them lost in

their own memories of the girl with the voice of an angel, whose time on earth was too brief.

'And what about you, Poppy?' Sal said eventually. 'When are you and Freddie off to the country, then?'

Poppy shot a glance over at her handsome husband, who stood by the bar chatting with Archie, and her eyes flashed with love. Poppy and Freddie had married one year after Vera and Archie, with no more pomp or ceremony. In fact, it had been the smallest, quickest wedding Sal could ever remember. They had tied the knot in a registry office with her and Vera as witnesses. Poppy wore a second-hand skirt and jacket, and not a scrap of make-up adorned her pretty features, but she was still the most radiant bride Sal had ever seen.

'Well, Freddie's just waiting to get his demob orders and then we'll be off. I should think sometime in the next six months.'

'Well, it won't be the same around these parts without you, love,' replied Vera. 'But I know where your heart truly lies – you never made any bones about that – and if you and your Freddie can make a go of that farm, well, good on you, I say.'

'And so say all of us,' smiled Sal, winking at Poppy and privately thinking what a long way she had come from the nervous slip of a girl who'd arrived all those years ago. They had never again talked of what happened to Poppy that night in the scullery, but meeting Freddie had been an enormous boost to Poppy's confidence and somehow Sal sensed she would always be safe in his hands. After all, he had saved her life from the very first moment they met, and since then the trust between them was implicit.

'Oh, but you will come down to visit, won't you?' she gushed.

'Of course,' smiled Vera.

'Crikey, I should say,' added Sal. 'My Billy and Joey are already planning it. They miss their days in the countryside, so it will be marvellous to have somewhere to take them.' She knew she was taking a chance on her next question, but curiosity got the better of her. 'And your mother? Will she be down to visit?'

Poppy shook her head. 'I'm not sure. I wrote to tell her I was married, but all she said was Lord Framshalton and his family lost everything in the war. They've had to let all their domestic staff go. They're ruined, apparently, down to their last farthing. Mother's staying on to help them out of a misguided sense of duty, I think, as even the cook and butler have gone.'

'Oh, what a terrible shame. They've had the silver spoons wrenched from their mouths; my heart bleeds for them,' snorted Sal. 'I'll say this for the war – it's been a great leveller, and I'm not just talking about the slums. The classes have never been so equal. The hoity-toity lot will have to get off their backsides and get real jobs now. Let's see how they cope in this new world of ours.'

'Who knows?' said Poppy. 'I shan't spend much time thinking about it, though, I can assure you. Skivvying's in the past for me now. Thanks to you girls and the factory, I feel ready to turn the page and take on a new chapter.'

Sal found herself smiling in awe at her brave friend. Poppy hadn't just survived her secrets; she had actually emerged a stronger woman, not in spite of them but because of them.

'And what about you, Sal?' Poppy asked. 'Now that so many women will be quitting Trout's and returning to life at home, there'll be a fair few empty seats on the factory floor. I worry you'll have your work cut out for you.'

'Well, there might just be one more empty seat and all,' she replied with a determined twinkle in her eye.

'What do you mean?' Poppy asked, puzzled.

'Well, this war, and all that I witnessed that night of the Tube disaster, made me realize that maybe I have something more to offer,' she said. 'No disrespect to factory work, but I thought I might try and retrain as a nurse. Vera's said she'll help me, and I'm going down to the children's hospital to talk to Matron tomorrow about what I need to do.'

'What a wonderful idea, Sal. You will make a really excellent nurse,' Poppy gushed. 'You were a natural with the children on the ward when we visited, and you were a true hero that night at the Tube. You dealt with the casualties so calmly.'

'I don't know about that, Poppy.' Sal shrugged modestly. 'I don't think that terrible night was anyone's finest hour, but I will say this: now Reggie's no longer around, I have a freedom I've never had, and I don't want to be dependent on a man again, or live in fear of one. The slavery years are over for me, in a funny way thanks to the war, and now I'm free to make my own way in life.'

Vera nodded sagely.

Just then a commotion at the far end of the street caught their attention and Sal found her gaze suddenly drawn to the figure of a tall man in uniform marching towards them.

'As I live and breathe, is that who I think it is?' marvelled Sal, squinting her eyes into the sunshine.

Robert looked so handsome and tall striding down the street, his chest proudly puffed out in front of him. The buttons on his uniform sparkled in the sunshine. He may have left for the D-Day landings in Normandy eleven months previously little older than a lad, but he had come back a hero.

As he walked, many of the men patted him on the back to show their respect. Sal smiled to herself as she looked pointedly at Pat, who had the good grace to look embarrassed after all she'd put Daisy through.

Robert returned their smiles, but he didn't stop walking until he reached the group. Carefully, he removed his hat and nodded with deference to Vera.

'Please excuse me interrupting your party, ma'am,' he said politely.

'Nonsense.' She smiled back. 'I doubt very much we'd even be having this party if it weren't for you GIs. It's good to see you, Robert. Hope, sweetheart, come and say hello to this nice gentleman.'

Sal watched in silent fascination. She knew that Vera and Robert had kept in touch by letter when he was abroad fighting, and the GI had lived for the photos Vera sent him of his little girl. No one had really dared to bring up the subject of the future, for throughout the war, every day had to be lived as if it were the last. But the war was over now and Sal realized with a jolt that Robert might wish to contend custody and take his little girl home to America with him. Sal could hardly bear to look at Vera's face and she felt a stab of panic. Hope was her goddaughter and she had grown to love her like her own sons. Losing her again was unimaginable.

Hope tottered over and hid behind Vera, peeking out curiously from behind her skirts to gaze at the tall stranger in the street.

Robert crouched down to her eye level and his brown eyes were at once filled with love.

'Well, hello there, little lady.' He smiled broadly. 'Would you like one of these?' He pulled a lollypop from his pocket and Hope's mesmerizing brown eyes went out on stalks as a sticky little hand shot out.

'You sure got your momma's good looks,' he said wistfully.

'Say "thank you", darling, and you can go and play now,' coaxed Vera.

When Hope had scampered back under the trestle table, Vera took a deep breath. 'I've been waiting for this moment, Robert,' she said in a shaky voice. 'I know we've never discussed it in our letters, but now the war's over, I assume this is why you've returned. She's yours and Daisy's daughter, and I won't stand in your way.'

'I'm afraid it's not that straightforward, Mrs Gladstone,' he replied. His voice, as rich and deep as molasses, was one of the things that Daisy had always said she loved most about Robert – that and his perfect manners – and listening to him now, Sal could quite see why.

'You see, my unit's being posted off to the Far East next week. The war may be over in Europe, but it's still being fought over there and we are still needed. But in any case, even if I weren't, I think . . . No, I *believe* her rightful place is here with you, Vera. She belongs in the East End, not in America with me. It just isn't practical, as much as I love her.'

Sal saw Vera sag with relief.

'Very well, Robert, if that's how you feel,' she replied. 'We'll take great care of her, I promise.'

'I know you will. It's what Daisy would have wanted,' he added sadly. 'All I ask is for photos as she grows up.'

Sal had barely noticed Archie come up behind them and thread his hand protectively through his wife's.

'I will always remember England, you know,' Robert said sadly. 'And I will always remember Daisy. Our time together on this earth was brief, but she taught me so much. On our very first date, she told me you only survived in the East End thanks to camaraderie and loyalty. I remembered that. Carried it with me, in fact, when we landed at Omaha. I truly loved her.'

Vera placed a shaky hand on his. 'War has left us all a lot poorer than it found us,' she replied.

Archie stepped forward and shook his hand. 'And England will always remember you, Robert.'

At that moment, their voices were drowned out. Someone had struck up a verse of 'Land of Hope and Glory' and everyone was joining in with great gusto.

'Come on, lad, you look like you could use a drink,' smiled Archie, clamping his arm around Robert's shoulder and leading him towards the bar.

'Well,' shrugged Sal, 'that's that, then, girls. Best foot forward. There's a few more songs to be sung before nightfall.'

With that, the Singer Girls linked arms and burst into song, their triumphant voices lifting high up over the rooftops of the East End. Life continued. Not as before, but finally unburdened.

Author's Note

I would like to dedicate this book to the 173 people – 62 of them children – who died in the Bethnal Green Tube disaster on 3 March 1943. These stoic folk had already endured so much suffering since the war began. They had survived the Blitz, not to mention poverty, rationing and unrelenting hard work. For so many to die in such an unimaginable and preventable disaster is nothing short of heartbreaking. It was the Hillsborough of its day, and yet few people know anything about one of the worst civilian disasters of the Second World War. The powers that be hushed it up under the Official Secrets Act, for fear of it being picked up and publicized as part of Nazi propaganda.

My interest in this sad event was sparked after learning about it from two venerable Bethnal Green ladies, Kathy and Vera, who took me to the memorial and told me about the terrible events of that fateful day. Both well into their eighties, these formidable women survived the Depression of the 1930s, post-Second World War slum clearance and the reign of the Krays, but the Tube disaster is the event that has had the biggest impact on them.

'My son says, "You want to forget it, Mum – it's done,"' explains Kathy. 'But it's not done as far as I'm concerned.

I'll never forget standing there looking at all those dead bodies lined up on the pavement, with fat tears trickling down my cheeks.' Kathy's pain is palpable seventy-two years on.

Discovering that I share a name with one of the victims, Kate Thompson, further fuelled my interest. Little is known about Bethnal Green Kate, other than that she lived in Russia Lane, and she was fun, hardworking and a devoted mother of seven sons and two daughters. She doubtless lived a life of abject poverty and work, incomparable to my modern, pampered life. I only wish I could have sat and shared a pot of tea with Kate. I'm sure I could have learned so much from her.

Kate's youngest son, Bill, was in the army. He worked as part of a bomb disposal unit, helping to defuse high-explosive bombs. It was a deeply dangerous occupation, but he survived the war. His mother, a civilian on the home front, did not – she was just sixty-three years old when she was crushed to death on the steps leading down to the Tube. We don't know what Bill made of this tragic twist of fate, for he never breathed a word about his mother's demise to either his wife or his daughter.

Today, an impressive bunch of people are working tirelessly so that the memories of Kate Thompson and all the other men, women and children who lost their lives that day are never forgotten. For years all that marked the disaster was a small faded plaque over the entrance to the Tube.

Now, thanks to the Stairway to Heaven Memorial Trust, a beautiful and fitting memorial is underway. However, there are insufficient funds to complete the final phase, which is to put a teak stairway on top of it with all the victims' names carved into the wood. The charity will not rest easy until it is completed, and it is testament to the unshakeable power of human love and devotion that it is there at all.

As Sandra Scotting, who lost her grandmother and cousin in the disaster, explains, 'It is so important we finish the memorial before the last remaining survivors die. We must never forget their suffering that dark evening.'

Vera agrees: 'Bethnal Green survived and triumphed through so much because we are a true East End community that has always looked out for one another. We lived, worked, fought and sadly died side by side.'

It is that very essence of community, heartfelt loyalty, camaraderie and, above all, friendship that I wanted to pay tribute to in *Secrets of the Singer Girls*. I hope you have enjoyed reading it as much as I enjoyed writing it. For more information on the memorial trust, please visit:

www.stairwaytoheavenmemorial.org

Read on to find out more about author
Kate Thompson's research in
The Story Behind the Story

The Story Behind the Story

Every man and woman who can recall life in Britain during the war has a story to tell, but the brave, vibrant and wickedly funny factory workers of the East End have a rich and never-ending wealth of tales. The many kind and inspiring women who gave up their precious time to help me with research opened my eyes to a side of life that has long since vanished from this country.

The majority of the ladies who used to work as seamstresses in garment factories are now in their late eighties, but as sharp as tacks and fiercely independent. Nearly every machinist I spoke with began work at fourteen. It was commonplace for children to finish their schooling on a Friday, only for them to be marched to the nearest factory to start work at 8 a.m. sharp the following Monday, without them bemoaning the abrupt end to their childhood. Indeed, they were proud to hand the precious brown-paper pay packets that they received at the end of each week straight into their mothers' hands, and thus be able to contribute financially towards their households. The East End mother was the lynchpin of her family, and her daughters were utterly devoted to her. Girls were pleased to be going out to work, making their way in the world and 'doing their bit'.

Tragically, when war broke out, this phrase took on a whole new meaning.

Many of the women who worked in the then-thriving East End rag trade were suddenly no longer stitching exquisite dresses and delicate children's wear bound for the smartest stores 'Up West', but instead found themselves sewing army battle dress, surgical field bandages and, once the fighting began, repairing uniforms peppered with bullet holes.

Much is made of the efforts of munitions workers during the war, but the work of machinists is often overlooked. It must have been hellish repairing uniforms and stitching bandages bound for the battlefields, to say nothing of how it brought the horrors of war into sharp focus. After all, how could a mother not worry about her serving husband, son or brother, when it might well be his uniform she was repairing? But for East End women who fell out of the cradle as machinists and for whom hard work was bred in the bone, they tackled the long hours and gruelling workload with great aplomb and guts. Not that they had much choice even if they did object. The job was classed as 'essential war work', and upping and leaving in most cases simply wasn't an option.

So instead, they stayed seated behind their Singer sewing machines and they sang their hearts out while they sewed. Singing along to *Music While You Work* or *Workers' Playtime* on a crackly wireless alleviated the boredom and kept up that all-important morale and work momentum.

'Oh, the factory singalongs were just wonderful!' recalled

one lady. 'One woman would start humming a tune, the worker next to her would pick it up, and it would travel down the line, until the whole factory floor was belting it out at the top of their lungs. "Show Me the Way to Go Home" and "On Mother Kelly's Doorstep" were favourites or, if we were feeling sentimental, "Silver Wings in the Moonlight".'

Some of the younger, more inventive of the women workers also found ways to amuse themselves. Slipping love letters and notes into the pockets of army uniforms or stitching them into the bandages, out of sight of the ferociously strict foreladies who oversaw the running of the factories, was commonplace. A risqué but doubtless thrilling pastime! What serving soldier aching for news from the Home Front wouldn't have been delighted to find a note in his pocket saying, 'If you're in the mood, come to me and I'll be in the nude'? It was an imaginative response to the lack of young men on the streets of London, and typified the Cockney machinist, who had always been used to trading on her wits.

One has to admire the woman who worked out how to fuse her sewing machine by 'holding the wheel and keeping her foot down on the treadle', thus craftily earning herself an extra ten-minute break, or the lady who proudly told me that she didn't regard herself as a proper machinist until she had accidentally impaled her finger on the sewing machine needle three times! Her descriptions of the forelady carefully turning the wheel until the needle was extracted from her thumbnail made me wince, and she said that after she had been deftly bandaged up she was told to get on with her work.

These two women, like every other machinist I spoke with, calmly worked their way through the raids of the Blitz until the bombs got too close for comfort and they were forced to seek shelter. The Luftwaffe weren't going to stop their sewing machines from humming if they could help it!

Today, the East End is unrecognizable, but back then, the streets of Bethnal Green, Bow, Spitalfields, Stepney, Hackney, Aldgate and Whitechapel were teeming with garment factories, all crowded with women working 'in the rag' and struggling to make ends meet through piece work. Many of the women I spoke to preferred piece work, where they were paid a set amount per item they produced, as it gave them the chance to earn more money.

The blistering poverty of the 1930s and 1940s can never be underestimated. London's East End was a compelling and mysterious world, a place of gritty hardship, aching hunger and staunch loyalties, unimaginable to much of today's pampered society.

The Boundary Estate, built in Bethnal Green, was the world's first council housing. Strong moral codes of honour governed the cobbled streets and ruled the redoubtable women who lived cheek by jowl in its terraces and tenements. The Welfare State hadn't been dreamt up and the streets were filled with the poor and hungry. Children walked about with bare feet or wore shoes patched up with cardboard. Strips of newspaper were used in place of toilet roll – or, as one woman told me, 'Mum just dried my bum with a handful of flour' – and many ragged children queued for a free breakfast from the East End Mission. The staple diet of many was stale bread dunked in watery Oxo.

Mothers often bore the brunt of extreme poverty and many women in Bethnal Green held down three jobs, from charring (cleaning) to assembling matchboxes, working their fingers to the bone from morning to night, and somehow managing, against the odds, to raise their children decently and put food in their tummies. It's little wonder that so many of the machinists I interviewed were fiercely loyal to their mothers. They had witnessed their mothers' many sacrifices.

'My father used to knock my mother about and clout her in front of us kiddies,' one woman confided in me. 'She was too scared to leave him. Where would she go? She went without food so me and my brothers and sisters could eat, she worked so hard to keep the family together. I used to call her the Duchess.'

Despite the phenomenal work ethic and efforts of these mothers, two centuries of uncontrolled development and a large poor population led to chronic overcrowding and by 1931, a census recorded that 18,156 dwellings were housing 27,978 people in Bethnal Green. Unemployment, low wages and overcrowding were the characteristics of a borough that was the backyard of the richest square mile in Britain.

A 1936 pre-war report on the health of the Borough of Bethnal Green, which is now held at Tower Hamlets Local History Library & Archives, observed wryly: 'There is a paradox that in a borough noted as a centre of the boot, shoe and clothing trade, only a reported five per cent of children are well clothed and shod.'

This was a world I needed to attempt to understand in order to write about it with any degree of authenticity. So just how does a mother-of-two who has been lucky enough to lead a comfortable life with all the trappings of modern convenience attempt to understand a world of teeming slums, and get beyond the nostalgic clichés?

I have written about the memorial to the Bethnal Green Tube disaster in the Author's Note, but researching more about this tragedy really did open my eyes to the suffering of the people who lived and worked in the East End during the war.

I went to see the steps that led down to the Underground at Bethnal Green and on a bright spring day, with streams of commuters descending them, it scarcely seemed credible that so many people perished there in scenes of undiluted horror. But seventy-two years ago, as a war-wearied Britain fought the evils of Nazi Germany, tragedy unfolded on those steps.

Not a single German bomb was dropped in Bethnal Green that evening and scarcely a broken bone was reported, but in the time it took for the air-raid siren to sound, the narrow corridor was converted into a charnel house as people piled helplessly one on top of the other. After the search-lights went on, an anti-aircraft battery in nearby Victoria Park launched a salvo of new rockets and, fearing that Hitler had unleashed a new kind of warfare, the crowd surged forward. A mother carrying a baby tripped on the stairs and, like a pack of cards, the shelterers fell one-by-one.

The scenes were unimaginable on that damp, blacked-out and bleak March night in 1943. Faces bulged in terror, slowly turning lilac as the air was forced from their lungs; protective arms thrown around loved ones squeezed the life out of them. The descriptions I've included within the book are harrowing, but they happened.

Reporters tried to bribe children who had witnessed the spine-chilling event to describe what had happened.

For a wartime government obsessed with propaganda and keeping up morale, news of this leaking out would have been disastrous. So instead, the shattered survivors put up, shut up and said nothing, condemned to carry their silent torment with them to their graves. No counselling, no acknowledgement of what we now call Post-Traumatic Stress Disorder or compensation that today's society demands. Their suffering was sealed off like the countless bombsites that peppered the neighbourhood.

It was whilst I was reading through a copy of the memorial service held each year in honour of the victims that I felt compelled to find out more, for there in black and white was a sobering reminder of precisely how privileged my life truly is. I share a name with one of the victims. Kate Thompson was just one of the women who suffocated to death on those dank, dark steps. It's hard to put into words the emotions of seeing your namesake in a grim roll call of death, but it set me thinking and leant a deep poignancy to my research.

Just who was the other Kate Thompson and what led her to flee to the so-called sanctuary of the Underground that fateful evening? Did we share more than just a name? From that moment, I knew that whatever it took, I would write this book so that Kate, and all the other people who died that night, would have a voice.

Apparently, Kate was down the Black Horse pub in her favourite fur-collared coat when the sirens went off that fateful night. She was also a sixty-three-year-old mother of nine, living in one of Bethnal Green's roughest areas when she perished in the disaster. It would have been easy to dismiss Kate as just another victim who'd been battling for survival in the narrow cobbled streets, but to do so would be foolish, because a closer examination into her life revealed some surprising facts.

Consulting a genealogist, whose job it is to trace back through historical records and piece together family history, provided me with a far more illuminating picture of her life than hearsay.

Kate Hammersley was born in September 1880 in Poplar, East London – the setting for the popular BBC drama *Call the Midwife* – the impoverished daughter of a cabinet-carver father. At the age of eighteen, in July 1898, she married a cooper or barrel-maker by the name of William Thompson and moved to Bethnal Green, where she bore him seven sons and two daughters. They resided at Quinn Square in Russia Lane for most of their married life. Pre-war, Bethnal Green housed some of the worst slums in London and of them, one of the most notorious was Quinn Square, a place where locals say you never went after dark and policemen only dared visit in pairs.

Booth's Poverty Map notebooks, written in 1897, singled out the six-storey buildings containing 246 flats as 'very rough, very poor, very noisy'. Writing in 1928, the *East End Star* newsletter was less charitable, describing the dwellings as 'one of the worst of the human rabbit-warrens in East London, these wretched flats house hundreds of men, women and children under conditions scarcely fit for cattle'.

Some of the flats contained illegal gambling dens and when the police were about, quick-witted residents would whistle off the balconies. 'There was a lot of whistling in them days,' one former resident laughingly told me.

The dark tenement block was built around a central square and the mostly two-roomed flats housed large families. One woman I interviewed recalls a mother of twenty-five children looking after them in just two rooms, making Kate's nine children seem a fairly modest family.

None of the flats had their own water taps or toilets, and tenants shared facilities on the landing between four families. Washhouse facilities were housed on the roof and the women of the square had to drag their laundry up six flights of stairs or down to the local bag wash. According to one local resident, the stench from the toilets was unholy. Perhaps that's why Russia Lane had its own bathing centre, known as a Personal Cleansing Station, though I'm sure it was referred to by other names. In 1936, records show that 3,831 children attended for infestations of bugs, mites and nits and a further 1,287 were treated for scabies, or as it was otherwise referred to, The Itch. So far, so depressing.

By August 1938, Kate Thompson and many others lived in a squalid, dilapidated hell-hole. Quinn Square was in a serious state of disrepair. Residents reported broken steps, broken handrails on the stairs, lavatory doors with no locks and broken facilities in the washhouse. Inside fared no better, with falling ceilings, damp walls, peeling wallpaper and no cupboards to put food in. Not only that, but the landlords were having a merry time at the tenants' expense, charging exorbitant rents for such miserly facilities. How did the fiercely house-proud and feisty East End women put up with this? The answer is, they didn't.

According to the electoral register, Kate was registered

to vote from as early as 1923: highly surprising for those times. Women had only been given the vote five years earlier, in 1918, and even then, it was only for women over thirty whose husbands were householders. Perhaps it was this interest in politics that led Kate to insist on her right to a decent standard of living. Far from being a passive victim, Kate and the other residents of the square issued a call to arms and got ready to show the landlords exactly what they were made of. The facilities may have been poor, but the community spirit was strong. All the residents promptly formed a Tenants Association and, supported by a local Member of Parliament and members of the Council, the tenants of the 246 dwellings flatly refused to pay their rents until the rapacious landlords reduced them to more reasonable amounts. They also demanded that necessary repairs to the property be carried out. Their argument was simple: Why pay high rents for broken facilities? Why should they be forced to take their washing elsewhere at added expense? This was in the depression of the 1930s, after all, at a time of widespread hardship and great unemployment. The added battle must have felt like a kick in the teeth.

One landlord responded by attempting to evict a tenant, claiming she was in arrears. When the agent, accompanied by bailiffs, arrived on eviction day, the tenants, wielding placards stating 'Less Rent, More Repair', barred their way, and the landlord was forced to make a hasty retreat. This was the biggest rent strike ever seen in the East End and it sent the press wild.

Buoyed by their success, the tenants of Quinn Square paraded around Bethnal Green with their placards, held daily meetings and picketed the estate office from morning until night. Showing the kind of stoicism that fared them so well during the Blitz, they refused to be beaten.

Apparently, every time the landlord went into the square – on one occasion even accompanied by a group of Sir Oswald Mosley's fascists, who attempted to break up the tenants's meeting by organized hooliganism – a huge crowd of women and children followed them and booed them out of Russia Lane, pelting them with hot potatoes! And so it was that Kate and her neighbours scored a resounding victory for the working-class underdogs of Quinn Square. It would take more than an unscrupulous landlord and some bullyboy fascists to scare them into submission. They may have been housewives in pinnies, but they were made of stern stuff.

The landlords acceded to their demands to lower the rent and carry out repairs, and this case made history, paving the way for success for other Tenants Associations.

Of course I have no way of knowing whether Kate was the one wielding placards and hot potatoes, but a woman I spoke to who knew her is in no doubt. Gladys, aged eighty-eight, is too young to remember the rent strike, but her memory of Kate as a formidable mother burns bright.

'Mrs Thompson was best friends with my nan and by God they were tough. They were sturdily built, upright women who always wore black and feathers in their hats. She and my nan stood up for their rights and weren't scared of any man. I'm surprised she didn't strangle that landlord when he tried to take liberties with her.'

A year later, war broke out and Kate and the other residents began the second great fight of their lives.

The dramatic events that took place in Quinn Square

perfectly illustrate that you should never underestimate the fighting power of a woman when her home and her family are under threat. Whether it's 1938 or 2015, it matters not – a mother will fight tooth and nail to protect the roof over her children's heads.

Reading about the success of the tenants of Quinn Square in Tower Hamlets Local History Library & Archives filled me with an enormous sense of awe. The other Kate wasn't afraid to stand up to corrupt landlords, fascists marching on her street or the might of the Luftwaffe. My 1940s namesake was indeed a far stronger, finer lady than I. It would appear that a love of a fur collar is about all we have in common. I wish I had one ounce of her courage and pluck. What a pity therefore that this indomitable woman had to die in such a pitiful and entirely preventable accident in 1943. That is why I have made a donation in her name to the Tube disaster memorial fund.

This book is a tribute to feisty Kate and to all the remark-able, brave women of the East End.

Acknowledgements

With sincere thanks to:

Kate Burke and Diane Banks at Diane Banks Associates.

Mollie Moran, author of *Aprons and Silver Spoons: The Heartwarming Memoirs of a 1930s Kitchen Maid* (Penguin, 2013), an amazing character, sadly no longer with us, who gave me the low-down on what life was really like 'below stairs' with great humour and zeal.

Terri Coates, consultant midwife on *Call the Midwife*.

Major Kevin Pooley, social historian at the Salvation Army.

Sandra Scotting at the Stairway to Heaven Memorial Trust.

Joy Puritz, writer and researcher.

Jennifer Daley, historical researcher.

Kathy, Vera and all at the Sundial Centre in Bethnal Green for sharing their memories of Bethnal Green.

Henrietta 'Minksy' Keeper for sharing her memories of singing and sewing in Bethnal Green.

Emily Shepherd for her memories of life as a machinist during wartime.

Monica Roberts for her insights into growing up as the illegitimate daughter of a black American GI.

Amy Condon and Kate Williams for proofreading.

Jenny Smith, domestic violence pioneer and author of *The Refuge* (Simon & Schuster, 2014) for her insights into domestic violence.

Staff at the Museum of Childhood in Bethnal Green.

Staff at the Imperial War Museum Archives.

Library staff at the Bishopsgate Institute.

Books and sources I have found helpful:

BBC Radio 4, *Bandits of the Blitz*, presented by Duncan Campbell.

If You're Reading This . . . Last Letters From the Front Line, Siân Price (Pen & Sword Books, 2011).

Nella Last's War: The Second World War Diaries of 'Housewife, 49', Richard Broad and Suzie Fleming (Sphere, 2006).

'*Over Here': The GIs in Wartime Britain*, Juliet Gardiner (Collins & Brown, 1992).

Keep Smiling Through: The Home Front 1939–45, Susan Briggs (BCA, 1975).

Aprons and Silver Spoons: The Heartwarming Memoirs of a 1930s Kitchen Maid (Penguin, 2013).

Secrets of the Sewing Circle

Coming out May 2016

Secrets of the Sewing Circle, takes us from the vibrant factory floor, deep underground, to the burgeoning community blossoming in the tunnels. You'll meet new Trout's characters, from handsome but frustrated boxer Lucky, to shy orphan Flossy, beautiful but aloof Peggy and salt of-the-earth tea lady Dolly, as they fight for their right to safety.

As the Blitz reaches its peak and the girls come to feel as if they are living underground, tensions are at breaking point. How will Flossy and Peggy cope as their lives and destinies are shaped and moved by forces outside their control? Can Lucky prove his worth in the war? Will Flossy ever discover the complex truth of her heritage? And, cooped up below ground, cheek by jowl, can Dolly manage to contain the explosive secret that binds them all?

It's time to relax with your next good book

THEWINDOWSEAT.CO.UK

If you've enjoyed this book, but don't know what to read next, then we can help. The Window Seat is a site that's all about making it easier to discover your next good book. We feature recommendations, behind-the-scenes tales from the world of publishing, creative writing tips, competitions, and, if we're honest, quite a lot of lists based on our favourite reads.

You'll find stories and features by authors including Lucinda Riley, Karen Swan, Diane Chamberlain, Jane Green, Lucy Diamond and many more. We showcase brand-new talent as well as classic favourites, so you'll never be stuck for what to read again.

We'd love to know what you think of the site, our books, and what you'd like us to feature, so do let us know.

 @panmacmillan.com

 facebook.com/panmacmillan

WWW.THEWINDOWSEAT.CO.UK